11/18

‖‖‖‖‖‖‖‖‖‖‖‖‖‖‖‖‖‖‖‖‖‖‖‖‖

W9-BRR-969

Discarded By
Easttown Library

EASTTOWN LIBRARY &
INFORMATION CENTER
720 FIRST AVENUE
BERWYN, PA 19312-1769
610-644-0138

EMPRESS
OF ALL
SEASONS

EMPRESS
OF ALL
SEASONS

by Emiko Jean

HOUGHTON MIFFLIN HARCOURT
Boston   New York

Copyright © 2018 by Emiko Jean

All rights reserved. For information about permission to reproduce selections from this book,
write to trade.permissions@hmhco.com or to Permissions, Houghton Mifflin Harcourt
Publishing Company, 3 Park Avenue, 19th Floor, New York, New York 10016.

hmhco.com

The text was set in Adobe Jensen Pro.

Library of Congress Cataloging-in-Publication Data
Names: Jean, Emiko, author.
Title: Empress of all seasons / Emiko Jean.
Description: Boston ; New York : HMH Books for Young Readers, 2018. |
Summary: During a once-in-a-generation competition to find the new
empress, Mari, who hides a terrible secret, Taro, the prince who would
denounce the imperial throne, and Akira, a half-human outcast, will decide
the fate of Honoku.
Identifiers: LCCN 2018007165 | ISBN 9780544530942 (hardback)
Subjects: | CYAC: Fantasy.
Classification: LCC PZ7.1.J43 Emp 2018 | DDC [Fic—dc23
LC record available at https://lccn.loc.gov/2018007165

Printed in the United States of America
DOC 10 9 8 7 6 5 4 3 2 1
4500728515

To Yumi and Kenzo,

you're all my wishes come true.

And to Erin,

thanks for asking me: have you ever thought about writing a

Japanese-inspired fantasy?

IN THE BEGINNING, dark water flooded the earth.

Kita, the Goddess of Land and Rice, built a staircase out of lightning and stepped down from the sky.

She dipped her nimble fingers into the black oceans and sculpted from the rocky depths the lands of Honoku. From her body, she made the terrain. Her eyelashes became forests, dense with trees. Her tears of joy became the oceans, rough with salt. Her breath became the desert, hot with sand. And with her fingernails, she created an impassable mountain range, one of extraordinary danger and height.

Delighted by her cleverness, she bragged to her fellow gods and goddesses.

Sugita, her brother, God of Children, Fortune, and Love, perpetually prone to jealousy, refused to be overshadowed. From the land, he gathered clay and molded figures.

The first were yōkai.

Sugita's imagination ran wild, and he fashioned these spirits, monsters, and demons, these otherworldly creatures, with blue, white, and yellow skin. Some he fashioned with horns; some without. Some he locked forever in childhood. To others he gave two mouths or fifteen fingers, long necks, ten hundred eyes, or shriveled heads. The yōkai were as limitless as the magic within them.

The second were human.

These he made in his own image, relatively uniform in appearance, with ten fingers and ten toes, each with a single mouth, and with hair upon their heads. Soon enough, Sugita recognized the weakness in his design. He had given yōkai vast powers, whereas he had given the humans none. So he gifted the latter with a second language — curses that may be spoken or written to ward off the yōkai, strip them of their powers. In this way, a balance might be established.

And to all — yōkai and human alike — he bestowed a mortal heart.

Finally, he took the human that bore him the strongest resemblance and set him upon the most fertile land. He touched the human's brow with his thumb and drew a smudge between his eyebrows. All would know that he was favored by the gods and goddesses. So it was.

The human was called Emperor.

Sovereign. Blessed.

Ruler of the land.

PART I:

One inch forward is darkness.

— Proverb

CHAPTER 1
Mari

BREATHING IN THE DARK, and not her own.

Mari tilted her head. She couldn't see in the pitch-black, but she closed her eyes. It helped her focus. She knew this space well, this room with no windows and an almost airtight door. Sometimes the musty smell invaded her dreams, morphed them into nightmares. The Killing Room, and Mari was executioner.

She inhaled, holding the stale air in her lungs. There, in the right corner, two feet away, someone waited. *Afraid.*

Mari stepped forward, the floorboards creaking under her weight.

"P-p-please," a high-pitched male voice wailed.

"I'm not going to hurt you," she said, letting a note of reassurance enter her voice. *Not yet, anyway.* She probed the wall. Her fingers brushed against a wooden ledge, then paper pulled tight over a bamboo frame. Matches rested next to the lamp. She struck one and lit the cotton wick, illuminating the room in a soft glow. The scent of rapeseed oil crept through the air. When her eyes refocused, she saw that the man was dressed in *hakama* pants and a surcoat. Samurai garb. The uniform of the military elite.

"Gods and goddesses," he said, mouth lifting into a sneer, "I thought you were one of them. Why, you're no taller than a sapling! What happened, little girl, did you lose your mommy?"

Mari regretted her paltry effort to comfort him. *That's what you get for being nice. Men. They always underestimated her.*

Opposite the man, a variety of weapons leaned in the corner: a sickle and chain, a bow and arrow, a *nunchaku* . . . Mari gestured toward them. "Choose." She liked to give the men a fighting chance. *I'm sporting that way.*

The samurai huffed. "You don't know what you ask, little girl. I trained at the Palace of Illusions with the *shōgun* himself."

Mari clenched her teeth. This was growing tedious. "I said, choose your weapon."

The samurai strolled to the corner. He rifled through the weapons and selected a *katana* and a *wakizashi*.

Predictable. The long and short swords were samurai weapons. Her opponent brandished them, sharp-edged steel blades glittering in the lamplight.

Mari sauntered to the corner and quickly chose her own instrument. Always the same. The *naginata*. The reaping sword was a long bamboo pole culminating in a wicked curved blade. Thought to be a woman's weapon, none of her opponents ever selected it. It was the only weapon Mari knew how to wield. "If you train on all weapons, you will master none," her mother always said.

Mari stamped the *naginata* on the ground. Dust billowed around the hem of her navy kimono. "I'm very sorry, but from this moment, you're dead," she said, unsheathing the blade.

The samurai laughed, the sound robust and biting.

Mari cut his chortle short. She dipped into a crouch, letting the pole end of the *naginata* swing out in an arc, clipping the back of the samurai's knees.

He collapsed with a loud thud. Mari winced. *The big ones always fall the hardest.*

"That was a mistake," he said, clambering to his feet. He crossed the swords in front of him, a dangerous glint in his eye.

At least he's taking me seriously now. "No," Mari corrected. "That was intentional."

The samurai rushed her, and she followed suit. The blade end of her *naginata* clashed against his big sword. Sparks flew.

The samurai jabbed with the smaller sword, and Mari dodged. A hairsbreadth from being impaled. *That was too close.* Her pulse quickened with fear and excitement. *This samurai is well-trained.* Before the samurai could pull back, Mari began twisting the *naginata*, catching both of his weapons in the windmill. Forced to let go, the samurai dropped his swords, which scattered to the ground, a few feet away. *Well-trained, but not as well-trained as I.*

She couldn't allow him time to take a breath, to reach for his weapons. *End this.* She snap-kicked, her right foot connecting with his abdomen. The samurai grunted and doubled over. He clutched his stomach as he tipped to the ground.

She stood over him, breath ragged, victory sealed. Warmth radiated through her body. She felt the beast rise within her, felt her brown eyes dissolve into twin black abysses. Her hands flexed as muscles spasmed and bones popped. Her fingernails grew into black pointed talons. The skin on the back of her hands bloomed with leathery, charcoal-colored scales as tough and thick as a rhinoceros hide. She ignored the agony of transformation. She had trained herself to shut it out.

The samurai stared, horror-struck.

She knew she looked hideous — still part human, but with the eyes and hands of a monster. She brought her face close to the samurai's, and when she spoke, her voice came out as a rasp. "You were right after all. I *am* one of them."

CHAPTER 2

Taro

TARO RUBBED THE MARK between his eyebrows, where pain blossomed. For someone chosen by gods and goddesses, he'd certainly suffered his fair share of ailments during his seventeen years of life.

The ache between his eyebrows pulsed, beating in time with the hive of activity surrounding him. In the Main Hall, servants bustled, scrubbing the zelkova floor on hands and knees, dusting the rafters with peacock feathers, polishing the four sets of statuesque doors, one for each season. Preparations for the competition had begun weeks ago.

Most days, the commotion was enough to grate on Taro's nerves, a reminder that his hard-won solitude would soon end. But today, that was not what annoyed him. Today it was a disturbance so great that he'd heard it from inside his workroom, clear on the other side of the palace.

His features darkened at the spectacle before him. Two imperial samurai, clad in black lacquered armor, dragged a screaming *kappa* into the Hall. A muscle ticked in Taro's jaw at the sound of nails scraping across metal. The *kappa*'s green webbed feet left a trail of slimy, muddy water on the high-glossed floor. A servant girl who had just finished cleaning it gasped and skittered off, vacating the space with the rest of the workers.

Behind the *kappa* trailed a retinue of priests. Their dove-gray robes brushed the ground, their steps careful and measured. Their voices were synced as they chanted curses in a song so beautiful, it made humans weep.

Unfortunately for the prisoner, the words were earsplitting to *kappa*, indeed to all *yōkai*. Chains, shackles, and wooden cages were unnecessary. The priests' chants kept the *kappa* locked tight in an invisible torture chamber.

Smaller than a human child, with a turtle-like shell on his back and an orange beak protruding playfully from his feathered face, the *kappa* didn't appear to be a threat. He was sweet-looking. Cute. Seemingly benign.

Things are rarely as they appear. Taro knew this to be true. He lived in the Palace of Illusions, after all. He also knew that *kappa* were notorious for their strength, possessing five times that of a human man, and for their love of entrails, usually harvested from live victims. Taro placed a hand over his stomach. *No wonder the servants fled the Hall.*

The *kappa*'s screams ceased, quieting to a coo. The language he spoke was unintelligible to humans, but Taro recognized the plaintive tone of his voice. *The* kappa *pleads for his life.* As they passed, the samurai and priests bowed to the emperor's son. Taro inclined his head, the barest hint of recognition.

8

The entourage slowed at a set of mahogany and cypress doors. A bar, made from the trunk of a thousand-year-old oak tree, rested across, blocking what was inside from getting out. A relief of a mountain covered in gleaming snow was carved into the wood.

The Winter Room. As with each of the Seasonal Rooms, it could be used for pleasure, or for pain.

Today, it is pain.

A sick feeling took root in Taro's gut, but his countenance remained stoic. He was good at wearing masks. His favorite was a formidable expression. He used it often. So often that sometimes he forgot who lay beneath.

The samurai dumped the *kappa* just outside the Winter Room doors. The creature whimpered, its spindly limbs curling in like a dried leaf. Unwilling to watch, Taro flicked his gaze to the tattooed priests. Cobalt ink covered their bodies. Even their faces were permanently branded with swirling, calligraphed curses. If a *yōkai* touched a priest's skin, it would burn.

Grunting, the samurai lifted the oak bar, then stepped back, the heavy wood weighing down their shoulders. The doors sprang open. Snow flurries escaped, melting in the warmth of the Main Hall. Icy air brushed Taro's cheeks, and his lips twitched. From the depths of the room, he thought he heard the echo of his long-gone laughter. As a child, he'd played in the snowfields and hidden in the Ice Forest. Now only death walked there.

Footsteps echoed behind him. The priests and samurai sank to the ground. Stillness descended, punctuated by the low hum of the priests' chants. Only one man commanded such a reception. Taro's father, the emperor, divine ruler of humans and *yōkai*, Heavenly

Sovereign, paused beside him. Heat rose on Taro's neck as his father's shoulder brushed his.

They were the same height now, almost mirror images of each other, except for the fine lines of aging that had settled around the emperor's mouth and eyes. Their broad shoulders swathed in purple robes cut imposing figures. Their hair was shaved on both sides but left long on top and pulled into knots. On their left hips, they wore the long and short swords, a nod to their samurai training. It was not enough to be chosen by gods. Ruling an empire required strength and force, the fierceness of a dragon. Traits Taro had always lacked. *Until now.*

Born prematurely, Taro had been a sickly child, small and given to coughing fits. In the last two years, he'd undergone a semi-metamorphosis, shedding his frailty. His lungs had cleared, and his muscles had thickened, his build now as massive as a bear's. Sometimes when he gazed at his hands, he didn't recognize them, the blunt strength in his fingertips, the power of his grip.

Taro kept his eyes forward as the emperor cast him a searching glance. If his spine straightened any more, it might snap. His father studied Taro often, now that he'd grown.

"Father," Taro said in a monotone.

"Son," the emperor replied. The emperor's voice always made Taro think of rusted iron — cold, hard, crusted, *useless.* "I thought you would be off *playing* in your workroom." Taro swallowed against the bite of his father's tone. The emperor had very definitive views on what made a man. Men did not cry. Men were not small. Men sought power and dominion. Taro spent most days avoiding his father.

The emperor's driving purpose was to rid the East Lands of

yōkai. Taro craved privacy, quiet spaces where he could invent things. *If I didn't know better, I'd think you were made up entirely of gears and springs,* his childhood nurse had often commented. The emperor certainly never understood his son's passion for engineering. Rumors swirled that there was a time when the emperor had been softer, that he had loved deeply and without judgment. If this was once the case, Taro had never witnessed it. And as for Taro, he knew what the servants and courtiers whispered about him. *The Cold Prince.* More metal than human. A man without a heart. Perhaps this was true.

"I heard the commotion." Taro didn't bother to hide his annoyance. A muscle rippled along his jaw.

"We caught a *kappa* in the moat," said the emperor.

Taro expelled a breath. The *kappa* must have been starving to risk coming so close to the palace.

His father arched a single silver brow. "Unbelievable, isn't it?" The emperor waved an impatient hand and spoke loudly. "Enough."

The chanting ceased.

The *kappa* stilled. His eyes — black, wounded, beseeching — rested on the emperor.

"His odor is offensive," the emperor intoned. The Main Hall did smell like fish and pond water. The emperor jerked his chin. "Throw him in the Winter Room."

Kappa may not understand human words, but this one clearly comprehended a death sentence. The *kappa's* eyes sharpened into resolute points. The creature opened its beak, screamed, and shoved the samurai.

For one glorious moment, the imperial guards were airborne, their bodies graceful arcs, hyperextended in space, and Taro marveled

11

at the small *yōkai*'s strength. The samurai crashed into the wall with a dull *clunk*, slumped and dazed.

A gust of snow from the Winter Room swirled into the Hall, obscuring Taro's vision. Out of the white, the *kappa* barreled toward Taro and his father, webbed hands outstretched, beak open in a shriek.

Taro squared his shoulders, counted his breaths. *One. Two. Three.* His mask did not slip. Nor did the emperor's. For all their differences, they shared a few traits. A cold air. Pride. No one would dare defy the emperor or the prince. To do so would be to court the wrath of the gods and goddesses. Religion was the emperor's greatest weapon.

The priests quickly resumed their chanting, climbing to their feet and beginning to sway. The *kappa* paused, clasping his webbed hands over his ears. A futile effort. The air thickened and crackled with the priests' incantations. The Hall grew colder. The *kappa* toppled to his knees, doubled over. Paralyzed.

The emperor barked at the dazed samurai. "Get up."

Slowly, the samurai regained their wits and dragged the *kappa*'s limp body to the threshold of the Winter Room. Taro turned a cheek as they threw him in.

If the *kappa* was lucky, the frigid temperatures would kill him before the predators did. The Seasonal Rooms created their own weather, aided by Master Ushiba, the revered Seasonist. A blizzard could come. In the Winter Room, that might be the quickest way to die.

A final wave of cold air blasted Taro as the doors swung shut. *At least it isn't the Summer Room.* His features tightened at the thought.

12

The blazing heat pressed down like a hot iron, blistering the skin of its victims.

The oak bar thudded back into place. The *kappa* screamed, beating tiny fists, rattling the doors. Another futility. The doors would hold against the *kappa*; they held against *oni*, the strongest *yōkai*. Taro turned and began to stride away.

"You won't stay?" his father called after him.

Something inside Taro clenched. A sound of disgust emanated from low in his throat, and he allowed his mask to slip, just this once. "I'm afraid not everyone has such a taste for death as you," he replied.

The emperor laughed. "Go hide in your workroom. But I will expect you at dinner tomorrow night. We need to discuss the competition."

Taro bit his tongue. *The competition.* His heavy footsteps matched the dull thud of his heartbeat. In a matter of days, hundreds of young women would descend upon the palace, armed and hopeful. The rules were simple: Survive the Rooms. Conquer the Seasons. Win the prince.

Taro seethed at the threat to his hard-won solitude and the ridiculousness of his being reduced to a prize to be won, a thing to be auctioned off. He shook his head. *No.* He would not stand idly by while his entire life was taken from him. Girls may come. They may conquer the Rooms. One may even win. But Taro would not marry her. He had a plan.

CHAPTER 3
Mari

THE SUN WAS just an orange flicker on the horizon, and the green trees appeared black against the encroaching twilight. Slushy snow dotted Mari's path, winter's last stand against the spring. She hastened her steps toward home, hunching her shoulders against the crisp wind. *Best not to be caught in the forest after dark.*

Just as the final ray of light sank beneath the horizon, Mari exited the woods. A clean scent hung in the thin air. She inhaled deeply. *Home.*

A few steps, and Mari arrived at the gates of Tsuma, her village. Paper tied to the iron bars flapped in the wind. Below were gifts, tributes left for her people, their packaging absurdly bright against the black gates and gray stone wall surrounding Tsuma. Travelers rarely ventured up the mountain. Those not acclimated to the altitude often suffered headaches, insomnia, and dizziness — *Mountain Madness.*

But some — human and *yōkai* — would risk it.

They came to leave offerings for her clan — fish, flowered hairpins, silk embroidered *obi*, even copper coins. Affixed to each tribute was a *mon*, a familial crest in the shape of a mandarin orange, a three-leaf hollyhock, or intersecting loops. *A fool's errand.* Mari's top lip curled as she bent to collect the bribes. Her clan would enjoy the gifts, but they would not spare those families. Everyone was fair game. *Prey.*

Mari navigated Tsuma's barren roads by memory. Though the village was small, it was built like a puzzle. The streets had no names, and the houses no numbers. The homes were all similar — wooden and unadorned. The steep thatched roofs always made Mari think of hands clasped in prayer. Many feared Mari's clan, and just as many would like to see them destroyed. Only Tsuma's inhabitants knew who resided in each home, how each piece of the puzzle fit together.

Two left turns, fourteen steps, and Mari was home. Light glowed behind the shuttered windows of her cottage. Hand on the door, she paused, taking a breath to steady herself. Facing imperial samurai in the shed was one thing. A more formidable opponent awaited her inside. Mari shook her head and laughed at her childish fear. *It's only your mother.*

Inside, she slipped off her sandals, dumped the tributes, and padded into the *tatami* room. Under her feet, the floor squeaked. Another small measure of protection: boards that sang so that no one could sneak up behind you. Warmth prickled her hands and cheeks as the wooden interior of her home came into focus. Save for a low table, the *tatami* room was intentionally bare. To any who entered, the home appeared simple. Poor. But beneath the singing floorboards was hidden untold wealth.

"You're late." Her mother's quiet, even voice drifted from the kitchen.

Usually, a screen partitioned the rooms, but tonight it was folded aside. Framed in the archway, her mother made a pretty picture as she bent over the *irori*. In the small hearth, an orange flame licked the bottom of a cast-iron teakettle. Steam charged from the spout, unleashing a low whistle. Mari's mother, Tami, poured the boiling liquid into a ceramic teapot on a plain wooden tray. Flowery notes scented the air. Jasmine tea. Mari's favorite. With practiced grace, her mother shuffled into the *tatami* room and placed the tray at the center of the low table. "How did it go?" Her mother knelt and began to pour. "Mari?"

Shaken from her cold trance, Mari stepped forward. "People will look for an imperial samurai."

Her mother delicately shrugged a shoulder, taking a sip of tea. "A disgraced imperial samurai. He liked the hostess houses too much, frequented ones with young girls." Mari shuddered. "No one will come for him. Sit," her mother commanded. Mari obliged, settling across from her. "Now, how did everything go?"

Mari sighed, folding her hands together atop the table. "Everything went fine. He didn't even take my weapon." Her chin jutted up smugly.

Her mother's dark eyes flickered. "It is the last one."

Mari's heart tripped in her chest. Her smugness slipped away, unease taking its place. Soon a far more perilous journey would begin.

Her mother ran a manicured finger over the lip of the ceramic cup. "It's a shame you didn't inherit my looks."

At her mother's words, Mari felt the tiniest pinch, as if a needle pricked her side. *If only your hair had the same shine as mine; yours is so dull and lifeless. It's too bad your teeth overlap in such an unfortunate way. Perhaps if you stood straighter, you wouldn't look so . . . substantial.* As always, Mari couldn't help staring at her mother, at everything she should have been and wasn't — long hair the color of the midnight sky, golden skin that never needed powder, a graceful, lithe body.

These days, Mari rarely looked in mirrors. She had abandoned hope that her reflection would change a long time ago. She'd stopped growing at five feet. She wasn't fat, but she was thickly muscled, sturdy. Her face was round, the shape of an apple. She wasn't ugly. She was plain. And in a village of preternaturally beautiful women, average meant unattractive.

The only trait Mari shared with her mother, shared with all Animal Wife *yōkai*, was the beast hidden inside her human form. Animal Wives were born for a singular purpose: to trick men into marriage and then steal their fortunes. *Men are conditioned to take. Women are conditioned to give,* Mari's mother once told her. *Long ago, our clan decided to stop giving and start taking.*

Mari ignored her mother's comment. She refused to apologize for her many deficits.

Wind beat against the shuttered windows, and a cry drifted through the slats. Not wolf, bear, or owl. Animal Wife. Mari startled to attention, her mother's words forgotten. She knew the origin of the wail. "Hissa is still in labor?"

"You are pale. I've saved you some dinner," her mother said, pushing a covered tray toward Mari.

Mari lifted the cloth from the tray, revealing a bowl of sticky rice topped with strips of dried seaweed. Her stomach roared. *Hissa can wait a few seconds more.* She dug her fingers in and shoved a scoop of rice into her mouth.

"Mari," her mother chided. "Have you forgotten how to use *hashi?*"

Mari shrugged. It was a small victory, offending her mother's delicate sensibilities. "It tastes better this way." She licked her fingers with a smack. "Hissa?" she prodded.

Her mother's lips pressed together. She shot a pointed look to the unused chopsticks. Mari's fingers curled on her lap. A standoff. Her mother would not dole out information until Mari complied. With a sigh, Mari picked up the two sticks and proceeded to eat with them. She should have known better than to spar with her mother. *She is the one opponent you'll never beat. One look, and you shrivel like a slug doused with raw salt.*

Her mother was slow to answer. "Still in labor. But her time approaches."

Mari chewed a bite of rice and swallowed. "I hope she has a girl."

"That would be nice." Tami smiled, an odd combination of bitter and biting. At this, Mari tensed. She was an only child, but not the only child her mother had given birth to. Two boys had come before Mari. Two half brothers she would never know. Because Tsuma kept her daughters and discarded her sons. Animal Wives' traits passed only to females, making them full-blooded *yōkai.* Boys were halflings — abominations.

Mari focused on filling the pit in her stomach. A knock sounded at the door. Mari's chewing slowed. *Who can it be?* Visitors past dark were uncommon.

18

The door slid open, bells tinkling. Ayumi entered, her sandals still on, a sure sign of bad news. "Forgive me, Tami-sama," she addressed Mari's mother.

"Hissa?" Mari asked, her heartbeat quickening under her ribcage.

"Yes. She's had her baby." Ayumi scowled furiously. "A boy. She refuses to let him go."

Mari's mother sighed and stood. "I will come."

Mari rose to her feet as well. Tami regarded her daughter, indecision etched in her expression. *She is going to order me to stay home.* A little ball of rebellion loosened in Mari's veins. She inhaled through her nose, ready to argue, to insist she be included. *I won't be left behind.* She'd never attended a delivery. But this was Hissa. Her best friend.

A year ago, Mari had kissed Hissa's fair cheeks, bidding her good-bye before she departed Tsuma. Two months later, Hissa returned, her hands spilling over with riches, a triumphant smile lighting her face. Hissa had tricked a wealthy merchant into love and marriage, and on their wedding night, she stole away with his most valuable wares — heavy silk kimonos, *washi* paper, umbrellas wrought from the finest bamboo . . .

Everything would have been perfect.

If only Hissa hadn't been pregnant.

As her pregnancy bloomed, Hissa grew zealous in her belief that the child would be female. "It will be wonderful," she told Mari, stroking her abdomen where the baby kicked. Mari remembered how lovely Hissa looked then, beaming and radiant. Glowing. "I'll have a little girl. You will be her auntie. Auntie Mari! We'll dress her in silks and play puppets."

Mari's heart lodged in her throat. Her friend had been so high on hope. How far she'd fallen. But Mari would be there to catch her.

Tami's mouth opened and then shut with an audible click. She jerked her head toward the door. "Come on, then." A flush of relief spread through Mari's limbs, and she stowed the little ball of rebellion away for another time.

She followed her mother and Ayumi out the door. *I'm coming, Hissa. Through thick or thin*, the friends once had promised each other. *Through boy or girl*, Mari amended. A new life had come into their village, and just as quickly, it would be snuffed out.

CHAPTER 4
Taro

FIVE MINUTES PAST MIDNIGHT, and Taro wasn't sleeping. Exhaustion chased him like a dog, but he would not succumb. While he waited for the rest of the palace to slumber, Taro worked. Deep in the palace, in an all-but-forgotten room, the prince built . . . *things*.

His eyes grew bloodshot, and his limbs ached as he hammered copper into thin sheets. Grease coated his hands and gummed up under his nails. With every bang of the hammer, he sought to drive out the *kappa*'s cries, his begging in his native tongue.

It's no use. Taro's throat constricted with emotions he refused to feel. The *kappa*'s screams haunted him, a battering ram bashing at his self-control, daring him to react. A fitting punishment for standing by and watching as the tiny creature was executed — *and for what? For swimming in the imperial moat? For being born* yōkai?

What if he had spoken up, opposed his father? It was unfathomable. The emperor considered any expression of sympathy for *yōkai* a weakness. Taro had learned his lesson long ago.

Only once had he asked for the life of a *yōkai* to be spared. Taro was ten and didn't understand the depths of his father's hatred.

The *yōkai* was a *tanuki*, a small gray-and-black-furred animal with the head of a raccoon and the body of a dog. Taro had found the starving cub in the tea garden. He cuddled the emaciated creature to his chest, repeating the comforting words his nursemaid would whisper to him. *There, now. It will be all right.* The *tanuki* pressed its small wet nose into Taro's neck and purred, a deep rumble that stirred Taro's lonely soul. He carried the creature's limp body to the emperor, presenting it like a sacred offering. And in the way of a small boy who yearns for something with acute desperation, he said, "I want to keep it as a pet."

The emperor's smile was thin and cold. To this day, whenever Taro remembered it, a chill settled around his shoulders. "Men do not keep pets. Especially *yōkai* pets," he said, his voice thick with scorn.

"Oh," said young Taro. "What should I do with it, then?" He wheezed, for he was small and sickly then.

"Put it back where you found it." Taro listened to his father and released the *tanuki* into the tea garden, but not before feeding it an apple and letting it lap at a bowl of rice wine. *Tanuki* were fond of alcohol. Perhaps the little fellow would find a home elsewhere.

But the next day, Taro found the *tanuki* in a cage in the garden. His father had had it imprisoned for the entertainment of the courtiers, who were mocking the creature mercilessly. A couple of days later, it died.

From then on, Taro found solace in his metal workroom. He did not need his father's love. He would never again find room in his heart for a creature that could be taken from him. His metal creations kept him company. They did not talk back, they did not demand, and they could not die.

Lost in his memories, Taro failed to notice the hammer in his hand drift from the copper sheet. The hammer smashed his thumb, and Taro grunted in pain. Tossing the tool aside, he palmed his head. On his workbench, a wingless mechanical bird jumped on tin feet — Taro's latest companion. Just last week he had placed a tiny heart made of gears in the bird's chest. His miniature creation was nearly ready. All it needed was wings. He'd been working on making the copper malleable enough to carve metal feathers. A rare smile touched Taro's lips. Perhaps the bird would soar high enough to overtake the palace walls. *Wouldn't that be something?*

The hands of the clock ticked. Early morning had arrived. It was time. Taro's smile dissolved. He unwound the bird, and it shuttered its steel eyelids. With a single breath, he extinguished the candle and slipped from the workroom.

Taro regarded the pelts lining the hallway: boar, lion, great bear, even a *kirin*, a rare chimerical *yōkai* beast that resembled a deer, only with dragon-like scales and a golden fiery mane. Torches blazed in metal sconces, the light reflecting the gilded walls and creating dancing shadows on the high ceilings.

At inception, the Palace of Illusions was built plainly and without nails, the interior nothing more than an open room. There had been no grand Main Hall or painted rice-paper panels. Since then, the dwelling had evolved, shedding its humble origins. To best his predecessors, each emperor had added new features: sprawling gardens with exotic plants, an imposing gate with snarling stone *komainu*, fierce lion dogs that acted as guardians and represented the beginning and the end of all things. The palace became a monument, a building of legends, where emperors would be immortalized.

Each emperor knew that all the gold and varnish couldn't protect them. If given the chance, there were always those who would try to take it for themselves. Thus, the palace was safeguarded with priests' curses. Illusions. A bottomless moat. Underground tunnels as intricate as lacework. Someday it would all be Taro's: the riches, the command of the land, the power. *I don't want it. I don't want any of it. I especially do not wish to be a prize in some stupid competition.*

His lip curled in disgust as he pushed aside a tiger pelt. The decorative furs concealed trapdoors. In this hallway alone, there were ten. And in the Main Hall, the entry point to the Seasonal Rooms, there were more than one hundred. Dozens of samurai patrolled the tunnels below, ready to spring from the floorboards, surprise-phantoms of death hungry to mow down marauders.

As a boy, Taro had been forced to memorize the lacework tunnels, an easy task, given his nimble mind. His brain stored millions of memories, each like a painting chronicling the seconds of his life.

The hidden door opened and closed with noiseless ease. The hinges were kept well-oiled. Taro descended the stone stairs. He didn't need a light. Sixteen steps, and he'd reach the bottom. Even if Taro hadn't had such a fine memory, the tunnels had a simple key. Steps were measured in multiples of eight. Always sixteen steps down. One hundred twenty-eight steps to the Main Hall, with eight lefts and eight rights and eight steps in between.

Taro inhaled. The air was cool and musty. His broad shoulders brushed the walls. The tunnels were narrow in this part of the palace, widening as they drew closer to the Main Hall. A rodent scampered across his path, followed by a cat chasing its prey.

A hazy light flickered. He'd come to the section of tunnel where samurai patrolled. He let his feet fall heavily, announcing his entrance. Two spears crossed and blocked his path. Taro arched a brow.

"Your Majesty." They bowed, lowering the spears. It wasn't unusual for Taro to walk through the tunnels. As a boy, it had been a game to him, playing to see if he could sneak up on the samurai. He passed the samurai without acknowledging them. Taro's nightly walks served a purpose. The guards were used to his presence. Unsuspecting. Soon these lacework tunnels would be his way out. Every day Taro walked these tunnels and dreamed of all the directions he could go. He longed for only one: the one that led to freedom from the castle walls. He'd vowed to be liberated from this fancy prison before the start of the competition.

Eight steps and a left turn, and Taro came to another set of guards. These two slept at their posts. Taro flattened against a wall and waited for another two guards to vacate a section of the tunnel. Their patrols left certain parts unguarded, but only for a few seconds. He'd memorized every guard's movements, the sound of their individual breathing, even what times they took breaks to relieve themselves. He knew their habits, their distinct quirks. If he were planning to be Emperor, he'd warn them not to be so predictable. But their flaws were his gain.

Taro slipped from his hiding spot and up the stone stairs. Again, this trapdoor lifted and closed effortlessly. Taro was in the Main Hall. While pelts hid the trapdoors near Taro's workroom, they were unnecessary here. The doors camouflaged seamlessly with the high-glossed zelkova floor.

Taro cracked his knuckles, the sound echoing through the cavernous space. He didn't need to worry about guards here. The samurai in the tunnels were trained to keep their ears open for the slightest sound. Intruders would be detected before they made it to the Hall. Another chink in the palace armor.

The Winter Room doors rose above him as he faced them, dark and ominous. Moonlight danced through skylights. He pressed an ear to the door. *No sound.*

Placing a shoulder under the oak, he pushed up. Even with his newfound strength, the weight was nearly unbearable, and Taro swore foully as he removed it. The doors creaked open. Against a rush of cold air, Taro slipped inside. His feet immediately sank into inches of crusted-over snow, his toes curling at the freezing temperature. The night was clear in the vast Winter Room. The moon was thin, but the stars shone bright, making the snow appear like spun glass. Hundreds of thousands of meters of Ice Forest stretched before him. In the middle of all the trees was a river upon which he had skated as a child. In the distance, wolves bayed. Closer, a white owl screeched in the trees, and beneath the owl was the *kappa*.

As Taro had suspected, the *kappa* had frozen to death. Its mouth was open, strained in a perpetual scream. Little icicles hung from its orange beak. Something in Taro's stone heart cracked. The *yōkai* had spent his last moment of life cold, afraid, alone. *This is not how it should be.*

Wind swirled, kicking up snow around Taro's ankles, billowing his purple robe. He stared down at the *kappa*. Tucked into the belt of

26

his *hakama* was his hammer. Usually, he used it to create. Today, he would destroy. He brought the hammer above his head and slammed it down upon the *kappa*. The resounding crack was inordinately loud in the silence. Startled owls and crows flew from their trees. Snow loosened from branches, falling in clumps to the ground.

The *kappa* shattered into icy crystals. One by one he gathered the *kappa* shards to his chest and strode through the forest until he came to the frozen river. He hammered a hole into the ice and cast the shards into the running water beneath. He had returned the creature to its rightful home.

There, he hoped, it would find peace.

CHAPTER 5

Mari

MARI STEPPED INTO Hissa's bedroom and covered her mouth. Inside, it was hot and humid, crowded with Animal Wives.

The Animal Wives, her lovely sisters — if not by birth, then by heart — parted like curtains, revealing her friend. Hissa lay on a cypress bed, all her attention focused on the tiny white bundle she clutched. White cloths stained with watery pink scattered the wood floor.

Hissa's cheeks and lips were as pale as snow, her eyes shiny, red-rimmed, and bleary with fever. Despite that, Hissa was lovely as ever. Almost incandescent. "Tami-sama," she cried. Mari's lips twitched. It stung that Hissa had cried for her mother and not for her. *I know why, though.* Tami was Alpha of their clan. With a single word, Tami could bend rules, break customs, allow Hissa to keep her baby.

"My dear one." Tami brushed past Mari and knelt beside Hissa. Another Animal Wife appeared over Tami's shoulder, handing her a damp cloth. Mari watched as her mother blotted the sweat from Hissa's brow.

"I've named him Yutaka." Murmurs ran through the room. Hissa should not have given her boy a name. It wasn't done. It only made things worse, made it harder to let go. A sob broke on Hissa's lips. She tightened her hold on the bundle. "I — I can't give him up." The Animal Wives lowered their heads, embarrassed for Hissa. "Tami —"

"Shush." Tami touched Hissa's cheek and thumbed away her tears. "You don't have to do anything. Give the boy to me." Gently, Tami reached for the small bundle.

Hissa's arms loosened. She was going to release him. Mari's fingernails dug into her palms, suppressing a desperate need to grab the baby and run. Cool logic overruled Mari's wild impulse. She wouldn't get far. A hundred beastly Animal Wives would hunt her. Just as Mari's hands unclenched, Hissa seemed to gather her wits. In a sudden burst of willpower, Mari's friend wrenched the baby back. Hissa's arms tightened around him. "You won't take him from me," she whispered. The tone of her voice carried a warning, a threat. Hissa's eyes flashed. Her pupils expanded until only black fathomless pits remained.

Fear beat in Mari's throat. She stumbled back, along with the other Animal Wives, their collective breath held.

Tami was quick to react. With a thin, lithe hand, she pinned the new mother to the bed at the neck. She drew forward, speaking quietly in Hissa's ear. Mari couldn't hear her mother's words, but she witnessed their effect. The fight drained from Hissa. Her eyes returned to their soft, natural brown, her face mottled with fear and sadness, *defeat.* Hissa thrust the baby into Tami's arms, giving in. Giving up. Mari clenched her fists, feeling her friend's surrender as her own.

Silent tears streamed down Hissa's cheeks. "Take him," she said. "Take my baby, but know that today you kill me, too!" With that, Hissa sank onto the bed, shriveling into herself. The baby boy let out a mighty wail, as if sensing its watery future.

Hissa's body shook with sobs, her hands shuttering her face. "Get him out of here! Don't make me listen to him cry."

Tami stood, her mouth set in a straight line. She tucked the bundle in her arms and strode from the room, not even sparing Hissa a backward glance. The Animal Wives filed out behind her, moving like sunbeams dancing on water. So graceful. The opposite of Mari. *They don't know how to swing a sword,* Mari consoled herself.

The room emptied, leaving Mari alone with Hissa. Mari's hands trembled. Mere hours ago, she had faced an imperial samurai in a game of death. The navy kimono she wore was still specked with dust from their combat. And now, she hesitated with what to say, how to comfort Hissa. *Sometimes words are so much more difficult to form than fists.*

As girls, Mari and Hissa had been the very best of friends, running barefoot through the streets of Tsuma, catching cherries as they fell from the trees, the red flesh of the fruit still warm from the sun. When Hissa's beauty blossomed and Mari's did not, the other girls abandoned Mari, but Hissa refused to desert her friend. Mari used to envy Hissa's looks, thinking they were the key to happiness. Now she realized that no one was above suffering.

Mari crept closer to her friend. Faintly, she detected pine and cucumber on Hissa's skin. *Night flower.* The Animal Wives used it to treat infections. Mari swallowed, her throat dry. "Do you want a cup of tea, something to eat?" she asked. Hissa continued to weep. Mari stepped around the futon and crouched, bringing her face level to her friend's. "Hissa." Her friend's name emerged like a plea. *Say something. Talk to me. Show me how to make this better.*

Hissa fought to still her quaking jaw. "I was so silly, so desperate for a girl. Now it's as if the gods and goddesses are laughing at me. You can't possibly understand what it's like to think you have the world at your feet, only to have it pulled out from under you like some cheap rug." Hissa's hands balled into white-knuckled fists, her tears continuing to flow unchecked. "I should have stayed with him."

Hissa's words weren't treasonous, but they were taboo. "Don't say that." Mari's voice was unsteady, cautious.

Animal Wives never stayed with the men they married. From birth, it was ground into them to honor and provide for the clan. *Duty and home, the whole before the self.* How many times had Mari heard those words?

She'd been seven when the last Animal Wife defected. Akemi fell in love and decided to stay with her husband, a farmer. When she'd shown him her true nature — the beast inside the beautiful woman — he'd rejected her. She returned to Tsuma but was rejected there, too. Animal Wives punished by ostracism. Refusing to leave her mountain home, she starved to death. Her bones, bleached from the sun, wrapped in woodbine and half-sunk into the ground, could still be found nestled near the iron gates.

Hissa's eyes dimmed, her laughter laced with bitterness. "I'm a monster. We're all monsters. No man, no human, will ever love us. That is the curse of the Animal Wife, never to be loved for who we truly are." Hissa's lips twisted. "You're lucky that you'll never have to face this."

Heavy hurt flourished in Mari's midsection. *Hissa is right.* When it became apparent Mari would not be beautiful, her mother had altered her daughter's destiny. *If you won't be beautiful,* Tami had said, as if it were a choice, *then perhaps you will be Empress.* From that day on, Mari no longer schooled with the other girls, no longer suffered through lessons on charm and etiquette. Instead, she was trained on a *naginata,* and then shoved into the shed. A boy around her age had been in the musty dark room. *Only one comes out,* Tami said before slamming the door. Mari had swung first, cracking the *naginata* against the boy's knee.

Mari chewed on her lower lip, willing the memory away. "I know," she replied to Hissa. Mari had fought her last opponent tonight, but it only meant that she would leave soon for Tokkaido, the Imperial City, carrying the weight of her mother's expectations. *You will enter the competition, conquer the Seasons, become Empress, and steal the prince's fortune, or . . .* Her mother had left it at that, but Mari could fill in the blank. *Or you will die trying.* The right to rule was paved with bloody stones. Not only would Mari have to survive the Seasonal Rooms, beating out the other girls, but *yōkai* were forbidden to participate. Even to set foot on palace grounds was an act of treason. So yes, Mari would probably never have to let go of a baby boy. Most likely, she'd die first.

"I'm sorry," Hissa said, her face falling. "That was cruel."

"It's all right." Hissa was just a cornered animal lashing out.

Hissa's gaze drifted to a crumpled pink silk blanket. Her fingers caressed the delicate fabric. For the last few weeks, Hissa and Mari had worked tirelessly, stitching bright orange and red poppies on that piece of cloth. "I was going to wrap her up in this." Hissa thrust the blanket at Mari. "Please, please take this to the river. Make sure they don't let him go without it."

Mari gathered the blanket in her hands. She kissed Hissa's salty cheek. "He won't even feel the water," Mari vowed.

The Letting Go ceremony took place at night, outside the gates on the banks of the Horo River, a lazy body of water that cut down the mountain, curved across several towns, and filtered into the Ma ni Sea.

Mari followed the sound of the river and the baby's cry — *Yutaka's voice*. The moon was just a hangnail in the sky. By the time she broke through the cedar trees, the Animal Wives had already gathered at the shore, waves lapping at their bare feet. Each wore a simple white kimono. Their long, glossy black hair hung loose. In their hands, they held lanterns. The yellow light limned their features, giving them the appearance of apparitions. Ghostly brides.

"Wait!" Mari shouted, nearly out of breath.

Yutaka was in a reed basket, half floating in the water, the other half anchored by Tami's hand. Mari shoved her way through the Animal Wives, almost slipping on the moss-covered rocks. Her chest heaved, and she caught her mother's eye. "Hissa wanted him to have this." She held up the blanket.

Tami dipped her chin. Permission.

Mari knelt by the basket. The baby's face was red and scrunched, wrinkly like a dried plum. *If I'd been born a boy* . . . Mari shook her head. *It's too terrible to contemplate.* An Animal Wife sniffled.

Probably Noriko. She had given birth to the last son. The day after his Letting Go ceremony, his reed basket was spotted on the other side of the river, shredded and soaked. The white blanket that had covered him was snagged on riverbank branches.

Mari tucked the pink blanket around Yutaka. She closed her eyes and said a little prayer to the gods and goddesses for the lost boy.

May the river keep you safe.

May the river keep you warm.

May the river guide you to a loving home.

Tears blurred her vision. The weight of the day pressed down upon her. Most of Mari's life had been spent pulling away, burying her sorrow, building walls around her private pain. All her safeguards failed her now. Mari couldn't watch as the Animal Wives pushed the little basket into the river, or set their lanterns to float after him. Instead, she looked up, past the jagged mountain peaks and into the endless night sky. A scream locked in her throat, choking her. *What is it all for?* She turned and walked toward the edge of the forest, then paused, feeling her mother's gaze on her back like a taunt.

You wouldn't dare.

That little ball of rebellion loosened in Mari's veins again, rolling like a boulder down a hill, picking up weight and speed. Mari broke into a run, allowing the trees to swallow her up.

It was not wise, her decision to flee.

Mari would pay for her defiance. Perhaps her mother would strike her, or maybe she would disown her, cast Mari from their mountain village. In her heart, Mari knew the latter would never happen. Her mother wanted the imperial fortune. Badly. Tami liked the comforts of life — maybe even more than she cared for her child.

A sharp pain in Mari's side stole her breath and stalled her thoughts. She slowed to a walk, massaging the stitch above her hip. The wind tapered off; the forest grew peaceful and still. At her feet, white flowers opened like hands to the moon.

She leaned against a gnarled oak with a gigantic trunk. Angry tears welled in her eyes. She brushed them away with a furious hand and pressed her lips together, steeling herself to return to Tsuma.

In front of her, a patch of trees shook. Mari stilled. There was no wind. Panic inched up her spine, and gooseflesh broke out on her arms. *I am not alone.*

Her breaths grew shallow and ragged as she listened. Every sense sharpened. The beast within stirred, a sharp tickle against the inside of her skin. She blinked; her eyes dissolved to black. Her nails elongated to talons. Ebony scales popped out along her hands. The shift ground to a halt. This was all the beast would give her — a partial transformation. Another of Mari's deficits, and her mother's greatest shame: a daughter with only half a beast. Plain and powerless.

The trees rustled again.

Mari's hands flexed as she wished for her *naginata*. She was weaponless, but not defenseless. Her talons were as sharp as knives. She dropped her body into a crouch, her lip lifted in a snarl. *Arm-to-arm combat it is.* She waited. *Let my enemy show his face first.* Her skin prickled the way it did when the mountain air was charged before an approaching storm.

The brush parted. A form appeared.

Mari sprang, her arm hooking around her assailant's neck and forcing them both to the ground. She landed atop her foe with an undignified grunt. She wrapped her hand around his neck, her talons nearly puncturing the thin skin. She could feel his pulse pounding beneath her fingertips. Mari pulled back to study what she'd caught. A boy.

He wore a simple black *uwagi* tied with twine. His skin was a shade lighter than hers, and his hair was dark and long, woven into braids to keep the locks from his eyes. A black cloth covered the lower half of his face. She wrenched the mask away.

She let out a soft breath. The boy's face was terribly scarred. A slit emerged from one corner of his mouth, extending in a graceful arc to the upper part of his cheek. Her gaze lingered on his ghastly half-smile. More slash marks covered the same half of his face, one across his eye, another bisecting his forehead. The other side of his face was unmarred, beautiful, with a high cheekbone and straight nose. Her hand twitched. She kept her hold even as he smiled, revealing straight, white teeth and gleaming eyes. He knew her. And she knew him. *The Son of Nightmares.*

CHAPTER 6
Akira

THE SON OF NIGHTMARES grinned like he'd won a prize.

His gaze settled on the girl, her face half illuminated in a single shard of silvery moonlight, half shadowed by her curtain of thick hair. The trees around them stilled as if the forest were holding its breath. "Animal Girl," he murmured.

"Akira." Her talons withdrew against his throat. Her black eyes faded to brown. With a disgruntled noise, she scooted off him. "You know I hate it when you call me that."

The Son of Nightmares grinned wider. He could count on one hand the number of people who knew his real name, and it sounded particularly lovely passing through Mari's lips. He sat up and placed both hands on her cheeks. She leaned into his touch just as the last scale on her hands receded. He was used to seeing her charcoal scales, her talons, her black eyes. Gently, he thumbed away tracks of dried tears and a scrape of mud. "You're a mess."

Her eyes fluttered and met his. *Squish.* That was the sound his heart made every time she looked at him, her brown eyes alive with recognition and light.

Akira remembered the first time he saw her, ten years ago. He was a gangly boy at the edge of the forest, and Mari a scrawny kid in a too-fancy kimono. Each was surprised and frozen silent, fascinated by the other. At first sight, he thought she was a vengeful ghost like his mother. But soon he realized who she was. He'd heard rumors of her clan: Animal Wives, a village of women who preyed on men. Whether or not those rumors were true, she was something different. *Something more.*

"I don't like it when you look at me that way."

"What way?" he asked, a rueful smile touching his scarred lips.

"Like you're thinking how best to handle me."

"That's not what I was doing at all." Although he kind of was. Years of friendship, and Mari remained an enigma — eyes that flashed from anger to fear, mouth that frowned more often than not, hands capable of killing but gentle when holding his.

Mari stood. Akira's fingers fell from her cheeks. He missed the warmth of her skin. "Then what were you doing?" she asked, turning her head away from him, a stubborn set to her jaw. Akira wished Mari could see herself as he did — beautiful, wanted, *beloved.*

"Why were you crying? You never cry." His smile faded. "Hissa had her baby. A boy?"

Mari crossed her arms over her chest. She still wouldn't look at him. "My mother put the baby in the river. I couldn't watch," she said, her voice thin, watery.

Akira rose, dusting loose dirt from his sleeves. "He will live," he assured her. "Besides, I've told you, there are no blemishes on the souls of Animal Wives." Every being, *yōkai*, human, animal, every living thing carried a distinct, colored aura that the Son of Nightmares alone could see. Mari's was pure blue, the color of a glacier. And when a soul killed another, a piece of it went missing, a hole appeared.

Mari snorted. "But how long will he survive, and how well?"

All his talents, and Akira had no idea. "All I know is that the river doesn't kill them. Perhaps the monks will find him," he said, trying to offer some comfort. The Taiji monks fostered children. They lived in a monastery with doors hung so low, you had to crawl through them. The monks would never turn a baby away. But the monastery was north, and the current of the river ran south.

"Maybe," Mari said stiffly.

"Sad girl," Akira crooned. "I have something that will make you happy."

Her body loosened, and she settled her gaze back on him. His heart made that squishing noise again. She sniffled. "I can't be gone long."

Akira nodded, understanding. A hidden friendship. Stolen moments. This was how it had always been between them. How it would always be.

"Come." He caught her fingers, interlaced them with his. Her palm was warm and soft. A perfect fit.

They walked deep into the forest. The light of the moon played hide-and-seek beneath the canopy. Giant-winged moths and spotted beetles fluttered and buzzed past.

Akira closed his eyes and breathed, absorbing the dense

sweetness of the land. He knew every inch of this forest, every blade of grass, the bark of each tree. He spent most days in the canopy, swinging from the branches as easily as a monkey. Although his mother was *yōkai*, a ghost, he hadn't inherited her ability to float through walls. He *had* inherited other things. The power to move as the wind, to leave no trace on the ground, to behave like a shadow. And his scars. The deep, silvery trenches on half his body were reminders of the painful story of his mother's death.

Before his mother was *yōkai*, a ghost, she was human and named Mizuki, the most beautiful girl in her city. She married Takumi, a local *sake* brewer. Takumi was as jealous as Mizuki was vain. One night, Takumi accused Mizuki of being too free with her smiles. He killed her, but not before carving the marks on her face. Mizuki awoke transformed, a *yōkai* vengeful ghost. She haunted docks, alleyways, abandoned apartment buildings, prowling for men who followed women too closely or held them too tightly. Upon these men, she heaped brutal punishment.

Akira slowed. A creek blocked their path. Water tinkled over rocks. He hopped across and went to lift Mari, but she shook her head and jumped over herself. So like her. "You surprised me back there. I didn't think you would return before morning," Mari said, walking beside Akira.

Their shoulders brushed, and Akira relished the touch. He chewed his cheek. He'd hoped she wouldn't bring it up. "He didn't want my help."

Mari paused. She inhaled and exhaled with a deep breath. Worry scrunched her brow. "But he's headed down the mountain?"

"Yes. I made sure he knew never to venture back here."

Mari gave a curt nod. "Good."

Akira scratched the back of his head. "Did you have to break his nose?"

"He laughed at me." Mari's expression grew pained. She kicked a rock. Too often, Mari bloodied a man and then sobbed in Akira's arms. Quick to anger and quick to regret it.

Akira would do anything for her. Mari had come to him, years ago, on a night like this. Her eyes bright, fearful, and full of liquid. *Akira, help me.* Unable to refuse, Akira followed her to a shed where a boy rocked, holding his busted knee. Akira put the boy on his back and carried him all night to the main road leading down the mountain.

From then on, Akira became the keeper of Mari's greatest secret. Mari maimed but never killed. If her mother ever found out that Mari let her captives escape, and how Akira aided her . . . He fought a shudder. Nothing good would come of it.

Mari stopped short at a wall of trees blocking their path. They had arrived at their destination. "The ginkgo tree?" she asked with a note of disappointment. The Animal Wives had been here a dozen times before, meeting under the thousand-year-old tree to celebrate the twelve festivals of the gods, goddesses, and seasons. The last time they'd met, winter was nearing its end. They'd smeared mud onto one another's faces and whispered spring blessings of luck and health.

A smile twitched at the corner of his lips. "Wait and see," Akira said, stepping through the trees.

Mari grumbled but followed. Her face lit with a smile. She was the most beautiful thing in Akira's world. "It's shedding!" she exclaimed.

Akira felt proud, like he'd given her a rare and precious gift. The tree's crown spanned a hundred feet. Bright yellow leaves drifted from the branches to the ground, soft and silent as snow.

Mari caressed the rough bark, reverence in her touch. To the Animal Wives, the ginkgo tree was sacred, a symbol of their duality, endurance, and longevity. Akira had asked Mari to tell him the story over and over, mainly just to hear her voice.

The first Animal Wife came to the peak of the mountain during a harsh winter. Nearly frozen, she stumbled upon the ginkgo and found shelter beneath its branches. She thought it must be magical, a tree with leaves in winter. The trunk kept the vicious wind from slicing her apart. When a lightning storm swept through, branches split from the tree, and the Animal Wife scooped up the timber. With it, she built the first home in Tsuma.

The Animal Wives believed that as long as the ginkgo tree stood in the Tsuko funo Mountains, they would survive. Some of the older Animal Wives were even superstitious about the tree's annual shedding, regarding it as a dangerous time for their clan. A naked tree is vulnerable, and thus so were the Animal Wives.

"I knew you'd like it," he said with a grin.

Mari didn't speak. She took a deep breath. Strife brewed in the murky depths of her eyes. Nestled in the branches were *kodama*, the ginkgo tree's soul manifested in small white figures, just the size of Akira's forearm. They were round-bellied, dark-eyed, and silent, but their mouths were open as if lost in a deep, childlike sigh. Full of innocence. Akira wondered how his soul might appear. Dark? Scarred? *Weak?* It was the only one he couldn't see.

"What are you thinking?" Akira asked, reading Mari's forlorn expression.

"Hissa says that we are monsters, that Animal Wives are cursed never to be loved for who we truly are."

Akira's heart lodged in his throat. He thought of his scars, his vengeful ghost mother, and his human father. Half *yōkai* and half human, he was the real monster. He would never be accepted among either group. He existed in a state of in-between, never human enough, never *yōkai* enough. Worse, his father wasn't just a human but a foreigner, a trader from the Ollis Isles with fair skin and hair. He came to Honoku as a merchant and fell in love with a ghost. "I don't see you that way," Akira told Mari.

A giant gust of wind swept through the tree, and its leaves fell like rain, catching in Mari's hair. "How do you see me?" Mari asked with a distant smile.

Perhaps she was fishing for a compliment. Akira didn't mind. He would always take the bait if it were offered from her fingertips. "I can't say." His smile teased. He drew even closer. "If I told you how I saw you, your ego would become unmanageable." Mari laughed, and Akira's soul lightened. *You cannot fathom all the ways I adore you,* he wanted to whisper. Confessions hovered on his tongue, words of love and devotion, but then Mari circled the tree and sighed. He knew that sound. It was time for Mari to go.

With a sad goodbye and a delicate wave, Mari slipped through the line of trees and disappeared. She was always the first to leave.

Akira slumped to a sitting position under the ginkgo tree. He rolled his head up and gazed at the *kodama*. Farther above, the stars shone like sprinkled sugar on a black mat.

Every time he saw Mari, Akira had a crushing feeling it might be the last. A feeling that wasn't unwarranted. When he was thirteen, he ran away from home. Not to escape, but to follow. Curious by nature, the mystery of the Animal Wives had obsessed him. So when Akira spied one departing Tsuma, he pursued her.

Only he didn't think to cover his face. The first villager he came across spat at him. Akira remembered wiping the phlegm from his cheek and touching his scars. After that, he remained in the shadows.

Two weeks passed. He never told Mari about what he saw. At first, he thought nothing of it. The Animal Wife checked into a boarding house and caught the attentions of a local jeweler. Within days, they were married. A few nights after their wedding, Akira watched through a latticed window as the Animal Wife robbed the jeweler. She stuffed her pockets with vials of powdered gold, coral gems, and chains of silver, then snuck away before dawn.

The Animal Wife's deception wasn't what bothered Akira. His own family survived by relieving mountain travelers of their coin. It was what happened afterward that deeply unsettled him. When the Animal Wife returned to Tsuma, she was changed. Her smiles became forced. At night she wept, and nine months later, she placed her baby boy in the river. Her soul became discolored, turning from radiant lemon to pale yellow. No blemishes marred the surface. She had not killed. The color change, Akira came to understand, was from sadness.

Mari's fate would be far worse. Her future was death or marriage

to the imperial prince. When he thought about their inevitable sep-
aration, it was as if a torch had been pressed under his ribs, burning
him slowly from the inside out. He knew that one day he'd have only
the memory of Mari to cherish — and the knowledge of how grand
it could have been.

THE FIRST EMPRESS

FROM THE SKY, Sugita watched his favorite human. His son, the first emperor, whom he had crafted in his image, was sad. On his golden throne, the human wept. Sugita called for the lightning and descended Kita's staircase.

He approached the weeping human. "What ails you, son?" he asked, for he was at a loss. From the heavens, Sugita saw all the gifts he'd bestowed on the human: fertile fields that yielded enough rice for eternity, mines with iron and gold and precious gems, humans who worshiped at his feet, who praised him as a god. "I have given you so much," Sugita remarked, unsettled by this human condition of wanting more.

His son's lips trembled. "I have everything, and no one to share it with."

Sugita's mouth parted in surprise. He had not considered love as a human need. To love was divine. He thought only gods and goddesses capable of it. "You wish for a partner, a woman to share your life?" Sugita asked.

"Yes." The human's eyes lit up. "I want a woman," he told Sugita. "But she must be worthy of me."

Sugita nodded. So Sugita scooped up human women from every clan and placed them in the farthest corner of Honoku. He left them in a cave carved by water and wind in the middle of a desolate cliff. Among the women were two sisters, Makoto and Tsukiko, daughters of an umbrella merchant.

Armed with silk umbrellas, Makoto and Tsukiko fought the other women for pieces of rope discarded in the cave. Using the rope, they climbed from the cliff.

At the bottom of the cliff, Tsukiko moaned. "I want to go home."

Makoto grasped Tsukiko's hand, holding it to her cheek. "Little Bean, as your older sister, I vow I will see you home or die trying."

The girls followed the Drum constellation, hoping it would lead to their small village. With the first heated wind of summer, they came to a mountain. "No way to go but up," Makoto said. They climbed. At the summit, Honoku spread out before them. The sisters realized that they were no closer to home than the stars to Earth.

They journeyed onward. Fall kissed summer goodbye. Just as the first leaf fell, they came to an abandoned village. They didn't question their good fortune. They raided the homes, stuffing their mouths with strips of wild boar meat, pickled beets, and mushrooms soaked in miso. But the village hadn't been abandoned. And while the sisters slept, the inhabitants returned. Oni. Eight-foot-tall demons with four eyes and six black horns curling from the crowns of their heads. The strongest of the yōkai. Again, Makoto and Tsukiko used their umbrellas as weapons and fought their way out of the oni encampment.

But for every victory, a price must be paid.

Tsukiko was badly wounded. Makoto refused to leave her sister. As clever as she was fierce, Makoto built a sled from branches. Then she lifted Tsukiko onto the makeshift stretcher.

"Little Bean, I will see you home or die trying." Makoto dragged the stretcher. Winter stripped fall. It began to snow. To keep Tsukiko distracted, Makoto sang to her. Tsukiko hummed along, and Makoto could just hear her over the howling wind. Soon, Makoto realized that Tsukiko's voice had faded.

Makoto stopped.

The stretcher was no longer behind her. The wind had bled the warmth from Makoto's hands. She'd thought she'd been holding the stretcher, but she'd really been grasping air. Makoto wailed and backtracked. She found Tsukiko nearly buried in the snow. Her lips were blue and her eyes closed. Ice crystals had formed on her lashes. Tsukiko was gone.

Weeping, Makoto curled up next to her sister's body. "Little Bean, I will see you home or die trying." They were not home. Makoto resolved to perish next to her sister. She slept through the raging storms. Snow covered their bodies. But the winter would not take her. Nature protected her. When the snow melted, it pooled on her lips, forced her to drink. When the spring wind shook the trees, fir branches fell and covered her like the warmest quilt. And when the first apple dropped from a nearby tree, it rolled into her open hand. She would not die. Nature would not let her. By this time, Tsukiko's body had sunk into the earth, only her delicate fingers still aboveground.

A man approached. Disoriented, Makoto grabbed her umbrella and pressed the tip against the man's throat. Blood trickled down his neck.

The man knelt. "My bride, my equal!" he exclaimed.

At once she recognized the man. The emperor. "I want to go home," she said, dropping the battered umbrella.

"You are home," the emperor replied. His arm swept behind him where the palace rose, golden and glimmering in the spring light.

She cried. "I have failed my sister."

The emperor smiled gently. "Success and failure are merely illusions. They are not yours to hold." Then he whispered all she was and all she was meant to be. "A ruler," he said. "Mine," he said.

Beloved by nature.

Revered by her husband.

An Empress of All Seasons.

CHAPTER 7
Taro

WATER POURED FROM THE SKY, splattered on the tiled roof of the palace, flowed into the gutters, and out the mouths of golden *shachihoko* — tiger-carp hybrids that summoned rain and protected against fire.

Inside, Taro turned his cheek to the emperor's hacking cough. Over the last twenty-four hours, the cough had grown raw and violent. They sat at the low table for an evening meal of fish-paste cakes and vegetables simmered in sesame oil. The emperor could barely hold down his food. A servant rushed forward, a silver pitcher of water sloshing over in his hands, but the emperor shooed him away.

"Has one of the theorists looked at you?" Taro asked dutifully.

The emperor took a sip of *sake*, his cheeks blushed red, and his eyes watered. He shook his head. "I'd rather choke to death than let one of them near me."

Taro arched a brow but said nothing. Theorists had been called to tend to Taro's mother when she was in labor with him. They had failed to deliver Taro, and his mother had grown sicker and sicker with the delivery. Desperate, the emperor was forced to summon another kind of help. Known for their midwifery, a *futakuchi-onna*, a *yōkai*, was the emperor's only hope. The two-mouthed woman had ushered Taro safely into the land of the living, but she had also aided in the empress's exit. Or so the emperor concluded. This was the root of the emperor's intense hatred of *yōkai*. *Funny how love can drive you to hate.*

There was a tight, awkward silence. Taro stared over the emperor's shoulder, out the window. The rain continued. Beyond, the Dry Garden stretched; white sand had been combed in parallel circles, mimicking the ripple of raindrops as they fell into water.

The person next to Taro cleared his throat. "It's been going around the palace." Taro cut his eyes to Satoshi. With his round face, dimples, and long lashes, Satoshi looked more boy than man. He wore white robes, and a sash of red hung from his shoulder, then wrapped around his waist, declaring his status as High Priest. *The priest of all priests.* Tattoos blemished his hands but not his face. *An odd personal choice.* Most priests tattooed their entire bodies, but always their hands and faces. The swirling cobalt markings were curses. They had the same effect written as spoken, only when a *yōkai* touched the ink, it burned.

Satoshi joined Taro and his father for dinner often. He filled a variety of roles within the palace. Priest. Adviser. Peacemaker.

Satoshi was also Taro's half brother. The son of a concubine, Satoshi posed no threat to the throne. Yet for some reason, their father

51

seemed to favor his bastard son over Taro. *Seemed to.* In reality, the emperor viewed both his children as blemishes, warts to be tolerated but never loved. It didn't stop Satoshi from seeking the emperor's approval any chance he got. Satoshi treated Taro in much the same way, seeking out the emperor and prince's affections as a stray dog nuzzles a friendly hand.

"I visited the Winter Room this morning," the emperor said, drawing Taro's attention from Satoshi.

"Not wise for an old man with a cold," Taro replied.

"I wore a *yamabiko* pelt," the emperor said through his teeth. Rare and elusive *yōkai*, *yamabiko* inhabited the lower elevations of the Tsuko funo Mountains. Their voices caused false echoes and mimicked sounds, including terrible screams. The emperor had hunted them nearly to extinction. Their thick brown fur was desirable for its warmth, and their ivory teeth were favored in jewelry; both fetched high prices in the markets. Taro worked to keep his expression serene as his father continued. "It seems my *kappa* has disappeared."

The memory washed over Taro. The dark Winter Room. The cold as it seeped into his clothing. Hammer in his hand. In a flurry, Taro thought of all the other *yōkai* frozen and hidden in the Ice Forest. A *kijimuna*, a redheaded, one-legged being that dwelt in Banyan trees. A *nure-onago*, a matted, wet-haired girl, birthed from the tears of drowning victims. The *futakuchi-onna* that had delivered Taro.

"Strange," Taro said to his father, and popped a piece of dried fruit into his mouth.

The emperor grinned, a predatory gleam in his eyes. "Yes, indeed. I'd hate to think we have a *yōkai* sympathizer in our midst."

Worry knifed Taro's gut. Executions awaited sympathizers. *Would the emperor do that to his own son?* He wasn't sure. "I'll keep an eye out."

"Perhaps the Resistance had something to do with it," Satoshi interjected.

Taro bit back a groan. Whatever good humor the emperor had possessed evaporated. His father's lip drew up in a sneer. "Impossible." Another cough rumbled from his throat.

Satoshi blushed and focused his gaze on his lap. "You're right," he said. "I don't know what I was thinking."

The Resistance was bigger in name than in action. Groups of same-species *yōkai* banded together and popped up like weeds. To date, the Resistance had chosen merely annoying, almost childish acts of rebellion: Blowing up a convoy carrying rice to the palace. Setting fire to a mine that provided iron to the royal forge. But Taro had a feeling that something larger was brewing. A few weeks ago, the Resistance had gone silent, and rumors had begun to swirl. Rumors of a *yōkai* Weapons Master, a trained assassin, accompanied by an *oni*, come to Tokkaido to unite the factions and build an army.

Somewhat appeased, the emperor took a long drink of *sake* and wiped grease from his mouth with a silk napkin. "Tell me, what kept you so busy this afternoon?" he questioned Taro.

Taro's mouth parted in surprise. The emperor never asked about his inventions. The only time his father had shown the slightest bit of interest was when Taro created a metal collar of unbreakable iron. Satoshi had the collar engraved with curses and slapped it around the neck of an *oni*, enslaving him. When the demon tried to remove it, his hands burned. His supernatural power, the strength of a thousand men, was subdued. The emperor used the once-mighty *oni* as labor to renovate the Spring Room. A few days later, the giant demon broke his back hauling a hundred-year-old cherry-blossom tree.

Production of the collars was removed from Taro's charge. The emperor had razed a temple and, in its place, installed an iron forge. Blacksmiths worked around the clock manufacturing the collars. The distant clang of metal on metal reverberated at all hours of the day, and the smoke blotted out the sun. Now all *yōkai* were collared and registered at birth, treated as less than dogs on leashes.

Of course, some slipped through the emperor's fingers. Collared mothers paid handsome prices to humans to ferry their babies away to the West Lands. Some humans sympathized with the *yōkai* plight, but most took advantage of it. A secret journey from the East Lands to the West Lands cost a pretty penny. And there were some *yōkai* clans that hadn't yet been conquered. High in the Tsuko funo Mountains, too high for the emperor to be bothered to expend the resources for an attack, was the Taiji monastery, where *yōkai* monks resided, locked forever in childhood.

Since the invention of the collars, Taro made sure his creations were inconsequential, nothing that could enslave an entire race.

Taro regarded his father through narrowed eyes. "I've been working on a mechanical canary." At the thought of the small bird, Taro's heart lifted.

"A canary?" Satoshi pressed gently.

Taro turned to the priest. "Yes. I've made it a small heart out of gears, and I'm in the process of creating feathers for its wings so it can fly —"

The emperor waved a dismissive hand. "You won't be able to do that once the competition starts. You'll have obligations. No time to fidget about in that workroom of yours."

Taro's lip curled. *Of course he wants to speak of the competition. Too bad I won't be here.*

"His Majesty is right," Satoshi said, a flush creeping across his cheeks. Taro wondered if it rankled Satoshi to address his father as "Your Majesty." "Your presence will be required at most of the festivities. Already the inns are nearly at capacity with girls and their clan members." Then he added, "I spoke with Master Ushiba today, and he says that this will be the toughest competition in generations." Master Ushiba, another thorn in Taro's side. The imperial Seasonist took his job seriously, often chasing Taro down to ask inane questions. *What do you think of swarms of honeybees in the Summer Room? How about a hailstorm in the Fall Room? Regarding the Winter Room, snow is so cliché. How about giant shifting ice sheets?* The small man with white eyes, sneaky and powerful, popped up everywhere.

Once every century, a human was born with eyes but no irises or pupils. This signaled a blessing. The goddess Kita had gifted the child with a singular talent — the ability to wield nature. Ushiba could bend the four elements — flame, water, air, and earth — to his will.

Taro shoved his plate away, too disgusted to eat. He took a few seconds, choosing his next words with care. "Girls have died in the Rooms. Have you no sense of decency? Are you so bloodthirsty?" he asked Satoshi. Although there were rules set before the start of the competition, "No killing" being foremost, the Rooms had predators in them. Nobody was safe. Satoshi had the good sense to look chastised. "It is an archaic tradition and should be abolished. The thought of being a prize —"

The emperor's fist slammed down, rocking the table. Little bits of jellied fish trembled, as did Satoshi. "I've had enough of your apathy." He leaned in close. "You will do this. If not for me, then for your mother. Have you forgotten so easily that she was once a competitor?"

At the mention of his mother, grief and guilt weighed down Taro's heart. *She would be alive if not for me.* Taro's nursemaid loved to tell stories of the empress and how wildly, how deeply, how madly the emperor had loved her. *How could a man love a woman so much, but not the son she bore him?* Taro returned his gaze to out the window. Raindrops blurred his vision.

The emperor continued. "She was radiant when she won ..." Taro knew what road his father headed down. A street lined with memories. He didn't need to listen to the words. He'd heard them often enough.

I remember with perfect clarity when she conquered the Seasons.

How she looked in the Winter Room, cheeks flushed and a smile like a secret hovering on her lips.

Gods and goddesses, I loved her.

Unwilling to listen once more, Taro pushed up from the table and left.

In his apartment, Taro looked at his platform bed. In a few mornings, attendants would come to rouse him and dress him for the competition. He would be a pretty peacock on display. Samurai would wait

outside his chamber doors, ready to escort him to the opening ceremony.

He painted a new future in his mind. An empty bed. A vacant
workroom. A missing prince. He saw this vision as real as day or
night or a coming storm. Soon he'd be gone. Satisfaction seeped into
Taro's bones; the future was bright and without imperial ties.

CHAPTER 8

Mari

IT WAS MORNING, and Mari stood at the entrance of the kitchen. Her body buzzed with adrenaline and lack of sleep. She'd stumbled home just before dawn. She had expected the lights to be ablaze, her mother waiting in the *tatami* room. She had expected a reckoning. But inside the house, darkness and emptiness greeted her. Tami was asleep. And Mari, too tired to question the momentary reprieve, took herself to bed.

Now, scant hours and little sleep later, Mari studied her mother, bent over the *irori*.

She doesn't appear angry.

It seemed like any other morning. Tami puttered around, scooping rice from an iron pot into an amber glazed bowl. Sensing her daughter's presence, she glanced over her shoulder. "I see you slept as poorly as I did," she said, her gaze sweeping over Mari's pale face, half-moon shadows under her eyes.

Mari made a noise of agreement as she settled into a sitting position at the low table. The room smelled of boiling rice and fire. Mari continued to track her mother's movements. She was a study in serenity. Mari didn't like it.

Remember, she is an accomplished actress. She fools men into love. How hard would it be to fool her own daughter?

From a blue porcelain jar, Tami dug out strips of pickled ginger. "You need to bring Hissa her gifts. They should have been delivered yesterday." Two packages sat in the corner. Mari had passed Hissa's house last night on her way home. Already, bereavement gifts littered her front porch. The parcels were wrapped twice in stiff *washi* paper and tied with twine, and would most likely contain coins or incense. There were also silver bowls overflowing with persimmons, pears, apples, and peaches. Fruit was the food of grief. Even in death, sweetness would be found. Her friend would be allowed to mourn forty-nine days and no more, just enough time to recover from childbirth. Then she was expected to venture back into the world and find another man with a fortune. Mari's pulse dulled at the thought.

Tsuma's survival depended on new life. *New female life.* Once an Animal Wife bore a girl, her duty was complete. She was celebrated. Revered. Most importantly, she could retire, raising her daughter in the quiet solitude of their mountain village.

The last baby girl was born five months ago. Yuka's daughter, Mayumi, was beautiful, with a round face, pink cheeks, and the longest eyelashes Mari had ever seen. All the wives doted on her. Mari would look at Mayumi and wonder, *Is this all there is? Marrying men, stealing their fortunes, and having babies?*

Tami slid a steaming bowl of rice topped with pink ginger and black sesame seeds in front of Mari, then sat down opposite her.

What game is she playing? Clearly, her mother didn't want to discuss the previous evening. *So be it. I can act as well.* Coolly, Mari reached for her *hashi.* A wooden trunk rested just under the window. "Is that new?" she asked, holding the chopsticks with a bite of rice near her mouth.

Her mother smiled, and Mari had a sudden sinking feeling. "It's for your trip."

She blinked. "My trip?"

"Yes. The competition begins in two weeks. It will take you at least a week to travel to the Imperial City. I thought to keep you here for another few days. But in light of recent events . . ." Tami shrugged. "You will depart tomorrow."

A tremor started in Mari's fingers, snaked its way down her spine. She'd known she would have to leave soon, but not having time to say goodbye? Now she understood: this was her punishment for running from Tami, for staying out all night. Tami smiled serenely as she continued sipping her tea. Cold. Calculating. *Cruel.* This was her mother's true nature.

Tami chuckled. "You think I don't know about him?" Her derisive laughter faded; her fine eyes narrowed. "You think the Son of Nightmares will take you away from here?"

Mari lowered her gaze. An angry flush crept up her cheeks. She hadn't ever considered that option. She only knew what she didn't want. She did not want to marry. She did not want to go to the Palace of Illusions. She did not want to bear baby after baby in hopes of having a girl. To all this, there was a single antidote. *Freedom. That is what I want. A life without obligation, without expectation.*

"You have nothing to say?" Tami spat. "You are a disobedient child, an ingrate."

A woman's worst trait is her temper, Tami had advised Mari. But white-hot anger beat in Mari's chest. She would most likely die in the competition and never see Tsuma or her mother again. Why measure her words any longer? Why play the part of obedient daughter for one more second? Why pretend? Lip curling, Mari growled, "I may be a disobedient ingrate, but that is far better than what you are! You are a child killer. Two of your own boys you've put in the river, and how many others? And now you sacrifice your own daughter." Her hands, her voice, shook. Though she knew it wasn't true. The boys didn't die in the river. Her mother didn't know that, however. And Mari used that information like a weapon.

Tami's eyes widened, and she leaped across the table. Rice, tea, pink ginger, and *hashi* scattered across the *tatami* mats. *Thwack.* Mari's head whipped with the force of her mother's palm. Her mouth tasted of blood.

"You think you know everything," her mother said, voice raspy and raw. Tears shimmered in Tami's eyes.

She never cries.

Tami wrapped her arms around herself, a shaking shield. "But you know nothing of sacrifices. You do not know what it is like to cast your sons into the river. You do not know what it is like to have a daughter and finally think your life has begun. Or what it is like to watch that daughter grow, to receive pitying glances when her plainness becomes evident and her beast remains all but hidden. Even though you think she is the most beautiful thing in the world." Her mother rocked. Mari's anger deflated, and in its wake, numbness set in. Words tumbled from Tami's mouth, tiny boulders that shook the foundation of Mari's world. "You do not know what it is like to have the Animal Wives whisper about your child. *Mari must be sent away; she is of no use to us; she is not beautiful; she has only a partial beast; she is not one of us*, they told me."

A thickness built in Mari's throat.

Her mother continued, undaunted; her eyes dulled, and her hands opened in front of her. "Don't you see? The training, the promise of an imperial fortune — it was the only thing I could think of to convince them. It was the only way I could keep you."

Mari's mouth parted, but no sound formed. Tami gathered herself and strode from the room. At length, Mari rose too. The weight of her mother's confession slowed her movements. She picked up the overturned bowl and teacup and swept up the sticky rice and ginger from the floor. *Hissa was right.* Animal Wives were cursed. Mari's chin trembled, but she did not allow herself to cry. *I am an accomplished actress too.*

A quickly drawn breath, and Mari's eyes sprang open, the last vestiges of sleep stripped away by fear. Someone was in her room. She could feel eyes upon her, watching her. Her mother? Not likely. After her confession, she would be keeping her distance. She'd spent the rest of the day staring out the window at the gray sky. The silence in the cottage was heavy with what remained unsaid. Another standoff. Their relationship had been reduced to a battle of wills.

Fear beat in Mari's throat. She lay still. Listening. Waiting. Outside, the wind was spiteful, rattling the windows, shaking the walls.

Her eyes adjusted to the dark, and in the shadows, a form began to materialize. She recognized the lithe movements as the figure stepped from the corner. *Akira.*

Only the Son of Nightmares could sneak over the gates of Tsuma undetected. He'd never been in her room, but Mari had shown him her cottage once. "My room faces the east. I wake with the sun," she'd said.

"Gods and goddesses, you nearly startled me to death. You were this close" — Mari sat up and pinched her fingers so that they were an inch apart — "from meeting the blade end of my *naginata.*"

Akira chuckled, leaned against the wall, and unhooked his mask.

At Akira's dry laughter, Mari frowned. *Something is off.* "What are you doing here?"

The Son of Nightmares sobered. "I dreamt you were gone." He pivoted to the wooden trunk, which she had dragged into her room. The trunk lay open, spilling over with heavy silk embroidered kimonos, *obi,* cords, gold pins . . . items worthy of an empress. "Apparently, I was right."

Wind whistled and slipped through the shutters, bringing with it a cold chill. Mari pulled the covers farther up. "I am going to the East Lands. To Tokkaido, the Imperial City."

Akira nodded. "Your mother is making you." He understood Mari's sense of duty, but he couldn't accept it. He gripped the back of his neck, frowning. "It doesn't have to be this way, you know. I've spoken with my mother and father. We're prepared —"

"I don't have a choice."

"There is always a choice," he said, hands falling to his sides and fisting.

"Not for me, there isn't." Mari shuddered, knowing that it was true. Even without her mother's admissions and threats, Mari's choice was clear. Her fate sealed.

Akira paced the length of her room, perhaps seeking the right words in the cadence of his footsteps. "Why?" he finally ground out.

Such a simple question. Such a complicated answer. She shook her head, looked away. "My mother — you don't know what she's capable of."

"I know exactly what she's capable of." He stepped forward, the floorboards creaking under his weight. "That's why I've made plans to leave this forest. We can go together. Tonight."

Mari whipped her head back to Akira. How bright his eyes burned; how they glittered, so many promises within their depths. Mari licked her lips. *Run away with him?* The idea lit up like a firework inside her. But it quickly fizzled out. *You could never go home.* She would never again see Hissa, her mother, Tsuma. She had the chance to do something big, to make them proud. *Duty and home. The whole before the self. It is an honor to serve your clan.* Her mother had drilled it into her.

And there was something else she only now saw. *Love.* From Akira. *Akira loves you.* The thought struck Mari as an arrow to the chest. *I don't love him, not like he does me.* It would be cruel and unfair to marry someone she didn't love. It would make her no better than her mother.

At Mari's silence, Akira ran his hands through his hair. "Nothing I can say or do will change your mind, will it?"

Mari's mouth tightened; she was unwilling to speak, unwilling

64

to give Akira any splinter of hope. Space and time stretched between them, a chasm as wide as the Ma ni Sea.

Akira glowered. But then he crossed to her, knelt, and gripped her hands. Akira's fingertips were cold and callused, roughened from climbing so many trees.

She looked at their joined hands, took a deep breath for bravery. "I cannot accept your offer. It means more to me than you will ever know, but it wouldn't be fair. I don't lov—"

He unclasped his hands from hers. And just as quickly as the Son of Nightmares had come, he'd gone.

Long after Akira's abrupt departure, Mari lay awake, counting the rises and falls of her chest. She blinked, memories resonating inside her like a bell. She was six, and it was the first day of her training. Tami had bid Mari to come to the courtyard.

"Mama." She'd bowed, eyeing the Animal Wives who had gathered. *Why are they here?*

Tami thrust a *naginata* at Mari. Before her fingers could wrap around the weapon, her mother charged, a *naginata* in her own grip. The hit was swift and direct, and Mari's legs gave out. She crouched in the dirt, liquid running from her eyes and nose. Tami moved to strike again, but Mari held up a small hand. "Mama, please."

By the mercy of the gods and goddesses, her mother halted. Tami's fingers pressed under Mari's chin, tilting her face up, forcing her to meet her steely eyes. She spoke low, so only Mari could hear. "You are not pretty. But you have all the skills of a lean tiger in winter. Do you understand?"

Mari's eyes shut tight; a chasm opened up in her chest. "No," she moaned.

Tami squeezed her chin, forcing Mari's eyes to open. "You *are* a lean tiger in winter. Nothing matters but survival. Now, pick up the *naginata* and fight me. You must do what you think you cannot do."

Mari wiped her cheeks and blew her nose on her kimono. She stood, *naginata* in her shaking hands. The Animal Wives tittered. They'd come to witness her humiliation, her defeat. Mari spent the rest of the afternoon crouching, hands covering her head, enduring the hits. Between knocks, Tami imparted wisdom. "Through pain you will achieve greatness." *Strike.* "Through suffering you will gain honor." *Strike.* "Through sacrifice you will rise." *Strike.*

Two years passed, and Mari learned how to wield the *naginata* as an extension of her own arms. She advanced and withdrew, cross-stepped and sidestepped, swung the blade with the precision of a butcher.

Still, defeating Tami remained out of her grasp. Until one fall day. The trees were changing colors, and the slope of the mountain looked like a perpetual sunrise. As usual, Mari met her mother in the courtyard. No Animal Wives had come to watch, having tired long ago of the spectacle. Plus it was raining. Gods and goddesses forbid the beautiful women should ruin their makeup. Heavy drops plastered Mari's hair to her head.

She bowed. Tami returned the gesture. They clashed, poles butting against each other, the sound echoing down the mountain.

All the time spent in a protective crouch, Mari had been observing her mother, learning Tami's favorite *naginata* position: the *waki-gamae*. It was performed by holding the reaping sword below your torso before swinging it out. In the rain, Tami moved to do this, and Mari saw her opening, her conquest. Her mother went low, so Mari went high. *Crash.* Mari landed a crippling blow to Tami's shoulder.

Her mother splayed on the ground, and Mari stood above her. She should have felt guilt, but all she felt was pride ballooning in her chest. Tami smiled; the flint in her eyes darkened. "You are ready for the shed."

Mari pulled her thoughts from the past to Akira. After they'd met, despite Mari's best efforts to harden her heart, Akira had wormed his way in. In truth, he was a constant well from which she drew strength.

In her short lifetime, she had played many parts: Obedient daughter. Compliant clan member. Aloof girl. But being Akira's friend wasn't just a role to be played. She wouldn't survive the competition without something to live for. Love. Friendship. Freedom. Those were all worthy causes. In her mind, she made a banner out of them. "I am a lean tiger in winter." A lump formed in her throat. She spoke past it, whispering into the dark. "I will survive. I will be free. And I will return to Tsuma."

CHAPTER 9
Akira

JUST OUTSIDE THE GATES of Tsuma, Akira felt himself being watched. It was in the darkest part of the night, when most creatures still slept, that he felt something stalking him. Heat crawled up the back of his neck.

Slowly, he turned. Mari's mother stood a few feet away, as still and silent as death. Her long hair was slicked back by the wind. Her skin glistened. By the light of the moon, Akira saw her eyes melt to black, then back to brown. Red haze clouded her shoulders. Her soul wasn't quite crimson. It was darker than that, the color of a currant.

Akira bent his head under the weight of her displeasure. As always, courage eluded him. If given the choice between fight or flight, he always chose flight. He readied himself to run.

"I smell your fear," Tami whispered. She stepped toward him, her bare feet crunching pine needles and dried leaves. "What does my daughter see in you?" *Not much, it turns out.* Akira swallowed. *I don't love you,* Mari had almost said.

Hot breath skimmed his neck, sending shivers down his back. At any moment, Mari's mother could call her beast forward. He imagined what he would do if she attacked. He would not give her the pleasure of a struggle. What would dying feel like? *Not very many people would miss you.*

"You are a strange boy," Mari's mother said. Her hand wrapped around his upper arm quicker than lightning, fingers squeezing his flesh. Sweat gathered along Akira's brow. His vision blurred. *Trapped. No way to run.* "My daughter has always had a soft heart, a fierce need to love. And you are desperate in your need to be loved. But you are weak; you are not worthy." Akira bit back a whimper as she released him. Then she whirled away, disappearing into the forest.

As soon as he regained his breath, Akira did what he did best. He ran.

Akira did not go home.

He sought safety in a chestnut tree, leaping into the foliage as easily as a bird. He perched on a low branch, his location concealed by hand-sized leaves. When the tremors in his limbs subsided, he hooked the black mask over his face. His arm hurt where Mari's mother had grasped it, although there was no mark. *A bruise on my pride, that is all.*

He swung onto a higher branch and then another, until he was nearly at the top. From this vantage point, he could see all of Tsuma — the thatched roofs bathed silver in the starlight, the jagged mountain peaks ringed with snow, dark silhouettes against the night sky. He settled in, forced his breaths to even out, his body to still, his mind to empty.

❀ ❀ ❀

As always, Akira's dreams were haunted.

He dreamed of *before*—before his family was chased out of town by armed villagers, before they were forced to scale a mountain and live as recluses, before he became the Son of Nightmares and met a beautiful animal girl.

They had lived in Hana Machi, a Pleasure City, where rules and common decency were elastic, things to be thinly stretched. Every evening Akira accompanied his mother on a walk. In his dream, Akira strolled with her, their arms linked. Recently, he'd had an obscene growth spurt, topping his mother by a whole foot. His gangly body no longer fit his seven years of age.

The dark cobblestone street shone with summer rain. Pink paper lanterns crisscrossed overhead and swayed in the breeze. The melancholy notes of a *shamisen*'s plucked strings coasted past on an errant breeze, and Akira wondered if it was his father playing the traditional three-stringed instrument, as he often did for tips.

Drunken revelers stumbled out onto the street. "Look at this woman with her scars! It's the Slash-Mouthed Girl!" one cried.

"Please," Mizuki said, her voice measured. "My son and I are just trying to enjoy our evening."

The man sneered, a gray tooth flashing. Its color matched his soul. "And look at her child—he's got them too!" The man pointed a finger at Akira. "You are the son of a murderer! The Son of Nightmares."

Akira and his mother ran all the way home.

Hours later, Akira awoke to a gang of armed villagers gathering below the window of their apartment, chanting: "Murderer, murderer, murderer!"

At first light, they fled Hana Machi. The Pleasure City was no longer safe. As they disappeared into the wild of the Tsuko funo Mountains, his parents breathed free for the first time. They had found a true refuge. But Akira gazed at the trees, saw how their branches swayed, closing in on him, like bars of a cage.

Until Mari.

Akira shook the dream from his head and righted himself, checked his hiding spot. Leaves obscured him. *The Animal Wives will not take kindly to the Son of Nightmares so close to their village.*

The Son of Nightmares, again the moniker.

He'd started using the name — as if taking ownership stripped it of its power. He leaned back against the giant tree trunk and picked at his teeth. The sun climbed higher. Birds woke and sang, their song bright and alive. Opposite of how Akira felt. Tami's words sank into Akira's chest. *My daughter has always had a soft heart, a fierce need to love. And you are desperate in your need to be loved.* There was truth there. The realization startled Akira. He had always been grasping for someone to tell him he was good, worthwhile.

The gates of Tsuma squeaked open. He came to attention, watching through the branches as half a dozen samurai arrived with a black lacquered and pearl-inlaid palanquin. Four of the samurai carried the enclosed carriage, and on either side of them, two others rode horses, clearly the leaders. The shorter of the leaders held his side and sat stiffly. Was he injured? Each of the six men possessed two swords, one big and one small, strapped over his left hip, and all wore traditional gear. Akira frowned. The samurai seemed . . . askew.

Their wide-leg *hakama* pants were stained and missing the traditional seven pleats, representing the seven virtues. Their tops were wrinkled and fraying. Their topknots were sloppy. In a lifetime, samurai could serve a dozen different masters, working their way up from *daimyō*, the great lords, to *shōgun*, military dictator, to emperor. They changed allegiance based on the amount of coin offered. These samurai clearly pledged no master. They were rogues, mercenaries for hire with no allegiance to the emperor. "*Rōnin*," Akira whispered. Their souls were only ever shades of black. So dark that it was hard to see any blemishes.

This band of misfits will escort Mari to the Imperial City? Gods and goddesses only knew where Tami had rustled them up. The tallest samurai dismounted and split from the group, a slight limp to his step.

Akira studied him. There was something familiar in the curves of his face. Did he know him from somewhere? *Probably Hana Machi.* Samurai were supposed to eschew pleasures of the flesh. But plenty visited the pink city, usually in masks or elaborate costumes.

An Animal Wife greeted the samurai. Yuka. Mari spoke of her often, the last Animal Wife to have a daughter. More Animal Wives filtered from their homes. A wayward breeze brought the stink of perfume to Akira's nose. Dressed in their finest kimonos, the Animal Wives lingered, colorful peacocks with white-powdered faces. From behind fans and umbrellas, they surreptitiously eyed the samurai, a rare spectacle in their sleepy village of all women.

The samurai kept his face impassive while Yuka chattered, then led him around a dusty bend in the road. Akira's heart stuttered. He knew the direction they headed. Mari's cottage. This was it.

The samurai reappeared with Mari's wooden trunk on his back. Mari and her mother trailed close behind. Akira would not have recognized her except for the color of her glacier-blue soul. Her face had been dusted white, her lips painted and eyes lined in red. Her black hair was pulled back in a rather painful-looking bun. Silk cherry blossoms adorned her hair. She glanced at the sky, not spying him through the branches. But he saw her. Despite her makeup and her heavy kimono, Mari was naked, exposed. Alone.

Animal Wives fell in line behind Mari and Tami, waving fans and ribbons. A parade and death march all in one. Mari stumbled near the gates, pressing a hand to her throat. Akira shifted, ready to leap. But Mari lifted her chin, shaking off whatever plagued her, and even attempted a smile. Steady. Resolute. Unflinching. How he admired her courage. How he envied it.

A shout rang out, and the processional parted. A girl dressed in a filthy, wrinkled *yukata*, with tangled hair and a soul the color of a bruise, pushed through, then skidded to a halt. *Hissa*.

Hissa opened her palm, unaware or uncaring of the samurai and the glaring eyes of the Animal Wives. The item glinted in the sunlight — a piece of silver metal with five interlocking circles.

Tentatively, Mari accepted the object. Hissa bowed low, the utmost sign of respect. Mari returned the gesture. Then she kissed her mother's cheek. Tami placed a necklace over Mari's head, a piece of twine strung with copper coins. A stocky samurai smiled and helped Mari into the jeweled palanquin. The samurai with the limp slung in her trunk and remounted his horse.

Akira watched as they set off, became dots on the trail, and disappeared completely. The trees were closing in on him for the first time in years. Smothering him. *You are not very good at being brave.* But perhaps he could be. Perhaps he could be worthy of Mari.

In that moment, Akira made a decision. He'd lived most of his life in the shadows and hated it, existing in the dark, on the fringes, but he was always too frightened to step into the light, to let people see his mangled face, his cowardly soul. He needed to be stronger. *Isn't that the foundation of bravery, resilience coupled with an iron will?* He'd never grow past his fears if he stayed in the mountains. The trees provided too much cover, too much safety.

"I'm sorry, Mother. I'm sorry, Father," Akira said as he dropped from the tree. "But I have to go. I have to see what I can become."

He thought it was fate, the force of his love for Mari propelling him on an uncharted, treacherous path. He would follow Mari and the band of misfit samurai. He would go to the Imperial City. In his heart, he promised Mari that everything would be all right. He would make sure of it. One last look up at the canopy, at the whisper of green trees. *You must take this leap. The jump always makes the fall worth it.* At least he hoped.

CHAPTER 10

Mari

THE SAMURAI WAS BLEEDING.

Red liquid seeped through a cloth wrapped around his upper arm. In the palanquin, Mari had moved the curtain aside. She squinted against the bright day. Not a cloud was in the sky. She watched the stocky samurai waver in his saddle and grip his injured shoulder. The man didn't look good. His face was pale, his brow moist. Mari recognized the symptoms of fever. If you weren't careful, the infection would take root, ravage the body. *It might be too late for this samurai.*

She sighed, brushing a wisp of loose hair from her face. Her backside ached. Only a few hours on the road, and her skin was layered in a thick coat of dust. First chance she got, Mari would wash her face, unbind her hair, and strip off this ridiculously ornamented kimono in favor of her more comfortable plain navy one. Her mind raced like wolves on a hunt. Every inch they traveled, they drew closer to the Imperial City, to the Palace of Illusions, the most dangerous place for a *yōkai*. Her opponents would all be human, and she wouldn't be able to call upon the beast during the competition. Too many eyes would be watching. No one could ever know what she really was.

The injured samurai pulled his horse away from the front to trot beside her. "We're about four days out from Tokkaido. We'll stop in a couple hours and camp at a temple."

Mari nodded. "I hope you'll live to see it." She gave a pointed look at his shoulder.

He barked a laugh. "Don't burn my body yet. I'm too stubborn to die." He inclined his head. "Masa."

Mari reciprocated the gesture. "Mari." She noted that his right hand, his injured side, couldn't quite grip the reins. Not a good sign. "Have you lost feeling in your arm?" she asked. Her gaze darted around the landscape, searching for a particular flower with velvet leaves and a dark-purple, almost black, bloom.

He flexed his hand, and his fingers trembled. "This is nothing compared to what I've faced before." Masa tilted his head back, revealing a jagged scar that traveled from just beneath his chin to his neck, then disappeared into his collar. "*Kappa* almost ate me alive during my first trek over these mountains." The green water creatures were well-known in the lower parts of the mountains. They favored entrails but liked cucumbers more. If you fed them the green vegetable, they'd let you pet them or bring you a fish to reciprocate the gift.

The lead samurai, the one with a vicious limp, glanced over his shoulder, brows drawn and eyes intense. A stagnant breeze ruffled his topknot. His gaze lingered; then he whipped it back forward. "I don't think he likes me very much," Mari confessed. The entire journey, she'd suffered his assessing looks.

Masa smiled. "Hiro doesn't like anyone. He has two expressions: angry and less angry."

Mari chuckled and snuck another glance at the imposing samurai. "What about now? Is he angry or less angry?" she asked in a conspiratorial whisper.

Masa leaned in, crinkles forming at the corners of his eyes. Mari wondered at how a man in such pain could be in such good humor. "Less angry. Escorting you to Tokkaido has made us wealthy men. We could hardly believe our luck when your mother's messenger found us. She's already delivered half her payment. This is our biggest payday yet."

Mari returned Masa's infectious smile. They rode on in companionable silence. Towering trees fenced the road. A breeze like the gentle stroke of a calligraphy pen caressed Mari's cheek. The trot of the horses echoed through the mountain. After a time, Mari felt the weight of Hiro's gaze settle on her.

Mari straightened her spine and shuttered her gaze. She told herself she didn't care what he thought of her. It was a lie. The first and foremost lesson taught to Animal Wives was to be likable. *A woman must be gentle and kind, never outspoken,* her mother had said before Mari's training shifted from traditional Animal Wife teachings to combat. But this early lesson stuck. She resisted the need to apologize. *I'm sorry you don't like me.*

Masa sighed and drummed his thumbs on his saddle. "Hiro says your people trick men into marriage and steal their fortunes." Mari started. "Don't worry. Your mother paid enough for our silence. Our lips are sealed." Mari released a breath. She wondered if this was a trait of all samurai, to speak the truth whether pleasant or not.

Anger stirred in Mari. It was one thing for her to hate her people's archaic customs. It was something else entirely coming from a stranger. "It's easy to pass judgment; far harder to understand," she said, teeth on edge.

"I agree. When Hiro called you a pit viper and said you're not to be trusted, I told him the same thing," said Masa.

As if he could hear them, Hiro whistled, summoning Masa.

"He doesn't want me talking to you," Masa said. "He fears you will trick me into marriage, then leave me desperate and wanting. As if that could ever be so." The samurai laughed airily.

You are not pretty enough. She cleared her throat, hardened her heart. "Whatever he thinks about me, whatever you think about my people, you are both wrong." She remembered Hissa's words. *We are monsters.* The words of her mother. *It is the only way I could keep you.* "Not everyone is all good or all bad. It is a mistake to think so."

Masa's mouth thinned. He took up the horse's reins in his stubby fingers and began to canter away, but not before turning back. "You'll want to hide your necklace and anything of value before we are off the mountain. No use drawing extra attention."

Mari's hands went to the piece of cord strung with copper currency. She tucked it under her kimono. On her lap, she cradled a silver pick, Hissa's parting gift to her. *It's for good luck. I wore it when I met my husband,* her friend had whispered. Mari turned the silver pick over in her hands, the precious metal glaring in the orange sun. The end tapered to a vicious point, a weapon as well as an ornament. Just like an Animal Wife. Mari slipped the pick into her kimono sleeve just as the crooked roof of a decaying temple rose on the horizon. A dark tide of fear rolled through her. With a long inhale and exhale, she steadied herself.

Duty and home, Tami had whispered in Mari's ear one last time in lieu of a heartfelt goodbye. So many things between them had been left unsaid.

I am a lean tiger in winter. I will survive. I will be free. And I will return to Tsuma. I will fix what is wrong between us.

Mari crept from the campsite. Her breaths came in short bursts, and the darkness felt heavy, unknown. She'd slept for only a few hours, uncomfortable on a thin pallet and wooden block beneath her neck to prevent her hair from becoming mussed, before Masa's moans had roused her.

At her back, the temple loomed. Dilapidated and forgotten. Hiro had stuck one foot in and declared it unsafe to spend the night in. A few yards from her was a grove of hemlock trees. And there, growing at the base, were night flowers. She plucked them easily from the ground, discarding the actual flowers. The purple blooms turned your insides to liquid. But crushed and mixed with water, the velvet heart-shaped leaves made a poultice that calmed the most ravaging infection. It was a wonder, a plant that could kill as easily as it could save.

Mari bit her lip. Masa didn't have much time.

Back at the campsite, the samurai slept, all except for Hiro. He reclined on his bedroll, tracking Mari's movements with his eyes. Mari ignored him. Quickly, she mixed the poultice in the wooden bowl she had used to eat dinner earlier. She knelt next to Masa's pallet. Before she could place the healing mixture on his wound, he whimpered, and his eyes fluttered open. "Am I dreaming?" he asked, one side of his mouth tilting up.

"I'm afraid not. You are very much awake. And very much in trouble, if that wound on your shoulder isn't taken care of soon." She snorted. "Your friends may not care about it, but I certainly do."

Masa chuckled, his lips chapped and white. Though a fire blazed nearby, he shivered. "Do you hear that, Hiro? She thinks you lack basic friendship skills."

"I'm glad you have your sense of humor," Hiro said, standing just above Mari's shoulder. "I hope you're still laughing when we have to cut off the arm."

Masa half smiled. "Please," he huffed. "I've never liked this arm anyway. It's always giving me trouble." Masa's laugh ended in a dry cough.

Mari fetched a gourd of water and trickled the liquid on his lips and then into his mouth. "Stay for a while," Masa said, eyes fluttering shut. "You're much prettier to look at than Hiro. Your hands are softer too." Then he was asleep.

"You're going to cut off his arm?" Mari asked, watching Masa's chest rise and fall with deep breaths.

The samurai said nothing. Mari's muscles coiled.

Hiro sighed, weighty and lengthy. "If it isn't better by tomorrow, we've agreed to sever the limb. It's his sword arm. He won't be able to fight again."

"What will he do?" Her brow dipped in concern.

"His father is a farmer. He'd have to go home."

Mari's jaw clenched. "You wouldn't keep him as one of your *rōnin?*"

"Not if he can't fight. He'd be a liability."

Mari stared at the poultice, hesitating. What if she was wrong about the night flower? She'd seen Yuka pluck it from the ground. But had she gotten it mixed up? Were the flowers the fever reducer and the leaves the intestine liquefier? She breathed in deeply and peeled away the cloth covering Masa's wound. She grimaced at the gashes, and her stomach rippled at the sour smell. "What happened?" she whispered.

Hiro crouched beside her, eyeing the wound impassively. Sparks shot from the dying fire, crackling and popping. "*Namahage* got him." Mari shuddered. Animal Wives didn't fear much, but the demons were a natural enemy. "They attacked us at night. We killed the tribe but not before one dug its claws into Masa." Three deep gouges ran down Masa's side. Claw marks. These *rōnin* had killed an entire tribe of *namahage?* Newfound respect with a healthy dose of fear blossomed in Mari's belly. The beast inside her stirred. She risked a glance at Hiro. She couldn't make out much of his expression because of the darkness, but she could detect the hard angles of his face. *He's a true warrior.* Something rough-hewed and born on a battlefield. Every minute that ticked by brought Masa closer to death. She reached for the bowl.

Hiro's arm snapped out; his fingers grasped her wrist. "If he dies because of you, I'll have your head."

"He's dead either way. This is his only hope."

Hiro released her wrist.

Mari brought the poultice closer in to her body. Using a clean cloth she'd ripped from her undergarments, she dipped into the paste.

Hiro sniffed. "What is that?"

"Night flower," she answered. "We used it in the village to treat women after giving birth. It cures infection." Masa's eyelids twitched, and sweat coated his forehead. He'd fallen into a deep, feverish sleep.

Hiro was quiet, his eyes glowing, reflecting the flames of the fire. *Perhaps he's imagining all the ways to kill me.*

Finally, he spoke, soft and earnest. "He's like a brother to me."

Mari leaned forward and began dotting the paste on Masa's injury. The man flinched but didn't wake. She kept her face placid.

Mari gave a slight nod and went back to work. She dipped two fingers in the poultice and spread it thickly over Masa's wound.

Hiro stood by the entire time, a silent guardian. When she was done, Mari cleaned her hands, wiped the sweat from Masa's brow, and covered him with a fresh blanket. Then she walked to her pallet. "Good night, Hiro."

"Mari," Hiro called out across the fire. Her back stiffened. "If you save him, I'll be in your debt."

"Imagine that," she said, a wicked gleam in her eye. "You, indebted to a pit viper." Then she scurried under her blankets and turned her face.

CHAPTER 11
Mari

MASKED CITY.

That was Mari's first thought as she glimpsed Tokkaido, the Imperial City, sprawled before their caravan. There was a gold-and-silver tint to it — half in shadow, the other half lit up in the dying sunlight. Forested hills, mountains wreathed in mist, and the Ma ni Sea fortified the capital. Overhead, a flock of wild geese flew, their desolate call bouncing off the rooftops.

They crested a hill, and Mari saw that the infrastructure had been designed in a systematic fashion. Streets ran parallel and divided at regular intervals. But the edges seemed raw and unfinished, as if the artist had run out of ink near the frame of his painting.

Another hour passed, and they reached the city's earthwork walls. Two snoozing samurai guarded the gates. The caravan passed without notice. Children with sunken eyes and bloated bellies ran behind the processional, begging for coins. Mari dug out the copper necklace from beneath her kimono, but before she could unstring the coins, the children were shooed away by *dōshin*, lesser samurai who patrolled the wards, brandishing steel wands with hooks.

The cobblestone streets teemed with humans, carts, and animals, all darting in different directions. Mari sucked in an uneasy breath as her samurai guards were forced to slow their pace and draw closer to one another. They kept to the main street, which ran across the whole city and ended at the Palace of Illusions. To the left and right of the road were the markets, brimming with a life of their own, a city within a city.

Masa sat with Mari in the palanquin, curtains pulled back. His fever had broken that morning, thanks to Mari's night flower, but he was still weak. "Eleventh ward," he told her, gritting his teeth and holding his shoulder. "Best to stay out of the commercial district unless you absolutely have to go."

Mari nodded absently, fascinated by the bustle. The air smelled of grime and smoke and sesame oil, but underneath there was freedom, opportunity. She had the chance to do something big. *You can be anyone you want here.* She thought of a dark, endless hallway with doors on either side, each room full of hidden possibilities and secrets.

The litter jerked, forced to the side of the road, and Mari grabbed her seat, narrowly avoiding being thrown. A large cart carrying eight human passengers rattled by. Instead of oxen, four *oni* demons were yoked to the front. Their horns and teeth had been ground down to nubs. Each wore a shining collar with curses engraved in the metal. Mari searched for the locks, but the seams had been soldered together. As they pulled, their muscles strained with the effort.

Mari's joy turned to ash, to fear and disgust. She'd forgotten she was *yōkai*. She'd forgotten the danger. The reality was stark, and she saw all too clearly her place in this city — at the bottom, where anyone could step on you.

"Careful," Masa warned. "If you let your emotions show, the priests will ask questions."

Ahead, a trio of gray-robed priests loitered outside a glassblower's shop. Their heads were shaved. Their faces and hands were covered in cobalt tattoos, giving their skin and lips a faint bluish tint. *Curses.* The Animal Wives carried home terrible tales of human priests with inked flesh. A brush of their skin against hers would burn. She kept her head down as they rolled by, but she felt a pulsing heat radiate from them and tasted burnt cinnamon in her mouth. She couldn't see it, but she could feel it, taste it. Painful magic. The blood stilled in her veins. Danger surrounded her here.

The road narrowed and dimmed. The markets shifted to neighborhoods full of rickety row houses that leaned up against one another, blotting out the light. Mari eyed the inhabitants with morbid curiosity. A hag that appeared human except for her eyes, which were black with no lids. A man dressed as a monk but with a red face, bulbous nose, and giant feathered wings dragging on the ground, sweeping filth from the street. All had sad, vulnerable faces. All were bent from a lifetime of looking at the ground. All were *yōkai*. And like the *oni*, all wore metal collars. Mari ached to leap from the palanquin and run to them, to help them. But self-preservation and cowardice kept her rooted to her seat.

"The eighth, ninth, and tenth wards are the only places *yōkai* are allowed to live," Masa whispered.

Mari swallowed hard against the painful lump in her throat.

A life lived in chains is no life at all. Unwilling to see any more, she snapped her attention to the road ahead, to where the golden palace loomed, like a giant watching over its city.

Around the seventh ward, the streets widened. Bunches of clover and lavender matted the cobblestones, masking the smell of filth, fish, and rotten vegetables.

Hiro whistled, and their processional slowed to a stop in front of a wooden building with a simple shingled roof. A piece of dyed cloth hung from the eaves, displaying the name of the establishment. The Gana Inn — Mari's home for the next few days. And quite possibly, the last place she would ever sleep.

"This is the only room you have available?" Mari asked, arching a slender brow at the innkeeper. There was no window, and the only light emanated from a single lantern on the floor. There was a thin mat in the corner, presumably to be used as a bed. The place stank of tobacco and pickled radishes.

The innkeeper nodded, his ruddy cheeks jiggling. The mustard-colored kimono he wore did nothing for his complexion, and the way he stroked his abdomen made Mari think of a preening cat. "Yes. We've been booked solid for a month. There are no vacancies in the city, at least not in the first seven wards. Many have come for the competition. You might be able to find lodging in one of the upper wards, but you'd have to share a room . . ."

She might almost prefer that. This one was stifling. Mari's nose twitched. "What is that . . ."

"Smell? That's the communal toilet next door." The innkeeper's lips pursed. He was growing impatient. "Do you want the room or not?"

"She'll take it," Masa announced, leaning heavily against the door. He'd insisted on accompanying Mari inside. Hiro had followed, dragging her trunk, grumbling the whole time.

Mari shot a scowl in Masa's direction, which made him grin. "How much?" she asked the innkeeper.

"Only ten *mon*," he said.

Masa snorted. Ten *mon* was half the worth of her necklace. She searched the innkeeper's face. Mari untied the cord from around her neck and slipped off ten coins.

"Excellent. I'll have a servant come and help you unpack." The innkeeper departed in a swirl of robes.

"You overpaid," Masa said. "This room is worth *two mon* at most."

Hiro pushed Mari's trunk to the center of the room.

Mari shrugged. "You heard the innkeeper. There aren't any other rooms available."

"Masa, we have to go," Hiro said, already halfway out the door, in a hurry to be out of Mari's sight, no doubt. Despite her having saved Masa's life, Hiro maintained his disdain for Mari.

Masa bowed. "It was lovely meeting you, Mari. I hope we'll see each other again. Friends?" he asked.

She liked the samurai. Mari gave a decisive nod. "Friends." Then she turned to Hiro. "Thank you."

Masa exited, but Hiro lingered. They stared at each other, the Animal Wife and the *rōnin*.

Hiro's head tilted as he scrutinized her. His jaw worked. At length, he said, "When I was a little boy, I was brought to the mountains. I almost died."

"Oh?" Something in Mari's chest began to flutter, butterflies with barbed wings.

Hiro snorted. His hand drifted to the swords at his left hip. The tips of Mari's fingers itched, her talons threatening to burst forth.

Hiro glowered at the lamp. "Throughout the journey, I questioned myself. Could it really be her? I've waited for this day a long time. I wondered what I would do if I ever saw you again. I figured it was impossible. The chances of finding you . . ." He shook his head.

Mari stepped back, her calves pressed against her trunk, blocking any farther retreat. Her brain fired as it tried to make connections and missed them.

Hiro squinted, appraising her. "I never imagined you were an Animal Wife. I've looked year after year, trek after wretched trek, for that shed. I trained as a samurai, became a *rōnin*, took any job that involved the mountains. I'd almost given up. Imagine my surprise when I saw you, my latest commission." Hiro's eyes locked with Mari's. "I still limp because of the broken knee you inflicted on me."

Mari's breath caught. Hiro had been her first. The boy she was sentenced to kill. She never would have recognized him. Of all those she'd injured, she thought of him the most. How he'd trembled. His jagged breaths. The slick tears on his cheeks. "What is it you want?" she asked. Her hands flexed; talons sprouted from her fingertips. Hiro's height put him at an advantage. She wouldn't be able to reach his neck or throat with much precision. She'd have to swing low, slice open the abdomen. *Did I save this boy's life only to kill him ten years later? What a shame.* Despite her mother's order, she had never killed. But she could if she had to.

Hiro inhaled. His mouth twitched. But he did not draw his swords. Hiro flicked his hand. "I fear no death but death with dishonor," he said, repeating the samurai code. "You saved Masa. You are not the evil I believed you to be. I — I am in your debt." He swept his body into a bow. "A life for a life, Mari-san. Someday I will repay the favor. I vow it."

At Hiro's words, Mari's claws retracted. She swallowed against her waning fear. By all rights, her life should be forfeit. This man had spent his life hating her. The whole journey, she'd been vulnerable. Every minute she slept, Hiro could have reaped his revenge. She may have been strong and able to wield a *naginata*, but she bled like everyone else. And now, not only did he forgive her; he felt in her debt. It was too much to process.

A soft knock at the door, and Mari's eyes darted to the intruder. A girl stood in the frame. She bowed low, splotches of pink washing over her cheeks. "My name is Sei. My master bade me to help you unpack. But I see you are engaged. I will return at another time." Sei turned to go.

"No. Stay," Mari said a bit too loudly. "I'll just be a moment." She stepped closer to Hiro. Her blood ran like honey, thick and slow. She whispered so only he could hear. "I won't insult you by providing all the reasons I had to do what I did. Nor should you be compelled to feel sympathy for me. So, silly as it may sound, I'll offer you the only thing I can: an apology. I'm sorry. I'm so very, deeply sorry." Mari bowed.

Hiro nodded, his gaze steely. "A life for a life. Someday our scales will be even." He grinned, and it was a terrifying thing, ferocious and toothy. Like a wolf. Her mother loved to hunt the wild packs near Tsuma. *Wolves never give up. They fight until the death*, her mother had said. "I will return to the mountains. But if you should ever need me, find the red cliff daisy," said Hiro. Mari frowned. She was familiar with the flower. It grew in sunny patches on the mountain. Its garnet petals were sticky and stained the skin. "When burned, it turns the smoke red. I'll find you." Then the *rōnin* left, his shoulders filling the width of the door frame, forcing Sei into the hall.

As Hiro's footsteps disappeared, Sei reentered, head bent so that Mari could see only the crown of her dark hair.

Mari exhaled, trying to calm her jangled nerves. *Don't throw up. Don't throw up. Don't throw up.* Once the tremors in her hands subsided, Mari said, "Sei? That's your name, correct?"

The servant's head popped up. A metal collar peeked out from under the top of her stiff brown kimono. She was *yōkai*. But what species? She looked human. "Yes, my lady. Would you like me to help you unpack?"

Mari looked about the bare room. "There's really nowhere to unpack."

Sei hesitated. "Perhaps you would like a bath after your journey? The communal bath is down the hall. I know for a fact that it's empty right now."

Mari regarded her fingers, her nails caked in dirt. She hadn't bathed the entire journey. "Okay," she said, giving Sei a decisive nod.

The servant led Mari down the windowless hall. Oil lamps lit the way. All around were pleasant odors. Candle wax. Rice paper. Sesame oil from the inn's restaurant. Homey smells. It would be just after dinner in Tsuma. The Animal Wives would be retiring after their day's work. She already missed the rhythm of the consistency she had thought a constraint.

Their village acted as a small city. Yuka ran an apothecary out of her cottage. Ayumi sewed and mended clothes. There were cooks, weavers, and healers. Hissa had a special skill in patching roofs. In every way but one, the Animal Wives had evolved past their need for men. But still they had to continue their traditions. *Duty and home. The whole before the self.*

CHAPTER 12
Taro

TARO'S MECHANICAL BIRD was ready to fly. Last night, he'd placed the final copper feather in its tail. He'd slept restlessly, imagining how the bird would look with its wings spread for the first time, how its metal chest would glint in the light. Soon the bird would be free, and so would Taro.

The prince dressed with care in simple *hakama* and a surcoat, peasant garb. He didn't bother to pack anything, only stuffed his pockets full of coins. Money would buy the essentials. He conjured thoughts of a storefront, a place in a market in a different city where he would sell his creations, where mothers with their children would stop and gaze with wonder at the creatures he'd built.

Tonight, he'd make his escape.

With the metal bird and coins heavy in his pockets, he slipped into the palace tunnels. This time, instead of veering toward the Main Hall, Taro took a series of eight rights and sixteen lefts. In this portion of the tunnels, the samurai patrolled only every sixty-four minutes. Deeper and deeper he went, until the smell of wet grass clung to his nostrils. He'd reached the outer tunnels, those under the gardens.

A set of stairs led him to a trapdoor located in the dragon-shaped maze. He alighted from the underground, hair slipping from his topknot and ruffling in the breeze. The night had grown darker, and fog clung to his ankles. He navigated the maze. The key was to walk counterclockwise alongside the dragon's coiling back. His steps slowed as a green wooden door set in a stone wall came into view. He'd reached the outer hedge. He fished a key from his pocket and slipped it into the lock. The door opened with a groan. Taro stepped over the threshold and locked it behind him.

When he was alone, something inside Taro uncoiled, released. No one — no servant, samurai, priest, or courtier — would dare enter this long-abandoned garden. And freedom was just a few feet away. Earthwork walls rose up in front of him, and, just beyond those, Tokkaido. Soon, he'd be gone.

Dead pine needles and twigs crunched under his feet as he walked the wild terrain, overgrown with shrubs and weeds and *kudzu*, a creeping vine where snakes often hid. The tea garden was a shell of its former glory. He'd heard that, once, it had bloomed with fiery maple trees and glowed with lanterns, the air alive with laugher. In the center of the garden was a dilapidated house. Its roof sagged, and its floorboards stank of rot. This had been his mother's tea garden. When she'd died, so had it.

Taro carefully removed the mechanical bird from the folds of his robe. The bird's eyes were closed, its wings pressed neatly against its body. Sleeping. Cradling the bird in his large palm, Taro wound the crank on its back.

The bird's eyes flitted open and blinked. Its head turned left and right with sharp clicks. He wound the crank again, and the bird's copper wings spread. The sight was magnificent. One more crank, and the bird's wings flapped. With a thrust of his hand, Taro set the bird to flight. His chest inflated with pride.

Like any newborn creature, the bird was tentative at first, flitting from branch to branch. But its bravery grew with each passing moment. The bird launched from a scraggly bonsai tree, entering the sky as straight as a spear. Its wings began to flutter erratically, and too late, Taro remembered its lifespan was only the entirety of three cranks. Two minutes. The bird was dying in the sky. All of Taro's hard work, months spent toiling, would disappear like the flash of a firecracker.

Taro ran, arms outstretched, ready to catch his little bird, to save it. But he was too slow. Taro could only watch as the bird spun from the sky, preparing to crash to the earth below.

CHAPTER 13

Mari

STEAM ROSE AROUND Mari as Sei sponged her back in the long, wooden tub. "Have you been employed here long?" Mari asked. Her hands drew gentle circles in the opaque water, where specks of dirt from the journey floated around her. Tendrils of hair plastered her cheeks.

"Yes. My mother was a servant here before me. When she passed away, I was bequeathed to the innkeeper, Mr. Adachi," Sei said meekly.

"Bequeathed?"

The cloth on Mari's back stopped moving. "*Yōkai* are not free citizens in the Imperial City. We must serve a human master. My mother was Mr. Adachi's property, and thus he owned any children she had."

Bequeathed: What a gentle word for enslaved.

Sei rose from her kneeling position by the tub and fetched a bar of rose-scented soap. Mari glimpsed hooks nestled into Sei's tight bun.

"You're a *hari-onago?*" A Hook Girl. Mari didn't mean to speak it aloud, but she couldn't believe it. They were practically cousins, molded from the same clay, Tami had told her. Like Animal Wives, *hari-onago* were often mistaken for human. But they had a distinguishing characteristic — barbed, needle-like hooks graced the tips of their hair. She had heard the stories. In the cloak of darkness, Hook Girls wandered the streets, searching for unsavory men. When approached by one, the *hari-onago* smiled. If the man smiled back, she would sink her barbed hooks into her victim's flesh, trapping him. Once the man was rendered helpless, the *hari-onago* devoured him. But this Hook Girl, Sei, didn't resemble the creature of Mari's childhood imagination. Sei was tall and gaunt. Her vicious hooks were rusted and dulled from a lifetime of neglect.

Hearing Mari's accusation, Sei dropped the bar of soap and fumbled for it on the floor.

Mari sat forward, water splashing over the tub. "I'm sorry."

Sei plucked up the soap and continued scrubbing Mari's back, her movements jerky and her breaths quick. Mari muttered another apology over her shoulder.

Sei spoke in a low voice. "You didn't say what village you hail from, but it must be far away. Here in the Imperial City, we don't speak of . . ." The words died on Sei's tongue. But Mari understood what she was failing to say. *We don't speak of who we really are.*

Mari's toes curled. "Is it forbidden?"

"It is . . ." The Hook Girl hesitated. ". . . unwise."

Mari grew thoughtful. She let her head fall to the lip of the tub and closed her eyes. "In the village I am from, *yōkai* are free. No one is collared. And no one is forced to live in separate wards." Technically all true, although perhaps it was not quite so idyllic as it sounded.

The sponge paused on Mari's arm. "Forgive me if I offer unwanted advice, but for your own safety, I would discourage you from speaking of such things."

Mari's heartbeat pulsed. "Does it hurt?" she asked, indifferent to Sei's warning.

For a tense moment, there was no sound but the drip of water. "Does what hurt?" Sei finally asked.

"Your collar," Mari clarified. "Does it hurt?"

"I've worn it so long, I've forgotten it's there."

Lie. Mari could feel Sei thinking, contemplating if Mari could be trusted. Sei's voice dropped to a whisper. "But sometimes my hand accidentally brushes up against it, and it burns like the heat of a thousand suns. The last time I burned myself, I lost all feeling in my fingertips." Sei opened her hands. Thick, callused scars covered her skin.

Mari didn't ask any more questions. Sei scrubbed her with rice bran until she was fresh and pink. Then she cleaned under Mari's nails with a wooden pick. Guilt blossomed in Mari's stomach, for while she grieved Sei's enslavement, she couldn't help but revel in her own freedom, however fleeting it might be.

Mari was lost. She had tried to sleep after her bath, but to no avail. She blamed her restlessness on the thin, sour-smelling mat, on the too-small room. Seeking fresh air and a reprieve from her chaotic thoughts, Mari left the inn and began to walk away from the markets. Somewhere, she had turned from the city's main thoroughfare and into a neighborhood.

A wealthy one. Willow trees lined the streets, their branches sweeping in the wind. Ahead, a half-moon bridge arched over a stream. Sprawling mansions took up whole blocks. Mari was lost in the dark.

She tilted her head back, hoping to spot the golden roof of the Palace of Illusions, hoping it might orient her. *Nothing.* The shifting branches of the willow trees blocked the sky. A stone wall nearly twenty feet high hugged the sidewalk. *It must lead to something.*

Each pad of her echoing footsteps reminded Mari that she was alone. She wished she had brought her *naginata. A girl unaccompanied in a strange city . . .* Cautionary tales started like that. A subtle shift in the temperature had Mari pausing. Then she tasted it, her tongue tingling with burnt cinnamon. Around a slight curve in the wall, two priests smoked tobacco from a *kiseru.*

Mari blinked rapidly, but her vision didn't change. A high whine of panic filled her head. A single drop of sweat slid down Mari's spine. The priests hadn't seen her yet. With haste, she turned and started back in the direction she had come.

"Hey, you!" a priest called out.

She nearly groaned at her mistake. She should have continued past the priests, fought through it. *Guilty people run.* She glanced over her shoulder. The priests hadn't rounded the corner yet. The empty street stretched out in front of her. If she continued on, they'd spot her like a deer in an open field.

Mari looked around frantically, noticing pieces of stone jutting from the wall. The brush of the priests' footsteps drew closer. Mari placed her foot on a stone and launched herself up. Her small stature had its benefits: she could climb fast. In her peripheral vision, she saw a flash of copper, but she didn't have time to process the oddity. With a grunt, she pulled herself over the wall.

She landed in an overgrown garden, just as that flash of copper crashed at her feet. *A metal bird.* It lay on its side, its eyes blinking furiously before shutting with an audible click. Mari picked up the bird, studying it. *How strange.*

She didn't hear the snap of twigs, didn't see the body barreling forward. She let out a cry as a hand pinned her to the wall. The stone bit into her back. The bird tumbled from her fingers.

She heard one of the priests on the other side of the wall. "Sounds like one of the guards got her." A muffled laugh, then the tap of fading footsteps.

Mari grabbed her assailant's wrists, her fingertips ready to sharpen into claws, pierce and slash whomever it was to pieces. *Men are conditioned to take. Women are conditioned to give. Never let a man take anything from you. Your smiles, your humor, your body.* She remembered her mother's words. Mari gazed at the soon-to-be-dead man.

The samurai was large, his face made up of sharp, unrelenting angles. He was imposingly handsome — in the way a *katana* blade was beautiful. His hair was long and kept in a sloppy topknot. And he had a smudge of dirt between his eyes. For a moment, there was nothing but the sound of Mari's ragged breathing.

She slammed her foot down on the samurai's, then thrust her knee into his stomach. His body bent. He emitted something between a snarl and a grunt. She bucked the same knee into his face. *Crack.* She'd broken his nose. The hand around her throat tightened, squeezed. Mari struggled, hands and feet swinging.

"Cease!" the samurai roared.

Mari stilled. Not because the samurai commanded it, but

because she needed a few precious seconds. She put her hands behind her back, calling to her half-beast.

The samurai moved toward her, his cheek almost brushing hers.
Blood dripped from his nose onto her feet. "You should know," came
the low voice, "you have breached a wall of the Imperial Palace. Who
are you, and what are you doing here?"

CHAPTER 14

Taro

TARO DREW BACK, gazing at what he'd caught.

A girl. Her long, black hair was woven into a thick braid. Her mouth was set in a thin line, and her russet-colored eyes shot daggers. Her kimono was simple, plain, but made of fine cloth. Not a servant, but not a courtier, either. Perhaps she was from out of town, here for the competition. The thought made Taro's blood run hot.

"If I let you go, do you promise to stop fighting me?" he asked.

She made a hissing sound. He decided that meant yes. Taro eased the pressure on her throat, but he moved his body closer, keeping her trapped. He felt her tremble. "Who are you?" Her eyelids lowered. She didn't answer. "What is your name?" he asked more forcefully.

She gritted her teeth, a slight sheen of sweat on her forehead. "Mari," she said.

Taro's arm dropped to his side. "Mari?"

"Yes." She lifted her hand, fingers caressing her neck, dancing over her stuttering pulse.

"And what are you doing here?" he asked.

Her eyes flashed, caution dancing in their depths. "That's a complicated question." He advanced. She put a hand up, warding him off. "I walked too far from the inn where I am staying and got lost." Taro stepped back. She straightened from the wall. He found her height unimpressive.

He supposed she was expecting an apology for his rough handling. Too bad; the heir to the imperial throne apologized to no one. She brushed her kimono and stooped down, collecting something from the high grass. Copper glinted in her hand.

"That's my bird," he said, reaching for it.

Mari shoved the bird behind her back. Her little chin jutted up. "I don't see your name on it."

What she lacks in height, she makes up for in confidence.

"You don't even know what my name is," he said. He cupped his nose. It made a sickening crunch as he set it back in place. He winced at the sting. The girl fought dirty. "If you look, you will see a *T* etched into the tail. It is my initial."

Mari's mouth pinched as she examined the bird's tail. "What does the *T* stand for?" she asked.

"Taro," he replied. He waited for recognition, for her to notice the smudge between his brows, for her to bow and kiss his feet. Nothing. This girl had no idea who he was. She thought he was a mere lesser samurai. He was struck by the novelty — and annoyed.

"Well, it is a very lovely bird," she said, handing it back to Taro. "Forgive me for not believing you at first. I assumed your heavy hands could never make something so delicate."

An apology and insult all in one. Against his will, one corner of Taro's mouth drew up.

"Gods and goddesses, is that the first time you've ever smiled?" she asked, eyes drawing wide. "You need more practice."

Another barb wrapped in soft cloth. He broke into a full smile. It felt unnatural, like ill-fitting clothes.

Mari turned her back on him, feeling along the wall. "No stones," she muttered.

"You are staying at an inn," Taro blurted out in an effort to make her stop, to stay, to look at him, to make him smile again.

Mari made a humming noise that sounded like agreement and glanced over her shoulder. "Give me a boost, samurai."

Taro scowled. He didn't want her to go. He wanted to demand she stay and amuse him some more. Alas, he realized how spoiled that sounded. He set the bird down on a rock carpeted in thick moss. Then he crouched and interlaced his fingers, inviting her to use them as a step. He didn't mention that there was a secret door just behind the mass of vines. With all the dignity and haughtiness of an empress, Mari placed her foot in his palms.

He hoisted her up, and she sat on the wall, the moonlight behind her. She was no great beauty, yet there was something arresting about her. He couldn't look away. Taro had never put much stock in looks. Porcelain bowls faded and gathered dust. Women and men grew old, their faces lined with age. With time, all things withered. *Except your spirit.* The soul always remained.

Wanting to keep Mari's company just a little longer, Taro shouted, "What brings you to the Imperial City?"

Mari faced away from him, ready to slide from the wall, to disappear. She paused, her head tilted, thick braid swaying in the middle of her back. "I've come for the competition."

Frustration cut a bitter path across Taro's chest. His lips tugged into a sneer. "So you hope to be an empress? You wish for the prince to fall in love with you and to wear pretty gowns and live in luxury for the rest of your life?"

Mari sighed. "It is disappointing how little you think of the opposite sex."

Taro grunted. "I know the prince. He does not like to be considered some prize to be won."

"Women are regarded that way all the time," Mari replied. "And just so you know, I have no desire to be Empress." With that, Mari slipped from the wall.

Taro listened as her footsteps faded into silence. Then he plucked the copper bird from the ground. The door to his freedom lay just a few feet away, nestled behind thick vines. In seconds, he could be on the other side of it. By morning he could be outside of Tokkaido, ready to start a new life. Taro looked to the sky, to the moon, round and glowing. He tried to forget Mari, shake loose the memory of her from his mind. He sighed deeply. It was no use; the girl was stuck, wedged in his brain. Placing the metal bird in his pocket, he turned away from the door and began to walk back to the palace.

She won't make it past the first Seasonal Room, he reasoned. Still, whether she lived or died, Taro wanted to see the girl again. Freedom could wait just a little longer.

CHAPTER 15
Akira

IT WAS WELL PAST DINNER, and Akira's stomach rumbled. He shouldered his way through the crowded commercial district. He swiped a rice ball wrapped in seaweed from a food cart and pulled down the black cloth wrapped around his face to shove it into his mouth. A few hours ago, he'd seen Mari enter the Gana Inn. Assuming she was safe and sound for the evening, he made his way back to the eleventh ward.

As soon as he glimpsed the commercial district, Akira knew this was where he belonged. The district was crowded, the perfect place to disappear. It was also the best place to gather information. While Mari competed, Akira would not sit idle.

He'd already spent half the evening skulking in the shadows, watching and listening. Already, he'd heard rumors of a spreading Resistance and of a Weapons Master trained by an elite group of monks who was building an army.

Akira had no desire to become part of the brewing *yōkai*

Resistance. *What could I offer it, anyway?* But he did want to learn how to fight, to be worthy of his Animal Girl. Akira imagined himself as one of the *rōnin* who had escorted Mari from the mountain, with swords at his hips lending a swagger to his steps.

Akira wandered deeper and deeper into the commercial district, navigating its arteries. Rickety stalls, densely packed together, sold food, clothing, and supplies. There were *sake* brewers, silk merchants, plasterers, tobacco cutters, mat makers, stonemasons, idol makers, and druggists. He passed a curator, a man with a navy soul, his stall cluttered with nightingales in twig cages, brightly colored fish in jars, and giant tortoises on leashes. He even spied some Ollis Isle traders among the masses, their fair complexions standing out among the tan locals.

Akira loped past the entrance to the fish market. The smell of brine and salt and blood filtered through the cloth wrapped around his face. A few feet more, and the stalls ended abruptly, giving way to a clearing — the heart of the commercial district. In the center, a giant cherry tree bloomed. Akira blanched when he saw what was underneath — prisoners elaborately roped and awaiting public flogging. Their souls were a sickly yellow. Near the prisoners was a sword swallower. Next to him was a puppet show for children. Stray dogs lounged. The clock tower chimed in the distance.

Akira crossed the forum and melted back into the markets, traveling until the pathways turned to the dank alleys of the eleventh-ward apartments, tenement buildings where most *yōkai* gathered. In these unwatched corners, they huddled together, momentarily safe from humans and priests with their burning magic.

Akira entered an alleyway at random. Lines hung overhead,

clothes drying in the stagnant air. He slowed as he reached a dead end.

Two *yōkai* sat on crates with another crate as a table between them. Both had green souls, the color of moss. A single candle lit up the shadows. One smoked a *kiseru*. The *yōkai* were identical — three or four feet tall, one-legged, and with teeth sharpened into vicious points. Their bodies were covered in fine gray hair, and they had egg-shaped heads with one giant eye in the middle of their foreheads and a smaller one near their left temples. Both wore rusted collars. The two *yōkai* stilled, their pea-sized eyes darting back and forth, scanning the black alleyway.

Akira let loose a breath and stepped out of the darkness. "Afternoon," he called nervously.

The *yōkai* smoking the pipe looked Akira up and down. "Are you lost, boy? Need someone to help you find your mama?"

His companion grinned, running a split tongue over his teeth.

Akira tensed at the mention of his mother. His parents were probably worried. *Will they search for me?* No. His parents would not leave the security of the forest. They would wait for him to return. "I'm not lost," he said, laughing uncomfortably.

"Well, you aren't found, that's for sure, boy," the *yōkai* said. He took a drag of his pipe. Scented smoke filled the alleyway. Akira recognized the smell of sweet grass, a hollow reed that grew along the banks of the Horo River. When the reed was broken, a type of sugary substance flowed out — honey of the gods and goddesses.

Akira peered more closely at the *yōkai*, his gaze darting between their different-sized eyes. Their pupils were huge, almost eclipsing the irises. Relief blanketed Akira. These *yōkai* weren't dangerous, at least not in their drugged state. Sweet grass made its abusers slow, sluggish. If needed, Akira could outrun them.

He took a step closer. "I think I found exactly what I'm looking for."

The *yōkai* frowned. "I don't trust a man who speaks in puzzles."

"Then let me be clear." A trickle of sweat ran down Akira's neck. The eleventh ward seemed to trap heat. He inhaled deeply, lungs filling with sweet-grass smoke. The *yōkai* puffed on his pipe and exhaled in Akira's direction. Akira unwrapped his face, displaying the scars. "I seek the Weapons Master." If he was going to live in the light, if he was to help Mari, he must be well-armed, well-trained. He must be brave.

One of the *yōkai* chuckled. His laughter echoed in Akira's ears. Akira whipped his head back and forth, seeing double. Another chorus of laughter. Akira closed his eyes. When he opened them, one of the *yōkai* stood in front of him. Akira looked down, seeing his reflection in the *yōkai*'s giant eye. Half-scarred face, snarled hair, and wide eyes that appeared black. "You like riddles, boy? I'll give you one. You'll find the Weapons Master when you find the thing with hands that cannot clap."

Akira opened his mouth to speak, but words wouldn't form. His tongue felt numb; his body felt weighty, as if his ankles were tethered to a rusty anchor. *Gods and goddesses, I've been drugged!* Then down he went, falling into a dark, dreamless ocean.

PART II:

A bee sting to a crying face.

— Proverb

CHAPTER 16
Mari

MARI STARED AT the massive mahogany and cypress doors, at the reliefs carved into them. A blazing yellow sun set in a blue sky. *The Summer Room.* She didn't know what lay beyond the doors, but she could imagine. A mountain girl through and through, Mari hated the heat.

She stood on a red carpet in a swarm of girls, crunched so closely together that their hair appeared an endless ocean of black. *There are hundreds of us*, Mari realized. *Taiko* drummers corralled the group. Their chests were bare and their legs spread wide as they beat with thick sticks against the drums' skin. The fast beat announced the start of the competition and drew courtiers to the Main Hall. The opening ceremony for the competition had begun. Later on, there would be a grand ball and garden party for the winners of today's room. But for now, the heavy beat of drums, a death knell, was the only welcome. The weak would be weeded out first.

Women courtiers were swathed in glittering red, blue, and green kimonos. They carried paper fans, fluttering them over their mouths, painted crimson, and their dyed black teeth — a symbol of beauty. Men dressed in elaborate *hakama* pants, neatly pressed and made of fine linen, and surcoats stitched in gold thread. Priests dotted the crowd, their gray robes little clouds of doom amid all the joyful colors. *The brewing of a perfect storm.*

Mari swallowed, and she locked her knees. She was too warm. She wished she had worn her *hakama* pants, but Sei had outfitted her this morning and insisted on something more feminine. They'd compromised on her simple navy kimono.

In the crowd, metal clinked against metal. Each girl toted a weapon. Mari's *naginata* felt heavy and reassuring strapped to her back. She swallowed heavily again, seeing so many other girls carrying *naginata*. Collective fear rippled through the mass. The girls' eyes flickered, assessing their opponents — their enemies. It made for itchy fingers. If one drew her weapon, chaos would erupt.

The drums reached a crescendo and then tapered to a soft beat. A gong rang, calling the Main Hall to attention. A gaunt man, with a silver beard so long it brushed his chest, stood in front of the Summer Room doors. His eyes were a milky white, his skin paper-thin, and he carried a black lacquered cane. On his head was a pointed black cap. He opened his fingers, and little flames danced along his long nails, then extinguished with a single gust of wind — a small display of his powers. "Welcome, all of you, to this most sacred event. I am Master Ushiba, Imperial Seasonist. I will be your guide through this competition. The Seasons will be your judge."

A hushed murmur traveled through the crowd. Master Ushiba paused. One by one, like trees toppling, the courtiers dropped to their knees, pressing their chests and foreheads to the ground. The emperor had arrived.

Mari and the other girls bowed as well. Daring a peek, Mari spied a striking middle-aged man standing next to Master Ushiba. His black hair was streaked with gray and slicked back in a topknot. His jaw was square and his mouth a cruel, hard line. He wore a purple kimono trimmed in fur, and at his hip were two samurai swords — an "emperor" and a "warlord." Mari's lips curved down. *Hate-monger. Yōkai slaver. Despot.*

A flash of white behind the emperor drew Mari's focus. A High Priest. A *young* High Priest. His hands were covered with the familiar cobalt tattoos, but his face was unmarred. *Probably because he is too pretty.* He had a slightly round face, dimpled cheeks, and long lashes. *A man too full of himself is empty inside.*

Near the emperor was another man, shifting on his feet as if preparing to flee. *Not just another man.* Mari's mouth tightened in recognition. *Taro. The samurai with the copper bird.* She bit back a smile, seeing the purple bruises ghosting his face. Her grin faded. A samurai would bow like everyone else. But Taro didn't. That meant only one thing. The smudge between his eyes matched the emperor's. *Matched his father's.* He bore the mark of the gods. *Taro is the prince.*

A flush of stupidity caressed her cheeks. *Taro.* Of course she hadn't recognized his name. He was always referred to as "the prince." Or sometimes the Cold Prince. But she should have known him by the smudge. The god Sugita's thumbprint. Her folly turned to anger. *What a laugh he probably had at my expense.*

"Rise," the emperor growled.

Clumsily, Mari found her feet, knocking into a girl carrying a bow and arrow. The girl elbowed Mari in the ribs. "Watch it," she snapped.

Mari's hand went to her bruised side, and she bared her teeth. She wished she could bare her claws.

"Have the contracts been signed?" asked the emperor. Mari kept her gaze locked on Taro. He was scanning the crowd. Did he search for her?

"No, Heavenly Sovereign." Master Ushiba kept his head down.

"Let's get on with it, then. I don't have all day," the emperor said, his tone impatient.

"Yes, Heavenly Sovereign." Master Ushiba faced his audience. His hand opened, gesturing to a table near the Summer Room doors. On it, parchment was stacked. "Before entering the Summer Room and beginning the competition, you each must sign a contract, stating your name and your clan name. In addition, this contract states that your clan will not be owed any compensation in the event of your demise. Killing your opponents is strictly forbidden, but the conditions in the Rooms are treacherous. I may have created the Rooms, but they have a mind of their own. They will choose you as much as you choose them. From this point on, your life is forfeit."

Mari felt a change in the air, a sudden tightening as if invisible nooses had been placed around their necks.

Master Ushiba continued. "Once you have signed the contract, you will be admitted into the Summer Room." He produced a piece of rolled parchment tied with a red string from the depths of his kimono. "Ten scrolls are hidden within the Room. They are your admittance to the next Room. If you hear this . . ." Master Ushiba gestured

114

at a samurai standing behind a golden gong. The samurai struck the instrument once, and a sound like a heavy bell echoed in the cavernous hall. ". . . it means that all scrolls have been claimed and you have been disqualified. Your clan will be eligible to compete next generation." The girls shifted on their feet. Only ten scrolls; only ten out of hundreds would go on. The stakes were high. The odds impossible. The Seasonist fell quiet. He tapped his thin lips. "Along with being tested physically in the Rooms, you will also face mental strain. Solve the following riddle, and find the scrolls." Master Ushiba opened his hands like a book. In his palms, he cradled an orange flame that lit up his face and made his milky-white eyes glow. The courtiers sucked in a collective uneasy breath. *I have roots nobody can see and am taller than a tree. Up, up I go, and yet I never grow.* Raindrops fell in a perfect circle, extinguishing the flame and leaving behind a misty sizzle. Then a single gust of wind dried Master Ushiba's hands.

"Less theatrics next time," the emperor muttered.

Master Ushiba frowned and ducked his head. "Yes, Heavenly Sovereign." The pretty priest smiled smugly beside the emperor. Ushiba cleared his throat and addressed the crowd. "Now, if you are ready, please come forward."

No one moved. Mari could taste the fear, sour and bitter. *Treacherous conditions. The Rooms choose you.* How many of them would die? Were these Mari's last moments?

A girl holding a sickle and chain shouldered her way from the back of the Main Hall, through the frozen horde. She gave a deep bow to the emperor and prince, one fist covered by the palm of her other hand. She rose, turned, and signed her contract with flourish. The doors sprang open with a mighty gust of wind, a ball of heat escaping and touching Mari's cheek. The girl with the sickle and chain dashed through.

After that, girls scrambled to get to the front of the line to sign their waivers, crushing Mari, forcing her to the back. No doubt by the time she got to the Summer Room, the girl with the sickle and chain would already have solved the riddle, scroll in hand.

Nearing the front, Mari's stomach churned. Her chest felt as if an iron band were cinched around it. It was here. The final moment, a sword hovering right above her neck. She approached the emperor, the High Priest, and the prince — Taro. She bowed. When she rose, the purple bruises on Taro's face stole her attention. Striking a royal was a crime punishable by death. She waited for him to accuse her, to demand the priests or guards drag her away. She forced herself to meet the prince's gaze.

Taro lowered his chin, a deep furrow between his brows. "Good luck," he rumbled.

He hadn't spoken to any of the other girls. What could he possibly be thinking? *Don't do me any favors.*

At the table, Mari picked up the brush, dipped it in ink, and scrawled her name on the contract along with a fictitious clan name. If she died, her body would not be returned to Tsuma. Without looking back, because there could be no looking back at this point, Mari stepped into the Summer Room.

CHAPTER 17
Akira

AKIRA WOKE TO THE PHANTOM SMELL of wild mint and fresh water. He'd dreamed of Mari, of the way she smelled. As his eyes cracked open, the scent of mint turned to must. He tasted salt on his lips, and gulls cried out above him. *The docks?* The floorboards under his cheek felt grainy, covered in dust, and gods and goddesses only knew what else. Akira lifted his hands to his face, felt the uneven terrain of his scars. His mask had been pulled off.

What happened? Where am I? His body felt like lead, but he managed a sitting position. With a flash, he remembered. The alleyway. The two-eyed *yōkai*. Sweet grass packed one hell of a punch. He could use a drink of water. Once more, his fingers grazed his scars. A crumpled heap of black rested near his toes. His mask. He reached for it.

A soft grunt and the warmth of another presence made Akira pause. His gaze roamed upward. A brick-red behemoth greeted him.

An *oni*. He wore a tiger-skin loincloth. Piercings ran up his massive red chest. His neck was collared by a disk of metal inscribed with curses. The *yōkai* Akira had seen in the markets had similar collars. The cursed metal must steal *yōkai* powers. The *oni* grunted again and licked one of his double fangs. His yellow eyes narrowed. Two horns protruded from his forehead. Surprisingly, the *oni*'s soul was light pink, the exact shade of a cherry-blossom petal. Akira snickered.

The *oni* growled.

Akira clambered back, face cover forgotten. Fear burned a path up his throat. He was no match against the demon. His eyes darted, wildly searching for a way out. The *oni* blocked the only exit with his massive frame. The demon clicked his tongue. *Is he trying to speak?*

Akira couldn't breathe. He searched for a weapon. The room was bare, save for a spinning wheel bolted to one of the walls. *What in the world?* Then he saw the source of the light. A huge round window took up one of the walls. *No, not a window — the face of a clock.* Through the clock, the Imperial City could be seen, bathed in the orange light of sunrise. He was in the clock tower. *How did I get here?*

The door flew open.

Akira stood, paralyzed, as a girl sauntered into the room. The girl was tall, nearly reaching the *oni*'s chest. Her long, ash-colored hair was pin-straight and parted down the middle, cloaking her shoulders. Her eyes were milky bluish silver. Her kimono was crisp and white. The metal collar peeking from under her dress was highly polished, unlike the *oni*'s, which was caked in dirt. Her movements were as graceful as those of a dancer. A pure white ferret was draped around her neck, a living fur shrug. Most striking was her skin. It was see-through, like rice paper. Akira found himself equally fascinated and disgusted by the network of blue veins running rivers under her translucent skin. Her soul glowed, ivory and pearlescent, but was marred with black spots. A killer.

She was *yōkai*. But Akira had never beheld one like her. "What are you?" Akira whispered, transfixed.

The girl pursed her lips and crossed her arms. "What a rude thing to say."

The *oni* clicked his tongue in a sound of agreement.

"And after we saved his life and everything. Those geezers" — the *yōkai* in the alleyway — "were going to turn you over to the priests. An uncollared *yōkai* fetches a high reward."

Akira hung his head, duly chastised. "I'm sorry. Thank you for saving my life."

The girl's lips twitched, her smile calculating as she approached. "Already forgotten."

The *oni* clicked in rapid succession.

She pointed a thumb over her shoulder at the demon. "He's warning me not to get too close to you. He thinks you might be dangerous. But I don't think you're dangerous." She sniffed around Akira's neck. Her breath was cold and carried the clean scent of winter. "At least you don't *smell* dangerous. You smell kind of soft and sweet, like . . . almond cookies."

Akira resisted the urge to bring his shirt to his nose and inhale. "I don't intend you any harm. I'm Akira," he said, trying to sound good-natured.

The *oni* clicked.

The girl nodded. "I agree. A pretty name for such a pretty boy."

Akira gritted his teeth. "And you are?"

The girl turned to the *oni*, slapping her hand against his massive chest. "This is Ren. I've had him since he was a baby. Have you ever seen an *oni* youngling?" She cupped his jaw, squeezing his burnt-red cheeks with her veiny fingers. "Cutest thing you ever saw." The ferret around the girl's neck awoke and scampered into Ren's hands. The demon smiled, gently stroking the animal with a thick yellow talon. "And that's Large," the girl said, gesturing to the ferret.

"Your ferret's name is Large?" Akira couldn't stop himself from asking.

The girl's eyes widened. She covered the ferret's pink ears with her hands. "Shh, he's very sensitive about his rodent condition." She grew thoughtful. "He's also very sensitive about his size."

"And who are you?" Akira asked. Had he been drugged with sweet grass again? It felt like it, trying to follow the girl's inane chatter. She had the attention span of a fly.

The girl tapped her bluish lips. "I never said." The girl grew annoyed. Her head tilted; her eyes narrowed. "What were you doing in that alley? Tell me now, and make it snappy. Before I let Ren make your *bones* snappy." Ren flexed his jaw and cracked his knuckles, ready to mete out violence.

Even if Ren's collar zapped most of his supernatural abilities, he appeared to be quite *naturally* large and strong. The *oni* could harm Akira if he wanted to. No question.

"I was looking for the Weapons Master," Akira said.

The girl's annoyance faded; her bluish lips curved into a smile — the grin of someone who likes to dance on sharp edges. "Now ask me again who I am."

The words of the *yōkai*, the geezers, in the alley curled through

Akira's brain. *You like riddles, boy? I'll give you one. You'll find the Weapons Master when you find the thing with hands that cannot clap.* Akira's gaze flew to the window, to the face of the clock.

A clock has hands that cannot clap. Realization hit in quick succession. "Are you —"

She cut him off, dipping into a low, dramatic bow. "Over the course of my lifetime, I have been known by many names. My mother called me Hanako. Before I was collared, my touch froze anything with a heartbeat, and so I was called *yuki-onna*, Snow Woman. But now, most know me by another name — Weapons Master." Hanako rose, forehead scrunched. "What, no applause?"

Ren clicked.

Hanako nodded. "Yes, yes. I'll ask him," she replied to the *oni*. But instead of asking Akira anything, she examined her nails nonchalantly. The white ferret scampered down Ren's leg and into a hole in the wall.

Akira cleared his throat. "Are you truly the Weapons Master?" He couldn't believe it. This girl was the leader of the *yōkai* Resistance? She seemed *not well*, and that was putting it kindly. Other words came to mind. Off-balance. A few hairs short of a full wig. *Crazy.*

Hanako scowled. She stepped toward Akira. "Are you calling me a liar?"

Akira's hands rose in defense. "No! I —"

"Would you like me to demonstrate my skill? Take a sword and slit you from stomach to sternum? Wield a bow and arrow and fire it through your heart? Or maybe I should make some companions to those scars on your face."

Akira touched the white gouges in his cheeks. *Mean and blood-thirsty*, perhaps that described Hanako best.

Hanako smiled, wicked and joyful. "Ah, I see I've touched a nerve. It is not the threat of physical violence that hurts you. What wounds you most is inside." Hanako's smile changed, turning bright and young. She clapped her hands. "You are like Large, my ferret. He abhors his smallness, and so do you."

Akira was as tall as Hanako. "I'm not small," he sputtered.

"Maybe not in size. But here." She splayed her hand right above his heart. Her palm was icy, and gooseflesh broke out on Akira's skin.

The *oni* clicked, the sound aggressive and impatient. "Do you know what he's saying?" Hanako asked, letting her hand fall from Akira's chest. Warmth flooded back into his body.

Akira shook his head. "I don't speak Oni."

"What a shame. They say the most insightful things. Like just now, Ren is wondering why you've been looking for me. The absence of your collar makes him suspicious. He thinks you might have made a deal with the priests. Perhaps you've promised to hunt down the Weapons Master? Ren thinks you're a spy. Do you know what happens to spies, Akira?" she asked. Her milky-gray eyes swirled like a storm. "They end up dead. So I ask you, and answer carefully, for your life depends on it, why have you sought me out?"

Akira closed his eyes. He smelled the salt of the Ma ni Sea. The window clock struck seven. When Akira opened his eyes, Hanako was directly in his line of sight, her head tilted in a question. "I am not a spy. I wear no collar because my family has lived as outcasts in the Tsuko funo Mountains since I was young. And I want to learn to fight."

Hanako observed Akira for a moment, scrutinizing him. Her lips spread into a slow smile followed by laughter, the tinkling sound filling the room. Ren followed suit, only his laughter came out as a roar.

Humiliated fury rose within Akira. *I am a joke to them.* He bit his cheek hard, nearly drawing blood.

"You want me to teach you to wield a weapon?" She wiped tears from her eyes as she sobered. "Seriously?"

Akira folded his hands into fists. "I am serious. I want to learn to fight. I want you to teach me." He left out his other desires. *I want to be brave. I want to be worthy of love. I want to live in the light.*

Hanako circled Akira, an animal stalking its prey. Akira wished he were wearing his mask. Wished he were anywhere but here.

"Are you sure you know what you're asking? This is a serious undertaking. A weapon tempts violence, courts bloodshed. Once you've beckoned death, you cannot unbeckon it."

Akira nodded. "I understand."

Hanako tapped her chin. "I imagine you have not been in the Imperial City long. Nothing here is free. I command a high price. But since you remind me of my pet *and* you've made me laugh more than I have in seven moons, I will train you for the very small fee of . . . ten thousand *ryō*."

An absurd amount. Akira didn't have a single *ryō* to his name, let alone ten thousand. "I don't have any money," Akira muttered.

"A shame," Hanako said with a shrug. "I guess this is where we part ways. Ren will see you out." Hanako began to walk from the room

Akira sighed. *I have nothing to offer in trade.* But then he

123

remembered his footsteps that made no sound, his hands that left no prints. Perhaps there could be power in the shadows. Why had he never contemplated this? A vision of his mother flashed before his eyes. She had surpassed death and emerged on the other side, with a heart that still beat, with a soul that still raged. Her blood ran through Akira's veins. He was mightier than the sum of his faults.

"Wait!" he called to Hanako's retreating form. Hanako's steps halted, but she kept her back turned. "I don't have any coin. But I'm an uncollared *yōkai*. Surely that could work in your favor. I offer you my services for your training."

Slowly, Hanako spun on one foot. Her brows drew together. She held his gaze. "And how do you think you can be beneficial to me?"

Akira ducked his head. He spoke to the ground, but his words were clear. "My mother is the Slash-Mouthed Girl." Hanako gasped. Ren grunted. So they had heard of her. For once, he was thankful for her infamy. "I am the Son of Nightmares. I am half ghost and can move like one too."

Hanako stepped closer.

Ren clicked.

"Exactly what I was thinking, dear friend," she replied to Ren. Then, addressing Akira, she said, "You can get in and out of spaces easily?"

"I am the wind. None will capture me. None will remember me. None will see me."

"And why do you wish to learn to fight, Son of Nightmares?"

Akira's hands curled into fists at his sides. "I have been conditioned to be afraid." He thought of his family, forced to hide in the mountains. "I have been conditioned to come second." He thought of

Mari's mother, reminding him that he was not good enough for her daughter. "And I no longer wish to be either." He would keep Mari a secret. For now.

"At last, an honest answer." Hanako bowed. "I accept your offer of trade, Son of Nightmares. I will enlist your services as the wind, and I will train you in the art of weaponry." In a flash, Ren drew a knife and handed it to Hanako. She slit her palm. "Let us seal our bargain." Hanako held the hilt of the knife out to Akira. Blood dripped from her fingers. His face went pale.

Akira hesitated. "What will you require of me?"

"You are the wind, no?"

Akira nodded.

"Wind can go anywhere, even cut through illusions. I have need of an inside man at the palace. You'll be my eyes and ears."

Akira's brow scrunched. Blood continued to drip from Hanako's hand. "Why?"

Hanako clicked her tongue. "The student doesn't learn every lesson at once. You will go to the palace, gather the information I tell you to, and in exchange, I will make you a mighty warrior."

The Snow Girl's words were seductive, playing to Akira's desires. She would train him, help him breach the palace. He could watch over Mari. Still, Akira looked at Hanako's outstretched crimson palm and grimaced.

Hanako huffed. "Come now, Akira. How will you tear into an opponent if you can't handle a little blood?"

Akira straightened. He took the knife and dragged the gleaming edge across his palm. *What's a few more scars?* Squeezing his hand into a fist, he let his blood drip to the floor.

Hanako did the same, bringing her hand closer to his. Their blood pooled together on the wood beneath their feet. They watched as it was absorbed. "It is in the grain now," Hanako whispered. "Our deal is part of the earth. If we break our promise to each other, gods and goddesses help us." The air sizzled with their pledge. Hanako grinned wickedly and clapped her hands. "Tonight, we celebrate!"

CHAPTER 18

Mari

MADNESS GREETED MARI in the Summer Room. A wet blanket of thick, hot air wrapped around her. Sweat coated her face and neck. Above, a sun blazed in a cloudless sky. Ahead stretched a field of yellow and orange sunflowers. And beyond that, a white birch forest flanked a dry, dusty mountain.

The doors to the Summer Room closed, and Mari heard the unmistakable sound of the oak bar slamming into place. They were locked in. She'd faced this before. The shed had taught her well. Staying calm was the key to staying alive. *Do not lead with your heart,* her mother had said. *Lead with your head.*

Girls rushed into the sunflower field. They didn't seem to care that Mari stood still, surveying the landscape. Perhaps they thought her too small to pay attention to.

Swarms of bees alighted from the towering sunflowers. The girls had disturbed their hives. Just as quickly as they had flooded the sunflower field, they scrambled out of it, arms like windmills, batting away honeybees.

Mari blinked. The chaos melted away. She was twelve and back on the mountain, in the cold, crisp air. Tami was beside her. It was early morning. Hunting time. The forest beckoned them, tree branches swaying with the wind. Mari lurched forward, but her mother stopped her, arm across her chest. "No. We wait. There will always be something stronger, smarter, faster, better than you. Let it reveal itself. Patience is a virtue." And so they stayed as still and silent as the trees, but for the wind ruffling their hair and kimonos. Mari's legs ached, and her stomach rumbled with hunger. Then came the rustle of leaves. And through a set of bushes, a small pack of gray wolves alighted, sniffing the ground, unaware of the Animal Wives feet away. The beast inside Mari trembled and wanted to attack. But Mari followed her mother's cues. The pack left the clearing, and Mari and her mother followed, keeping just enough distance to stay down-wind. The wolves led them to a deer. Tami smiled at her daughter and whispered. "See? They do the work. We reap the reward."

Another blink, and Mari was back in the Summer Room. Sweat coursed down her spine. Out of the corner of her eye, she spotted two girls dart into the birch-tree forest. *Lead with your head.* Mari thought of the riddle. *I have roots nobody can see and am taller than a tree. Up, up I go, and yet I never grow.* She hadn't a clue what it meant. But those two girls looked as if they did. There was purpose in the direction they headed. Had they solved the riddle? Only one way to find out. She let loose a breath. *They'll do the work. I'll reap the reward.*

128

Mari kept to the side of the sunflower field, avoiding the swarm of bees. She maintained a quick pace, and, as she moved, she shed clothing, leaving her *obi* and kimono in a heap behind her. It was a bit of a struggle with the *naginata* strapped to her back, but Mari managed. In her thin, light undergarments, she was much better suited for the climate.

She reached the edge of the field. Her mouth felt dry, and her throat ached. She looked up, shielding her eyes. The sun glared, an open wound in the sky, and it had shifted ever so slightly. *Late afternoon?*

On the ground, she noted four sets of prints. The girls hadn't covered their tracks. *Too easy.* Before diving into the birch forest, Mari glanced over her shoulder. *Always look behind you*, Tami had said. *You don't know what could be stalking you.* A flash of red caught her eyes — a girl with a crimson ribbon in her hair. The girl carried no weapon. She raced through the sunflower field so fast, her body was a blur. Then the girl leaped, clearing the last of the sunflowers and skidding into the birch forest. Above, gray clouds filtered. Lightning wrenched across the sky like a reaching hand. Mari watched as it split a tree. A branch fell, landing on top of the red-ribboned girl, pinning her. More sparks flew, and thunder rolled. *The Rooms choose you as much as you choose them*, Master Ushiba had warned. Mari darted into the forest, applying her footsteps over those of the two girls.

The thunderstorm left just as quickly as it had arrived. Mari jogged slowly, tracking her prey. Soon enough, a stitch buckled her side, and she was forced to a walk. Her feet felt like they were on fire, swelling with heat. Determined, she continued on, trampling through the shrubs, using her *naginata* as a walking stick. Dappled sunlight and a hot breeze filtered through the trees. Flies swarmed, biting Mari's neck and face. Voices in the distance ruffled the air. The two girls. Mari had caught up to them. She slowed, lay down on her stomach, and shimmied forward, using a bush to shield her. Through the leaves, she caught sight of their dark hair. She recognized one of the girls, the one with the bow and arrow, the one who'd rammed into her side during the opening ceremony.

The bow-and-arrow girl laughed and plucked an apple from a tree. They were in a grove of some sort. Apples hung heavy from branches, along with oranges and lemons. Mari's mouth watered as she eyed them through the wavy heat. "When I am Empress," said the girl, "I will have this room completely remodeled. An orchard in the middle of a birch forest? How absurd."

Her friend frowned, *katana* sword held tightly in her hand. "I don't think we should slow down. There are only ten scrolls."

"Pfft," the bow-and-arrow girl chided, biting into the apple. "They are all still trying to solve the riddle. 'Up, up I go, but I never grow.'"

Her friend's frown deepened. "We should go. I feel like we're being followed."

Mari ducked farther into the bush.

The bow-and-arrow girl sighed and threw the apple. "I suppose so. The mountain will take some time to climb."

Mari bit her cheek. Mountain? Yes, of course. *Up, up I go, but I never grow.* A mountain. She could've slapped herself at her stupidity. *You live on a mountain.* The girls began to exit the orchard, but their steps stalled. A tree rustled, and from the branches a bright green snake fell, its body coiled and ready to strike. Mari startled violently.

130

The pit viper hissed, fangs dripping with venom, eyes focused on the girl with the *katana* sword.

The girl with the *katana* sword turned wide eyes to her friend. "Help me," she said, body wound tight. Any movement, and the viper would strike. Mari crawled forward, reaching behind for her *naginata*.

The bow-and-arrow girl smiled. "We can't both be Empress. Better our allegiance ends now than to drag it out."

The *katana*-sword girl gritted her teeth and took a cautious step back. The snake hissed and followed. "It's against the rules. No killing your opponents," she said.

The bow-and-arrow girl laughed. "I'm merely letting nature take its course." The bow-and-arrow girl plucked a rock from the ground. She tossed it up in the air and caught it. "Well, maybe I'm helping it along a little bit." She threw the rock at the *katana* girl's feet. The pit viper leaped into action and struck, biting through the *katana* girl's kimono. The *katana* girl's knees buckled, and she fell forward, hand clutching her throat, spittle forming at the corners of her mouth.

The bow-and-arrow girl didn't stay to watch. She left the orchard. The pit viper coiled again, ready to strike, guarding its prey. Mari drew to her feet and crept from the bush. The pit viper opened its mouth and hissed. She blinked the sweat from her eyes, and in one swift movement brought her *naginata* down, slicing through the pit viper's body.

He calls you a pit viper, Masa had told her.

Mari smiled at the dead snake. "You and I are not the same." She crouched next to the *katana* girl and felt along her neck. Her skin was still warm. No pulse.

Mari peered up, but branches blocked her view. How much farther to the mountain? She'd better get going. But she hesitated to leave the girl behind. Alone. It seemed not right. Mari gathered leaves and dirt from the ground and covered the girl as best she could.

She stumbled from the orchard. The birch trees were silent and eerie. Even the leaves that fluttered in the breeze didn't make a sound. She should have been able to hear the other girls — their cries of defeat and shouts of victory — but all was silent. The grass grew high, and the blades cut her arms. Thick swarms of flies appeared, and she knew this could mean only one thing: water.

Mari licked her cracked lips. A drink sounded good. She wouldn't be able to go much farther without one. The tall grass parted, revealing a pond that stank like rot and dead fish. An arched bridge stretched over the water. On the bridge, a girl and a giant boar were locked in a standoff. The boar was near the size of the girl. Its mouth frothed with spit, and its two sets of tusks were rimmed in red. The boar stamped its foot. Mari noticed that it was the sickle-and-chain girl, the bold one who had signed her contract first. *I thought she'd have a scroll by now.*

The girl with the sickle and chain put her hands up, eyes widening. "Easy, pig," she said, backing up. The boar shook its head and stamped its foot again.

It's not your fight, Mari counseled herself. She turned to go. Her feet, her conscience, held her immobile. She groaned and rolled her eyes. *I'll not see another girl dead if I can help it.* Mari swiveled and burst from the reeds. Her feet made no sound on the rickety wooden bridge. As she ran, she braced her *naginata* above her. The pole struck the boar in the temple. It waivered but didn't collapse. She swung up and struck again, three more times. The boar grunted and fell, uncon-scious, with an audible thud on the wooden bridge. Mari heaved and watched the boar for a moment, *naginata* ready to strike again.

"Thanks." The sickle-and-chain girl spoke. She had dark brown eyes, chestnut hair, and straight eyebrows. The only soft thing about her was her heart-shaped face. She wore an *uwagi.* The tunic was tied tight around her throat, covering her neck.

Mari nodded. "We've got boars where I'm from. Terrible animals. Messy eaters."

The girl laughed, a throaty sound. "I'll make sure I mind my manners when I'm around you." She bowed. "I'm Asami."

Mari returned the bow. "Mari."

"Well, thanks again, Mari," Asami said. She adjusted the sickle and chain. "Good luck." Asami turned, rambling off.

"Wait," Mari said. Asami paused. "We could work together." She thought of the two girls she'd followed and their short partnership, before one betrayed the other. "If we team up, it would strengthen our odds. I'd have your back, and you'd have mine . . . at least until the last Room." *Think with your head. Make an ally.*

"Sorry, Mari." Asami kept walking. "I work alone." Then she slipped into the birch trees and disappeared.

Mari hung her head. A black spider with white stripes crawled across her feet. Its body was near the size of her palm. With a tiny squeak, she shook off the eight-legged creature. Then she used her *naginata* to sever it in half. A soft cry echoed through the forest. The sound of another girl dying?

Night closed in, but the heat lingered, suffocating the endless forest.

Mari slogged on, sweat pouring from her body. Her muscles ached with fatigue, but her thoughts centered on the scrolls. They were probably all taken by now. But there was supposed to be a signal. The sound of a gong meant failure. And she hadn't heard one yet. Then again, she hadn't seen another girl for hours. Hadn't heard another sound, aside from the rustling trees and buzzing insects.

What if she was walking all for naught? What if she was walking in circles? What if the losers were meant to stay in the Summer Room and perish?

Twice she thought she saw a sparkling river through the trees, but when she dipped her hands into the water and brought them to her lips, she tasted dirt. She heard a crunch of leaves behind her. Was she being followed? She whipped around, *naginata* drawn. Nothing. No one. Her mind was playing tricks on her. Heat made people crazy.

Everything smelled of rotting earth, as if the ground were being overcooked. She kept going, running when she could, walking when she couldn't. Homesickness hit Mari like a punch in the gut. How was Hissa? What was Akira doing right now? *Will I ever see them again?*

Hard rocks bit into the arches of her feet. The sparse grass of the birch forest ended, and the slope of the mountain began. Mari drew her head up. The dry mountain had seemed so small in the distance. Now it rose above her, an imposing giant. She couldn't walk upright, so she had to settle for a sort of bear crawl. Her hands sank into dry dirt, and gravel dug into her palms as she began to climb. *One step down, a thousand more to go.*

Mari's muscles screamed and ached. She risked a glance down. All she saw was black, a yawning mouth waiting to swallow her whole. Heated wind swirled, kicking up buried memories. She focused on them instead of the pain.

The first time she'd spoken to Akira, she'd knocked him out of a tree. She'd been sent to collect tributes from the gates. She'd just picked up a basket of persimmons when movement in the trees caught her eye. She knew who it was. He'd been watching her for days, haunting the gates. She plucked an orange from the basket and launched it at him. He toppled from the tree.

"You've been following me. What do you want?" she'd asked, standing above him, hands on her hips.

He flinched.

Her glare intensified. "What's wrong with your face?" she asked.

He fingered the deep grooves of his silvery scars. There were more on his hands. "My mother is the Slash-Mouthed Girl. I am the Son of Nightmares," he said, as if that explained it all.

"You don't look very nightmarish," she'd said, nose scrunching. "Maybe a bad dream, but that's all." She grabbed the orange she'd thrown, peeled it, and offered him half.

As he took it, his fingers brushed hers. Touch has a memory. And Mari remembered that stroke as a song, the melody of one lonely soul calling to the other. "I think we ought to be friends," he'd said.

Mari had puckered her lips in consideration. Soon her mother would come searching for her. "I don't think that's a good idea."

The scarred boy grinned. "I think it's the best idea I've ever had."

Mari swallowed at the memory. She had to get back to him, to her friends. Whatever the cost, she must return to Tsuma. The rocky façade leveled off, and Mari bit back a shout as she hoisted over a rise. As she stood, her chest heaved. A hot, errant breeze rippled her hair. All her nails were broken, and her once-white undergarments were a filthy brown. Her knees were scratched from sharp rocks. But she'd summited the mountain. Accomplishment gave her new breath, new hope.

Hazy lights glowed ahead from sheltered flames. In between the craggy edges was a platform. Samurai were there, spears in hand, guarding a table. And on that table? A single scroll tied with red twine. *Mine.*

Behind the platform was another pavilion where nine girls, dirty and bedraggled, drank ladles of water from a wooden bucket. Each had a scroll.

Mari licked her parched lips, tasting victory. She flung herself forward. Her feet fell out from underneath her. She landed hard, her palms cut by sharp rocks. Her side ached as if punched by a giant fist.

Mari turned her head. Black beady eyes met hers. A boar stood above her. *The* boar. She recognized its red-tipped tusks, the wound at its temple. Something *had* been stalking her. Too late, she remembered how smart these animals were, how *patient.* The boar stamped its foot and drew back, ready to charge.

Mari closed her eyes and prayed for it to be quick. Air whooshed by, followed by a *thunk,* the sound of a body falling. Tentatively, Mari opened an eye.

Asami had taken the boar's place. Her sickle dripped with dark red. "You should've killed it when you had the chance," said Asami. She extended a hand to Mari. Her wrists and palms were tattooed. Fear burned a path up Mari's throat. *Curses?* She looked closer. The ink color was wrong, but she couldn't tell exactly what they were. Mari took Asami's hand.

A scroll was tucked into the fold of Asami's *uwagi. She left the protection of the samurai to help me?* Mari couldn't make sense of it. Asami gestured to the low table. "Take your scroll. I'll watch your back."

Cautious, Mari stepped between the samurai and onto the platform. Her fingers trembled as she reached for the scroll. She grasped it and held it to her chest.

A gong rang. The samurai stomped their spears on the wooden platform. The sound echoed through the Summer Room, and the doors opened.

Mari's whole body shook, but she kept the scroll tight in her grip. Nobody would take it from her.

Asami stepped to Mari's side. "I've thought about your offer. I accept."

Mari swallowed. Dirt coated her throat, making her voice rough. "What changed your mind?"

Asami shrugged. "The Rooms are no joke. And two opinions are always better than one." The girl smiled. "Especially when one of them is mine. We'll help each other until the final Room. And then . . ." She shrugged.

Mari understood. "Then it's every woman for herself."

"Deal?" Asami asked, wiping her sickle on the arm of her tunic sleeve. A streak of red stained the fabric. Boar blood.

Mari stared at Asami. *She's your enemy in this competition. Don't trust her.* Mari nodded. "Deal."

Asami smiled.

They were allies now, bound by a fraying thread.

CHAPTER 19

Mari

MARI KEPT A TIGHT HOLD of her *naginata* as she strolled the perimeter of the lavish bedroom. She couldn't shake the feeling of being followed. She couldn't believe that the Summer Room was over.

The zelkova floor was bare but lacquered and shiny, warming instantly beneath her feet. A platform bed with periwinkle silk cushions took up one wall. Suspended above was a pair of gold-tipped rhinoceros horns flanked by two mirrors that faced each other — an antiquated superstition to ward off evil spirits. The wall opposite the bed was coated in linen wallpaper with an illustration depicting an arched wisteria. Mari inhaled. The room even *smelled* luxurious, spiced faintly with cedar, candle wax, and incense. This room, the Wisteria Apartment, inside the Palace of Illusions, would be Mari's home for the duration of the competition.

The other ten girls had accommodations in the same wing, in the East Hall. She'd seen Asami escorted into the White Plum Apartment next door.

With a knock, the door slid open, and Mari dropped to a crouch, *naginata* in front of her. Sei stepped through, and Mari relaxed.

"You survived!" Sei exclaimed. "When the samurai came to fetch me, I thought . . ." She shook her head. "I thought the worst, that you were dead or I was being punished for the taxes I owed . . ."

"Taxes?" Mari leaned her *naginata* in the corner so that it was still within reach. She didn't like the idea of sleeping in her enemy's home, surrounded by her competitors.

Sei moved farther into the room. She bit her lip, her head lowered. "It's nothing, my lady."

Mari wanted to prod Sei, but . . . *another time.*

"I didn't bring your trunk with me," Sei said apologetically.

Mari strode to a black-and-gold lacquered chest. Atop it was a copper dish decorated with persimmons drooping from a tree branch. The oranges reminded Mari of Akira. *I think we ought to be friends . . . I think it's the best idea I've ever had.* Mari caught her reflection in the golden rim — the curve of her full cheek, her heavy-lidded eyes. The bowl was worth a small fortune, to be sure. She might take it with her when she left. She felt Sei's questioning gaze upon her.

"Each of the competitors is allowed to have an attendant." Next to the bowl was a matching tray laden with dried octopus, fruit, and rice biscuits. Mari popped a bit of apple into her mouth. "I didn't bring anyone with me from my clan, and I don't know anyone in Tokkaido. I was hoping that you might consider staying here with me."

Sei sucked in a breath. "My master —"

"Would not deny this request, especially coming from a potential empress." Mari gave Sei a smile full of confidence she didn't feel.

A light sparked in Sei's eyes. She nodded. "I'd like to stay. I've never been in a place so beautiful."

Mari's chin dipped decisively. "Good." She ate another piece of fruit. On the chest was also a vase of white chrysanthemums. The flower symbolized long life. At Mari's touch, the petals shed, scattering across the table. The memory of the Summer Room rolled over Mari, a dark and dangerous tide. "Sei," she called over her shoulder, "would you open the windows, please? It's warm in here. I can't tolerate the heat."

Mari frowned, seeing samurai guards posted by her door.

"They're outside all our doors," Asami said, striding forward. Her ally had decided not to dress for the banquet this evening. Asami's pants and simple top were clean and of good quality, but they were clearly peasant clothing. Again, her tunic was laced high and tight around her neck. Asami snorted, looking Mari up and down. "Hoping to impress the prince, are we?"

Sei had fetched Mari's trunk from the inn. And Mari had chosen her kimono with care — a black silk stitched with red poppies. The most striking piece of Mari's outfit was the *obi*. The wide decorative sash looped around her waist, but instead of bustling in the traditional way, the ends were left dangling, showcasing the two deer embroidered in gold and copper on the back. She had borrowed the *obi* from Hissa. *Remember me,* Hissa had said. As if it were possible for Mari to forget.

"I dressed for the occasion," Mari said stiffly, "not for the prince." A partial truth. Mari still held the Animal Wife desire to be beautiful and wanted, pleasing and perfect, goals she would never accomplish. She remembered raiding the stores of precious silk kimonos from under the singing floorboards as a child, and playing dress-up with Hissa. It was a fun game that resulted in fits of giggles and mismatched outfits. She had felt beautiful then. But somewhere along the way, the game of dress-up became less fun and more like hard labor, especially when her mother joined them one day. Tami had dusted the girls with perfumes and powders and imparted advice: *Men like the smell of self-worth, confidence. You must know your mind and speak it, but not too often. Men fear intelligent women. It means they are capable of anything. You must laugh, but not be funny. You must be spirited, but not strong* . . . Mari shook the memory away. "I just want to blend in. That's all," Mari told Asami.

Asami huffed. "I don't care about those things." Her chin jutted out, as if daring Mari to call her bluff. "Let's go," Asami ordered one of the samurai. *She may dress as a peasant, but she gives demands like a courtier.*

The samurai muttered a gruff, "This way."

As they trailed the samurai, Mari scanned her ally, her eyes traveling over Asami's hands. "I thought . . ." Mari said, uncertain. "I thought I saw tattoos on your wrists and palms when we were in the Summer Room."

Asami's dry laugh bounced through the cavernous hall. "Tattoos? Never had one in my life."

She was certain she'd seen ink on Asami's hands, and Asami's laugh seemed forced, her smile falsely bright. *Why hide your tattoos?*

They reached a set of open double doors. "The Wet Garden," the samurai said. He bowed and withdrew.

Together, Asami and Mari stood, hovering at the threshold, staring at the opulent sight before them. *A place where heaven meets earth.*

An artificial lake sat in the middle of the garden, placid water glowing in the moonlight. In the center of the lake was an island, dotted with black pines and white sand. Lanterns hung from the pines' twisted branches. *No, not lanterns.* Glass bubbles filled with fireflies. Two streams flowed from the lake, and the current carried dragon barges, their backs carved to hold cups of *sake*. Courtiers laughed, picking up glasses of rice wine as they drifted by.

At the farthest point in the garden was a sandpit. Large men with rotund bellies and loincloths stomped their feet and threw salt in the air, purifying the ring. Closer in was a table with a wooden box that contained satchels of incense, each held wood shavings from different parts of the empire. Participants were guessing from which region each satchel hailed. Mari wondered if there was a scent from the Tsuko funo Mountains. She ached for home with a sudden acuteness.

A gong rang, and Master Ushiba appeared beside them. "Lady Asami, representing the Akimoto Clan, Fourth Finisher in the Summer Room," he announced in a sonorous voice. "Lady Mari, representing the Masunaga Clan, Tenth Finisher in the Summer Room."

The courtiers grew silent, twisting their necks to watch Mari and Asami descend the staircase. Mari tensed, and her throat ran dry. She scanned the crowd and found the girl with the bow and arrow. She held up a cup of *sake* and tilted it toward Mari and Asami, a toast that seemed more like a warning. Mari caught sight of Taro. The prince stood, just past the bow-and-arrow girl, under a sugi tree. Quickly, Mari averted her eyes.

143

"Smile," Asami mumbled behind her own tight one. "Remember, sharks circle only when they smell blood."

Mari pasted on a smile, bright and blinding, and gazed at the sea of courtiers, at their grinning mouths, their black teeth. Inside, she hardened, willing her soul to be dry earth. *Duty and home. Conquer the Rooms. Marry the prince. Steal his fortune.*

EOKU:

God of War, Military, and Night

EOKU, GOD OF WAR, MILITARY, AND NIGHT *sought to make an army of followers on earth. His army would be made of the strongest men, with the toughest skin and the fiercest tempers. The army would carry out his will and worship him so that he would always be remembered, always live in the hearts of men. Gods and goddesses fed on worship, and when they faded in human and yōkai memory, they fell into a deep, dreamless sleep.*

Eoku snuck away to Honoku, entering through a cave in the northeast-most corner of the land. He invited yōkai and humans to compete in battles to the death. The champion would be Eoku's namesake, his right hand, the most feared being in the land.

As a test of courage, Eoku created a gate of fire that all had to pass through before competing. Many tried to breach the threshold but burned up instantly.

Only four succeeded.

All were yōkai.

The tengu, *a giant birdlike creature, flew through the center of the ring of fire, his wings only singed by the flames. The* ashura, *a demon with six arms, three faces, and three eyes, walked through the fire unharmed, his slick skin protecting him like a fireproof robe. The* jorōgumo, *a mammoth spider that could shift into the shape of a woman, used its web to smother the flames. And the* oni, *a pale-skinned lesser demon, inhaled a massive breath, then exhaled, extinguishing the hellish fire before walking through.*

The four creatures battled, and Eoku watched with wicked delight.

The ashura *snared the* tengu, *caging and crushing the bird's hollow bones in his six arms. The* jorōgumo *wrapped the* ashura *in a web of unbreakable silk and suffocated him.*

Only the jorōgumo *and* oni *remained.*

They circled each other, their bodies tense, coiled snakes ready to strike. The jorōgumo *shot a web from its abdomen, hoping to ensnare the* oni. *The* oni *caught the web in his hand and pulled the* jorōgumo *forward by her own thread. The* jorōgumo's *eight legs scrambled on the dirt ground, kicking up rocks, trying to find purchase. But the* jorōgumo *was no match against the* oni's *massive strength. Once the* jorōgumo *was close enough, the* oni *climbed on its back and bit into its neck. The* jorōgumo *collapsed. The* oni *painted his body with his victim's blood, staining his skin red. Eoku made the color permanent. From that day on, all* oni *were born with red skin and pledged their lives to Eoku. And they were no longer regarded as lesser demons. Through blood and might and the strength of Eoku, they were the strongest of the yōkai.*

CHAPTER 20
Taro

"SOMETIMES MY FATHER forces *oni* to fight here," said Taro. Mari jumped visibly. She'd been watching the sumo match for some time. And Taro had been watching her, unsure how to approach. He did it with his usual finesse, speaking in a near bark and scaring the daylights out of the recipient.

"Your Majesty," she said, bowing low. Salt, thrown from the ring, crunched under her wooden sandals.

Taro's lips twitched, and his frown deepened. "Please don't call me that."

In the soft lamplight, he saw her anger flare. "How should I address you, then? Prince? Samurai? Taro?" *Liar?* She didn't say it. But she didn't have to. The accusation was present in her narrowed eyes, in her quivering lips. She wasn't just angry. She was hurt. Taro didn't like that he'd caused her pain.

With a small sound, and before he could say anything else, she fled with a swish of her kimono.

Taro gave pursuit, muttering an oath. Once he was within feet of her, he used his most imperious tone, the one that made samurai, priests, and peasants shake and bow. "Mari."

She stopped, her spine rigid, tiny hands clenched. A glass bulb of fireflies hung from a tree, lighting the path. The two deer embroidered on the back of her *obi* shimmered, black eyes silently watching him. Slabs of obsidian stone paved the pathway. The air smelled sweet, loamy, and cool.

Taro gulped, waiting for Mari to turn. She didn't. "Will you not look at me?" he asked roughly.

Mari made the slightest movement. Taro shifted on his feet, ready to pursue her again. He would insist she accept his apology, insist she banter with him as she'd done in his mother's tea garden.

She didn't run.

Instead, her voice floated to him, soft and demure, a light mist of rain. "I'm afraid," she said. "And embarrassed. And angry."

"You fear me?" Taro asked, surprised, dismayed.

"I struck you. With a snap of your fingers, you could order my death."

Taro inhaled. What courage it had taken her to admit that. His breath made little fog clouds. The bruises didn't even hurt anymore. Taro had told the emperor that he'd gotten them while sparring with a samurai, catching a clumsy elbow to the face. His father had seemed pleased. Until Taro explained that he'd lost.

"I do not wish to be a pawn in your cruel game, Your Majesty." Her shoulders squared.

"You think I play a game?" Taro asked.

"Isn't that what a man does when he dresses as someone other than himself?"

Taro ventured forward. Gently, he touched Mari's shoulder, then pulled back. Gooseflesh rose on her small neck. He sighed. "I am the heir to the imperial throne. This is the truth. I cannot change the status of my birth any more than a tiger can change its stripes. The person you met in the garden the other day, wearing samurai clothing and holding a metal bird, that is the real me." He stepped around her so that they were face-to-face. "Twice now I have gravely insulted you. First, by assuming that your intentions for entering the competition were to live a life of luxury." Mari expelled a caustic breath. "Second, by not revealing to you who I really am. Please accept my most sincere apology." Taro swept into a sharp, formal bow. The low type of bow that you present to a superior. The type of bow an imperial prince never executed. "I owe you a penance. A boon. What would you like?"

Mari tilted her head, deep in thought. A signal her anger was yielding? "How big of a boon?"

"Ask me for anything," he demanded quietly. The need for her forgiveness, to make things right between them, burned under his skin. Why was this so important to him?

"What if I wanted a garden with a million roses?"

"Done," Taro answered swiftly.

She reached up and removed a lantern from the nearest branch, cradling it in her hands. Her lips pursed. "Now that I think of it, roses make me sneeze. What about a boat?"

"Of course. A yacht or a fishing boat?"

Mari's mouth relaxed. "I don't think I want that, either," she said softly.

"What *do* you want?" he asked.

Mari sighed, her expression unreadable. "Thank you," she said. "But I don't think anyone can give me the thing I truly want." Mari uncapped the top of the lantern. Unsure of their newfound freedom, the lightning bugs lingered for a moment before gliding away.

"Why did you do that?" Taro asked, studying Mari's face, trying to take her apart, figure her out like one of his contraptions. *Who are you? Why are you here? What are you doing to me?*

"Lately, I've found myself bothered by things in cages." He felt her shoulder brush along his arm as she turned. "But I am monopolizing the prince. You have many guests to entertain. I must say good night."

And with that, she left Taro alone in the dark.

CHAPTER 21
Akira

AKIRA AWOKE IN the clock tower with a pounding headache. *Again.*

But this time he knew how he'd gotten there. The night before, Hanako had taken him out to celebrate their new "friendship." They'd gone to a *yōkai* tavern on the docks with Ren, ordering a bottle of pomegranate rice wine as they entered. The night passed in a haze of drinks, toasts, and bar fights. The sun's rays had just begun to crest when Ren had thrown Hanako and Akira each over a massive shoulder and brought them back to the clock tower.

Akira rolled and groaned, softness grazing his cheek. He was on a futon. His headache spiked as the door opened, the squeaky hinges like nails scraping across his brain. He grumbled, burying himself farther under the covers.

An ice-cold foot crept under the blankets and nudged Akira's side. Hanako's voice followed, clear and sharp. "Get up. It's time to train."

Hanako stood over him, looking amazingly refreshed. Today she'd dressed in a black leather kimono. Her feet were bare. Still fascinated by her see-through skin, Akira watched the delicate veins running through her toes. Ren leaned against a wall, muscled arms crossed over his chest. He picked something from his teeth. Probably hummingbird, apparently the demon's favorite.

"Go away. I need to sleep another hour," Akira said, a queasy hitch in his voice. *Or maybe the whole day.* He couldn't possibly learn to fight in his current condition.

Hanako crouched, bringing them nose-to-nose. "It's funny. You think you have a choice. Come, new friend, Son of Nightmares. Today we choose your weapon."

Akira's interest was piqued. He held up a hand to shield his eyes from the sun streaming through the window. "I won't be trained on all weapons?" he asked.

Hanako laughed. "Only a Weapons Master can wield all weapons. I trained for sixteen years with the Taiji monks in the art of war."

So the rumors are true. Akira had heard that the monks adopted children and trained them, male or female, to be courtesans. But when children were too ugly, the monks trained them as assassins. But all assassins were supposed to report to the emperor for duty, to serve in one of his legions. How had Hanako come to live in the Imperial City but not serve the emperor? And how had she become the leader of the *yōkai* Resistance?

"A weapon is a very personal item. It must choose you as much as you choose it," she explained.

"Interesting," Akira murmured. Still, his head pounded, his eyes drifted closed . . .

Hanako clapped twice. "Ren. The bucket."

The *oni* grabbed a bucket of ice-cold water and dumped it onto Akira's head. He gasped and jumped up. "Gods and goddesses, that's cold!"

Hanako broke into a poisonous smile. "That's nothing. Compared to the blood that runs through my veins, an ice bucket is a warm bath." She tossed an apple and a cloth at him. "Eat, dry yourself off, and meet me in the room directly below. Be ready to bleed."

Akira threw open the door. A hallway and a rickety staircase lined with *yōkai* greeted him. They filled the corridors: Red-skinned *oni* with various metal body piercings, one even with an iron hoop punched through a tusk. A trio of *kamaitachi*, weasel-like creatures with hedgehog quills and a dog's bark. A *yamawaro*, a stout *yōkai* with long, greasy hair and a single eye in the middle of its head. It could mimic the sound of falling rocks, wind, or even dynamite.

"Be careful," Hanako had warned last night, "Ebisu, the *yamawaro*, will sneak into your bed and take naps. He leaves behind a greasy outline and stray hairs."

Akira eyed the *yamawaro*. It smiled at him, a single line of drool dripping from the corner of its mouth. All were collared. All eyed Akira with a hint of distrust.

Akira closed the door firmly behind him. Maybe he could find a lock in the markets. A few steps down, he passed the geezers sitting on the stairs, the ones who'd drugged him and brought him to the clock tower. They were brothers, identical twins, hatched from the same egg. As Akira walked by, they sniffed. "New pet," one said.

He didn't stop. But he studied his surroundings carefully, as he'd been too inebriated the night before to take note of anything. The clock tower was circular and built around a set of winding steps. Narrow hallways shot off on each floor and housed small rooms. From the rafters, giant logs had been strung up. With a knife, the strings could be cut, sending the massive pieces of wood down the staircase. Last night, Hanako had gleefully explained her traps to him. She'd rigged the whole clock tower with swinging logs, explosive tripwires, even nail spikes along the windows. It was clear that the Snow Girl was preparing for something. Whatever it was, Akira planned to clear out before it happened. A few more steps, and Akira reached the room below his. He opened the door and stood, stunned.

Wall-to-wall weapons filled Akira's vision — *katana* and *wakizashi* swords, sickles and chains, bows and arrows, miniature cannon launchers, throwing daggers, and on it went. *Does Hanako truly know how to use each of these weapons?* Below were glass cases. Akira's eyes rested on a set of *tantō* knives, their blades catching the light. A chill ran through him. A *tantō* knife had killed his mother.

"What do you think of my collection?" Hanako asked, strolling amid the armory, running nimble fingers along the edges of the glinting blades. "I am skilled in all. You will be skilled in only one." Slowly, the Snow Girl approached Akira and circled him, rubbing her hands together. "Let's see what you're made of. Then I will determine what weapon you shall have."

For the rest of the day, Akira endured Hanako's endless torture. She measured the span of his arms, had him balance on his toes until the next bell on the clock sounded, demanded he flex. She timed how long it took him to run from one end of the room to the other. She made him do jumping jacks. Then he had to drag himself across the floor with just his arms. Hanako's *yōkai* comrades filtered in, laughing when Akira fell and wincing when he lost his lunch all over one of Hanako's glass cases.

By late afternoon, Akira was sweaty and dirty and more tired than he'd ever been. He was also incredibly hungry. The apple he had in the morning and the bit of rice in the afternoon had barely sustained him. Akira collapsed into an exhausted heap. "Have you decided what weapon yet?"

Hanako made a pffting sound. "Oh, that. I knew the moment we met. All this was just for my enjoyment." Laughter among the *yōkai* ensued. Ren's rumbled like thunder.

Akira scowled. "I believe a sword would suit me." He thought of the *rōnin* who had escorted Mari from the mountain. *Swords discourage enemies. I would never have to fight.* Akira chastised himself. *You think like a coward.*

Hanako made another pffting sound. "Your arms are too thin to wield a sword, even a light blade such as the *katana*. You have neither the body nor the heart of a samurai. You are a poet. Someone born to string pretty words together and contemplate the soul of man. What rhymes with *killer*?" She didn't wait for him to answer. "Also, I don't think you have the stomach to watch your enemy bleed out." Hanako marched to a glass case and removed a small cedar box.

She brought it close to Akira, holding it under his nose. Notes of stale lemon oil and must swirled up. "This is the weapon that was meant for you. Can you hear it?" She held the box a little higher. "Can you hear it, Akira? They're singing for you."

Yes. He could almost hear it. Like the high pitch of a tuning fork, whatever was inside vibrated for him, wanted him. His fingers twitched, aching to open the box.

"The Taiji monks presented these to me on my initiation day. The day I killed my first man. Every weapon has a destiny. Do you know what the monks told me about this weapon's destiny?"

Of course Akira didn't know, couldn't possibly know, but he wanted to find out more than anything. He licked his lips. "Tell me," he said hoarsely.

"They said: *Cold steel in scarred hands will save the world or destroy it.*"

Akira opened his palm, where the white, puckered flesh of his scars crisscrossed in silver arcs. More slash marks. When Takumi had cut his mother's face, he had also sliced her hands, her chest, her throat — no patch of skin went uncut. His mother's scars passed to him like hair or eye color — a reminder that Akira should not exist, that he was a mistake, a deformed creature. Worse, they covered only part of his body, marking him as a halfling. What a shame it was to look in the mirror and see what you could've been, how handsome, how lovable.

"Akira, Son of Nightmares, every weapon has a destiny. I always thought these weapons were supposed to be mine. But I was merely a courier meant to bring them to you." Hanako opened the box. Maroon velvet lined the interior. Cushioned in the soft fabric were *shuriken*, the most ancient of weapons. Throwing stars. With shaking hands, Akira removed one of the stars. The metal warmed under his fingers as if welcoming him home.

His life had been drawn inside heavy lines. He'd been cursed at birth to live as an outcast. He'd stayed in his box, never daring to leave. Soon enough, the box had become a prison. With the throwing stars, Akira would finally break free.

Akira's body felt heavy with fatigue and pain, as if he'd been in a horrible scuffle. But the injury was self-inflicted. He'd asked for it, and Hanako had delivered twofold.

After the Snow Girl had gifted the throwing stars, she'd ushered Akira back upstairs. Hanako stopped at the spinning wheel hanging over Akira's bed. "You will train on this. The wheel represents everything you need in order to be proficient in the throwing stars. The hub is your center, your moral discipline. The spokes are wisdom. The rim is concentration. You will need that above all else." She spun the wheel. "When you've mastered the wheel, you've mastered the throwing stars."

For hours, Akira had thrown the stars at the wheel while it spun, hoping his aim would be so precise that the metal star would slip through the spokes and sink into the wall. No luck.

Every time he threw a star at the wheel, it pinged off the spoke and flew back at him with twice as much force. It was fortunate he wore black. Black didn't show bloodstains. His upper arm had been cut, his forearm, part of his ear, even a chunk of his hair had been severed when a star flew back. Each time, Hanako laughed, sent the wheel spinning, and told him to try again. "You must know the pain your weapon causes." And oh, did he know it now, the sting of a thousand paper cuts all over his body.

After dusk, Hanako ended their training day. Akira felt sleep tug at him, but he forced himself from the clock tower. A chill crept through the alleys and chased Akira as he looped through the fish market, a shortcut he'd discovered. He stepped into the district center. The cherry tree shook in the wind, petals drifting to the ground. It reminded Akira of the gingko tree, of the precious moments he and Mari had shared beneath it.

Below the tree, a gaunt man with a thin wisp of gray beard read names from a scroll. Akira was late. The recitation of the dead had already begun. He inched closer out of the shadows, wrapping his black piece of cloth around his shoulders and to cover most of his face. Others had gathered for the recitation. Family members, Akira presumed.

"Fukumi of Clan Akamatsu, dead in the Summer Room, fell from the great dry mountain." A *dōshin* with a narrow chin and deep-set eyes let out a wail and sank to his knees. "Arisu of Clan Goya, dead in the Summer Room, bitten by a pit viper." A courtier in a red kimono burst into tears.

The gaunt man lowered the scroll. "The recitation is complete. Please come forward to claim the bodies." Two men assisted the weeping lesser samurai. They staggered to a cart covered with a thin sheet, but Akira could make out the distinct lines beneath. *Bodies* — girls who had come to compete and perished in the first Room. More family members emerged from the crowd, their steps dragging, laden with grief. Akira's vision blurred.

The names of all the dead and disqualified were nailed to the cherry tree. Carefully, Akira wound around the families. Some quietly rejoiced. Their daughters, sisters, or cousins had survived the Summer Room. Some would move forward in the competition. Others were eliminated but would return alive, perhaps injured but not gravely so.

Akira read the list twice. After, he stood, shaking and cold. Mari's name wasn't on it. Not under the dead or the disqualified. He squeezed his eyes shut. Mari was alive. She was moving forward to the next Room.

Akira didn't know whether to laugh or to weep. Soon, he'd go to the palace. Hanako had assured him that his time to be useful would come quickly. Today he trained. Tomorrow he conquered illusions.

CHAPTER 22

Mari

THE RICE-PAPER SCROLL summoning Mari to the Fall Room felt brittle in her hands. A new day. A new Room. A new challenge. *And more will die.*

"Sei," Mari called.

The Hook Girl slid open the door that connected their rooms, entered, and bowed. "I'm to report to the Fall Room in an hour," said Mari.

Sei's lips flattened in displeasure. "That's not very much time. What kimono —"

Mari shook her head. "No kimono. It will just weigh me down. I'll wear pants and an *uwagi.*"

"Yes, my lady," Sei replied, turning. "I'll get them from your trunk."

The Hook Girl helped her dress, handed Mari her *naginata,* and slid the door open. Mari saw Asami waiting in the hall.

Sei bowed low. "Good luck, my lady," she whispered, a slight tremor to her voice.

Mari frowned at the servant's fear. A thought sobered Mari. *Our fates are tied together now. Whatever happens to me affects Sei.* If Mari lost the competition, Sei would be cast from the palace, forced to return to the Gana Inn. Unwittingly, Mari had taken responsibility for another. *What will happen to Sei if I win the competition and disappear? She won't go back to the inn. I'll find somewhere else for her, someplace better.* This Mari promised with her whole heart.

With a muttered thank-you, Mari went to join Asami, but the hall was empty. She heard the echo of her ally's quick footsteps fading away. Mari started to follow but stopped, and turned back to the Hook Girl.

"If I don't come back," Mari said, heart clenching like a fist, "at the bottom of my trunk is a silver hair pick and my copper necklace. I want you to have them." There was more. Things she wanted to ask of Sei. *Find my village in the Tsuko funo Mountains, and tell my mother I'm sorry. If you can, look for the boy with the scars on his face, and tell him that I thought of him often. I couldn't love him the way he loved me, but I did care.* But Mari didn't say any of those things. Sei nodded. "Yes, my lady," she said just before sliding the door shut.

Samurai escorted Mari to the Main Hall. But there wasn't any need. The sound of the drums would have led her just fine. Once again, *taiko* drummers lined the hall, their beats fast and furious. But today their sticks were lit on fire. Flames danced in graceful arcs. The doors to the Fall Room were open, the Main Hall fragrant with earthy rain and rotting leaves. A cool breeze caressed her cheeks. She kept her body calm, even though inside she spiraled in turmoil. A red carpet had been laid out, and Mari instinctively followed it into the Fall Room. The samurai left her, and she felt strangely alone as she walked toward the other girls, standing shoulder to shoulder, their backs to her.

Master Ushiba stood on a dais. Rain fell in a pretty veil around the small platform, but no drops landed on Master Ushiba. Courtiers shuffled in, oohing and aahing at the water trick. Women carried paper umbrellas adorned with swirling pink lotus blossoms. Master Ushiba fluttered his hands, and the rain ceased. A warm mist rose in its place, and a series of rainbows arched from the puddles on the ground, touching some of the courtiers' hands. The women of the court tittered, cradling the rainbows in their palms.

None of Mari's opponents laughed. For them, there was no joy in the Fall Room. What animals lurked here? What dangerous conditions did this room have in store?

Mist coated Mari's cheeks as she joined the line, standing next to Asami. For a moment, Mari's eyes lingered, willing her ally to look at her. But Asami's chin stayed set and her gaze fixed forward. Mari's focus changed. She eyed the other eight girls, deciding only two were worthy of her attention — the girl with the bow and arrow, the one who had let the pit viper kill her friend, and a tall girl who carried a huge *ono*, a battle-axe.

Mari knew the strength it took to wield such a weapon. Only once had she faced an opponent with an axe. A farmer had chosen it from the cache of weapons. He'd swung it wildly but precisely, breaking Mari's *naginata* in half. He nearly made a red ruin of her chest. The secret to winning against a battle-axe was proximity. Just as with a *naginata*, a battle-axe was most threatening when you were at the end of its arc. When the farmer swung a second time, Mari had ducked and rushed his legs. She defeated him, and buried the axe in the forest. Blinking, she shook away the memory.

At her first full view of the Fall Room, her breath caught. Neat rows of hundreds of maple trees tunneled before her. *Trees on fire.* Each crown was tipped in red. The branches swayed in the light wind. Above the tree line, heavy fog gathered and ringed the gentle slope of mossy hills.

A gong sounded. Crows startled from the maple trees and launched into the milky-gray sky. A retinue of samurai marched in, announcing the arrival of the emperor and prince.

The courtiers bowed on the thick carpet of rotting leaves, ruining their precious silks. Mari dropped, her face turned toward Asami. She willed her ally to speak, to look at her.

At Mari's entreating stare, Asami spat out, "You keep a slave."

"Sei?" Mari whispered, taken aback. "My attendant?"

Asami bristled, her fingers, with ragged nails, curled in the slimy leaves. "*Attendant.*" She snorted derisively. "She wears a collar around her neck. A slave is a slave no matter what pretty word you use."

The emperor barked for all to rise.

Mari regained her feet, brushing dirt and sticky leaves from her *hakama.*

"I thought I said fewer dramatics." The emperor gave an irritated shake of his head.

The Seasonist's papery cheeks blushed. "Apologies, Heavenly Sovereign." The rainbows disappeared, and the mist cleared. Master

Ushiba bowed. "Welcome, competitors. Today you face the Fall Room." His arm swept out, encompassing the maple forest.

Mari focused on the imperial family. As always, the emperor stood proud, severity etched into his expression. The beautiful priest and Taro flanked him. And as always, Taro looked ready to flee. The harsh lines of his jaw seemed to be carved from granite. Mari could almost hear his teeth grinding. For a split second, she felt a pang at being a part of something the prince detested. She knew what it felt like to be forced into a ritual you didn't choose.

"Again, you seek scrolls," Master Ushiba went on. "This time, there are only five to be had. You will follow the same rules as the last room. Any deadly combat amongst competitors is strictly forbidden." Though Mari had seen firsthand how the rule could be circumvented. She'd have to watch the bow-and-arrow girl carefully. "Solve the riddle, and you will find the scrolls. *Feed me, and I thrive. Water me, and I die.*"

Mari's eyebrows darted in. The girls shuffled, each wearing a countenance of unease. *What prize is worth your life?* Mari knew her reasons. *Duty and home. The whole before the self. A chance at freedom.*

"Let the Fall Room begin!" Master Ushiba shouted. The clouds appeared first in the Seasonist's eyes, swirling, gathering for a storm. A great gust of wind hit Mari full force, and she nearly toppled over. The sky had turned the exact shade of Master Ushiba's eyes, and there, too, swirling clouds gathered. Courtiers fled the Room, women dropping their fine umbrellas. Ushiba laughed. Fat drops of rain as cold as ice began to fall, quickly plastering Mari's clothes to her body. A glance at the imperial family showed them unaffected. No wind ruffled their hair as they left the Fall Room. The doors slammed shut, and Ushiba was gone. In his place was a cyclone, hovering just above-ground.

"We need to get to cover!" Asami shouted. The wind began to pick up. Tree branches wrenched back and forth with a mighty force, cracking from their trunks. One skidded along the ground, almost clipping the bow-and-arrow girl as she ran into the forest. The other girls scattered as well, seeking shelter.

"Do we still have a deal?" Mari shouted, hair lashing her face. She wasn't sure which posed a greater threat: the vicious storm or her supposed ally.

"In the Seasonal Rooms, we are allies. But I won't be friends with someone who keeps slaves." Leaves whipped Asami's cheeks.

Shame spiked in Mari's belly. "What if I saved her from something worse?" she asked. Immediately, Mari realized her words were unwelcome and unwise.

Asami shot her a look of such contempt that Mari flinched. "She is better off free. To serve or not to serve; everyone should have the choice."

Mari knew it was true. *I'll do right by you, Sei, whatever comes.*

"We need to find shelter before that thing" — she pointed to the cyclone — "touches down," Asami said.

Without speaking, they ran into the forest. The wind pressed them forward. Together, they dodged or jumped tree branches. Rocks lifted from the ground and pummeled them. Mari touched her cheek, and blood came away on her fingers. A wave of panic overcame her. The storm was getting worse. A maple was torn from the ground, roots and all, and toppled forward just feet from Mari. Seeking shelter in the forest was a mistake. A howl of pain ghosted by on the wind. A girl had been injured.

"We need to get out of the forest," Mari shouted over the din. Rain fell in thicker sheets, pummeling through the canopy.

"There!" Asami pointed to a cluster of gray boulders slick with rain. She took the lead and disappeared into a small hole in the rocks. Mari followed, diving feet-first into the darkness. A little cry escaped her as she slid down and then hit the bottom. Immediately, her teeth set to chattering. The cave was cold. Wind whistled at the entrance. Farther inside the cave, water dripped and echoed.

"Okay?" Asami asked, startling Mari. Other than a single slice of light from the hole, the cave was pitch-black.

"Okay," Mari said, regaining her breath. She noted that her ally was not nearly as winded as she. *Asami is in better shape than I am. She is a mystery. The way she disdains keeping* yōkai *slaves. How she scorns the prince's attention.*

"There's wood in here, and it's not wet. We can make a fire, dry off," Asami said from somewhere down the cave.

Mari stepped forward, into the light. She peered up. Raindrops splattered her face. The storm raged on. "Don't you think we should go back out there?" she called. The scrolls awaited.

"Nobody's finding anything in this storm. The smart move is to wait it out and solve the riddle." Asami's voice sounded farther away.

A desolate cry echoed through the cave. Without thinking, Mari ran toward the sound, *naginata* in hand, stumbling over the uneven surface. Her eyes had somewhat adjusted to the dark. The cave widened. Rain and light poured in from openings above. Seeing Asami hunched over, Mari slid to a stop. *Is she weeping?* Mari crept closer, and her racing heartbeat shuddered to a stop.

There before Asami was a *yōkai*.

But not just any *yōkai*. A *kirin* — a sacred, untouchable *yōkai*. The deer-like creature lay near a boulder, its hooves tucked underneath it and its rainbow tail and mane sopping wet. Even in the shadows, the *kirin's* iridescent scales shimmered.

Mari's eyes grew watery. She'd never seen a *kirin*, but she knew they were the gentlest of creatures. Knew they could not harm a living thing, human, insect, or *yōkai*. And this *kirin*, this beautiful beast, had been collared, its eyes dull and lifeless. Its ribs jutted out under its scales. Its eyes were open. Unseeing. Dead.

"It starved to death. But I don't understand why; there's plenty for it to eat." Asami turned to Mari. Tears tracked down her heart-shaped face. *Kirin* were vegetarian. And along this section of the cave grew giant ferns.

Mari remembered Akemi, the Animal Wife who was ostracized, who camped near the gates because she had nowhere else to go. Mari had gathered a handful of nuts and left them near the gate, but the Animal Wife wouldn't touch them. Akemi had lost the will to live, and so had this *kirin*.

"Asami," Mari said as gently as possible. Mari put a hand on Asami's shoulder. "Some things would rather die than live in chains."

"We have to remove its collar." Asami looked up, dark eyes wild and searching. "Do it," she demanded of Mari. "I won't allow it to be a slave in death."

Mari squeezed Asami's shoulder. Asami shuddered, again giving in to tears. Mari considered her ally's deep grief, her disgust at seeing

167

Mari with Sei. Asami had a secret. And Mari knew exactly what it was.

"I can't," she said quietly. *Gods and goddesses, I pray I'm not wrong.* "I can't remove the *kirin*'s collar, and I don't think you can either." Because one touch of the engraved curses would burn them both.

Asami bowed her head in her hands. It was all the answer Mari needed. Asami was *yōkai*.

They covered the *kirin* with ferns and walked back to the entrance of the cave. Suddenly, they were not alone. A figure slid down the hole, landing with an *oomph*. Mari and Asami drew their weapons. A girl unfurled, hands and battle-axe held aloft. "Just looking for somewhere to wait out the storm."

Mari relaxed, remembering Master Ushiba's rules. No deadly combat. She jerked her chin. "All right," she called to the girl. The girl lowered her hands and drew closer. When she neared, Mari had to crane her neck, the girl was so tall. And she was quite striking — her dark hair fell in waves, her eyes were chestnut brown, and her lips were full and red. *She's pretty enough to be an Animal Wife.*

"Name's Nori," the girl said, introducing herself with a small bow. Asami ignored her and gathered wood to make a fire.

"I'm —" Mari began.

Nori cut her off. "I know who you are. I saw when you were announced in the Wet Garden. The prince spoke to you during the banquet. It seems you have his favor." She said this without ire.

"What's it like out there?" Mari asked.

Asami began to rub a couple of sticks together, her hands quick and sure. Soon enough, a tiny blaze lit the kindling.

Nori flipped her battle-axe and rested her hands on the butt. "I found a giant maple and settled against the trunk to wait out the storm. Before, I passed two girls with legs broken from errant tree branches. The storm picked up, and I knew I wasn't safe. I figured it was better to keep moving. Then I saw the entrance to the cave."

Mari inched closer to the fire, splaying her hands above it. A tiny bit of warmth. "Did you see any other girls? What about the one with the bow and arrow?"

"Oh, yeah, I know her. Sachiko. We're from the same clan. She's the daughter of the *daimyō* in our town. She's been training for this her whole life. She likes to hold things over other people — her father's position as a lord, his wealth, her belief that she'll be Empress one day . . . She's never lacked confidence."

Asami added more wood to the fire. A flash of purple-black ink inside Asami's wrist caught Mari's attention. She blinked, and the ink was gone. A tattoo that moved? What kind of *yōkai* possessed that? "You seem to dislike her," Asami said. "It'd be easy enough to do away with her. You can make anything look like an accident."

Dread coiled in Mari's stomach at Asami's cavalier attitude.

Nori shrugged, a contemplative expression on her lovely face. She didn't seem disturbed by Asami's suggestion. "I didn't come here because I like to kill people. I don't think that's what any of us want."

"That's right," Asami said, a snide tone to her voice. "We want to marry the prince and be rich."

Nori smiled ruefully. "Maybe that's what you want, but not I."

"What do *you* want?" asked Mari.

"A farmer's daughter doesn't have very many options," said Nori.

"You're a pretty girl," Asami said. She sat, feet propped up near the fire. "I'd bet you could have made an advantageous marriage."

Nori laced her fingers together and looked down at them. "I've often been told that I'm beautiful." Her lips twitched in disgust. "Most of the time it is because someone wants something from me, usually a man — a smile when I was young, and later, my body. Before I left, a farmer named Jun proposed, and I remember looking into his face and thinking, *He doesn't know me at all.* When I rejected him, he grew spiteful, like I should've been elated that he wanted me. He said unkind things about me. I can't even repeat them. Then he set his tongue to wagging, spreading rumors about me. People are always so eager to believe what is untrue. He said we spent the night together. It was enough for my family to stop speaking to me. I was a leper in my own home." Nori shot Asami a pointed look.

Asami's shoulders hunched forward. "Sorry," she muttered.

Nori shrugged. "It's no matter. My parents don't know I'm here. I don't know why I came. I can't believe I'm still alive."

Mari drew a deep breath as a memory came, swift and sharp. She'd overheard two Animal Wives gossiping about her. *It's appalling how unattractive she is. And her beast, so deformed. Are we certain she's one of us?* They'd laughed. Mari had run home, crying to her mother. Tami had clucked her tongue, pinching Mari's chin between her soft but strong hand. *Look me in the eye, daughter.* Mari complied. *Those foolish women forget: our bodies are not ornaments; they are instruments.*

Asami grunted, cutting into Mari's thoughts. "I know why you're here. It's why I'm here too. Why we all are, I imagine." Asami's eyes glowed, two burning coals. "We've been pushed around and forced into quiet rooms our whole lives. Nobody's ever asked us what we wanted. The prize isn't the prince. It's the power."

Mari's eyes lifted from the fire to Asami. Her gaze pivoted back and forth between Asami and Nori, sweeping over them like water.

Nori bit her lip. "You're right. After I rejected Jun, my father sat me down and said, 'You are pretty and want too much.' I asked him, 'What is too much? Love? Equality?' He said, 'Yes. You are pretty. That should be enough.'"

Mari sneered.

So did Asami. "He shamed you for speaking your desires. Don't apologize for what you want." Mari's ally rose. "We should be solving the riddle. We've wasted enough time already."

Mari blinked at the fire.

"*Feed me, and I thrive. Water me, and I die,*" Nori said. "I can't make heads or tails of it."

Water dropped from the cave ceiling and into the fire, sizzling. Asami had chosen a poor location for the fire. The answer to the riddle came suddenly and with fierce certainty. Mari glanced back and forth between Nori and Asami. "Fire," she said. "It's fire. *Feed me, and I thrive. Water me, and I die.*"

CHAPTER 23

Mari

ASAMI BEGAN FURIOUSLY throwing more wood on the fire until it blazed five feet high. "If the other girls solve the riddle, they may see the smoke and think it's the fire."

Mari smiled. A clever distraction.

Nori linked her fingers together to help hoist Asami and Mari from the hole. Once free, Mari stuck a hand down and pulled Nori up. Smoke billowed from the cave. The storm had calmed some. But great gusts of wind still accosted tree branches.

Weapons in hand, the three girls climbed to the top of the cave, nearly above the tree line. Mari's hands were covered in scratches and dried blood. She wondered how her face looked. Probably worse. The girls huddled against one another, afraid of being blown off the edge.

Nori was the first to spot the fire. She pointed. "Looks to be north of here, a few hundred feet off." Dark tendrils of smoke curled up and licked the sky. All at once, the storm rolled away, the wind stopped, and the rain ceased. *The Rooms choose you.* A blue sky replaced the gray. Even birds sang in the distance. Still, tension filled the air. The peaceful weather felt even more dangerous. What awaited them in the forest?

They scrambled from the top of the cave and walked through the dense forest in silence, weapons drawn and at the ready. Each rustle of a tree had the three whipping around, weapons raised. Each time, it was just the wind. A squirrel. A crow. But Mari kept her eyes peeled for pit vipers and her ears open for wild boars.

The scent of fire filled the air. The girls exchanged glances. Asami jerked her head to the right, and Mari and Nori followed. Their pace slowed as they crept from tree to tree, the scent of the fire intensifying as they closed in. The blue sky began to fade. Twilight descended, much faster than it would in the outside world. Asami nodded, then mouthed, "I'll go first." Then she disappeared. Mari gazed up at the tree branches. A squirrel stood frozen, ears flattened. It sensed a predator. Something big.

A low whistle, followed by Asami's voice. "It's safe."

Nori and Mari started toward her. The forest gave way to a small clearing where, inside a metal pen, a large fire burned. Asami opened her hands. "Where are the scrolls?" she asked.

Mari swallowed. "Someone must have thought of the same trick you did."

Asami kicked at rocks and uttered curses.

Mari examined the scene before her. "Look," she said, gesturing to the ground. Five metal collars lay discarded. Mari circled the pen; behind the blazing fire was a body. A mangled priest. She arrived back at Nori's side, gaze still set on the pen. "Something was caged here. There's a dead priest just over there. And —"

"Uh . . ." Nori elbowed Mari.

Mari snapped to attention. Five *oni* emerged from the maple forest, yellow eyes gleaming in the near darkness. Eight feet tall, red-skinned, tangled hair, tusks like fangs, foaming mouths, horns.

Mari breathed in and out, shifting her *naginata* in front of her, trying to calm her shaking hands. The skin on her palms grew slick when she saw the wooden clubs the *oni* carried. The weapons were unnecessary, merely decoration. An *oni's* true strength was in its arms, in its massive body. They could crush a skull as easily as a human could squish a grape. Their sharp talons could peel away skin from bones like the rind from an orange. *Most of their strength will be undercut by collars.* Mari felt comforted by the thought. She stood a fighting chance. Mari squinted in the darkness, studying the *oni*, looking for any sign of weakness. Her pulse skipped a beat; cold fingers of dread traced her spine.

"No collars," Mari whispered.

"Look what they *are* wearing." Asami inched closer to Mari.

Iron chains dangled from their throats with glass pendants attached, each containing a red scroll. Mari's hand tightened around her *naginata*, a chokehold of steely resolve.

Oni didn't speak, but they could communicate. After a series of growls followed by clicking, one stepped forward. *Their leader?* Mari wished she had paid more attention to *oni* lore when her mother spoke of it. She didn't know their customs, their weaknesses.

"What should we do?" Nori asked, a tremor in her voice.

"We can't take them on uncollared. That would be suicide," Mari said.

"What about the scrolls?" Nori asked.

Mari's hands grew clammy around her *naginata*. "This isn't right. They should be collared. We can't defeat them at full strength. We need to run."

Asami shook her head. "The scrolls —"

"We're dead if we try to wrangle those from their necks," Mari said. One of the *oni* had lifted its massive foot and stomped, shaking the ground. Blood dripped from its club. It licked it off, mouth curving into a wicked smile.

"We're running," Mari said. Their only hope lay in reaching the Fall Room doors. If samurai were posted outside it, maybe they would help. "On three, each of us runs as fast as she can to the front doors, no looking back, no stopping, even if one of us —" She couldn't finish the thought.

"No looking back, no stopping," Nori agreed.

"On three," Asami said, tears choking her voice. "One, two, thr —"

The *oni* lifted its massive club and brought it down. Dodging just in time, the girls broke into a frenzied run. *No looking back. No stopping.* Wind whipped Mari's cheeks; her pulse hammered. Together, they leaped into the maple forest.

Nori led, and Mari hoped she knew where she was going. The *oni* were right behind them, their footsteps heavy, striking the ground in tiny earthquakes. Rotten leaves squished under Mari's feet, propelling her forward. A ripping sound. Mari risked a backward glance. One of the *oni* had pulled up a tree by its roots.

Mari ducked and rolled, the trunk missing her by a hairsbreadth. Asami easily sidestepped, but Nori wasn't quick enough. She collapsed underneath the massive tree.

Gaining her feet and breath, Mari crouched by the battle-axe girl's side.

Asami drew close. "No stopping," she reminded Mari and continued jogging, disappearing into the maple trees.

The *oni* closed in, only a few feet away.

"Go," Nori said as she struggled under the weight of the tree. "If you stay, we're both dead. I'd leave *you* behind."

If you stay, we're both dead. The better gamble was to keep going, try to lure the *oni* away from Nori.

"Wait," Nori gasped. "My axe." The weapon had fallen inches from her fingertips.

Mari kicked the axe to Nori. "We'll come back," she promised.

Nori smiled, her fingers wrapping around the wooden axe handle. "Sure you will."

Mari stepped away from Nori and watched as the *oni* approached her, clubs swaying back and forth, like pendulums on a clock. Her new friend's time was quickly dwindling.

"Hey!" Mari shouted. She plucked rocks from the ground and threw them. Her aim landed true. Each rock hit an *oni* square in the head. The *oni* grunted. Their eyes set in vicious slits and trained on Mari.

"That's it," Mari taunted, backing up a step. "Follow me, you ugly creatures."

The *oni* gave chase, and Mari bolted, running zigzag. In the mountains, this worked on wolves, kept the canines guessing. She heard the *oni* clicking at one another, strategizing, trying to flush her out. *They're smarter than wolves.* Up ahead, lights shimmered through a break in the trees. Lanterns. The front of the Fall Room. *Salvation.*

Mari's calves screamed. She gasped, struggling for each breath, but she felt a renewed energy. At last, she reached the edge of the forest. Her confidence withered and died in her chest. The Fall Room doors were barred shut. Still, she raced to them and pummeled her fists against the wood. "Help!" she screamed. Nothing.

Salvation found. Salvation lost.

Slowly, Mari swiveled on her feet. The *oni* neared. *Where is Asami?* As they drew closer, Mari got a whiff of the demons. They smelled putrid, a mixture of decay and puss. Mari blanched. She counted their shadowed bodies along the tree line. Three *oni* against one girl. So two had broken from the pack. She wondered if they'd gone back for Nori or if they'd found Asami.

In unison, the *oni* smiled, crazy, warped grins with white fangs and black gums. *This was just a game to them*, Mari realized. She backed up. The *oni* advanced.

An arrow flew through the air, piercing one of the *oni* in the chest. The bow-and-arrow girl, Sachiko, stepped from the forest. She notched another arrow and released it. It flew and joined the first in the *oni*'s chest. The *oni* grimaced and broke the arrows off, tossing them to the ground. He swiveled and raced toward Sachiko. Quick as lightning, she notched two more arrows and sent them sailing into the *oni*'s chest. Then she disappeared into the forest, *oni* hot on her heels.

One down, two to go.

A sickle and chain flew through the air. The chain wrapped

around an *oni*'s neck. Mari's ally jumped on the *oni*'s back, strangling it. "Gods and goddesses!" Asami yelled to Mari. "Don't just stand there. Do something!" Asami ripped the scroll from the *oni*'s neck while tightening the chain around its throat. The *oni* thrashed. It was as if Asami were riding a wild bull. They tumbled to the ground.

Suddenly, a shadow cast over Mari. She scrambled back, her spine meeting the rough bark of a tree. The last *oni* shifted closer, and his hot breath fanned her cheeks. She stared at the demon, still frozen in fear. In the twilight, she saw that his eyes were rimmed in kohl and the lightest shade of blue, startling in their beauty. *So this is what my death looks like.*

Mari raised her *naginata*, but the *oni* tore it from her grip, tossing it out of reach. The *oni*'s hand clamped around her throat, cutting off her cry. Mari looked past the *oni* to Asami fighting her demon. "Hel — !" Mari's cry was cut off. The *oni*'s hand tightened around her neck. Mari grasped and scraped at the *oni*'s wrist, but to no avail. The demon would not let go. Her breath stilled.

She had no choice but to risk exposure. Kill or be killed. The bones in her hand broke and reformed; her skin shifted to black scales; her fingernails lengthened to claws. Her partial beast emerged.

The *oni*'s mouth opened, so wide it could bite through her skull. Saliva gathered in the corners of the demon's lips and dripped onto Mari's cheek. She went limp. In the wild, some animals played dead. The *oni* paused, sniffing her. Then she swung at him, sinking her claws into his ugly face. The *oni* howled. Its hand squeezed her neck. Mari saw stars. She screamed, a war cry. *No. It doesn't end here. It doesn't end today.*

She swung again and again, carving deep grooves into the *oni*'s face. The *oni* swayed, its hand still around her neck, guiding her like a puppet. The hand eased, and Mari found her first full breath, followed by a sob. The *oni* collapsed, convulsed, and stilled. She'd killed it. Quickly, Mari hid her claws behind her back and retracted them. No one had seen. The *oni*'s body blocked the others' view of her.

Mari crawled over its body and yanked the scroll from its neck, stuffing it into the folds of her *uwagi*. The Fall Room grew eerily quiet. The battle had ended. In the moonlight, Mari surveyed the carnage. Two *oni* littered the ground. In the middle of it all, standing tall and breathing heavy, were Sachiko and Asami.

"The rest of the *oni*?" Mari choked out.

Asami's chest rose and fell deeply. "I killed two in the forest, plus this one." She toed the dead *oni* in front of her.

Sachiko chimed in. "I got one with my arrows." Sachiko coughed, spitting out blood, and maybe a tooth. In her hand she held a scroll.

Mari gazed down at the *oni* she'd killed. *All five are dead.* The threat had passed. For a while, Asami, Sachiko, and Mari stared at one another, not sure what to do, whether to celebrate or weep. The stillness was profound.

A queer sense of detachment settled over Mari. Her body felt weak, and she collapsed to the ground. Her eyes caught Sachiko's. Through her fatigue, she inclined her head to her. She smiled at Sachiko. *I am a lean tiger in winter. Come for me. I dare you.*

CHAPTER 24
Taro

TARO ARRIVED AT the Fall Room doors before the others.

A single, muffled scream bled through the door. Taro's heart clamored. He put his shoulder under the oak bar and pushed up, shouting for assistance. Footsteps pounded as samurai stormed the hall. Taro dropped the oak bar, and the Fall Room doors cracked open, allowing cool, wet air to touch his cheeks. It was dead of night in the Fall Room, though only a few hours had passed since the *oni* had been released on the girls. A trick of Master Ushiba's — not only could he bend the weather, but he could speed the time of day.

Taro drew his swords and moved to the threshold.

A samurai stepped into his path and bowed. "My prince." The samurai wanted to go first, protect the heir, but he awaited permission. Taro looked past the samurai. The maple forest looked as if it had been crushed by a giant fist. Two giant *oni* blanketed the ground, wounds gaping, throats uncollared. Blood soaked the dirt. Taro shouldered past the samurai and saw that whatever had transpired was now over. All was calm. All was quiet.

He gritted his teeth. *Where are the girls?* Slowly, he began to pick through the wreckage, overturning branches and kicking up dirt. He tried to remember what Mari wore into the Fall Room, but couldn't. He vowed to pay better attention next time. *If there is a next time.* The chances any of the girls survived against uncollared *oni* were slim. But then again, two *oni* were dead. Treacherous hope dug in and took root. *Let her be alive.*

"Gods and goddesses!" Satoshi exclaimed. "What has happened here?" The priest stood next to Taro, his face leached of color.

Taro gritted his teeth. "I don't know. Why don't *you* tell *me?* Your priests were in charge of the *oni.*" With his sword, Taro nudged a third dead demon. Claw marks covered it, as if it had been attacked by an animal. Mari's *naginata* lay discarded nearby. Taro's anger peaked. "Where are their collars?" he bit out. *No way she survived this.*

"I — I don't know," Satoshi stammered.

"Are you telling me you have no control over your priests? You were responsible for Ushiba," Taro snarled.

"I'll find out what happened," vowed Satoshi.

"You do that. Now go and find all the theorists you can. It's unlikely we'll discover any survivors, but if we do, they will need healers." Taro left Satoshi and strode toward the maple forest, ready to search for survivors, ready to find a short girl who freed fireflies. He stopped short.

Three girls emerged from the pulverized woods. Mari and another girl with a heart-shaped face were supporting a third girl whose most distinguishing feature was her impressive height. A large wound in the middle of the tall girl's chest seeped blood, and her face was pale. A scroll dangled around each girl's neck.

Taro shouted for help. Two samurai sprinted forward, taking hold of the tall girl and carrying her from the room.

Taro's eyes glued to Mari. He studied her with great intent, scrutinizing every inch for any sign of harm. A mottled ring of black-and-blue bruises circled her neck. Dried blood stained her face. But it wasn't hers. He exhaled and approached her. "Are you all right?" he asked, sheathing his swords.

"I am alive," Mari said, her tone flat, her voice raspy.

"I'm alive too," the heart-shaped-faced girl piped up.

Taro regarded the girl for a beat. "Apologies," he said. "Are you well?"

"I am dirty and hungry. I'd like to go to temple and thank the gods and goddesses for my life. But first I would appreciate a bath and a meal, in that order. Or perhaps a meal while I bathe." At that, Mari smiled weakly. It warmed Taro's cold heart. His firefly girl was battered but not broken.

Taro gave a swift nod. "You shall have all those things." He shouted, bringing two samurai forward. "A bath and a meal are required. Please see the lady back to her apartment so she may receive both. Then escort her to the palace temple."

The girl bowed to Taro and then whispered something in Mari's ear. Mari's eyes widened, then collapsed. With the squish of rotten leaves under her feet, Asami was gone. A light wind rustled Mari's hair, errant strands sticking to her cheeks.

Samurai hoisted the bodies of the *oni*, piling them for burning. Another group of samurai, a search party, had gone into the forest and now emerged, carrying the limp bodies of six girls. All dead. Mari muffled a cry. *It could have been me*, he thought he heard her mutter. "There's another girl, Sachiko. She's alive. She has a scroll."

"We'll find her," Taro promised. Mari seemed to relax, but her eyes remained cautious. "You are injured," Taro said, stepping closer. Without thinking, he brushed a fingertip along the bruises on her neck.

Mari stepped back. "Your Majesty."

"Taro. Please, call me Taro."

She hesitated, glancing at Satoshi, who was busy speaking to another priest, and the samurai, before complying. "Taro."

"It would displease me if you had died," Taro admitted softly.

Another weak smile accompanied by an even weaker laugh from Mari. "It would have displeased me even more."

"You laugh, but I am serious." Should he tell her how much he had feared her death? How he had imagined what it might be like never again to be at the receiving end of one of her barbs?

Mari studied him. Her mouth parted. "You *are* serious," she said. A half-smile curved her lips. "Don't worry, Prince. I'm much harder to kill than I appear. Perhaps it is because I am so small; nobody ever believes that I can do big things."

Taro watched Mari exit the Fall Room. She'd requested the same as the other girl: a bath and a meal. But no temple. He'd wanted to sweep her up in his arms, to shield her from more harm, to wipe the blood and dirt from her face. He'd offered her accompaniment, but she'd insisted she was fine alone. Still, Taro nodded at a couple of samurai. A silent command to follow her, keep her safe.

Satoshi paced near Taro, waiting for the prince's attention.

"Your Majesty." Satoshi bowed.

"News?" Taro asked.

"It seems one of my priests took it upon himself to make the Fall Room more exciting. He uncollared the *oni* and lost control of them. He is dead, Your Majesty. He was found near the *oni* pen at the back of the Fall Room."

Taro's contempt grew. Satoshi lingered. "Something else on your mind?" Taro asked, his countenance cool.

Satoshi cleared his throat. "We've examined the bodies of the *oni*. There were a few . . . discrepancies."

Taro waited.

Satoshi hurried to explain. "One of the *oni* was particularly damaged. It looked as if an animal had gotten to it."

Taro recalled turning over the body of an *oni* with its face destroyed beyond recognition. "Strange."

Satoshi nodded. "Yes. It's strange. The only creature in the Fall Room aside from the birds and squirrels was the *kirin*, and that looks to have died days ago. And either way, a *kirin* wouldn't be able to inflict such damage."

Taro filed away the information. "You said discrepan*cies*."

Satoshi played with the sleeves of his robe with his tattooed fingertips. "The samurai who retrieved the bodies of the deceased girls informed me that three of the girls had no physical injuries. It appears they were suffocated or smothered. Not exactly an *oni*'s style — they are usually much less elegant."

"What do you think happened?"

"My best guess is that one of the girls saw an opportunity to get rid of some of the competition."

"Find out what happened," Taro commanded.

"Of course, Your Majesty." Satoshi's pretty face scrunched up. "If I may be so bold . . ." Satoshi paused, waiting for permission to go on. Taro remained silent, impassive. "If I may be so bold, I wonder what has changed. Originally, you showed so little interest in the competition."

Taro didn't answer. What could he say? So much had changed. And it started and ended with a girl who climbed a wall. For the first time in his life, Taro found himself wanting something other than solitude, something other than creatures made of metal. This desire was new. Uncertain. Intoxicating. *Alive.*

CHAPTER 25
Akira

LATE IN THE AFTERNOON, Akira cut through the streets of the second and third wards. The sun blazed, and heat skulked even in the shadows. Humans moved sluggishly, but Akira's movements were quick and sure.

The clock had just rung one hour past noon when Hanako had approached Akira, a note clutched between her see-through fingers. The shine of her collar caught the light streaming through the clock-tower window. The Snow Girl clearly still polished her chains while plotting a revolution. "Take this to the palace temple," she said. "A girl will be waiting there. Make sure you put it in her hands only, and don't let anyone else see you. Be the wind you promised me, Son of Nightmares."

Akira slipped the note inside his surcoat, secured a rag over the bottom half of his face, and went. The geezers escorted him as far as the eighth ward, but beyond that, *yōkai* were forbidden except with a human escort. "The temple is located on the far-most corner of the palace, the eastern corner. You'll have to hop the palace wall and avoid the samurai patrols. Don't be seen in any of the wards. If a priest catches you, you'll be collared. The Weapons Master will have no use for you then." With a laugh and a hard pat on the back, the geezers left.

Silence was second nature to Akira. He cloaked his movements easily, moving from shadow to shadow when humans turned their heads. The sharp corner of the envelope poked Akira's chest as he stepped into the first ward. Though lavender lined the streets, smoke choked the air, making it rancid.

Spying a group of priests, Akira ducked into an alley. Though the first ward was dedicated to housing, samurai and priests were in abundance. Traveling on the ground level was no longer safe, even for him. Akira followed the alleyway all the way back, seeking alternative modes. He located a drainpipe. *Perfect.* He shimmied up, alighting on the blue tiled roof. There he perched, surveying the city.

The golden palace rose nearby, almost within reach. The Palace of Illusions was surrounded by a moat. "It is bottomless," Hanako had said. "Hope you can swim." He spied the temple, recognized it by its five stories, one for each element: earth, water, fire, wind, and sky. The temple was exactly where the geezers had said it would be. As he looked closer, he saw that one didn't need to cross the moat to gain access to the temple. It lay outside the main structure of the palace, with only a section of wall to fortify it.

Akira jumped from rooftop to rooftop, landing with the grace of a cat. *I am the wind.* His mask rippled in the breeze as he leaped onto the wall. He paid the price for overconfidence. A metal spike stabbed into his foot. He clamped his mouth shut from yowling in pain and fell from the wall, landing in a heap within the temple confines.

Voices roused him from his daze. Priests, discussing the weather. He scrambled back behind a small wooden building just as the hems of their gray robes came into view. Gravel crunched under his feet as he crept farther into the shadow. The injury to his heel stung, but he'd hurt even worse if he were found, so he swallowed the pain.

Akira followed the building all the way to its end, as far away as he could get from the voices. Back pressed against the building, he risked a glance around the corner. There was an open courtyard with white gravel and a single well. *Gods and goddesses, priests are everywhere.* He must have fallen into their lodgings. In the distance, the clock tower chimed. Nightfall. Akira's time dwindled. Whoever he was supposed to meet wouldn't wait forever.

Akira felt something inside him changing, a purpose growing. *Cold steel in scarred hands will save the world or destroy it,* Hanako had said.

On the ground, he couldn't orient himself. Again, he found a drainpipe and shimmied up. Sweat coursed over him. His breath came in little puffs.

A light patter of rain began to fall. He scaled the slick tiles in a crawl, body tilted precariously. The angle of the roof hid him from the courtyard. Still, Akira kept his ears open. He spied the temple once again. *It is painfully close to the priests' lodgings.* Hanako could have mentioned that.

A quick leap from one rooftop to another, and he was next door to the temple. He inched along the golden spine of the roof, then slid down from it, the moon's light disappearing behind a building. Cold air caressed his face, and white gravel crunched under his feet. The din of the priests' quarters quieted. The decaying temple loomed. He stilled, listening. Nothing. Just the sound of the wind and a rustle of trees.

Inside was empty, but there was evidence of worshippers — lit candles with dripping wax, smoldering incense. He approached the altar. A figure darted from the shadows, and suddenly a blade was placed at his throat.

"Shh," a female whispered in his ear, pressing the blade deeper. "Priests are coming." Then she pulled him back behind the altar. They waited a few heartbeats. Akira's chest rose and fell with panicked breaths. Footsteps sounded outside the temple, then faded. Once all was quiet, the pressure of the blade loosened. "If you do not enter the tiger's cave . . ."

"You will never catch its cub," Akira finished.

The blade, which would have slit him from sternum to stomach had he not completed the saying just right, left his neck. Akira spun around. The girl was of medium height with a heart-shaped face and severe brow. Bruises littered her cheeks and neck. Who was she? What was she doing at the palace? His eyes filtered down to her hand, to the blade. But it wasn't a knife she held. It was an envelope. He'd been threatened with death by a piece of paper. The girl's mouth tilted up in a sardonic smile. "I watched you on the roof. You're fast and quiet. Hanako did well. I'm Asami." The girl swept into a bow. Her soul was the lightest purple, the color of lilacs. And blemished. Akira counted at least ten lives taken.

"Akira," he introduced himself, bowing in the same manner.

"You have something for me?" She held out a hand, thin fingers open and waiting.

Akira waited a few seconds before reaching into his surcoat and withdrawing the note. Asami held it to her nose and inhaled before she cracked the seal and scanned the contents. When she looked up, her dark eyes shone bright. "Tell her I understand, and give her this." Asami handed Akira the envelope. "The plans aren't complete. There are more rooms and hallways in this place than a Hana Machi brothel. But I did find out that there are tunnels underground. I've mapped what I could."

"How . . ." Akira hesitated. "How did you get this information?"

The girl smiled again, the glint of it dangerous. "Hanako didn't tell you?" She tilted her head, candles lighting one half of her bruised face. "I am a spider. We can go anywhere." She snickered, and Akira thought her a little mad, like Hanako. Asami turned to go.

"Wait!" Akira called out. He wanted to ask about the competition, about Mari, find out if she was alive or dead. But Asami was gone, and with her, all the answers to Akira's questions.

Akira's journey from the palace and through the wards was brief and without incident. Under the curtain of night, he truly was a shadow. Before returning to the clock tower, Akira had one more stop to make. He arrived at the cherry-blossom tree, after the recitation of the dead had concluded. He approached the tree, where the names of the dead and disqualified were listed. He held his breath and expelled it in a twisted wheeze. Mari's name was not there. Once again, she had evaded death.

CHAPTER 26
Mari

SEI GASPED. Mari offered the Hook Girl a reassuring smile. "I can't look *that* awful," she said, handing Sei her *naginata*.

"You look half gone, my lady. I overheard a couple of samurai whispering about an *oni* attack. They said most of you were dead . . ." Sei trailed off as she placed the *naginata* in a corner of the room.

Mari's attention drifted to her open trunk and the kimonos strewn about. She'd stake her life that the silver pick and copper necklace were missing from the bottom. The tips of Sei's ears turned red. She opened her hand. In her palm was the copper necklace. "I'm sorry, my lady," she croaked.

Mari shrugged. "What for? I said you could have those things if I died. You were just upholding my promise."

"It felt as if I were stealing from you."

"You cannot steal something that is given freely."

"I'm also sorry for doubting you. I should have known you'd make it out of the room." Sei moved to return the necklace.

"Keep it," Mari said.

Sei paused, surprised. "My lady —"

"Think of it: If I die, I'll have no use for it. If I win, I'll be Empress and have no use for it either. Keep the coins, Sei." Gently, Mari closed Sei's fingers around the pieces of copper. "I'll keep the silver pick for now, though. It has sentimental value." Mari's thoughts turned to Hissa, and her chest throbbed with a deep ache for home. She stifled the urge to sob. When she swiped her cheeks, blood smeared her hands. The ache turned into a tremor. Mari grew suddenly cold. She'd held it together in the Fall Room, but now she couldn't. Couldn't stop the shaking. Couldn't stop the fear.

"Come, my lady," Sei whispered, reaching for her. "I think you could use a bath and a well-deserved rest."

Mari jerked away at Sei's touch. *She shouldn't be so kind.* Mari wanted home, her cypress bed, and her mother's cool, dispassionate touch.

"Please, my lady," Sei beseeched. "Come, I will draw a bath for you and rub your feet. It's what my mother used to do whenever I was upset." Sei reached for Mari again, and this time Mari let the Hook Girl take her hand and lead her to the bathing room.

Mari didn't fuss when Sei undressed her or helped her into the steaming water or washed the blood from her hair.

Birds greeted Mari as she walked through her private garden. Each apartment had a small courtyard attached. This morning, Sei had roused her. "Fresh air will do you some good," she'd said, smiling brightly before dressing Mari in a plain red kimono and braiding her hair.

It was a fine day. The sun shone. Droplets of dew clung to the mossy path. At a small pond surrounded by irises, Mari watched brightly colored fish swim in circles. The cool air felt good on the bruises ringing her neck. She was jittery, on edge. She was alone. Then she was not. A shadow fell, and the fish darted deeper into the pond. She swiveled around, ready to attack.

Upon seeing the intruder, Mari exhaled. *Taro.* The Cold Prince loomed over her. By his feet, the garden was somehow upturned. A perfect square lay in its place, revealing a dark staircase leading down. A trapdoor. *How clever. Still . . .* "You aren't allowed to be here," she said. It was one of the rules. Girls stayed locked in their apartments unless competing.

At Mari's words, Taro's countenance remained cool. "I am a prince. I can do anything I want."

That drew a laugh from Mari. "Your issues of overconfidence concern me."

A very small smile twisted Taro's lips. "All the more reason you should come and spend the afternoon with me. I need your counsel."

Spend the afternoon with Taro? *Be wary of the prince. He invented the metal collars,* Asami had murmured in Mari's ear before leaving the Fall Room. Mari didn't want to believe it, that Taro had made the thing that enslaved her people. *He couldn't have.*

"Are you unwell?" Taro asked, searching Mari's face.

Mari shook her head. "No." Her body ached, and her throat burned, but pain didn't keep her from accepting Taro's offer. Fear did. *The bruises that ring your neck are nothing compared to what a collar will do.*

"Are you afraid, then?" Taro challenged.

Mari squared her shoulders. Denial came easily. She'd had her share of practice. "Of course not."

"Then come with me. I have something to show you. No one will ever know." He gestured at the open trapdoor. *A way out.* Sei had gone to do laundry, and Mari faced the day alone with nothing but her thoughts to keep her occupied. She'd packed the persimmon bowl in her trunk. Stealing the prince's fortune was proving harder than she'd thought.

Taro was already descending the stairs. In a moment, the hatch would shut. Her chance at respite would be lost. It didn't matter where he led. As long as it was far from the Wisteria Apartment, Mari wanted to go. She gathered the skirt of her kimono in her hands and followed. Down, down she went.

"Where are we?" she asked, voice dropping to a conspiratorial whisper, though she and Taro were alone. She'd followed the prince through the twists and turns of dozens of cavernous hallways, agog that such tunnels existed beneath the palace. Twice, Taro had paused and motioned for Mari to step into an alcove while samurai passed. Body pressed against Taro, she held her breath, excitement and fear somersaulting through her blood. As prince, Taro would never be punished. But Mari the *yōkai*? Anything could befall her.

At last, Taro turned a sharp right, and the tunnels narrowed, rocks and dirt brushing her shoulders. A staircase led them up, and Taro opened a trapdoor, extending a hand down to her. She let him help her, the feel of his palm warm and somehow right against hers.

Now they stood together in a dim hall, the only light from a single lantern on the wall. She hadn't known that this part of the palace existed. In contrast to the lavish details of the rest, this extension looked old and out of use. Forgotten. *This is what he wants to show me?*

Taro frowned, and Mari thought what few times she'd seen him smile. "These are my private quarters."

Mari arched a single brow. "Oh."

"Does that make you uncomfortable?"

Mari considered this. "Are you a threat?" she asked, only half joking.

"I believe the opposite is true."

Mari tilted her head. A wisp of hair fell into her eye. "I am a threat to *you*?"

"Most definitely." Taro reached up and, ever so gently, pushed the wisp of hair from Mari's eye. "Will you come in?" Opening the door, Taro stepped aside.

Mari strode forward, the door sliding closed behind her. Inside, lanterns glowed and wooden tables lined the walls. Strewn on these tables were pieces of metal — gears, rods, pipes. But no collars. Mari exhaled. Despite the clutter, everything seemed to have a place; it matched Taro's personality — orderly, methodical, studious.

In the center of the room was a steel drum, circled with brick — a forge. More metal, along with pieces of rope where drawings were clipped, hung from the rafters. Mari touched one of the pieces of paper on which was painted a picture of a butterfly with tin-plated wings and a steel-wire antennae. "What is this place?"

He cleared his throat. "It's my workshop. The bird you saw, I made it here."

"You really made it?" Mari asked.

Taro nodded, his mouth a firm line. "Yes. Look." He darted to the side. On a table were five metal butterflies, the drawings come to life. Taro wound a tiny crank at the back of each butterfly. Their iridescent wings fluttered, and they began to fly.

"Oh!" Mari gasped. The beautiful creatures swooped between the rafters, then floated back down. Their cranks slowed to a stop, and the butterflies fell to the ground, their little bodies clinking against the wooden floor.

Taro bent to collect them. He inspected the tiny insects with a quizzical glare. "We haven't really figured out how to stick the landing yet."

Mari grinned and continued to look through the drawings. It seemed that Taro was working on a collection of animals. There was a snake made of linked chain, a giant crane with copper wings, a frog with bolts for eyes. Her fingers grazed the worktable, stopping at a sheaf of papers wedged under a giant gear. Carefully, Mari slid the papers into view. "Collars?" she asked, eyeing the rough drawing, obviously done by a younger hand. The papers were brown with age. Mari's pulse raced.

Taro snatched up the papers, startling Mari. His lip curled as he set the papers away from him. "The metal collars all *yōkai* wear. The rumors are true. I created them."

Mari's blood ran cold.

Taro stared at her, eyes glinting, jaw working as if daring her to call him a monster, *wanting* her to call him a monster. *Is this a man seeking punishment?* Mari couldn't tell. "Are you proud of your invention?" Mari worded the question with care, mindful of the prince's mercurial moods, of his power. He could still have Mari jailed.

Taro averted his eyes and strode to the opposite side of the room. With a thick finger, he felt along the rim of a pole. It seemed he wouldn't speak. When he did, his voice was rough with painful honesty. "It's not easy for me, to admit a fault."

Mari considered this. "Do you find it difficult to trust?" She walked forward to peer at his profile.

Taro's hands flexed, then fell to his sides, his expression inscrutable. "I have trouble reading people, which leads to distrust. Metal, gears, and hammers are the language I speak." Taro turned from her. "You don't know how much you ask of me."

She stepped closer, breaching his space. Her muscles ached, and she was reminded again of the battle she'd fought, of the bruises ringing her neck, of her beast emerging and shredding the *oni*. "I ask only for what you are willing to give," she said softly.

His muscles bunched under his surcoat. "And if I give you the truth, what will you do with it?" he asked.

Mari put her hands to her chest, over her clamoring heart. "I will hold it close, and never betray your confidence." *Don't trust me. Duty and home. The whole before the self. Those are my loyalties.*

She watched Taro's chest expand and then deflate with a deep breath. He raised his head and leveled his gaze at her. "Then I will trust you. The collar is the only invention I've ever made that I am not proud of. It was a child's mistake."

"You regret it."

He gave a short nod. "I regret it."

Don't believe him. He tells pretty lies to cover his ugly deeds. But Taro's pained expression looked sincere, palpable in the dim room.

Mari suddenly felt unsure. Taro was brooding, and most thought him as cold as the metal with which he tinkered. But metal warmed at a touch. Perhaps that was what Taro required, a human touch to make his heart beat again. But Mari wasn't human. She was *yōkai*. "You know, you don't have to regret it," Mari said quietly. "You could do something about it. You are the second-most powerful man in this world."

Taro snorted. "I am subject to my father's whims like everyone else."

Mari nodded. What else could she do? What Taro said was true. Everyone was born with a chain. But some had a shorter leash than others. One day, Taro's father would die, and Taro would be Emperor. "I'm sorry," Mari said. "I don't mean to upset you."

"I'm the one who should be sorry," Taro said, closing the distance between them. "I am sorry I was short with you. My father is a dangerous man — he lashes out and asks questions later."

Unexpected tenderness welled up within Mari. Thoughtlessly, she opened her hand against Taro's cheek. The skin against her palm was warm, heated, *alive*. He turned his cheek into her palm. Then he withdrew.

Ever so lightly, Taro touched the pulse in her neck. "You are bruised. Do they hurt?"

"Yes," she said. "My muscles ache too."

His hand drifted down and settled on her shoulder. He squeezed, massaging the ache underneath. "Better?" he asked.

Mari scrunched her nose and gazed up at him. "No."

"Stubborn," he said.

Her shoulders sparked where his fingers lay, a lit firecracker with a very short fuse. Their breaths synced, and somewhere deep inside her heart, a little bit of room was made for Taro. Unsettled, Mari broke from Taro's hold and strode about the room. "Teach me how to make birds fly, Prince," she demanded haughtily.

Taro bowed. "As you wish."

CHAPTER 27
Akira

THE SUN BROKE the horizon as Akira mounted the clock-tower steps, painting the Imperial City in hazy pinks and oranges.

Hanako was waiting for him in his room. She lay on the futon, eyes closed, her white ferret, Large, curled up on her chest. "You've been out awfully late," she said, popping one eye open. "If I were the jealous sort, I might think you're seeing another Weapons Master."

Akira pulled down his mask. "You've got a *yōkai* spy in the palace." From his surcoat, he withdrew Asami's note.

The ferret scampered from Hanako's lap as his master stood. Her soul glowed particularly bright today — white, almost ethereal except for the blemishes. "Of course I do. She's in the competition. How else would I have gotten her into the palace?" She plucked the note from Akira's fingers.

Akira's blood ran cold. Mari had a formidable opponent, an uncollared *yōkai* with unknown powers. "What is she doing there?

What are you planning?" He gritted his teeth. How much danger was Mari in? Was it too late to save her?

Hanako regarded him. "It is funny you think you may ask such questions of me." She opened the note and read it. All the while, Akira seethed. He was growing weary of Hanako's games, her non-answers. A slow smile curved Hanako's lips. "Asami has done well." From her *obi*, Hanako withdrew a *tantō* knife. Akira thought of his mother's carved face. He remembered that she used to sing him to sleep when he was small. She had the sweetest voice. He'd inherited so many things from her: his scars, his fragility, his capacity to see souls . . . The curse of a soul-seer was the inability to see one's own. But Akira's mother didn't have one at all. *What color is my soul?* she would ask. *It is the loveliest shade of yellow, the exact color of the center of a lotus blossom*, he'd lie. He never asked her about his.

Hanako handled the blade deftly. Tossing the note in the air, she let the knife spin from her hand. It pierced the paper and sank into the wall, revealing an intricately drawn map. Akira's gaze roved over it. Asami hadn't done herself justice. The map was drawn with the finest hand, the sketch of a master cartographer. It had an almost three-dimensional effect, showing the palace buildings and the tunnels below. Not all of the tunnels were sketched in full, but Asami had starred one, a tunnel that ran under the palace gardens and into a private tea garden and then ended outside the palace walls. *An escape route.* An exit and an entry. What's more, *X*'s marked the samurai patrols.

"Gods and goddesses!" Akira exclaimed. "You're planning an assault on the palace."

Hanako came to stand next to him. "Of course I am."

His teeth ground together, and his anger bubbled up. It was worse than he'd thought. So many lives would be lost if Hanako lay siege to the palace. Innocent lives. *Mari's life.* Frustrated and without an outlet, Akira withdrew a star and launched it, closing his eyes. It sliced through the air, whistling low. The star thunked as it embedded in the wood wall. The wall was littered with gashes, and each time Akira looked at them, he was reminded of his failure. He had not mastered the stars yet. He had not mastered anything at all.

"Akira," Hanako whispered, wonder in her voice.

Akira shook his head and squeezed his eyes shut. He was in over his head.

"Akira," Hanako said more forcefully, "open your eyes."

Akira sighed. "I don't —"

"Open your cursed eyes!" Hanako demanded.

Akira reluctantly complied. Hanako's face was set in a wide grin. The clock tower struck seven. The throwing star glinted in the morning sunlight, embedded in between the spokes of the wheel. He'd done it. At last, his aim was true.

Hanako yanked the star from the wall. "Do it again," she said. If possible, her soul shone brighter. It glowed with happiness. And pride?

Akira shook his head. "That was an accident. I wasn't even thinking of a target. No way I can do it again."

"That's it!" Hanako shouted. "Your thoughts have been blocking you." She went to the wheel and sent it in a slow spin. "Close your eyes." Akira did so and felt Hanako place the star in his hand, the metal warming instantly in his palm. He ran his thumb along the edge of the blade. "Now listen to the room. Let it speak to you. What do you hear?"

Sounds bombarded him — the clicking hand of the clock, the scamper of Large the ferret, Hanako's shallow breaths, the squeak of the wheel as it turned, the chatter of other *yōkai* in the clock tower. One by one, he sorted through the sounds, separating them into individual threads. The clock was four strides behind him. Hanako was two strides to his left. The wheel was ten strides straight ahead. He allowed his mind to go blank. The star was heavy and sure in his hand.

Let go. Release. He pulled his elbow back and pitched the star. *Thunk.*

His eyes popped open. He focused on Hanako, too afraid to see his failure.

"You've done it!" A gleeful chortle escaped Hanako as she swept into an exaggerated bow. "Master of the Spinning Wheel." The throwing star was embedded in the wall behind the wheel. *Gods and goddesses, I've done it.* He retrieved the stars from the wall and threw them again, this time around Asami's map. Hanako frowned. "Easy, Son of Nightmares. We need that."

Stark reality rushed back upon Akira. "When will you attack?" he asked, steeling himself for the answer. He needed time to warn Mari. *Please let there be time.*

Hanako stared at the map. She traced the tunnel leading from the tea garden into the palace. "I don't intend to." She paused, drew a deep breath in consideration. "Aside from me, Asami is the most dangerous *yōkai* there is. She is to win by any means necessary. She'll marry the prince, and, once she does, she'll have his head, and his father's, on their wedding night. There will be no attack if it can be helped."

"And if she doesn't win?" Akira nodded to the plans.

"Plan B. If Asami perishes, *yōkai* will storm the palace." Her eyes flashed to his. "One way or the other, the emperor will fall."

AIKO:

Goddess of the Sun, Animals, and Day

AIKO, GODDESS OF THE SUN, ANIMALS, AND DAY, *was born the first time lightning struck a rock. From the remnants, she rose, cradling all the light of the land in her hands. She illuminated the world and ensured the fertility of the rice fields. Ever so gentle and kind, she had thousands of attendants. Many flocked to Aiko, if only to stand in her light.*

Eoku, God of War, Military, and Night, grew jealous of Aiko's power and popularity. He plucked a kirin, *an animal particularly beloved by the goddess, from the forest and threw it into the ocean. Devastated, Aiko dove from the heavens and into the churning sea. But she could not swim. She could not save the* kirin. *Aiko sank to the bottom of the ocean, and there she stayed, drowning again and again, a thousand times over. Without her, there was no sun. The rice fields perished. People grew hungry. Endless cold night descended.*

Aiko's attendants searched for her. But it was Umiko, Aiko's sister, Goddess of Moonlight, Storms, and Sea, who discovered her in the sea's depths. Umiko sent a large wave across the ocean, sweeping her sister to land. Aiko coughed, choking up so much water that the world's lakes were created. Umiko wiped Aiko's face and helped her home, back to the heavens, so that her light shone on earth once more.

Still, every year without fail, the cold season remained. The sun dimmed, and Aiko wept. Aiko thought this to be right, a reminder of what had come to pass. A reminder of the coldness and violence that hate begets. Winter would always be for regrets.

CHAPTER 28

Taro

TARO PACED THE DEWY GRASS of the wet garden. The banquet wasn't set to start for another hour. He was early. A new habit. One he wasn't sure if he liked or not.

He felt himself changing, all because of a short, abrasive girl who had pushed her way into his life. He liked his space. The quiet. And now she filled his silences. Every time she teased or challenged him, it felt . . . life-altering.

He'd sent a note requesting her presence prior to the banquet. He smiled at the thought of her receiving the summons. No doubt she would bristle at the command. But she would come. Taro was sure. He interested her as much as she him. Still, he felt like a lovesick fool, waiting for her, pacing the garden, a gift for her warming his pocket.

"Good evening."

Taro whirled around at the sound of Mari's voice. His words stuck in his throat at the sight of her. The sunset limned her body in a kind of celestial light. Her kimono was the color of a river. Curved white lines had been stitched into the fabric, mimicking ripples. In the current, birds swam, irises bloomed, and lilies floated. Taro feared that if he blinked she'd disappear. This creature of water and moonlight didn't belong to him. And perhaps she never would. There were two more rooms left in the competition. Master Ushiba had bragged about the Winter Room. *By my calculations, there are least a thousand ways to die,* he'd said. Taro's stomach clenched.

Mari's two samurai guards hovered nearby, and Taro dismissed them with a flick of his head.

"Your frown is so fierce, it looks as if it could set the garden afire." Mari stepped forward.

"I was just thinking of the girls from the Fall Room."

Mari nodded. "I've been thinking of them also. Have your investigations yielded anything?" When they'd spent the afternoon together in his workroom, Taro had mentioned the three girls who had died under suspicious circumstances.

"They were poisoned," Taro said.

Mari knitted her brow. "Poisoned?"

"That's how it appears," Taro explained. "Inquiries have been made into their deaths, but the *shōgun* is confounded."

Mari frowned.

Seeking her smile, Taro said, "I've brought you a gift."

Mari perked up. "What is it?"

Taro reached into his sleeve and withdrew the copper canary — the bird that had brought Mari to him. She grazed the bird's feathers with a careful touch. "You've healed her."

Taro had worked for hours, bent over his worktable, painstakingly hammering the feathers. He couldn't fix the dent in its abdomen, and the copper didn't shine as brightly as it once did, but the bird would fly again.

"Should we see how she fares?" he asked.

"I think it would be wrong not to," she replied.

Courtiers began arriving, the garden growing more crowded by the minute. "Not here," he said gruffly. He offered his arm.

The warmth from Mari's hand seeped through Taro's sleeve. He led her down the path they'd traveled at the first banquet.

"No fireflies," Mari mentioned offhandedly.

"No," Taro replied. "I had them all released."

Mari rewarded him with a glowing smile.

The path narrowed, then opened into a field. Thick moss carpeted the ground and crept up, covering stone lanterns and steps. A fine mist cloaked the base of the cypress trees. The Moss Garden, another of Taro's secret hideouts. He took in the musty dirt and rich greenery. It brought him a unique tranquility. One look at Mari, and he knew she felt it too.

"This reminds me of home," she said.

"Where is that?" he asked.

"Far away."

Taro frowned. Mari was careful with details. He hadn't missed how she artfully dodged questions about herself by turning them back on him. She was clever. Secretive, even? "But where *exactly*?" he pressed.

Mari walked farther into the garden, moss cushioning the sounds of her steps. She brushed a hand against the thick orange bark of a cedar tree. "The mountains. I am from a small village in the Tsuko funo Mountains."

Taro's suspicion eased. Why did he find it so difficult to trust? He remembered the copper canary in his hand. He wound the bird and let it go. The canary flew up and then back down, hovering near a stone lantern.

"It's flying a bit crooked," Mari said, stepping closer to the bird.

Indeed, the bird favored one wing over the other, giving its flight pattern an uneven tilt. "That's okay," he said. "She is wounded but still a warrior." When the bird's cranks ran out, the moss cushioned its fall. Taro retrieved the bird and cracked open its chest with his thumb. He traced the gears and explained how the mechanisms worked. "The most important thing is the heart."

Mari touched the bird, stealing Taro's attention. "You speak of the bird as if it were alive."

"What is life?" Taro asked, the corner of his mouth curling in a wry smile. "Most believe it is anything with a spirit, a soul. This bird has been a friend to me." He focused on his feet, searching for the right words. "Every time I create something, I put a part of my soul into it." Taro paused. "Even the metal collars." Bringing his head up, he saw Mari's stricken expression. "It doesn't mean that I'm proud of them. I still regret it, but I don't deny that they're a part of me." Carefully, he closed the bird's chest and placed it in Mari's hands. "My gift to you." *A piece of myself.*

Mari's hands shook as she closed her fingers around the copper canary. "Thank you." Her voice sounded strange, choked. But then she smiled, at once honest and mysterious.

"What are you thinking?" Taro asked. Her hair was pulled back in an elaborate bun and adorned with a silver pick. It caught the light, winked at him.

Mari tilted her head to the sky. "I grew up so far away from here, but you were just as isolated. It occurs to me that you, too, have been alone all your life." She leveled her gaze with his. "Is it lonely in your Palace of Illusions?"

Taro answered in a rough, uncultivated voice. "It is safe."

"That is not the question I asked."

Yes, he wanted to answer. *It is. So lonely.* Taro loved his creatures, but at the end of the day, they were cold. They could not speak or feel. Mari's eyes locked with Taro's. The air hummed. They stepped toward each other, magnets pulled together.

Taro grasped Mari's waist. At the action, she let loose a breath. Then he brought his mouth to hers. There were no lightning bolts. Or fireworks. Or blazing heat. But a gentle warmth crept through Taro, and, along with it, a fierce certainty. His lips mapped hers with care. Whole worlds danced before his eyes as Mari sighed and drew him closer. He felt something fierce and needy uncurl deep inside him. *This creature of water and moonlight.* He'd never let her slip through his fingers.

Abruptly, Mari broke the kiss. She stepped back. Her fingers went to her lips, and her eyes widened. Surprise etched her face, and something else. Fear?

Taro inhaled, wanting so badly to capture her lips once more, to silence any of her protestations. But he stayed in his place. "I'm sorry," he said, even though he wasn't sorry at all.

"Are you?" Mari asked.

His lips curved down, back into his usual frown. "No."

Mari's eyes narrowed. "I should go." She took another step back.

"No," he said again, his voice strangled. "I don't want you to." Now he sounded like a petulant child, but he couldn't stop the fear from climbing his throat and choking him. If he let her leave, he might never see her again.

Mari's lips toyed with a reproachful smile. "Do you always get what you want?"

Taro didn't have to think about it. "Yes," he answered. "But not what I need."

"You admit to being spoiled, then?" she asked, ignoring his last comment.

Taro gave a snort. "Yes. I am spoiled and stubborn." His two greatest faults. He looked down, shaking his head. "Mari . . . there are things I . . . things I need to tell you."

"Don't," she said in a warning, plaintive tone.

His words flooded out. "I ordered all the lightning bugs freed because you didn't like them in cages." They locked eyes, and his hands clenched. "I've been a coward, too afraid to stand up to my father, but I don't want to be that way anymore. I want to be different. And I think I could be, with you by my side. You make me want to be . . . better."

She pursed her lips before answering. "You should want to be better for yourself, not for someone else."

He didn't know how to respond, so he did in the only way he could. "There are two rooms left. I believe in you. I believe you were meant to conquer the Seasons and be my empress. Just as I believe it is fate that brought you to me in the garden. And now I believe in us, in what we can do together. I believe together we can make another way, a better way." He stopped, crippled by his vulnerability. It was as if someone had cracked open his chest, pulled out his heart, and was peering at all the nicks and defects.

"You are cruel, Taro," she said wretchedly, her eyes glistening with unshed tears.

"Mari —" He reached for her, but she put out a hand.

"It isn't fair. You promise me things I cannot have."

"I don't understand." He watched her.

"This isn't how it was supposed to be," she whispered the words to herself.

"What isn't the way it was supposed to be?"

She gestured at the space between them. "I never intended —" Her words cut off on a choked sob. She fled. And despite his earlier vow never to let Mari slip through his fingers, Taro lost her to the trees and the ink of night.

Taro returned to the banquet. He caught a cup of *sake* from a passing servant's tray and downed it in one gulp. The liquor burned the soft tissue in his throat, releasing the sting of Mari's departure. He'd upset her, but why?

"I never liked these parties." The voice startled Taro. The emperor drew close to his son. They stood shoulder to shoulder at the fringe of the revelry, twin stony stares shadowing their faces, making them unapproachable.

"No one likes them less than I," Taro said. He clutched the *sake* cup and tipped it to his mouth, hoping for another drink, but the cup was empty.

"Is this something else we should argue about? Who likes parties less?" the emperor asked. He sounded tired, resigned. Could his father be wearying of their discord?

Taro tapped his fingers against the *sake* cup. "Is there something you wanted, Father?"

Lines of irritation appeared on the emperor's forehead. "The Winter Room starts tonight."

Taro's brow descended in an ominous line of displeasure. "It was supposed to begin tomorrow."

The emperor sighed. "I've asked Master Ushiba to move it up. I'm tired of waiting." Another of the emperor's less desirable qualities: impatience. "I want to see this over and you married." He slapped Taro's back and returned to the banquet.

A frustrated wheeze escaped Taro as he watched his father go. A love like madness, that is how the people often spoke of the emperor and his empress, how they described what they shared.

"Be careful," his nursemaid used to warn. "It's catching. Your father's blood runs true. There is a flame in your veins, waiting to ignite." It was a warning never to love too deeply. But Taro no longer heeded his nursemaid's words. What if he did go mad with desire? If Mari were a fire, Taro would gladly burn.

CHAPTER 29
Mari

MARI FLED THE MOSS GARDEN. Her hair loosened, and the silver pick, Hissa's gift, dislodged. She tore it from her bun, holding it alongside the copper canary.

She could still feel the warmth of Taro's lips. The imprint of his hands gripping her waist. *Duty and home. The whole before the self.* The betrayal in her heart burned, and a sob wrenched from her lungs. She'd meant it when she'd accused Taro of cruelty.

How dare he dangle this life in front of her?

She'd come to care for Taro, the prince of metal and ice. But he was more than that. Taro was a lonely young man who created brilliant things.

It would be easy to love him. As easy as falling or breathing. Mari swiped at the tears on her cheeks, her thoughts in chaos. Her old desires and new desires clashed, leaving only wreckage in their wake. Taro offered her a chance at . . . love. Passion. With Taro, the possibilities were endless.

If she stayed with Taro, she could never go home to Tsuma. *Maybe that would be a bearable sacrifice.*

But what would happen if Taro discovered she was *yōkai*? Would she always have to hide the other part of herself, her *yōkai* existence? Would it be possible to trust Taro with the truth?

Cold air caressed Mari's face. The banquet's revelry grew muffled in the distance. She'd arrived at the Dry Garden. White sand, raked into waves, glittered in the moonlight.

Another way, Taro had promised. His words burned inside her chest, the force of a million suns. *A better way.* Was this her purpose? The glimmer of a new destiny unfolded before Mari, one in which she and Taro forged a path together, where *yōkai* were no longer choked by the metal collar.

The garden grew cold. Chilled wind brushed her cheeks. Her lips tingled, and she tasted . . . *snow?* Yes, snow! Little flakes began to fall, catching in her eyelashes and melting. It reminded her of home, and Mari smiled with wonder. Snow in spring. A clack of footsteps on the slate path drew Mari's attention. Out of the darkness, a figure took shape — thin, gray beard, milky eyes, papery skin that loosely hugged bones. Master Ushiba hurried forward. "There you are. I've been searching for you everywhere."

Mari's mouth parted, but she said nothing. The snowfall increased and began to layer on the pathway. Still, the sky remained clear, stars twinkled, and the moon was full and bright.

"Come, come." Master Ushiba gestured for Mari to follow. "The others are waiting."

Mari hastened to join the Seasonist. "Waiting?"

"Yes, the Winter Room starts now." He continued on his way, moving far too briskly for a man his age.

"I didn't receive a summons," Mari said. They exited the garden and wound through the banquet, courtiers parting and staring at the spectacle, Mari chasing the Seasonist while snow fell around them. As they mounted the palace steps, Mari glanced back, searching for Taro, but she couldn't find him in the revelry. Did he know the Winter Room began tonight?

Master Ushiba waved a thin hand and bobbed his head. "The emperor, our Heavenly Sovereign, said I have spent far too much on *taiko* drummers and red carpets. Less is more, he said. And I am ever his dutiful servant."

"My weapon," she uttered.

"No weapons in this Room. You will rely on your natural abilities."

They arrived at the Main Hall in front of the Winter Room entrance, the cloud of snow still hanging around them. Sachiko, Nori, and Asami were already gathered. None of the girls carried weapons. Six samurai lined up against the entrance, waiting to lift the oak bar and unlock the room. A snow-capped mountain was carved into the doors. Mari took her place next to her ally.

"Evening," Asami said, swallowing.

"I had hoped we wouldn't see each other again so soon," Nori remarked. The battle-axe girl's breaths seemed shallow. She hadn't fully recovered from the Fall Room.

"Welcome to the third season, the Winter Room." Master Ushiba rubbed his hands together. The snow ceased, evaporating into

217

thin air. "Behind these doors, a single scroll awaits you." Mari sucked in an uneasy breath. Beside her, the other three girls shifted on their feet. *One scroll. One winner.* It seemed her alliance with Asami was at an end. *But what about the fourth Room?*

As if reading Mari's mind, Asami spoke. "What of the fourth Season?"

Master Ushiba smiled. "Though only one girl will move forward, the competition *will* continue beyond this room. But that is all I can tell you. A Seasonist must have some secrets." He clapped his hands. "The doors, please." The samurai's motions were synced as they placed their shoulders under the massive oak bar, lifting it up and away.

Endless winter sprawled out before Mari, a vast field of rolling white hills. A blast of cold air pressed Mari's kimono against her body, and she shivered. In her hand she clutched the canary and her silver pick, the items forgotten in all the excitement.

Master Ushiba cleared his throat. "When you see the sun flare"—the gray sky in the Winter Room erupted with light, then abruptly extinguished—"you may begin your search. You will find the scroll at a place that always runs but never walks, often murmurs but never talks, has a bed but never sleeps, has a head but never weeps." Silence reigned. Mari mouthed the riddle to herself, committing it to memory.

"A warning before you enter." Master Ushiba's voice took on an ominous tone. "It has been brought to my attention that one of you may have used trickery to gain an advantage. Though I cannot control your actions once in the Room, beware that the Room sees and knows all. Do not try to cheat the Seasons, for they will collect twofold. Nature is the most vengeful of partners."

A sick sensation curled low in Mari's stomach. She glanced at Sachiko. The girl had let a pit viper do her dirty work. Was she also responsible for the deaths in the Fall Room, for poisoning the other girls? Or was it Asami? Mari didn't know what kind of *yōkai* the girl was. *She could be capable of anything.* Or could it be Nori? The battle-axe girl had been wounded. But could she have inflicted it on herself? *Never discount an opponent in last place. She has her own advantage. Your back is turned, unprepared for a stab between the shoulder blades.*

Master Ushiba smiled. "Now, Lady Asami of Clan Akimoto, your destiny awaits." He swept into a bow, gesturing at the open doors.

Asami's chin jutted out as she stepped forward. Once again, she was dressed simply, in a tunic and pants, far better suited for the Winter Room climate. Mari's kimono would only hinder her, but she couldn't afford to lose the warmth in favor of her undergarments. Snow crunched under Asami's feet, and wind whipped her hair as she entered the Winter Room.

Master Ushiba breathed deep, his white eyes filled with a swirling storm and the jagged edges of black frozen trees, and the landscape from Ushiba's eyes was brought to life before Mari. A vast field of snow unfurled and, beyond that, a frozen forest. The Seasonist bowed again and gestured toward the Room, the sleeve of his yellow robe flapping with the frigid wind. "Lady Mari of Clan Masunaga, your destiny awaits."

Hesitantly, Mari stepped forward. Wind lashed her cheeks, and her fingers numbed. Snow soaked her split-toe socks. A movement at the end of the Main Hall drew Mari's attention. *Taro.* The Cold Prince stood, face serious and impassive. His dark eyes glinted in

219

the torchlight. Ever so subtly, he nodded to her. *Good luck? Goodbye?* Maybe both.

Resolve settled in Mari's spine. *Another way.* But there wasn't time to think of that. To think of him. For a lean tiger in winter, survival always came first.

CHAPTER 30
Akira

THE MAP ASAMI had drawn worked.

Akira smiled to himself. Hanako would be pleased. However, she would not be pleased to learn that Akira had stolen the map and returned to the Palace of Illusions. His smile dimmed. Late in the evening, he'd plucked the map from the wall and snuck from the clock tower. Fortune had smiled upon Akira — the geezer guards were sleeping. *Too much sweet grass.* On his way out, Akira had stolen their pipes and stash. *You never know when sweet grass might come in handy.*

His trip through the wards had been swift. He'd scaled a drainpipe, inching along the gabled roofs. No one knew an assassin was among them, creeping atop their homes. That's what he was now. "You will be my wind and my assassin," Hanako had told him after he'd mastered the throwing stars. Too bad Akira had no intention of being owned. At least not by the Weapons Master. He had to warn Mari about Asami, about her unknown enemy, and Hanako's plan to storm the palace if it all went wrong. If it came down to it, he'd kill for

Mari. If he did have a soul and it could be seen, he imagined it might be darker now, fringed in soot or ash. The Imperial City had changed him. *For better? For worse? Only time will tell.*

He found the entrance to the tunnel leading into the palace easily enough. The tunnels connected to the city's sewer system. His nose scrunched at the smell. He tucked the map into his surcoat. In the tunnels, it would be too dark to read it. He'd have to rely on what he'd memorized. With a deep breath, he removed the grate in the sidewalk, climbed down, and then replaced it.

Water came up to his ankles. Akira trudged sideways in the narrow space. A couple of feet, and the sewer should give way. There was no sound but his breathing, the tinkle of water, and the squeak of rats. He kept moving.

He knew the moment he breached the palace confines. The water gave way, draining into an even deeper sewer system, and the tunnels opened up so that Akira could walk normally. From Asami's drawing, he knew that the tunnels in this section of the palace weren't guarded. He spent an hour combing the outer tunnels. Twice he took a wrong turn and had to light one of his precious three matches to illuminate the map to get back on the right path.

Hazy torchlight appeared in the distance, along with muted voices. *Guards.* He'd reached the main tunnels. Here, they would open up even more, and samurai patrolled in twos and at regular intervals.

Akira removed the pipe and stash of sweet grass from his coat. He struck his final match and lit the pipe, drawing out the smoke but being careful not to inhale it. The pipe smoldered. He wrapped his black cloth around his face, holding it tightly over his nose and mouth. For a moment, he stood still, letting the sweet grass gather, then disperse, chasing its way down the tunnels.

"Do you smell that?" a deep voice asked. Guards were close. Just around the corner. Akira's breaths became shallow. There was nowhere to hide. If he was discovered and the guards sounded the alarm, he'd have to run. And it would all be over. He'd be hunted by the emperor *and* Hanako. The Snow Girl wouldn't take kindly to Akira's betrayal, nor the emperor to treason.

"It smells like honey," the guard's partner remarked.

"I don't feel right."

The voices cut off abruptly.

Akira stepped around the bend. Two imperial guards lay slumped over, snoring softly. Carefully, Akira wrapped one of the guards' hands around the pipe. A few more feet, and Akira encountered his second set of guards, both sleeping, thanks to the sweet grass. His muscles relaxed, and he smiled under his mask. *If you do not enter the tiger's cave, you will not catch its cub.* He whistled all the way to the East Hall.

Akira was back in the rafters, high up where he belonged. He'd used a trapdoor to access the East Hall. The emperor had seen fit to drill holes in his trapdoors, a way to keep a lookout, and Akira had used these to ensure that the East Hall was deserted. But something wasn't right. According to Asami's map, the East Hall was where the girls were kept for the competition. It should be heavily guarded. But all was quiet. Abandoned.

Steps reached Akira's ears, and he scurried back into a shadowed corner of the rafters. Torches blazed and lit the hall. A silhouette of a robed man appeared, and as he approached, Akira saw that it was a priest. His hood was drawn, but Akira recognized him by his robe — white and adorned with a red sash. *The High Priest.*

During their drunken night, Hanako had spoken of him, calling him the "pretty" priest. "He's the emperor's bastard. But he walks around as if he's the heir. He thinks so highly of his looks, he doesn't tattoo his face like the other priests," she said with a sneer.

The priest's soul was marred with so many dark spots, Akira couldn't discern what color it was. *Most likely all* yōkai *kills.* Akira's gut twisted with disgust. No person, human or *yōkai*, should have so much power over another.

The priest paused at a door and knocked. A collared *yōkai* answered. Her dull brown eyes widened, beholding the priest's white robe. She bent her head and bowed low.

"Invite me in," the priest demanded.

"My lady Mari is not in," she explained meekly. Akira's muscles tensed. Mari's apartment? What was the High Priest doing there? Slowly, he inched across the rafter. He needed to get closer.

"I know. I didn't come to speak with her. I wish to speak to you." The girl froze.

"Lately, the emperor has been favoring the Summer Room for punishment. You are a Hook Girl, are you not?" Akira saw barbed hooks nestled in the girl's hair. He didn't know of her kind. *Yōkai* were as varied as blades of grass. "Hook Girls are particularly intolerant of the heat, isn't that correct? I remember reading that you flourish in the dark and cold. By nature, you are nocturnal creatures. I imagine a room drenched in perpetual sunlight is your worst nightmare."

The Hook Girl's face paled, and she slid the door open a little more. "My lady will be back soon."

The priest smiled with all the softness of a snake. "She won't. The third Season has started. She's in the Winter Room now. Let me in."

The Hook Girl's eyes darted down the hall. Searching for help? At length, she stepped from the threshold and gestured for the priest to enter the chamber.

Indecision kept Akira rooted to the rafter. *She's in the Winter Room with a dangerous* yōkai. He needed to warn her. With haste, Akira swung down from the rafters and entered the tunnels once more.

CHAPTER 31

Mari

ENDLESS WINTER, and Mari trudged through snow up to her knees. Her cheeks were red and wind-chapped. The kimono she wore was a mere scrap of warmth against the cold. Each step was like an icy dagger. She held the silver pick and copper canary tightly in her hands. To stave off the bitter chill, she conjured images of fire, thick blankets, and miso soup. She couldn't see three feet in front of her. A few moments ago, the sun had flared, lighting up the gray winter sky, brushing her cheeks with heat. Then it was gone. That's when the storm started, swirls of ice and snow obscuring her vision. She lost sight of the frozen forest. She lost sight of everything, save her two feet trudging forward.

Mari kept moving. To stop was to die, to give in to the cold and the numbness. She didn't know in what direction she headed. Amid the wasteland, she searched for a dot of black against the white, anything but the white. Mari's pulse drummed in her ears, and she thought of the new riddle. *You will find the scroll at a place that always runs but never walks, often murmurs but never talks, has a bed but never sleeps, has a head but never weeps.* The first riddle had been about a mountain. The next about fire. Both about natural elements.

Memories filtered forward. *Let nature work for you. The sound of the water will hide your footsteps,* her mother had advised. As when she'd solved the fire riddle, everything crystallized at once. *A river.* A river ran and never walked, murmured and never talked . . . Her whole life passed before her eyes — hunting wolves, the killing shed, sparring with her mother — each of these separate events had prepared her for the competition. Even when she hadn't thought she was training, her mother had been carefully teaching her — how to navigate the wild, how to channel the forest, how to survive the Seasons.

A sudden growl made Mari swivel to the right. Out of the white, five hunched black figures took shape. Mari recognized the curve of their backs, the yellow flash of their eyes. Wolves.

Without thinking, she'd drifted closer to the wolves. She ached for her *naginata*. But she had only the silver pick and the canary. She shoved the silver pick into her *obi* and tried the same with the canary, but her hands were stiff. The bird fell from her grasp and sank into the snow, lost. She didn't have time to dig.

The wolves snarled, but the growls weren't directed at her. They surrounded something else. A girl. Sachiko? Nori? Asami?

The wolves pounced on their prey. From the center of the pack, a flash of red kimono caught Mari's eye. Sachiko. The human who had betrayed her friend with a pit viper was fighting a wolf pack. *Fighting and losing.* She could not stand by and watch another girl die.

Mari inched forward, stepping over two slain wolves. She glanced to her left and right. No one else was present; no one else would see. She summoned her beast. The bones in her hands crackled and popped. Her fingernails lengthened to sharp talons.

The wolves had closed in on Sachiko. She lay pinned by their massive paws, their muzzles digging into her sides, shredding her kimono.

Mari lunged, hands swiping at the wolves just as they went for Sachiko's throat. Flesh tore. Everything blurred into yowls and screeches. Hot blood. Then silence. Stillness.

Mari withdrew, retracting her claws, her breaths hot in her frozen lungs. She'd killed the remaining wolves, but not in time to save Sachiko. The girl lay in the snow, her eyes open. *The Rooms choose you*, Master Ushiba had warned. Was this Sachiko's punishment for the Summer Room, for betraying her friend? It seemed the Seasons had collected, just as Ushiba had promised. Carefully, Mari closed Sachiko's eyes.

Nori and Asami were left. She didn't want to compete against her friends. Need coupled with dread burned inside her. *A lean tiger in winter has no friends.* She trudged on.

What if there was *another way?* Taro's words echoed in Mari's ears. Miles and hours passed. She couldn't make out the sun in the sky. She knew that the day grew long only by the decrease in temperature. Her steps were slow and staggered. Still no sign of a river.

Trees, scraggly and laden with snow, rose from the tundra like broken bones popping through skin. Mari nearly collapsed at the sight. *Shelter, respite from the wind.* She ran toward the Ice Forest. The trees blocked the cutting wind. Blood rushed to Mari's cheeks, her hands, her feet. Pain prickled where warmth tried to seep in.

A lump rose in the snow, and she fell, landing on a solid form. Not ice. Not rocks. *A body.* Mari scrambled back.

Nori's snow-dusted profile came into view. Her lips were blue, her eyes closed. Mari searched her for signs of injury. There were none. *No blood. No broken bones.* She felt for a pulse. The battle-axe girl was dead. Who would carry the news of her demise to her family? *My parents don't know I'm here,* she'd said. Mari sat back on her haunches, staring at the battle-axe girl's profile.

Nori's mouth twitched, and Mari stilled, terror-struck. A fat black spider with white stripes pried itself from Nori's blue lips. Mari remembered seeing a spider like that before. In the Summer Room. Mari's pulse pounded. *They were poisoned,* Taro had said of the girls in the Fall Room. But he didn't know by what. *By a spider, that's what.*

Mari's eyes traveled with the spider as it skittered onto a frozen river, where Asami crouched in the middle of the ice, an arm of her tunic pulled up to the elbow. In between them, almost equidistant, lay a red satin pillow. And on that pillow lay a scroll encased in a glass tube.

Mari rose, a dark sense of foreboding growing within her. She stepped onto the river. The ice whispered in complaint, but Mari didn't notice. She was too caught up in watching the black spider. Her former ally hadn't yet sensed Mari's presence.

As the spider drew closer to Asami, she smiled, her heart-shaped face softening. Purple-black ink began to swirl down her forearm, like a creeping vine. The spider crawled into Asami's palm. The ink then took another form. A web. It absorbed the spider, its body flattening and becoming part of Asami's tattoo, part of her skin.

All the puzzle pieces came together. "You killed Nori!" Mari yelled.

Asami stood. "Sachiko?"

Mari jerked her chin.

"So it's just you and me."

Mari turned her head up to the gloomy sky. Her teeth chattered. "So it appears." Another step closer to the satin pillow. She had to have the scroll. She had to move to the next Room. She called her beast forward. Her bones popped, her fingers receded, and talons appeared.

"An Animal Wife?" Asami asked, unmoved. "I wouldn't have guessed it based on your looks. No offense."

"None taken." Mari flexed her hands.

"It's a neat trick you've got," Asami said. "But I have something better." She splayed her forearms, and spiders appeared, rising from her skin like bodies from the grave, then dropping onto the ice. The spiders swarmed Asami's feet. The whites of her eyes receded and turned black. More ice splintered around Mari's feet.

"I don't want to fight you!" Mari shouted. "Let me have the scroll. I'll leave you here. You'll be disqualified, but you'll live."

Asami laughed. "That scroll is mine. What makes you think you would be able to defeat me? I am a *jorōgumo*, the most feared of the *yōkai*. You may be an Animal Wife, a formidable opponent, but my guess is that those claws are all you've got."

Mari took another step. If she threw herself, she might be able to reach the scroll. "What are you doing here?" she yelled. "What is it you hope to accomplish? You want to be Empress?" None of it made sense. Asami didn't answer. She moved toward the scroll. The spiders followed. The ice groaned. Vicious wind flung Asami's tunic open, and Mari gasped. Abrasions and burn scars covered Asami's neck and chest. "What happened?"

Asami tensed, her features tight. "My mother burned to death removing my collar. And I burned too. I can't transform anymore. My people have been reduced to nothing. Only a few of us remain."

The spiders scurried from Asami's feet, rounded the pillow, and headed toward Mari. She crouched and began smashing them with her hands.

"That hurts!" Asami cried.

"It doesn't have to be this way," Mari said, trying to reason with her while frantically squashing the spiders.

"What was your plan, Animal Wife? To steal the emperor's fortune? Crawl back to your village and hide? It's not enough! The emperor and prince must be punished!" Asami shrieked. More spiders cascaded down her arms. Mari couldn't contain the onslaught. She found a crack in the ice and slammed down a fist, scrambling back just as a fissure opened up. The spiders tumbled into the water. The pillow slid in. It wobbled with the current, but the scroll stayed intact, perfectly safe in its encasement.

Asami's words penetrated Mari's battle fog. "You plan to kill the emperor and the prince?" Mari asked in a choked whisper.

Asami laughed. "Of course I plan to kill them. Why do you think I'm doing this? What do you think my mother sacrificed her life for? My sister choked to death on her metal collar because she couldn't pay her taxes!"

Sei had mentioned taxes. The spiders began to circle around the fissure, creeping toward Mari.

Something inside her snapped. Her heart expanded and contracted at the same time. The beast inside her roared, hungry to feed. Her eyes melted to black. "I can't let you kill him," Mari said, surprised to find her voice low and roughly edged. The sound of the beast.

Mari charged, leaping over the crack in the ice and barreling into Asami. Mari's hands wrapped around Asami's throat, and they both tumbled to the ice, the weight of their bodies causing more shards to splinter off. Spiders slipped under Mari's kimono and onto her bare skin. She rolled, taking Asami with her. A deafening crack echoed through the forest. The ice tilted, and Asami and Mari slid, plunging together into the frigid water.

Mari's kimono pulled her down. It felt as if a thousand tiny, icy hands were grabbing at her legs, twisting her lungs. Desperate for air, she swam upward, fingers and legs numb. She broke the surface just as Asami climbed from the water. In her hand, Asami held the scroll. Mari watched as the red pillow saturated with water and sank. Frantic, Mari dug one claw into the ice to keep from being pulled under again. Asami approached Mari, hair dripping, a sneer curving her mouth. She lifted a foot and slammed it down on Mari's hand.

Mari howled, feeling the bones in her hands crushing. She couldn't keep a hold on the beast. It was drifting away. Her hands, arms, and eyes shifted back into their human form. Mari's teeth chattered so hard, they nearly cracked.

Asami bent down, a veneer of triumph on her face, but underneath was a shadow of something else. Regret? Asami put her hands on top of Mari's head and pushed down.

Mari struggled against Asami's hold. Still submerged, Mari fumbled with her *obi* and withdrew Hissa's metal hair pick. Mari surfaced, a scream on her lips, her hand poised to stab, but she withered. Asami sat on the ice, coughing and shaking, the fight drained from her. Spiders swarmed Asami's ankles and shoulders. A frantic hug.

The girls locked eyes.

"I've come so far, but I can't — I can't do it," Asami said. Her cheeks had turned the faintest shade of blue. "I can't kill another *yōkai*, watch another of my kind die." Asami crawled on the ice, hand outstretched. It reminded Mari of the Summer Room, when Asami had killed the boar, had saved her.

For one split second, Mari thought this might be a trick. But she didn't have a choice. She couldn't lift herself from the water without assistance. Mari took Asami's hand and allowed herself to be pulled up. Mari splayed out on the ice, gasping for breath. Asami sat next to her in pitiful shape.

Another deafening crack. A chunk of ice broke off, tipping into the water. Asami cast a look of terror toward Mari as she slid down, hands still fisted around the scroll.

"No!" Mari shouted, reaching for Asami. A second too late. Bubbles formed at the surface. The scroll floated to the top, pristine in its glass tube. Mari grabbed it, violent shivers wracking her body. A thump sounded underneath her. The chunks of ice pushed together and refroze, blocking Asami's way back up. Mari scraped snow off the sheet of ice. Asami's fist tapped uselessly on the frozen window. Her mouth opened, gulping water.

Mari clawed at the ice, banged on it, kicked it. It was too thick. "I'm sorry," Mari cried.

Asami's eyes fluttered closed, and she floated away. *She is gone.* The spiders found a crack in the ice and slipped into the water, lemmings going off a cliff, following their master into death.

A heavy ache settled in Mari's chest, and she sobbed. She'd won. But at what price? *Is the freedom of all worth the life of even one?* Mari didn't know. On hands and knees, she dragged her body from the frozen river and back into the snow, clutching the scroll. Inch by inch, she made her way. If she didn't make it to the doors soon, she'd die of frostbite. A new storm started, blinding Mari once again.

In the whiteness, a figure took shape. Clad all in black, a mask covering his face. An assassin? Another challenge? How many times must Mari fight for her life? How many more would she survive? The figure stepped toward her slowly, unhindered by the cold. She recognized him.

The outline of his body, the silvery scars that disappeared beneath his mask. Surely this was a hallucination. The Son of Nightmares in the Winter Room? He stopped in front of her. She looked up at him. He tugged a leather glove from his hand, crouched, and placed a warm palm against her cheek. "Animal Girl," he crooned. "I thought to help you, but it looks as if you've helped yourself." She blinked, and he was gone. *Definitely a hallucination.* But the warmth of his unreal touch spurred her on. She kept walking, and when she couldn't walk anymore, she crawled, scroll gripped safely in her hand. A snow-covered field came into view, and, rising above it, the frost-covered Winter Room doors. Two samurai guarded the exit, spears in hand, silent as statues.

"There are no more. I'm the last girl. Let me out," she said, voice trembling. Seconds burned away; they did not move.

234

Mari curled into a shivering ball. Vaguely, she heard the heavy doors open. Master Ushiba appeared. He bent, helped her stand. She wavered on frozen feet.

He bowed low. Draped over one arm was a dark brown *yamabiko* pelt, and in his hand was Mari's *naginata*. He placed the pelt over Mari's shoulders, and she drew the cape in, relishing the warmth. "Congratulations. You have defeated Summer, Fall, and Winter. Please follow me to the Spring Room. Your final challenge awaits." He thrust the *naginata* at Mari.

Mari's gaze hardened.

It was not over.

UMIKO:

Goddess of Moonlight, Storms, and Sea

UMIKO, GODDESS OF MOONLIGHT, STORMS, AND SEA, was so beautiful, so alluring, that to glance upon her was to experience uncontrollable desire, a lust like madness.

Eoku, God of War, Military, and Night, spied Umiko bathing in a river. He called a star into his hands and used it to lure Umiko to him. When she drew close enough, Eoku took her by force.

After, Umiko went to the god Sugita and begged him to strike down Eoku, to cast him from the heavens for his crime. "Punish him," she pleaded, her cry harsh and anguished.

Sugita stroked Umiko's tangled hair. With both hands, he held her bruised face and replied, "If you weren't so beautiful, this would not have happened."

"He hurt me," she beseeched.

"Ah, silly girl," Sugita chided. "He has no power over you save for the power you give him."

Umiko left, shamed. Vowing to never let her beauty tempt men again, Umiko covered herself from head to toe. She drank silver to dye her body blue, the color of sorrow. She hid her face behind the mask of a big-cheeked, laughing woman. Then she shaved her head.

Still afraid Eoku might catch her again, Umiko ran. Her terrified footsteps shook the clouds, creating the thunder and lightning, and the sweat from her body became the rain.

CHAPTER 32

Taro

TARO PACED THE PLATFORM, palming the swords at his hip. Courtiers waited, expectant. The Winter Room doors had opened what felt like an hour ago. Whoever was champion would meet Taro here, in the Spring Room.

Anxiety coiled in Taro's chest. What if it wasn't Mari? Back and forth he walked, the cadence of his footsteps the only sound.

The platform sat in the middle of a cherry-blossom grove. The air smelled of sweet rain. A breeze coasted by, dislodging some of the blooms. Petals spun in the wind, and delicate pink flowers squished beneath Taro's pacing feet. He caught his father's eye.

The emperor sat on a golden throne, his face grim. *Is this difficult for my father to watch? Does it stir up buried memories?* The emperor had been in Taro's position once. Behind the emperor, Satoshi hovered, always just within reach.

The crash of a gong was followed by the opening of the Spring Room doors. Taro turned. Framed in the massive doorway — small, delicate, and bloodstained — was Mari. Taro's knees buckled. He wanted to smile, but his mouth settled into a flat line.

Mari's steps were hesitant as she climbed the red-carpeted stairs to the platform. Master Ushiba followed, then diverted from the carpet to stand next to the emperor and Satoshi.

Taro studied Mari. She wore a simple white *yukata*. A *yamabiko* pelt was draped around her shoulders. Her hair was wet, and the *naginata* trembled in her hands. Looped around her delicate throat was a chain with a pendant containing a scroll. What had happened in the Winter Room?

"Taro," she whispered. He didn't like the vacant look in her eye.

He bowed low, every vein in his body pulsing. "I was born in the spring, during the mightiest of storms. The future empress must be an equal to the emperor. I am your final challenge." He withdrew his swords and crossed them in front of him.

Her eyes darkened. "I cannot kill you."

His expression softened. "You don't have to. The first to draw blood wins." This was a mere formality. A gesture recognizing the first empress, Makoto, who drew the blood of her betrothed before marrying him.

Mari nodded. She slipped the stole from her shoulders and unsheathed her *naginata*. "You will not go easy on me," she demanded firmly and loudly. *Such pride.* Worthy of an empress.

"No, I won't go easy on you. To do so would be an insult."

Holding the *naginata* across her body, Mari moved slowly toward Taro. "The first to draw blood?" she asked.

"The first to draw blood," he confirmed. Just as the last syllable left his mouth, she swung the butt end of the *naginata*, clearly intending to clip Taro at the knees. Taro jumped, avoiding the rod. Gasps rose from the courtiers. Mari withdrew and scampered to the corner of the platform.

Taro advanced, swords pointed. Mari blocked Taro's strikes. The metal of their blades clashed, and sparks flew through the air. Mari thrust the *naginata*, divesting Taro of his small sword. The *wakizashi* went aloft, pinning itself in the soft grass at the courtiers' feet.

Taro gritted his teeth. "You are well-practiced. You anticipate my moves."

"My mother taught me that I'd never be as strong as a man, so I must be smarter," she said, hardly out of breath.

"You shouldn't give away your secrets so easily." They circled each other.

She shrugged. "I never really believed in thinking before I speak."

All at once, he was a blur of motion. He had trained a year with the *shōgun*, and though he never had the heart of a warrior, he had the strength and skill of one.

Mari blocked Taro's strikes and rained down blows, which Taro deflected in kind. They were forces of nature. The clang of steel on steel was deafening. Mari managed a jab to Taro's shoulder. Taro grunted in pain, and his sword lowered for just an instant. At that moment, Mari struck. *Whoosh*, the sound of steel as it sliced through clothing to flesh. A rivulet of crimson ran down Taro's arm. She'd drawn first blood.

The *naginata* clattered to the ground. Taro's hand went to the shallow cut — a paltry wound. Taro hadn't been withholding, but he realized Mari had. She could have inflicted far more damage. *She is not my equal. She is far better than I.*

Wind swept the platform, banished the clouds, and warm sunlight filled the room. Taro caught Mari just as she began to fall.

"Is it over?" she asked.

"It's over." Then he cried to the courtiers, to his father, to all who could hear and would listen, "Behold, the Conqueror of the Seasons."

The samurai stomped their spears, hands to their hearts. A chorus of cheers rang out. Taro's eyes met his father's. The emperor's jaw clenched. They nodded to each other in mutual recognition. It was over.

The emperor stood abruptly and left. Satoshi hurried after him. His father would not stay and watch anymore. But for once, Taro didn't feel blistering anger toward him. No, all Taro felt was pity, and empathy. Imagining if it were not Mari before him, at last he understood his father's grief. *A love like madness.* Nothing would stand between him and Mari. He'd cut through death to get to her.

Taro held his empress tightly. How glorious she looked in her triumph, no longer a thing of moonlight and water but something forged in steel and blood. He spread his dreams at her feet. She had his heart.

Tread lightly, my love.

CHAPTER 33
Akira

SEAGULLS SHRIEKED, and the smell of fish and brine filtered under Akira's mask. Boats clunked against one another. He walked the docks in the dark and ruminated.

Akira had seen her, *seen Mari*, in the Winter Room. He had watched everything — the fight with Asami. He could have stepped in at any time, could have thrown a star and cut Asami off at the knees. But he'd done nothing. He'd watched and waited. He'd never get in her way. Victory would be hers, and hers alone. But he did allow himself one moment, to touch her cheek, to feel her strength, and, he hoped, to give her some comfort.

Then he'd followed her into the Spring Room and watched again. A silent sentinel in a cherry tree. It was his first time observing the Cold Prince, the man who had created the collars. Akira's insides squeezed when Mari drew blood and was announced Conqueror of the Seasons. Soon, she'd marry the Cold Prince. Mari would become a princess, the future empress, but that wasn't the end. She had the prince's fortune to steal, and Akira would be by Mari's side when she made her escape. They would travel together. *Go home.* Nothing had ever sounded quite so good.

A tavern door sprang open, and drunken *yōkai* spilled out. Among them were Hanako's geezers and Ebisu, the *yamawaro*. If the group was present, Hanako was sure to be close by. The tavern door swung again, and Akira saw a flash of red. *Ren.* The demon never strayed far from the Weapons Master. Akira swiveled on his heel. *Too late.* A beefy red arm hooked around his neck.

"Well, what do we have here?" Hanako was as lovely as ever: leather kimono, white ferret draped around her neck, see-through skin almost glowing in the dark, pearlescent soul a hazy shroud around her shoulders. Did Akira detect new blemishes?

Akira struggled against the hold. His mask slipped down to his neck. Ren tightened his arm, and Akira wheezed. Hanako's *yōkai* lackeys surrounded them. Akira turned his head, clearing his airway, then used his hands to grab onto Ren's arm. He tucked his chin, raised his shoulders, hunched, and stepped back all in one fluid motion. Then he hooked one leg behind Ren's and leaned forward, knocking Ren off balance. Akira swiveled and threw Ren down. The demon grunted as it hit the docks. Free, Akira cut through the line of *yōkai* and turned to Hanako, throwing stars at the ready.

Hanako held up her hands.

Ren got to his feet and clicked.

Hanako nodded. "I regret teaching him that move as well. Easy, Son of Nightmares. Let's talk." Large perked up, scampering down her body and into the sewer system.

The demon sneered at Akira. Akira sneered back.

"I believe you have something of mine." Hanako snapped her fingers and held out a hand.

Keeping a grip on a throwing star, Akira reached into his surcoat and withdrew Asami's map. He threw it at Hanako's feet. She raised her brow and bent to pick up. She unfolded it, making sure that the map was intact before addressing Akira. "Why did you steal this?" A whistle and then a popping noise sounded, and Hanako frowned as fireworks in the shapes of lotus flowers and turtles lit up the sky. "The competition is over," Hanako whispered. "There is a new Conqueror of the Seasons, a new princess."

Ren grunted.

Hanako smiled at her demon. "Asami has succeeded. I knew it."

Akira shook his head. "Your champion is dead."

The Snow Girl's eyes drew wide. "*No.*"

"I saw it myself. She fell into the river in the Winter Room. She drowned. Her spiders along with her." He remembered how Asami had laughed. *I am a spider. We can go anywhere.*

Ren moved forward and placed a meaty paw on Hanako's shoulder. The Snow Girl crumpled under the weight of her friend's touch and stifled a sob. Akira loosened his grip on the throwing star and stepped forward, only to be blocked by the geezers and drooling *yamawaro*. His mouth opened and closed. "She meant more to you than you let on." Above, fireworks continued to explode, the beauty at odds with Hanako's heartache.

"Of course she did," Hanako spat out. "Do you think me incapable of love?"

Akira glanced at the ground, shook his head. "I think you guard your heart. Perhaps you've built your walls so high, it's impossible for people to even see it anymore."

Ren clicked a soft agreement and stroked Hanako's hair with a thick talon. Hanako sniffled and wiped her nose. She straightened. "I thought she was invincible."

Ren clicked.

Hanako smiled sadly. "Yes, when you love someone, it is easy to think they are infallible." Akira rubbed the back of his neck. He thought of Mari. Of how far out of reach she always seemed. Hanako's face hardened, any remnant of grief gone. This was the true Weapons Master: cunning, decisive, *cold*. "Asami's life will not be in vain." The geezers rumbled their agreement. "She wouldn't want us to mourn." Another rumble of assent. Hanako's fist slammed into her open palm. "We will gather our allies. We will storm the palace. We will end this empire once and for all." She nodded to her followers. "You know what to do."

Their chins dipped in response. They turned to go, to drum up the masses.

"Wait!" Akira shouted. A tremor passed through him. "Let me go." *Mari will be safe.* "Let me be your wind and assassin. Let me kill the emperor and prince for you."

Hanako grew contemplative. "Why should I trust you? You stole my map. And you still haven't said why."

"I went to the palace to gather information — for you. The map works, but the tunnels are narrow. You won't be able to fit an entire army. But I can slip through the halls as easily as the rats that inhabit them."

Hanako snickered. "Did you just liken yourself to a rat?"

Ren clicked and crossed his arms.

"Ren is sure you're lying. He wants to break your arm and see what truth spills out."

Akira flashed the throwing star in his palm. "I'd like to keep both my limbs, if you please. I'm going to need them. Give me twenty-four hours." That would be enough time for Mari to marry the prince and steal his fortune. Enough time for them to escape the Imperial City. "I will do your bidding. No one will ever know I was there. They may even blame humans for the imperial family's deaths. No more *yōkai* would have to die, would have to be sacrificed." He braved a step closer to Hanako. "Asami wasn't the only *yōkai* in the competition. There is another girl, the one who won. She will help me." At that, Hanako's eyes glowed. "One day is all I ask. If I fail, you can go on with your plan."

Hanako pinched her lips. "One night. Twelve hours."

Akira jerked his chin. "The emperor and his son will be dead by morning."

PART III:

After the rain, earth hardens.

— Proverb

SUGITA:

God of Children, Fortune, and Love

ONCE UPON A TIME, the god Sugita planted a tree in the spring.

Then he thought the tree should have a partner, a friend with whom to witness the seasons. So the following summer, Sugita planted another tree. Through the years, the Spring and Summer Trees grew side by side, weathering storms and blazing heat alike. Each was as strong as metal mined from the deepest trenches of the earth.

Only, the Spring Tree was always just a little bit taller than the Summer Tree. At first, this was not a problem. The Summer Tree received enough sunlight and water to thrive. But soon enough, the Spring Tree grew so large that it eclipsed the Summer Tree, leaving it in its shadow. And the Summer Tree began to wither without sunlight or water.

Seeing this, Sugita wept. He went to his sisters: Umiko, Goddess of Moonlight, Storms, and Sea, and Aiko, Goddess of the Sun, Animals, and Day. "My tree needs sunlight and water. Save it, please."

Umiko removed her porcelain mask and laughed. With both hands, she held Sugita's sad face, in much the same way he had done when she'd asked him to banish Eoku. "If you hadn't planted the trees side by side, this would not have happened," said Umiko. "That tree was born to die."

Aiko, ever the loyal sister, smiled sadly. "You reap what you sow, brother."

The two sisters left. And Sugita could only watch as his beloved tree withered and died.

CHAPTER 34
Mari

SULFUR AND SMOKE, the scent of fireworks, drifted through the open window. Tremors coursed through Mari, aftershocks from the Winter and Spring Rooms. She winced as Sei pulled her hair in a high bun and shoved in a strand of silk cherry blossoms. The delicate flowers poured over Mari's right ear and temple.

In her lap, Mari flexed her hands. She could still feel the spiders crawling on her, feel the bite of icy water. Mari was wounded and weary, in no shape to attend a celebration, a wedding. *My wedding.* In a few hours, she'd be married.

"My lady, it's time to get dressed." Sei held up a red kimono with gold thread woven in an abstract flower pattern. Draped on the bed was a checkered *obi*. Mari sighed, biting back a shudder of pain as she stood. Every muscle protested. Sei seemed distressed by Mari's battle-worn body, but the Hook Girl kept her silence.

Once Mari was dressed, Sei stepped back, her lips curving in a triumphant smile. "You are the embodiment of Spring herself." Sei grabbed a polished silver tray. "Look." She held up the tray, and Mari started at her reflection.

The red of the kimono brought out a rosy glow in her cheeks that matched her crimson lips. The cherry blossoms framed her face. *A veil of spring.* Tiny water pearls the color of the moon were woven through her hair, catching the light. Sei had painted thick black kohl lines around Mari's eyes. Even if she wasn't beautiful, she felt like it.

Mari ran her hands over the cool silk of the checkered *obi*. Sei chattered on, but Mari was only half listening. The world melted away. She had accomplished what she'd set out to do. Conquer the Seasons.

And now, a new destiny unfolded before her. *Another way.* A *yōkai* empress and a human prince. Perhaps she could be *Oni* Slayer, Conqueror of the Seasons, *and* Peacemaker. At Taro's side, she would herald in a new golden era of Honoku. But the dream was but a tiny ember that, if not sheltered from the wind, would blow away.

Taro does not know you are yōkai.

A small kernel of doubt planted in her stomach, irritating her. If she stayed, she'd never see Tsuma, her friends, her mother again. *It has to be worth it. I will make it worth it.*

"You will turn many heads tonight," said Sei, drawing Mari's focus.

Mari smiled, but it was half-formed. "Thank you, Sei."

The Hook Girl looked at her feet. "You are welcome." Sei's hand jumped to her throat, nearly caressing her collar, but she stopped just before her skin made contact with the curses. *I'll make it better. You won't have to wear the collar soon.* "My lady, I was wondering, if it's not too much trouble . . ."

"What is it, Sei?"

"Back at the inn, you spoke so passionately of your home." Mari remembered. *Of a place where yōkai don't wear the metal collar.* "I know now isn't a good time, but I hope you may share more stories with me. It sounds wonderful."

Mari grasped Sei's hands. "Of course." *I'll take you there. You won't be afraid anymore.* A knock struck the apartment door. Mari hesitated. There was more she wanted to say. The knock sounded again. Sei rushed to answer it.

In the hall, two samurai bowed low, their eyes hidden beneath black lacquered masks. "His Majesty, the imperial prince, requests your presence."

Sei bowed. "When I see you again, you'll be a princess, the future empress."

With a small smile, Mari bid Sei goodbye. Outside the door, the ground was littered with gifts, presents left by courtiers in hopes of gaining the future empress's early favor. It made Mari think of the gifts left outside of the gates of Tsuma. What would her mother say if she could see her now? *You are a true Animal Wife. You have married the highest of us all.*

The samurai's steps were synced with the distant hammer of *taiko* drums as they escorted Mari to the Main Hall. The heavy thuds called all to the Imperial Palace. All except the *yōkai*, who were forbidden, kept on the outside as always. But humans, no matter what age, gender, or wealth, were invited to the palace tonight. They would be free to roam its exotic gardens, or stare in wonder at the Seasonal Rooms, a wedding gift from the emperor to the masses. They would come to set eyes on Mari, the future empress. Wife to the Cold Prince.

A pang of self-doubt seized her, and Mari paused mid-step. She was playing a dangerous game, one with smarter, better-equipped players. The guards stopped but did not speak. Though they seemed stoic, Mari knew that they were trained observers. *What secrets they must hold.* Showing any weakness was a strike against her. *Remember, sharks circle only when they smell blood,* Asami had told her. That seemed like so long ago. Mari stilled the trembling in her hands, squared her shoulders, and kept walking.

She rounded a corner and stepped into the Main Hall. Red banners with strokes of golden calligraphy hung from the rafters. Soon, this space would be crowded with people. Now it was empty, save for the prince, who stood by the open doors of the Fall Room. A few samurai lined the walls.

With small steps, Mari approached Taro, her betrothed.

Taro was dressed in a black surcoat and matching *hakama* pants stitched with gold thread. Swords rested on his left hip, swords Mari knew he could wield very well, but still she had bested him. The thought gave her the courage she needed to take the final few steps toward his imposing presence. *He is yours,* she reminded herself. But the words wouldn't settle in her spine. She had won the competition, but she felt no sense of victory, no sense of relief.

She smiled as she reached his side. "I wondered why Sei picked this kimono, but now I see. We match."

Taro's face softened, but a dark, uncertain gleam remained in his eyes. "No," he said.

Mari blinked, taken aback. "Are you displeased that we match?"

Taro swallowed, the ball in his throat working up and down. "We don't match, because I could never come close to your beauty, your spirit. Whatever I wear only complements you."

Mari relaxed and drew closer to him. "We complement each other."

A corner of Taro's lips twitched. He took her hand, pressing a kiss to her palm. "You best me in combat and in rhetoric."

Mari smiled, a flush spreading from her neck to her toes. She nodded at the Fall Room door. "I hold no favorable memories of that room."

Taro's eyes flickered to Mari's. "Someday, you will have to tell me how you survived it."

Mari kept silent, remembering the smell of the *oni*'s breath, the feel of its flesh as her claws raked its face. "I must have *some* secrets," she teased.

"Not from your husband," Taro corrected, dark gaze raking her up and down.

"Is that what you want? If I tell you everything, I'll have nothing left for myself," she jested again.

"I do not wish to strip you of anything. But I do wish to build a bridge between us." Taro breathed deeply. "I wish you to be my wife."

Mari's head snapped up sharply. "That is all but a certainty. In a few moments, I will be." The ceremony was less than an hour away. *Too late to turn back now. The moment you stepped into the Summer Room, your fate was sealed.*

"My wife in truth. I want to know that you come to me not because of some competition and whatever brought you here, but of your own free will, because you want me" — he paused — "as much as I want you."

"There are things you don't know about me. The things I've done, you would never understand."

Taro gripped Mari's hands. "Whatever you've done, whatever you were, it is in the past."

"You would forgive me?"

Taro nodded. "Anything. Be my wife in truth." It was a demand, an order from a man used to getting what he wanted. Taro didn't know any other way. "My subjects say that I am heartless. When so many people say the same thing about you again and again, you begin to believe it is true."

"I have some experience with that," Mari acknowledged.

He placed his palm against her cheek. She turned shimmering eyes to him. Taro went on. "But now I realize that my heart has only been missing. And you've found it, haven't you?"

The wedding took place in the Spring Room, on the same dais on which Mari and Taro had battled. But the Room had been transformed. The trees bloomed with fresh cherry blossoms. Butterflies with unnaturally blue iridescent wings swooped through the air. A simple pagoda covered the dais. And although it was night outside the Palace of Illusions, the sun shone bright inside the Spring Room.

Taro and Mari walked down the aisle arm in arm. At the altar, a white wedding hood was placed over Mari's hair, a red robe embroidered with gold cranes draped over her shoulders. Cherry blossoms rained down, a shower of soft petals thickening the air. Taro kept hold of her hand, and she was grateful. Without his support, she didn't think she could stand. She gripped Taro's hand tighter. While everything else raged, he was calm. He anchored her. And she needed an anchor. She had faced so much death. Taro was warm and alive.

The servants continued ornamenting, forcing Mari's arms through the red robe. She lost Taro's hand. Her knees buckled, but she managed to stay standing. *This is my wedding.* She almost laughed. A strange buzzing filled her ears. A ceramic turtle was placed in her palm.

The High Priest stood in front of Taro and Mari, the handsome one who always hovered near the emperor. He waved a smoking branch over their shoulders, a ritual purification.

The priest spoke, but she couldn't make sense of his words. She was too distracted by his cobalt tattoos, too afraid his skin might brush against hers. Expose her. She shook from adrenaline and fear. Everything was moving so fast. She wanted to stop time, to gather herself, build up her walls.

A cup of *sake* was thrust into her hands. She sipped from it and passed it to Taro. The cup circled back twice more.

Taro read from a large scroll, his voice deep and earnest. She tried to remember Taro's blood when she'd cut him. If it was the same as hers. *Yes. Inside we are the same. A sign.* It had to be. She was *yōkai*, and Taro was human, but they shared this. The first dazzling sparks of love. That would be enough. Enough for Taro to forgive her treachery. Mari managed a smile just as the ceremony ended, just as she was declared the princess and future empress of Honoku.

Taro clasped Mari's hand in his. The samurai guards opened the palace doors. The hall filled with noise — fireworks, *taiko* drums, the thunderous roar of the crowd.

Before Mari, the main garden stretched, rolling carpets of bright green grass, cherry trees heavy with blossoms, pathways of polished slate. All of it was packed with guests — peasants, merchants, *daimyō*, courtiers.

The imperial court would sit and watch the festivities from the platform in the middle of the garden. Thousands of lanterns hung, and the scent of burning wax and cooked almonds perfumed the air. It felt familiar, almost, in some strange way, like home.

Taro squeezed Mari's hand. Like dominoes falling, a hush ran through the crowd. A voice echoed to Mari's right, Master Ushiba. "Most loyal subjects, the Emperor of Honoku, Junichi Haito." The emperor stood to Taro's left. "The Prince of Honoku, Taro Haito, and the Princess of Honoku, Mari Haito."

Mari had never felt so exposed. She wondered if the people were tallying her faults. Small boxes of rice were thrust into her hands. "Distribute them," Taro whispered. As they descended, Mari handed out the boxes to peasants who lined their pathway. The crowd cheered, a victory roar. She wondered if the throng saw how her hands shook.

Taro's expression remained sober, but warmth steeped his eyes. "It seems they approve," he whispered under his breath.

Mari took Taro's arm. Seeing so much color, so much light, it almost hurt. Then she remembered the *yōkai* beyond the palace walls. These humans were not her people. Her people wore metal collars. She must not forget.

A lone samurai caught her eye. He'd removed his helmet to stare at Mari. Silvery scars marred half his face. A knot wound in her stomach. *No, it can't be.* But it was. *Akira.* She blinked, her eyes filling with tears. *He's real. As sure as night encases day, Akira is here.* But *yōkai* were not allowed in this celebration. Fear chilled her blood, froze her steps. Akira replaced his helmet.

She hadn't realized she'd stopped until Taro cleared his throat. "Mari?"

She offered Taro a wavering smile. "I thought I saw someone I knew. But I was mistaken."

Taro stared at her for a moment, searching her face, then returned his attention to the spectacle before them. Mari risked another glance at Akira. He still stood in the horde. She couldn't see his face anymore. Not with the samurai mask on. But she could feel his gaze, burning holes through her and Taro's linked arms.

Taro moved, gently prodding Mari forward. As they walked the last few feet to the dais, Mari searched for Akira again, but he was gone. *Lost.* She felt the brush of Taro's lips against her ear as he leaned down to seat her. "I'll give you whatever you want," he vowed quietly, so only she could hear. "I'll give you anything." She flexed her hand, lightly touching it to his chest, and almost buckled at the weight of the world at her fingertips.

CHAPTER 35
Akira

AKIRA WANTED TO SHOUT. His Animal Girl was alive and well. *And the Cold Prince's wife.*

His jaw clenched. He hated the manner in which the prince directed Mari, placing a hand on her back, propelling her forward, whispering in her ear. Next to him, she looked like a prop, an object to reinforce his status. Akira's hands twitched at his sides, desperate to caress one of the stars hidden in his belt. It would be a simple thing, to hurl a star. He imagined the blade lodging in the prince's throat. But Mari might be harmed in the resulting fray. He would not risk her life for his petty jealousy.

Akira grunted as a passerby rammed into his shoulder. Seeing Akira's samurai dress, the man muttered a hasty apology.

Akira scanned the throng. A band began playing, and he recognized the low notes of the *shamisen*, the instrument his father used to play. He wandered the revelry alone, an unseen thread pulling him toward the platform, toward Mari. The Cold Prince watched his bride with unconcealed fascination. Akira recognized the look on his face. That of a man deeply in love. The prince's soul was a lovely shade of lavender. It complemented Mari's ice-blue soul. The colors intertwined.

Across from them, the emperor laughed at something, then broke into a hacking cough. It grew to a violent fit, and he grasped for his *sake* cup. Quick as lightning, Mari's hand shot out, spilling the contents. Rose-colored liquid splashed the front of Mari's kimono. No one had seen her move. Everyone, including Taro, assumed that the emperor had doused her gown with his clumsy hands.

Mari gasped, blotting her kimono with a napkin. The Cold Prince whispered something in Mari's ear. Akira gritted his teeth, seeing such intimacy. Mari nodded and rose from the table. She turned her head, almost imperceptibly, toward Akira, then quickly escaped to the Main Hall.

Akira watched as she passed through the double doors and turned right. Her stride slowed, and again she tilted her head in Akira's direction. Akira plunged through the crowd. He had followed Mari to the Imperial City. He would follow her anywhere.

CHAPTER 36

Mari

"YOU SHOULDN'T BE HERE." Mari kept her back to Akira, her gaze lost in the wreckage before her. Uprooted trees. Overturned boulders. Slash marks in the ground. She'd sought refuge in the Fall Room. Since the *oni* attack, the room had been cordoned off for repairs. This wasteland was the only place Mari knew she would find true privacy. So much blood had been spilled here in this maple forest. Was this room haunted now? A gust of wind shook Mari's hair loose, making her think of the restless dead.

Twigs snapped under Akira's feet as he moved toward her. "Is that all you have to say to me?" he asked, unable to keep the confusion and bitterness from his voice.

She turned, her eyes luminous. He'd stripped the samurai mask from his head. Seeing him up close, talking to him again . . . something like a knife lodged in her throat. "If the prince or the emperor sees you —"

Akira's chin went up; his hands brushed his armor. "Let them come. I am not afraid." He looked every inch the warrior. Mari was surprised to see that this darker look suited him. There was a new power in his body, a crackling fire waiting for a sharp wind to set the world ablaze. The tension in Akira's body relaxed; his eyes softened. "I've missed you."

The knife in Mari's throat twisted and lodged itself deeper. *Tell him. Tell him about the Rooms, about what you did to survive, how it brought you to the edge and pushed you off, how Taro caught you mid-fall.* "I've missed you, too." She spoke the truth. She was happy to see him. "You were in the Winter Room." It was not a question.

Akira inched closer, his footsteps cautious as he navigated the uneven ground. He hopped over a fallen tree, moving like a shadow. "I thought to rescue you." He smiled wryly, the same smile she remembered from the boy in the woods the first time she'd met him. "But I should have known better. You no longer need the Son of Nightmares. You rescued yourself."

It was true she'd succeeded, but not without great loss. Wasn't that the way it always was, though? To succeed, someone else must fail. To win, someone else must lose. "So much has happened." *Coward! You can slice an* oni *in two, but you cannot speak the truth to your dear friend.*

"A princess now. I should bow to you." He did not. "You've accomplished what you set out to do. I suppose congratulations are in order." He smiled, joking.

"I don't feel like celebrating."

Akira sobered and nodded. "I understand. You're not finished yet. Tell me, how do you plan to steal the Cold Prince's fortune?"

Mari picked at the bark from a maple tree.

"Mari?"

"I'm staying."

For a long moment, Akira did not respond. Then he scoffed. "I'm sorry. I'm sure I didn't hear you correctly. You're staying? For how long?"

"I know it sounds preposterous, but —"

"There is no possible good reason for you to stay."

Mari licked her lips and whispered, "Do you believe we all have a purpose?"

He chewed on her question. "Yes. I believe it. Every one of us has a destiny."

"I used to think I knew my purpose — Tsuma, thievery." A fleeting smile graced her lips. Mari's hands skirted over Akira's chest. "But now I know I didn't understand at all. I didn't have a clue."

"You think your purpose is to stay here, married to the Cold Prince?"

"Yes, I believe I am supposed to be Taro's wife. And to help as Empress."

"Help?"

"Free the *yōkai*."

Akira staggered; his body slumped heavily against a cypress tree. "This is much more than stealing a fortune. You speak of revolution. And what happens when the prince finds out your true form?"

Mari remembered Taro's words. *Everything is forgiven.* "I have reason to believe he will understand." Somewhere between their kiss in the Main Hall and the banquet, Mari's hope that Taro would accept her had evolved into tenuous certainty. *He will not reject me. He cannot.*

"This is a fool's task." Akira's anger grew.

"Akira, please."

Akira rubbed a hand down his face as bitter understanding dawned. He pounded the bark with a backward fist. "You love him. The Cold Prince."

"Akira —"

"And I love you."

"I never promised you anything," she hotly defended.

He shook his head sadly. "No, you didn't. I am not such a fool as to believe my affections would be returned. You don't owe me anything. Still, the truth cannot be denied. Mari, Animal Girl, Conqueror of the Seasons, wife of the Cold Prince, you are so many things, but you are unwise in your love for him. The prince loves you like the summer loves the wild rose: only for a season."

Mari felt her cheeks flush with anger. "I am a rose, then?" she asked. "A cheap flower that catches someone's fleeting attention?"

Akira's eyes blazed. "No. You are not a flower, something to be admired, plucked, and kept, which is what the Cold Prince wants. He does not know what I know. You are so much more. And you will wither under the Cold Prince's thumb."

Mari sucked in a breath. If it were two months ago, she would have agreed with Akira. "You are wrong. Taro is not cold. He knows me."

"That's it, then. Your mind is made up."

Mari tilted her chin. "I'm sorry."

"You have nothing to apologize for," he said softly, stepping away from her. Back turned, he said, "You should know that the *yōkai* Resistance is building. Asami was part of it." Mari stiffened at the mention of her dead ally. How did Akira know her? He went on before she could ask. "I came here . . . I thought I could . . ." He shook his head. "It doesn't matter anymore. *Yōkai* will storm the palace soon. I've bought you a few hours. If you truly love your prince, you'll urge him to run." He melted into the darkness, helmet hanging from his hand.

Mari felt the loss of Akira like a battle wound. She closed her eyes, girding herself against the emotional onslaught. Tears burned behind her eyelids. When she opened them, she was alone.

CHAPTER 37
Mari

MARI SPRINTED THROUGH the Fall Room, slowing as she approached the doors. She wiped away tears and straightened her spine. The Main Hall was filled with drunken revelers. She kept to the walls, hiding behind the golden banners hanging from the rafters. Shapes materialized in the shadows. Mari stiffened. *Only two lovers embracing.* They paused as Mari passed. She deliberately staggered to appear drunk. They didn't recognize her. Who would expect a princess to be fumbling about in the dark?

Her thoughts churned. She couldn't return to the banquet. Taro would know something was wrong. What would she say? *My yōkai friend disguised himself as a samurai and snuck into our wedding celebration. He warned me of a plot against you. If you value your life, we should run.* She needed to tell him. Needed to save him. But not in the middle of a celebration the entire city was attending.

Mari burst into her apartment, bile rising in her throat. A pocket door, the entrance to Sei's servant's quarters, slid open. The Hook Girl stood at the threshold, hair down, *yukata* wrapped tightly around her body. Sleep lingered in her eyes. "My lady." She bowed low. "Forgive me. I did not think you would return tonight. I thought you would spend the night with —"

Mari managed a tremulous smile. "The emperor spilled some *sake* on my gown. I've come to change."

"Oh." Sei frowned, stepping forward. The front of Mari's kimono was damp but not stained. A few minutes by the fire, and it would dry completely. There was no need to switch gowns.

Mari held out an arm. "Would you help me, please?" She wondered if Sei detected the slight trembling in her fingers.

"Of course." Sei's hands settled on Mari's *obi*, deftly untying it.

Heat licked Mari's cheeks as she gazed into the fire while Sei worked in efficient silence. She'd woven such a tangled web. Akira's words replayed in her mind: Yōkai *will storm the palace soon. I've bought you a few hours. If you truly love your prince* . . . Would Taro run with her? Where would they go? Where would an imperial prince and a *yōkai* princess be safe? Would he forgive her betrayal? Or would he think her a monster? Like his father thought of all *yōkai*.

"You're cold," Sei said, placing a tentative hand on Mari's shoulder once she was stripped down to her undergarments. "I'll make you some tea."

I'll make you some tea. Mari had done as much for Hissa after her friend had given birth. A lifetime ago. Hissa's words rang sharp and true in her mind. *We're all monsters. No man, no human, will ever love us. That is the curse of the Animal Wife, never to be loved for who we truly are.* Tears formed in Mari's eyes. She realized that her bravado

268

with Akira had been false. A very small part of Mari did doubt Taro. What would that feel like, to see Taro turn from her in disgust?

Her heartbeat pulsed in her chest. A storm was fast approaching. Soon Mari would have to send for Taro and tell him the truth. Every minute that ticked by, *yōkai* were coming closer to the palace walls, armed and ready to take their revenge.

The silvery moonlight cascading through the open window, the crackle of the fire, the deep, even breaths of Sei — all of it was so tranquil. *Such a fragile peace.* Mari wanted to hang on to it a little longer.

So when Sei helped her settle onto a cushion, then presented her with a steaming cup of tea, Mari didn't protest. She'd give herself a few moments. Mari inhaled notes of jasmine. She'd requested the tea days ago. A reminder of home. Now a reminder of all that she stood to lose.

"Won't you join me?" Mari asked, peering up at the Hook Girl. In the firelight she seemed so frail, ghostlike.

Sei shifted. "I'm not allowed. *Yōkai* are not permitted to socialize with humans — much less royals."

Mari's mouth curved up. "It will be our secret."

Sei glanced around as if someone were watching. "Secrets have a way of worming their way to the surface."

"They do. But just for tonight, let us pretend that you are not *yōkai* and I am not a princess and that we are two friends sharing tea."

The Hook Girl bit her lip, hesitating. Then she fetched the tea from the brazier and poured herself a cup. She smiled as she sat across from Mari. "It smells good."

Mari stared into her teacup. "Have you been collared all your life?"

"Since birth," Sei answered, sipping.

"You've never known freedom, then?"

Sei felt the back of her head, where her hooks were nestled tight in a bun. "It is the small things I long for. Walking through the different wards without being chased by samurai." Her eyes met Mari's. "An apartment of my own where I could greet friends."

Such longing in Sei's face, a bone-gnawing hunger for something more. "You and I may have more in common than we know. The village I grew up in was isolated, and I had few friends. I was expected from a young age to accomplish unimaginable feats. That kind of pressure made me want the same as you, simple pleasures."

Sei chewed her cheek. "My grandmother and mother are gone. I never knew my father."

"I never knew my father either," Mari interjected.

"I have no siblings. I am alone in this world. I think about that often. If something were to happen to me, no one would grieve." *I would*, Mari thought. "I believe everything in life that is worth anything is people — those you love and those who love you. I love no one. And no one loves me. Even so, my life has some value, doesn't it?"

Mari set down her teacup with a decisive click. "Yes," she said unequivocally. "You are worth more than you know. I consider you a very dear friend."

At that, Sei seemed to tense. "As Princess you will not be allowed to keep a *yōkai* lady's maid."

"I have it on good authority that as the future empress, I will be allowed to do whatever I want," Mari jested, remembering Taro's words: *I am a prince. I can do anything I want.* Then Mari considered something. "But perhaps that is not what you want. Is there a different future you see for yourself?"

Sei lifted a shoulder. "Your village sounds like a lovely place — small, peaceful."

Mari glanced out the window. In the distance, she could just make out the jagged edge of a mountain. Homesickness hit her in the gut, nearly stealing her breath. "See that peak, the one that looks like it's been bitten off by a giant?" She pointed to the dark silhouette. Sei nodded. And finally, for what felt like the first time in the longest time, Mari told the truth. "My village is there. It is called Tsuma. My mother's name is Tami. The journey up the Tsuko funo Mountains is difficult, but for enough coin, you can buy guides."

Sei fingered the copper coins on her wrist. "I'd not make it very far with the metal collar."

"I'm sorry." It was all Mari could say, all she could do. And it seemed paltry at best.

"I'm sorry too," Sei said.

This startled Mari. She stared at Sei. "You have nothing to apologize for."

Sei smiled, embarrassed. "No, I guess not."

Mari thought of the *yōkai* Resistance Akira had mentioned. Each must be willing to die for the cause. For freedom. She regarded Sei as the Hook Girl stood and gathered the teacups. "What price would you pay for your freedom? What would you give to be free of the metal collar?" Mari asked.

Sei set the cups down on the writing desk next to a sheaf of writing paper and gold inkpot. The parchment had been delivered after the Spring Room, stenciled with Mari's name on it. A gift from the prince, from Taro. *So you may write your family and tell them of your victory and our marriage,* his note had said. The persimmon bowl used to be there, but now it resided in Mari's trunk. The first and only thing she'd stolen. "I don't know, my lady." She paused, considering. But Mari detected that Sei had thought about this before. "I guess I would pay any price. Any cost." Sei finished cleaning. "Thank you, my lady. You made me forget for a while." She bowed and bid Mari good night, slipping through her pocket door.

Mari chased after Sei, intent on telling her to run. She rapped once on the door and opened it. A small reed pallet. A lit bamboo lamp. But no Hook Girl. The room was empty. Mari opened her mouth to call out for Sei, but her words were cut off by screams. Mari snapped to attention.

It has already begun.

CHAPTER 38

Taro

TARO WAS THINKING OF MARI—her strong shoulders, the gentle curve of her cheek—when the first scream sounded. It coasted through the revelry, reaching the dais. The music screeched to a halt. Another scream, and Taro shot to his feet. The sound had come from inside the palace. Where Mari had disappeared. More screams, and Taro ran through the fray, knocking over startled courtiers and peasants.

Chaos reigned in the Main Hall. Samurai swarmed the Fall Room, and he followed. A crowd had gathered. He pushed his way through. When no one bowed, Taro realized that they were frozen in shock. Master Ushiba was there, his pale face even paler than usual. The Seasonist's hands twitched, and time moved from evening to breaking daylight, though it was still night in the rest of Honoku.

In the sun's first ray, Taro saw a waxen figure. His swords clattered to the ground. If winter were a feeling, that would be Taro's emotion. Cold. Numb. It was his father.

Everything moved very slowly.

All Taro could hear was his breath rattling in his chest. His father. The emperor. A giant ordained by the gods and goddesses had fallen. Taro struggled to believe it, but there it was. His father was dead. Assassinated. The emperor's neck and abdomen had been sliced open. *Only a monster could have done this.* Fury coursed through Taro. He barked an order at the nearest samurai. "Close the palace. No one comes in or out until every person is questioned. Find who did this!" he commanded.

The samurai swept into a bow. "Yes, Your Majesty."

Nearby, Satoshi quivered. The priest looked as sick as Taro felt. "Satoshi?" Taro asked. The priest moved closer, his face almost white. "Find Mari."

"The empress, Your Majesty?"

The use of the title "empress" didn't register in Taro's mind. He gritted his teeth at the question, at Satoshi's impertinence. "Yes. Until the assassin is found, she will have double the number of guards."

Satoshi bowed. "Yes, Your Majesty. Anything else?"

"Empty this room."

Taro waited for the Fall Room to clear before unleashing his grief. His knees buckled. Wet leaves plastered his clothing. A mist formed in the air, hugging his shoulders. His hands hovered over his father's body.

They would never have the chance to close the distance between them. Anger and grief swirled inside him, a dangerous alchemy. He would find his father's murderer. He would have his revenge. By gods and goddesses, he vowed it.

He passed a rough, shaking hand over his father's eyes and closed them. *His body is just a vessel.* The emperor's spirit was with the gods and goddesses now, seated in a golden throne high above.

Taro stumbled from the Fall Room and into the Main Hall. At the prince's entry, a hush fell. One by one, the samurai, priests, and servants bowed their heads and knelt before Taro. The new the emperor.

The room was suddenly stifling. Taro couldn't breathe. When he reached the double doors of the palace, he wrenched them open and halted at the top of the steps. Thousands of people crowded the courtyard. News of the emperor's demise had spread like wildfire. Mourners had replaced celebrants. A heavy shroud hung over the crowd.

A peasant near the front cried out. "Long live the emperor!" The masses echoed the declaration, stomping their feet and bowing. Taro felt the stranglehold of responsibility wrap its bony fingers around his neck and squeeze. He was their leader.

Long live the emperor.

Taro sought solace in his workroom. He couldn't face Mari — not until he had regained his composure. Here, he would be undisturbed. The dusty counters were lined with metal parts — gears, screws, sheets of copper. Taro cleared them with a single swing of his arm, but it did nothing to calm his anger.

At least he still had Mari. The thought calmed him, kept him from taking his hammer to the windows, lighting a fire, and letting everything burn. Taro hung his head. The sun rose. A new day. How had Taro's life changed so drastically in a matter of moments? A knock sounded at the door, and it slid open.

"Heavenly Sovereign?" Satoshi bowed his head in supplication. "Forgive the intrusion."

Taro sucked in an uneasy breath and wiped his brow. He wasn't used to his new title. "Do you have news?"

"I have much to tell you."

Taro waved the priest inside. "Have you found the traitor?" Taro asked.

Satoshi glanced down as if seeking answers from the floor. "Several servants have come forward. Others have been questioned. A maid recalls seeing a man dressed as a samurai leaving the Fall Room."

Taro's hands balled into fists. "One of our own did this?" An imperial samurai? He could not fathom it.

Satoshi shook his head. "No. We believe it was a disguise. The maid saw him before he replaced his helmet. He has unusual scars that cover half his face. I've put some inquiries forth to my *yōkai* informants. It seems he goes by the name the Son of Nightmares."

Taro scowled.

Satoshi continued. "He's a *yōkai*. My informants are looking more into him."

Taro gripped the edge of his worktable. "What type of *yōkai* is he?"

"Nobody is sure. He's not *oni* or . . ." Satoshi hesitated.

"How can we not know? Every *yōkai* is registered," Taro said through clenched teeth, his fury growing at Satoshi's ineptitude. He, the High Priest, above all others should know this *yōkai*'s location.

"We don't know because he doesn't have a collar."

Taro blinked. "There is an uncollared *yōkai* in the Imperial City?" His father had wanted to post priests at the city walls, but Taro had dissuaded him. *That's a little excessive, don't you think?* he'd said. His father never listened to Taro. Why had he done so then?

"I'm afraid it gets worse. We have reason to believe that there may be more uncollared *yōkai*." Satoshi paused, clearly debating what to say next. "I learned just last night. I didn't want to overburden you on your wedding eve. We've been cleaning the Winter Room, collecting the girls' bodies, restoring the ice on the pond, and we discovered that one of the competitors, Asami, was *yōkai*." Taro waited for Satoshi to continue. "It may mean that more *yōkai* have infiltrated the palace under false pretenses. We should trust no one." Satoshi's eyes met Taro's. "Not even the empress."

Taro took a step forward. "Careful, Satoshi. Your next words may be your last."

Satoshi held up his hands. Cobalt tattoos swirled in Taro's vision. "Please, let me explain. Last night, Mari disappeared from the celebration."

Taro's lip turned up. "And where were you last night, Satoshi? You were gone for a time as well. Perhaps I should be questioning you."

Satoshi's face paled. "I — I would never . . . my father," he stuttered.

"Now you see how it feels to be accused." Taro's eyes settled on Satoshi, impassive and firm. "My father spilled *sake* on her gown. She left to see to the stain and didn't return because she felt unwell." He lied about that last part. Why *hadn't* she returned?

Satoshi met Taro's gaze, jaw tightening. "But nobody else saw her, and then her servant —"

"Her servant what?" Taro couldn't believe what Satoshi was implying. Rage coursed through him at the accusation.

"I think it may be best to hear it from her." Satoshi strode from the room and returned with a small girl, a collar around her neck. A Hook Girl.

"Go on, tell him what you told me."

The girl bowed low. "Forgive me, Your Majesty."

"Stand up. You will look me in the eye when you speak. I will see your face as you betray your empress."

"My lady —"

"Her Majesty," Taro corrected.

The Hook Girl looked to Satoshi, a silent request for permission. He dipped his chin. She went on. "Her Majesty returned last evening near midnight. She seemed unsettled, and we had an unusual conversation."

Taro took a deep breath. "Unusual how?"

"She told me of her mountain village." Taro scoffed. Sei hurried on. "She explained how I might travel there by purchasing a guide. Days ago, she gave me these copper coins. She also said *yōkai* live there uncollared." Sei breathed deep. "She also asked me what price I'd pay to be free."

"And what did you reply?"

"I am a loyal servant." Sei bowed her head. "I told her I was happy in my position." The Hook Girl stopped, unwilling to say anything more. Taro didn't want to hear more anyway.

Satoshi shoved the girl. "Go on, show him the note," he commanded.

The girl let out a cry as the curses on Satoshi's hands burned through her kimono. With trembling hands, the Hook Girl removed a piece of parchment from inside her sleeve. Satoshi snatched it and handed it to Taro. "I found this on her desk," she explained. Taro recognized the stationery he'd gifted to Mari.

The emperor is dead.
Set all yōkai free, or the prince will be next.

Taro nodded, stoic mask in place. Note in hand, he strode from the workroom.

Satoshi chased after Taro. "Your Majesty, where are you going?" he asked.

"To speak to my wife." Taro quickened his pace, leaving Satoshi behind.

Throughout the last three days, it was as if time had ceased. In the Spring Room, when he had watched Mari draw first blood, when she had peered at him under her white wedding hood, when he'd grasped her hand and introduced her to his people as his princess, when he saw his father's body, bruised and broken in the Fall Room . . . But he'd never felt the vertigo of infinity stretching before him as he did now.

The impossible had just become possible. His mind roiled with unanswered questions. How had Mari killed Asami, a powerful, uncollared *yōkai*? Could Mari be a *yōkai* in disguise as well? *No*, Taro thought. He'd been alone with her several times. She had every opportunity to harm him, and she never had. But perhaps that was because she was waiting, biding her time so that she could kill the emperor first. Mari might have betrayed him. He couldn't fathom or stand the thought, and yet his doubt, like an insect, laid eggs and multiplied.

CHAPTER 39

Mari

THE WISTERIA APARTMENT had become a prison. Four samurai guarded her, by order of the emperor. She was not to leave her room.

"And what will you do if I try to leave? Run me through with your sword?"

The samurai's expressions hardened. "Stay in your room, Your Majesty. It's for your own safety," one of them responded.

A new servant brought her a morning and an afternoon meal. She hadn't seen Sei since their shared tea. She tried to question the new servant, but she would not speak. Mari's thoughts became a hurricane of activity. Had the emperor ordered her to be imprisoned? Had he discovered she was *yōkai*? Had Taro?

Frustration grew to anger. *Why hasn't Taro come?* He at least owed her a chance to explain her side of the story, a chance to tell the truth. She swallowed a lump in her throat. Perhaps Taro had already drawn his own conclusions.

The door slid open with a soft whoosh. Mari spun from the window where she was watching samurai pace the perimeter of the black sand garden. Taro entered, a dark, forbidding expression on his face.

She gripped her fists to keep them from trembling. "What's going on? Why are guards posted outside? Why won't they let me leave?"

"They were for your protection," he clipped, a muscle ticking along his jaw.

Her pulse skipped a beat. "My protection?"

"Or perhaps they were for mine," he murmured, laughing sardonically. "My father is dead." He stared at her, studying her reaction.

Mari shook her head. *What?* She couldn't make sense of his words. "How? I'm sorry, Taro."

"Are you?"

He watched her again. Waited. *For what?* "Of course." She crossed to him, tried to place a hand on his shoulder, but he jerked away.

He took her place at the window and looked out, hands linked behind his back. "A *yōkai* dressed as a samurai killed my father. It seems this *yōkai*, this so-called Son of Nightmares, snuck into the palace and killed him in the Fall Room."

Mari's knees locked. *That's not true.* It couldn't be true. Akira had been in the Fall Room, but he'd left before she had. She was sure he'd fled the palace. Sure he was safe, somewhere in the Imperial City. Then again, she thought of Akira, how different, how much *darker* he seemed. *Oh, Akira, what have you done?* Concern for her friend eclipsed her questions. She imagined Akira, sealed in the Winter Room, blood slowly freezing in his veins.

"You've caught him, then?"

Taro shook his head in disgust. "No, it seems he is uncollared and therefore unregistered. But my samurai are combing the city for him now. It won't be long before he is apprehended."

Mari's heart felt as if it were being cut slowly, with a dull knife. "What will you do when you find him?"

"What must be done to all *yōkai*. I will collar him and then put him to death myself."

"You don't mean that," she pleaded.

"Mean that I will execute the *yōkai* who killed my father, avenge his death? I have never meant anything more."

This Taro was a stranger. She did not know him. "You sound so cold."

With a searing glance, he said, "And you sound concerned for a piece of *yōkai* scum. It makes me wonder why."

Now she noticed the dangerous glint in Taro's eyes, the hostility burning just below the surface. She started to back away. "You spoke once of regret for interning the *yōkai*, for making metal collars. Violence only begets more violence. We could stop this war between *yōkai* and humans." *Another way. You promised.*

"That was before my father was murdered by a *yōkai*." *Tell him the truth. Tell him you are* yōkai, *that nobody is all good or all bad.* Taro advanced, forcing Mari to retreat. "There's more to what happened. Would you like to hear it?"

A piece of paper crumpled in Taro's hand. She recognized the color, the calligraphy — her stationery. "What —"

"You killed my father," Taro accused, voice dripping with venom.

Mari shook her head, hair whipping over her shoulder. "No."

Taro scoffed. "Where were you last evening?" He looked at her like she was a stranger, unrecognizable. "Your servant said you returned to your apartment and were in disarray. You seemed upset. She said you spoke of freeing her, a *yōkai*, and of your home where *yōkai* live uncollared." *Sei, what have you done?*

"I was in the Fall Room, but —"

"You admit it, then."

"No. I was alone." She shook her head. The night's events seemed muddled. "I wasn't alone."

"Well, which is it? You were alone or you weren't?"

"My friend . . . my friend . . . I told you I thought I saw someone I knew. I did, and we met in the Fall Room. It was the Son of Nightmares, but his name is Akira. And he isn't capable of doing what you think he did. He wanted me to leave with him, to abandon you, but I couldn't. He called me foolish. He thought you would hate me if you ever found out . . ." She paused.

"Found out what?" Taro's teeth ground together.

The beast moved under her skin. "If you ever found out that I am *yōkai*." Her voice broke. There. She'd said it. And it hurt only a little, seeing Taro flinch. As if a boulder were crushing her chest.

"No!" Taro's roar shook the walls.

Her hands transformed into claws. Taro froze, horror-struck. Mari reached out helplessly, accidentally cutting his cheek with a razor-sharp talon. "No! I'm sorry." Mari gasped.

Taro's hand went to his cheek; blood smeared on his fingertips. The note fell from his grasp. Taro unsheathed his swords, pointing them at Mari's throat. Her eyes grew wide, holding Taro's burning gaze. "You will tell me the truth. Did you plot with the Son of Nightmares to kill my father?"

Hot tears ran down her face. Her claws retracted. "No."

"You are lying. You plotted with him to get the emperor alone, and you killed my father in cold blood. Then you wrote a note boasting about what you had done."

Mari swayed, then plucked the note from the floor. Her gut clenched. She choked out a sob. "This isn't my handwriting. I didn't write this." Taro refused to look at her. *He doesn't believe me. He doesn't want to believe me.* "You ask for the truth, but you refuse to hear it."

"All along, my instinct has been not to trust you. You've kept yourself hidden, and now I see why. Why would I believe you when every word that spills from your mouth is a lie?" The swords dropped from Mari's neck.

Fear burned like an ember in her throat. "Don't do this."

"You have done this to yourself. You've played me for a fool."

"Akira told me the *yōkai* are storming the castle. We have to run. You can't stay here. They're coming for you."

Taro laughed spitefully. "You think I'm a fool?" His face settled into an impassive mask. "The time for explanations has passed. I cannot hear anymore. I loved you so . . ." He couldn't finish. "Guards!" he shouted. Samurai swarmed into the room, swords drawn. "Take the empress," Taro hissed, "to the Winter Room. See that she doesn't escape."

"Please —" Mari tried once more to reach him, to break through his anger. But Taro was immovable, his eyes turned to lifeless stones. Two samurai took hold of Mari's arms, but she shrugged them off. "I will go," she said quietly. She'd never felt such crushing shame. With as much dignity as she could muster, Mari let herself be taken to the Winter Room.

CHAPTER 40
Akira

ROUGH HANDS SHOOK Akira awake. "Hurry," Hanako said. "We don't have much time. Imperial samurai have surrounded the clock tower."

Ren stood behind Hanako, arms crossed over his massive chest, toe talons curling into the floorboards. The room was still and quiet, dark. "Go away," Akira muttered, rolling over.

He'd stumbled back to the clock tower in the dead of night. He could have left the Imperial City, could have made his way home alone. But he couldn't envision the journey without Mari. The clock tower had chimed, and he remembered the promise he'd made to the Snow Girl. What she had said in return. *Our deal is part of the earth. If we break our promise to each other, gods and goddesses help us.* Then, of course, there had been the thought that he could convince Hanako to save Mari. If she were foolish enough to stay. Those were his last thoughts before he drifted off into a deep, dreamless sleep.

"Get up, you lout. This is not a training drill. We have to go.

Those damn geezers ratted us out. They even told the samurai of all my traps. We have no defenses. Our allies have abandoned us."

Akira sat up, awake. "How many?"

Hanako shook her head. "I don't know. I'd say a hundred. Is what they say true? Did you kill the emperor? Is the empress a *yōkai*?"

Akira's heart jostled. Mari had been discovered. She wasn't safe. "The emperor is dead?" he asked. He wiped sleep from his eyes. This wasn't right. He'd passed the emperor on his way out. The man was three sheets to the wind but alive. Jovial, even. "What have you heard?"

Hanako's excitement bubbled over. "It's all over the city. You spoke the truth. Asami wasn't the only *yōkai* entered in the competition. This *yōkai* won. Someone had the same plan as me. Geniuses think alike, you know?"

Akira grew desperate. He grabbed Hanako's shoulders. "What's happened to her?" he demanded.

Hanako's gray eyes widened. "Gods and goddesses, everything makes sense now. She's the reason you came to the Imperial City, isn't she?" Akira let go of Hanako. His hands clenched. "You should have told me what you were up to. It seems we've had the same agenda all along. Why didn't you confide in me?" She grew thoughtful. "If I find out you had something to do with Asami's death, I'll eviscerate you myself."

Akira shook his head and started pacing the length of the room. Nothing made sense. "I didn't kill Asami. I told you the truth. She slipped into the pond. Mari is innocent in her death as well."

"Mari? That's her name? Mari the Emperor Slayer," Hanako said in awe.

Akira's frown deepened. "You revel in someone's death."

Hanako sneered. Her collar glinted in the moonlight, and her ferret curled around her neck. "I revel in the death of a madman who has enslaved our people."

Footsteps pounded on the stairs.

"What will happen to her?" Akira asked again.

Hanako looked solemn. "If the prince is like his father, he probably put her in the Winter Room."

A lump rose in his throat. *Mari has nine lives — she must be alive.* "I have to go after her." He pushed toward the door.

Ren clicked.

Hanako grabbed Akira's arm. "Didn't you hear me say samurai are storming the building?"

Akira hesitated. "I don't suppose you have a hidden escape hatch somewhere."

"I never had the time to install one." Hanako shrugged.

"Then we fight," Akira said, reaching for his throwing stars. He would cut through the samurai, all the way to Mari.

Hanako rolled her eyes. "Don't be ridiculous. One hundred against three? Hardly a fair fight . . . for them, of course."

The footfalls stopped just outside the door. A fist pounded so hard, the walls rattled. "Surrender now, and the emperor will be lenient," a voice boomed.

"And by 'lenient,' he means chopping off our heads instead of slowly torturing us," Hanako whispered, using a see-through hand to draw a line across her throat.

"Surrender!" the voice bellowed. Something rocked the door, a battering ram. Bits of wood splintered from the door frame.

"What do we say to surrender?" Hanako asked Akira.

Ren clicked. Akira blinked once. He had no idea.

"That's right," she said. "*No*, we always say no. Ren, the *ibushi-ki*." She thrust out a hand to the demon. Ren lifted a small ceramic pot with holes drilled along the sides. An acrid smell wafted from it. Akira recognized the scent. Explosive powder. A fuse was placed in one of the holes. Once lit, smoke would fill the room. Akira took a wobbly breath.

Large shifted on Hanako's neck. Something was clamped between his teeth — a length of fireworks wrapped in white paper. The ferret scampered down Hanako's body. Ren struck a match against his teeth and lit the firecrackers' and the smoke pot's fuses. Hanako shattered the glass of the clock with her elbow.

The battering ram wracked the door again. This time the wood splintered. Ren slid the smoke bomb to the middle of the room. The ferret squeezed under the door, firecrackers trailing behind him. Akira watched all of this in a daze. All he knew was that he wanted to fight, not just for Mari, but for Hanako, for Ren. His friends.

Hanako grabbed two ropes that dangled just outside the window. "My original escape plan was just for two. We're going to have to make do!" she yelled. Smoke began to fill the room. A loud popping noise sounded outside the door.

Ren clutched one of the ropes, and Hanako leaped onto his back. "I hope this holds us, big guy. Tell me you put the spikes in deep."

Ren clicked.

It could just as easily have been a no as a yes.

"What about Large?" Akira asked, snatching up the other rope.

Hanako winked. "He'll be fine. He's been training his whole life for this."

The battering ram rocked the door again, this time boring a hole. A samurai reached through the opening and unlocked the door. "On the count of three," Hanako said just as samurai burst through the door, swords drawn. "Oh, screw it, go! Just go!" She slapped Ren's massive shoulder.

They jumped. Akira held his breath. Buildings and houses zipped by in a dark gray blur. Akira yelled as the rope snapped to an end, slamming him into the clock tower's brick wall, nearly dislodging his shoulder from the socket. The streets below were empty, save for a few samurai. Most of the contingency had forced their way into the clock tower. Hanako and Ren landed in a similar fashion, bodies smacking against brick.

Hanako's see-through skin practically glowed in the dark. The Snow Girl hugged Ren's neck tightly. "The rope is holding! If I didn't like girls, and you didn't like eating seagulls, I would kiss you."

They rappelled the rest of the way down. As soon as their feet hit the cobblestones, Akira drew his throwing stars, confident he'd be able to defeat the few samurai on the street. A blur of white scampered by: Large, escaping into the gutters.

A dozen priests materialized out of the darkness.

Hanako frowned. "That's not good."

The priests began chanting. Curses thickened the air. The taste of burnt cinnamon coated Akira's tongue. It felt as if invisible hands were at his throat, suffocating him. Hanako and Ren were on the ground, writhing in pain, their skin smoking, their souls flickering. The circle of priests closed in, bearing shackles and chains.

A priest with a graying beard crouched beside Ren. The demon growled and flashed a fang. The priest laughed as he fastened manacles around Ren's wrist and ankles. Then the priest bound the manacles together with the length of chain, tying him up.

The priests chanted louder, faster. The soft tissue in Akira's esophagus felt as if it were on fire. He opened his mouth, and smoke seeped into the air. He was burning from the inside.

The priest with the graying beard advanced on Akira. Cold steel caressed his skin, a manacle looping around his wrist. *What do we say to surrender?* Something roared to life inside him. Like gunpowder touched by a match, Akira exploded. "Noooooo!" His roar echoed through the barren streets.

A window shattered. A flock of frightened gulls took to the sky. For one crystalline second, the priests stopped chanting. It was enough time.

Akira lifted his body, executing a roundhouse kick. He heard a sickening crack, the sound of the priest's jaw breaking. Akira's throat ached and burned, but breath passed into his lungs. Nursing his broken jaw, the priest with the gray beard was no longer a threat. Akira did a quick count. *One down. Eleven to go.* He plucked a star from his belt. He had only five of the precious weapons. *Each throw must count.*

The priests resumed the chanting. Their voices swelled to a crescendo and echoed through the streets. Flashes of movement caught Akira's eye. The streets were not as empty as he had believed. He felt his skin grow tight with anger. Agonizing whimpers filled the streets. He needed to shut the priests up. Through his haze, Akira realized that the curses did not affect him as they did other *yōkai. It is because of my blood. I am half human.* The curses burned, but they didn't completely incapacitate. The throwing star warmed in his hand. He bent his elbow back and let the star flow from his fingers in a calculated arc. It grazed a priest's throat and then another and another, until four priests were clutching their necks, red oozing between their fingers. He knew the minute their hearts stopped. Their souls flashed, then extinguished. Like the blink of an eye.

Akira withdrew another star, ready to launch. But he paused. The remaining priests, faces stricken, turned and ran. *Run, cowards. Run.*

He held his breath as he retrieved the star from its mark, then knelt by Hanako, his hands fumbling with the cuffs on her wrists. Footsteps clattered as samurai erupted from the clock tower.

Ren clicked.

"He's right. You don't have time," Hanako said in a rough voice.

The samurai descended.

The *yōkai* in the street stood, eyes wide, uncertain about what they had witnessed. A *yōkai* resisting curses? Unheard of.

"Akira, you must go," Hanako said more forcefully. How many times had Akira run in his life? Fled in fear? Or because he'd been told to? No more. Hanako could have left him in the clock tower. But she'd risked her life to save him. Akira stepped over Ren and Hanako's bodies so that he was a barrier between them and the samurai. An impenetrable wall. *One against one hundred? Hardly seems fair.* Akira smiled. *For them.*

Something brushed against his left shoulder. An *oni* stood next to him. Then a geezer flanked Akira's right side. More *yōkai* shuffled over, filling the street. Their hands fisted, ready for battle.

The samurai formed single-file lines. With a whoosh, their

swords were drawn. The priests had fled, which meant no more curses; the samurai were on their own. But the *yōkai* were collared, their strength reduced to that of mere humans.

Now, this seems fair.

Akira beckoned the samurai forward, a wicked gleam in his eye.

CHAPTER 41

Taro

TARO'S HANDS WERE COATED in grease. Sweat trickled down his forehead and cheeks. His eyes were dry and bloodshot. He turned the geared heart with his fingers, then let it drop to the table with a helpless *thunk*. It was mangled. Disfigured. It seemed that in grief, Taro could not bring anything to life.

Sleep eluded him. How could Mari have done this? Her deception clawed at his soul. How could he have been so wrong about her? Had he been that desperate to be loved, to love, that he had fooled himself? The thought made him feel angry, humiliated. And still he didn't want to believe it.

Taro hadn't left the workroom since Mari's capture. Now he glanced out the window and saw the moon hanging low in the sky. The clock-tower raid should be over soon. He had wanted to go and see the Son of Nightmares brought to his knees, but Satoshi and his *shōgun* convinced him to stay. "It is much too risky, Heavenly Sovereign. Let us catch him. We will bring him back to the palace, and you may do as you see fit," the head military commander had said.

A quiet knock interrupted Taro's thoughts. Satoshi stepped into the room, hands resting in the folds of his white robes.

"You bring good news, I hope," Taro barked.

"Good and bad, Your Majesty." Satoshi bowed.

"I'll take the bad first," Taro said.

Satoshi's mouth lifted in a thin smile. "Just like our father."

Before the emperor's death, Taro would have scoffed at being compared to him. But now . . . Taro had so many regrets.

Taro saw Satoshi's face change, and he cursed himself for his insensitivity over the last several hours. "You've lost a father as well." His half brother was his only blood relative left.

Dots of red blotted Satoshi's cheeks. "I guess we are both orphans now," Satoshi said.

Taro was just a boy when Satoshi's mother hanged herself from the imperial gate. Satoshi had discovered her body.

"The bad news it is," Satoshi said, his voice hoarse. "Unfortunately, the Son of Nightmares has eluded capture, Your Majesty. The priests who returned reported that he was immune to their curses." Satoshi's words were soft, but Taro heard them as if they had been shouted from atop a mountain. His father's murderer was still free.

"So what's the good news, then?" Taro asked.

Satoshi smiled. "The good news is that the revolt has been stamped out. The *yōkai* who took up arms against the imperial samurai will be punished and made examples of."

Taro nodded. *So many lives will be lost.* It was the Son of Nightmares' fault. When Taro caught him, he would make him see the pain he had caused others. *Look at how many of your brethren you've killed. It is your fault. Do not try to rise past the stair on which you are born.* If everyone stayed in their place, there could be peace. Just as his father had always said.

Satoshi continued. "We have also retrieved the Son of Nightmares' conspirators, a Snow Girl and an *oni* demon."

"That is good news how?" Taro grunted.

"We have reason to believe that he'll try to rescue them, and the empress . . ." Satoshi trailed off.

Taro's jaw tightened at the mention of Mari. Would the Son of Nightmares come for Mari? "Let him come, then."

Satoshi grinned. "I was hoping you would say that. I've laid a trap for him in the Main Hall."

Outside the window, the moon inched lower on the horizon. Dawn would come soon. Taro cursed the new day. No sunlight would wash away the bitterness of betrayal. He wished for eternal night, something to match his black soul. Despite Satoshi's plan, Taro felt weary. He flicked his hand. "Good work, Satoshi. You may go."

Satoshi took his leave, and Taro turned back to his metal heart. *What a waste.* He tossed it off to the side. He closed his eyes and breathed deeply. He'd never let another *yōkai* hurt him again. Mari's face appeared before him, and his throat constricted. *To love is to suffocate.* Mari should be made to know what that felt like.

CHAPTER 42

Mari

THE GROAN OF the wooden doors jolted Mari from her slumber. With her claws, she'd dug an ice cave in the Winter Room. Outside her cold home, she heard something click and then a voice like a tinkling bell. "I suppose we *have* been in worse situations. I just wish I had worn my fur kimono. I remember before I was collared, I couldn't even feel the cold. But now it's as if I'm human. Terrible."

Mari scrambled to sit up. Poking her head out of the entrance of her cave, in the full moon's light she saw a girl with ash-colored hair and see-through skin standing next to an *oni*.

Their eyes met, each measuring the other.

The girl's face broke into a huge smile. "Your Majesty!" She trudged forward, kicking up snow and ice. Then she bowed with a flourish. "The news of a *yōkai* empress has traveled through Tokkaido and beyond. It is an honor to meet you."

Mari's gaze fixed on the *oni* as she pulled herself up.

"Uh-oh," said the girl, eyes wide. "I don't think she likes you, Ren."

She positioned herself between Mari and the demon. "I am Hanako, Snow Girl, Weapons Master, and *yōkai* Revolutionist. And this is my lifelong companion, Ren. He means you no harm." The demon held up his massive hands in submission and swept into a low bow. Tufts of air curled from his nostrils like dragon smoke. Mari retracted her claws. The Snow Girl and demon watched Mari in rapt silence. *What do they want?* She couldn't find the will to speak. So quietly, deliberately, she crawled back into her ice cave.

Mari closed her eyes as the Snow Girl invaded her hut. The space inside the cave was tight, with barely enough room for one. Still, the Snow Girl managed to wiggle in and sit next to Mari. She stretched her legs out in front of her, crossing them at the ankles. "Well, this is cozy. You know, I grew up in a cave just like this one. Ours was a little roomier, a little homier. Maybe if you hung some pictures . . ." Hanako trailed off.

How could she be so cavalier? At the opening of the cave, Mari saw the *oni*'s ankles pacing, bare feet sunk into the snow. "Whatever it is you expect of me, you will be disappointed," Mari said. *I'm not the one you are looking for. My life does not serve a greater good.*

The Snow Girl looked down at her interlaced fingers. "And what if I only expect you to listen?"

Mari drew her legs in to her chest, laid her cheek against her knees. She was frozen, inside and out.

Hanako shifted, crossing and uncrossing her legs, adjusting her kimono. "When the emperor mounted his campaign against the *yōkai*, he targeted what he perceived to be the most dangerous first — *oni*, *nure-onago*, *hari-onago*, and *yuki-onna* — Snow Girls like me." She gave a wry smile. "Before my collar, I was really something. One breath, and I could freeze the blood of a grown man. Two breaths, and I could make it snow. Three breaths, and I could transform oceans into ice." Her smile faded. "I was four when the priests infiltrated the mountain pass where I lived with my mother. She saw them coming and hid me in a snowdrift behind a grove of trees. She told me to stay put, close my eyes, and wait for her to call. I can't remember much after that, but they must have come and gone. Night fell, and everything was silent, then morning, and still nothing." She glanced at Mari. "It's funny the stuff you do remember, you know? I remember my aching legs as I left my hiding place, and I remember the smell of pine trees. I found a few samurai and one priest — all frozen like icicles. But my mother was nowhere. I stayed in the mountain pass for days, waiting for her to come back." Hanako's eyes went soft and distant. "She never did. I don't know what happened to her. After many days on my own, the squish of softening snow underfoot awoke me." Hanako paused.

Mari's curiosity was piqued. For a moment, she forgot about her imprisonment. "Who was it?"

Hanako licked her lips, clearly pleased with her captive audience. "This is the best part. The winter snows had just begun to melt. That morning, I spied the first bud of a leaf on a tree. There were three children in the mountain pass — two boys and one girl, all with shaved heads and brown robes."

"The Taiji monks," Mari whispered. Nobody really knew the origin of the monks locked eternally in childhood, whether they were *yōkai* or human or divine. Tami had said that they were the children who "could have been but never were." They adopted orphans and lived in a monastery on the highest peak of the Tsuko funo Mountains. Mari often dreamed that the boys from Tsuma ended up there.

Hanako's smile was wistful. "I didn't know who they were at first. My mother never told me about outsiders. We were secluded." Her expression pinched. "That is how the emperor keeps such a tight rein on *yōkai* — he separates us, pits us against one another. Many of our species believe *oni* are all evil, but they're not."

Outside the cave, Ren grunted his agreement.

Hanako shook her head and crossed her arms. "Anyway, the monks had come for me. I looked at their scratchy robes and pink cheeks. And in that moment, I knew with certainty my life would change. But I was scared. When one reached for me, I darted away. But they stayed. Finally, one approached me as if I were a wild creature, with his hand out and a tentative step. He said eight words. Eight words that I've carried with me to this day so that I may give them to you."

"What did he say?" Mari asked.

"Do not let your fear decide your fate."

They went quiet for a moment. "What is it you want from me?" Mari asked.

"You are the Conqueror of the Seasons. The Cold Prince may have stripped you of your pretty gowns, the ribbons in your hair, even his love, but he has not taken everything from you. Already our people whisper about the *yōkai* empress chosen by the gods and goddesses. They have prayed for a champion, and a champion has been delivered."

"Their prayers are wasted. I'm no hero." Mari slunk back down.

"So, what? You'll wait here for the Cold Prince to deliver his final judgment? To collar you or let you freeze? He may put you to death, but it is you who are signing your own warrant." Hanako began to scoot from the cave. She paused, face twisted toward Mari. "This is not what Akira would want for you. It is not what you should want for yourself." She quieted. "And it is not why Asami sacrificed her life."

Mari's heart swelled and broke all at once. "You know Akira? And Asami?"

"Know Akira? Who do you think taught him to use those throwing stars?" the Snow Girl exclaimed. She smiled. "We are like steel to a blade, he and I. He told me all about you. But I can see he was wrong. As for Asami, she was part of the *yōkai* Resistance." The Snow Girl's expression flickered with pain. "I could have loved her in another life. But I wasn't born to love. I was born to maim and kill, to fell an empire."

Mari's hands curled into her kimono, and she turned her face toward the Snow Girl.

"Do not cling to the hand that holds you down," Hanako whispered, and scooted from the cave. "Let it go."

Slowly, Mari crawled from the cave. A few feet away, Hanako and Ren huddled together, teeth chattering, the demon's arms wrapped around the Snow Girl. Mari shuffled over. Heavy snow fell. How much longer would she survive in the Winter Room? *A day, maybe two?*

"Even if I did want to help," Mari said as she reached them, "we're still stuck in here."

A smile spread across Hanako's face. "I am the best assassin ever to be trained by the Taiji monks."

Ren clicked and rolled his eyes.

"It's not bragging if it's the truth." Hanako removed something from beneath her kimono. Between her slender fingers, Hanako held a book of matches. She shivered dramatically. "I am so very cold. A fire sounds nice, don't you think? I say we find something to burn."

All three of them turned toward the Winter Room doors.

CHAPTER 43
Akira

WITH THE SUPPORT of the *yōkai* at his back, Akira felt invincible. But he wasn't. And neither were the *yōkai*. When it was over, there had been so many bodies strewn about, poppies plucked from the ground and left to wilt.

Several of Akira's ribs were broken, a back tooth was missing, and there was a gash on his thigh. But he had escaped. Akira bound his ribs and closed the cut with sticky paste from a tree.

He didn't allow himself a moment of rest. Instead, he went to the palace.

With the death of the emperor and the Revolution afoot, the palace was near impenetrable. The sewer grate Akira had used to access the tunnels was now guarded. Akira perched high in a cypress tree and watched the stoic samurai.

The man hadn't moved an inch in over an hour. The tunnels were no longer an option. So Akira counted the guards and watched their patrols, noting the timing of their switching posts: every thirty-two minutes. This left some sections unguarded for sixty seconds. Not very long. But enough.

Akira patted the weapons concealed under his clothing. Peering down from the tree, he inhaled deeply, the smell of sap and cedar filling his nostrils. Carefully, he strapped the *tekko-kagi* he had salvaged from the clock tower to the backs of his hands. The iron spikes of the climbing claws curved over his fingers with bands that wrapped around his palms. He waited, trying not to let fear overcome him. *I am unstoppable. I am a force of nature.* That said, he began his assault.

Akira leaped from the cypress tree onto a willow branch, then onto another tree. The north wall, the one that backed the priests' quarters, came into view. Two samurai marched past. If he couldn't go underground, he'd go over. He preferred heights anyway. Inching along a sturdy maple-tree branch, Akira jumped onto the north wall, dodging the spikes jutting from the top of it. One heartbeat, and he hopped from the wall, rolling into a cluster of overgrown shrubs. He listened. Silence.

Akira crept through the weeds and thorny bushes, using them for concealment. The back walls of the priests' quarters rose up ahead. The guards weren't as heavy in this section. No doubt, the priests with their curses didn't need the extra security.

"We had a deal." A soft, meek voice reached Akira. The accusation piqued his interest. This was a private conversation. Akira crept along the wall until he came to an open window. Ever so slightly, he turned his head, risking a glance inside the room. The apartment was sparse. The only furniture was a platform bed and small writing desk. Inside was a priest — the High Priest, Satoshi. And a girl. Not just any girl, but Mari's servant.

"How did you get in here?" Satoshi asked. Carefully, the priest's gaze roamed the dim room. Akira jolted back, pressing his body against the wall. His heart beat double-time.

The Hook Girl spoke, defiant. "It wasn't hard. Samurai are looking for uncollared *yōkai*. They couldn't give two spits about us collared servants. We had a deal. You promised to remove my collar if I supplied you with information about Mari. I brought you her stationery. I lied to the emperor. I've done everything you asked." Fury rose in Akira as fierce and unforgiving as a bolt of lightning. Sei huffed out a breath. "What has happened to my mistress? What have you done with her?"

"Careful of your tone, Hook Girl," the priest warned.

"Where is Mari? Tell me now, or I'll march straight to the emperor and tell him everything."

"The emperor won't listen to you. I am the only voice he hears."

"I've done what you wanted. I've upheld my end of the bargain. It is time for you to uphold yours. The skin under my collar itches. I am ready for the metal to be removed," Sei demanded.

"Haughty creature." Satoshi laughed, low and malicious. Akira risked another glance. The priest's back was to him. In his hand, he held a *tantō* knife. He turned it over, and the knife caught in the lantern light.

The girl's eyes widened.

Satoshi's laughter faded, leaving just the wicked smile. "Do you know who my mother was?" he asked.

The Hook Girl shook her head, eyes wild.

"Once, she was a beacon of beauty and grace. Supposedly, the goddess Kita blessed her with cheeks the color of a red rose, hair the softness of spun silk, and a voice like the sound of a nightingale. She was raised to be an imperial concubine. But her favors were not wanted at court." Satoshi leveled Sei with his gaze. "The emperor had an empress he loved deeply.

"Then the empress died. And my mother was summoned to the emperor's bedchamber. For years, she was the emperor's favorite concubine. When I was born, His Majesty was the first to hold me, blessing me with the name he chose — Satoshi. Soon after, the emperor's affections waned. My mother spent more and more time laid up in bed. The theorists prescribed lavender oil for her melancholy. It didn't work." Satoshi ran a thumb along the *tantō* knife's blade.

"Sorrow can become a sickness," Sei said. Akira saw the Hook Girl shift, almost imperceptibly, to the right.

Satoshi nodded, considering. "Yes. So can hope." Satoshi advanced, his voice changed. "Did you actually think I would remove your collar? I knew you were stupid, but not this stupid."

The slave darted, but Satoshi caught her arm in a vicious grip. The tattoos on his hands burned through Sei's kimono, melting her skin. Akira nearly gagged at the scent of burning flesh. "Please!" she cried. "Let me go. I'll never tell anyone."

"You know I can't do that, Hook Girl. You're a loose end. And you know what happens to loose ends?" He clutched the *tantō* knife. "They must be cut off." He plunged the blade into Sei's stomach.

Her body buckled, and Satoshi let her crumple to the ground. Akira watched as blood pooled at the priest's feet.

He crouched next to her. Her eyes flickered; a single tear slipped down her cheek. Satoshi paused. He was savoring this *yōkai*'s death. "To answer your earlier question, your mistress is in the Winter Room. If she is not dead, she will be soon. She's been useful. Did you know she was *yōkai*?" The Hook Girl coughed, blood and spittle leaking from the corner of her mouth. "Ah, I can tell you didn't. I knew after the Fall Room. I am the one who should rule. Taro never wanted to be Emperor anyway. And soon I'll do him the same favor I did my father. I will steal the breath from his —" Satoshi stopped abruptly.

The girl's eyes were open, still and unseeing. Dead. The priest sighed. He bent down and smeared more of her blood on his robes. He sliced his hand so that it bled and mussed his hair. Then he ran from the room, face fixed in terror. Outside, Akira could hear him shout. "Help!" he cried. "A *yōkai* attacked me!" His hands went to his knees as he gasped for breath. "She had a knife and cut me. I managed to take it from her and turn it against her. Please," he said. "You must go. I don't know if I killed her."

Thundering steps ensued as samurai stormed the apartment. *Time to go.* Akira scaled the wall and pulled himself onto the roof. The slant hid him from view. He crept along the tiles, taking the same path as he had before. But instead of alighting from the temple roof, he kept going. Five minutes, and Akira was at the main palace garden, where he'd first glimpsed Mari as Princess. Again, he hid in a tree, a twisted pine. Below, two samurai guards lingered. He dropped from his perch. The guards swiveled, drawing swords. In an instant, Akira had one in a chokehold, swiftly cutting off his air supply. Just as the samurai lost consciousness, the other opened his mouth to shout the alarm. A kick to the gut silenced him. Both samurai lay in clumps at his feet.

Akira canvassed the open space ahead of him, charting a path. Then he cut through the grounds, ducking behind rocks and tall trees, narrowly avoiding samurai carrying lamps. Akira crouched behind a boulder near the great steps of the palace. Tension stilled the air as if every living thing were holding its breath. No flutter or buzz from insects. *Too quiet.* The hairs at the base of Akira's neck prickled.

The massive palace doors were open to the Main Hall, lights blazing inside, cozy and welcoming. *Something is wrong.* It all seemed too easy. Down the long hallway, he spotted the Winter Room doors. Hopefully, Hanako and Ren were in there with Mari.

His hands flexed, covered by the iron bands of the claws. *Now or never. Do or die.* He broke from his hiding spot and sprinted up the stairs.

In the Main Hall, Akira froze. His mind raced, confused. The hall was empty, as quiet as freshly fallen snow.

They materialized from the shadows.

They came out from behind banners, from the balconies, and the rafters. They emerged from the darkened gardens. Dressed in navy with hoods and masks, they blended into the night, into the dark. Like Akira, they were moving shadows in human form. He remembered stories of warriors who drank the blood of the crow to absorb its power.

Ninja.

One broke formation, *nunchaku* spinning in his hands. The ninja didn't pause for Akira to ready himself as honor dictated. He came at Akira with all the might of a boulder hurtling down a cliff. Akira ducked and rolled, barely avoiding the attacker.

Akira's chest grew tight, and his limbs shook. The ninja loomed above him, the sticks and chain spinning in a deadly arc, ready to swing and bash his head in. Desperate, Akira swiped with the metal claws.

The ninja stiffened as the iron ripped through his thigh. Blood soaked the front of his pants, darkening the navy hue. The ninja paused briefly, then set the *nunchaku* spinning again. A determined glint shone in his eyes, the only part of his face that was visible behind his mask.

The ninja raised the *nunchaku* above his head. Akira rolled, but more ninja blocked his path. They swarmed around him like bees. The Son of Nightmares closed his eyes. The flash of the sticks imprinted on the backs of his lids.

He waited for the blow, to feel the sticks strike his temples, render him unconscious. The smell of smoke curled up his nose. Then came bright light. Akira scrambled from the distracted ninja just as the Winter Room exploded.

CHAPTER 44
Mari

MARI VOLUNTEERED HER *JUBAN* as kindling. Her white undergarments were the only piece of dry material in the Winter Room.

Hanako bundled them near the doors. She struck the match twice before it blazed, the scent of sulfur exploding with it. Ren and Mari cupped their hands to guard the small flame as Hanako lowered it to the kindling. The cloth began to smolder and smoke.

"How long do you think it will take?" Mari asked.

Hanako lifted a delicate shoulder. "An hour at least. But as soon as the doors light and there is the smallest opening, we need to push through and run."

That was the extent of their plan. No one mentioned what they might find outside — samurai, priests, certain death. They would escape, or die trying. If they could not control their impending doom, then they would its timing. *There is always a choice,* Akira had said. Mari winced. Where was Akira? Was he safe?

Ren sniffed and clicked.

Hanako breathed in deeply. "No, I don't smell anything." She inhaled again. "Uh-oh. Do you know if these doors were painted recently?"

Mari shook her head. "No. Why?"

"It looks like our timeline has accelerated." Just as Hanako uttered the words, the doors exploded. Splinters of wood shot out with the crimson flames. Heat singed Mari's cheeks. She crouched, hands covering her head. Ren leaped, placing his massive body over Mari's, shielding her from the back draft.

Fire, dust, and snow rained down.

The last piece of the door fell, and Ren helped Mari to her feet. She coughed, expelling smoke from her lungs. "Thank you," she rasped. The *oni* patted Mari's back with his massive paw. "Where's Han—" Mari didn't need to finish her question. Ninja lined the Main Hall, and Hanako had already raced into the fray. Her kimono swished as she kicked and struck at navy-clad warriors, disabling one after another. The flames reflected off her see-through skin.

Hanako snapped up the swords of the fallen and tossed them to Ren and Mari. They couldn't be much different than a *naginata*.

"I counted twenty, but there might be more," Hanako panted.

Ren grunted, whipping his sword back and forth.

The fire was spreading down the Main Hall, leaping onto the red banners, eating the golden wallpaper as it climbed. Some of the rafters were already smoldering.

Ninja assaulted from all angles. "Like swatting flies," Hanako called out.

Ren lacked skill with a sword, but his colossal strength made up for it as he batted ninja away with single swipes of his meaty arms.

A whirl of navy caught Mari's eye. A ninja hurtled toward her. Mari brought her *katana* up, blocking the blow. Using her sword as leverage, Mari pushed the ninja back. With a low roundhouse kick, she clipped his knees. The ninja stumbled. Then in one swift move, she plunged the *katana* into his side. Not a killing blow, but a disabling one. The ninja would live to fight again, just not in this battle. This battle belonged to the *yōkai*. Mari felt it in her blood, in her bones.

A flicker near the doors caught Mari's eye. A figure clad in black was fighting off ninja.

"Akira!" Mari screamed. He had come. Their eyes connected across the struggle. The air whistled. Arrows rained down, piercing the wooden floor. Ninja with bows and arrows had gathered in the rafters.

One took aim at Akira, whose movements were a blur as he launched throwing stars. Ninja toppled like felled trees. Ren, Hanako, and Mari sprinted to the palace doors, driving swords into ninja as they went.

Escape was within reach.

They joined Akira, forming a circle with their backs turned toward one another, ready to fend off the remaining ninja. The hall buckled and hissed, a serpent on fire.

"Ruuun!" Hanako shouted.

Thousands of samurai were storming the main garden. Alarm bells trilled. A fire like this could spread, jump from rooftop to rooftop, and decimate the city. Mari paused, ready to defend herself, but the samurai raced past her. They weren't armed. Instead, they carried wooden buckets sloshing with water.

Mari didn't question their good fortune. She caught Hanako's eye, then Ren's, and finally Akira's. A silent agreement, and they bolted into the night.

Mari broke into a coughing fit. Blood and soot covered her arms. They stood by the north wall of the palace. Thick smoke billowed into the night sky.

"The whole city will be looking for us," Akira said between deep breaths. "It isn't safe here."

Ren clicked and cleaned blood from one of his horns.

"I agree with Ren. We should go to the West Lands. I have friends there," Hanako said. "We'll find sanctuary."

"Sei," Mari wheezed. "My servant. We have to go back for her." Mari turned, ready to climb the north wall. A hand wrapped around her arm. Akira's.

"The Hook Girl?" he asked.

Mari's eyes drew wide. "Yes. I can't leave her behind."

Akira's eyes shone bright in the darkness. "She betrayed you. She brought the priest your stationery. She helped frame you for the emperor's murder. Satoshi is the one who killed the emperor."

Mari's heart faltered. She remembered her conversation with Sei. *What price would you pay for freedom?* Sei had replied: *Any cost.* Sei's betrayal wounded Mari's spirit, but she understood. Desperate people do desperate things. "It doesn't matter. She's —"

314

"Dead," Akira ground out. "The priest killed her, stabbed her with a *tantō* knife."

The news buckled Mari's knees. "No." Her temples pounded as the word echoed through the night.

Akira reached for her but drew back. "It's true. I saw it myself. Satoshi wishes to be Emperor. He killed Sei, and he used you as a pawn."

Mari looked to the jagged silhouette of the Tsuko funo Mountains. Understanding dawned, fast and unforgiving. "I told Sei where my village is." She blinked, and images flashed before her eyes — Tsuma under attack, Animal Wives collared, the mountain burning. "Gods and goddesses, I've put everyone I love in danger."

Akira regarded Hanako. "Mari's village is in the mountains. My parents are there too, just outside. We have to tell them that the emperor's army is coming, give them a chance to flee."

"I understand," Hanako said. "And of course, we'll go there first. We'll give your parents the chance that was never given to my mother."

Mari bowed her head in her hands. If what Akira said was true, Taro's life was in danger. After all he'd done, still she wanted to save him.

"Mari?" Akira reached for her. "We have to go."

Mari looked up and into the eyes of the Son of Nightmares. Behind him, the palace burned, blurring the lines of her vision. "Okay," she said, wiping at her eyes. Was she crying? No, her eyes stung from the heat and debris; that was all. "We'll go home." She shoved past Hanako and Ren, and she let Taro go.

CHAPTER 45

Taro

STREAKS OF PURPLE parted the orange sky. Taro wandered amid the rubble of what was once the Main Hall. The Spring Room, the Winter Room, the Summer Room, and the Fall Room, all gone, burned down by Mari and her band of rebel *yōkai*.

He'd been too late to do anything except stand by helplessly, watch the Main Hall crumple like paper in an iron fist. The fire finally extinguished at dawn. As Taro walked, Master Ushiba's cries drifted on the wind, his life's work decimated. Snow, cherry blossoms, and dry leaves swirled in the air, the last remnants of the Seasonal Rooms. Taro counted the burnt ninja skeletons.

Samurai reported seeing the Snow Girl, the *oni*, the Son of Nightmares, and the empress fleeing the palace.

Satoshi stood behind him, rattling off his report. "It seems that the *yōkai* believe Mari to be some sort of savior. A *yōkai* empress. I have priests and samurai ready to canvass the city at your command. It is imperative that she be recaptured. We cannot —"

Taro cut Satoshi off. "They're not in the city anymore."

"We can't possibly know that."

Taro looked sternly at Satoshi. "The servant, the Hook Girl, what did she say about the empress's village?" He couldn't bring himself to say Mari's name.

"The mountains, Your Majesty. I believe south of the monastery, near the broken-topped ridge, a few days' ride from Hana Machi."

Taro felt something twist in his gut. Instinct. "That's where they'll go."

"You think they'll go to her village?"

"She's on the run now. Where do you go when you want to feel safe?" Taro took in the shell of the palace. "You go home. Prepare the horses and five hundred samurai. We leave at dusk."

Satoshi bowed. "As you wish." He vanished in a swirl of white robes and ash.

Taro crouched and scooped up a handful of the palace remains, then flung it into the air, dust in the wind. Hate burned his insides. Taro would track Mari to the mountains. He would find her village. He would locate her home. Then he would make her watch as he burned it to the ground. It would be a day all *yōkai* would remember with fear in their hearts.

A niggling voice in the back of Taro's mind said something else. He wasn't ready to kill the woman he loved. He might never be ready. But he wanted her to feel what he felt. *Punish her.*

CHAPTER 46

Mari

IT WAS NIGHT in Hana Machi, the pleasure city. Travel-weary and numb, Mari stumbled through narrow alleyways that stank of sweet grass and spilled *sake*. Scattered rose-colored gas lamps lit the way.

Hanako led the group. "I think it's just around this corner." It was the fourth time she'd said it. "I haven't been in Hana Machi in so many years," Hanako said, a concerned crease lining her brow. Ren grunted. Mari couldn't help but look at Akira. They'd barely spoken on their journey.

Laughter echoed in the dank alley. Ren clicked. He seemed agitated.

Hanako rushed forward. "Here it is! I remember this scrollwork." Just above a pink painted door, an intricate berry vine was carved into the stone. It was a brothel. Hanako rapped on the wood. Almost instantly, the door opened a crack, emitting the musky smell of incense. "No more customers today."

Hanako stuck her foot in the door and leaned down, addressing a small woman with whiskers on her chin. "Tell Madame Shizu her long-lost daughter has come to pay a visit." The woman huffed and slammed the door. Hanako smiled. "She'll be just a minute. When she answers the door, try not to stare at her neck. She's sensitive about it."

The door swung open. Lamps blazed, casting a very tall woman in dark silhouette. The woman's height came not from her legs or torso but from her neck, which stretched nearly three feet. Between the folds of her heavy silk kimono, Mari spied a collar. The woman looked down her nose at Hanako, her neck twisting with snake-like elegance.

"Hanako, to what do I owe the pleasure?" The woman's voice was low and smoky.

"Oyotsu." Hanako bowed. "My friends and I require a place to stay and supplies for a journey through the mountains."

Oyotsu clucked her tongue and crossed her arms. "You still owe me money for two nights' lodging. And the last time I allowed you to stay, you taught my girls how to put a man to sleep by pressing on his jugular. What makes you think I would do anything for you?"

Hanako shrugged a delicate shoulder and rocked on her heels. "They wanted to learn, and I am, above all things, a teacher."

Oyotsu flicked her hand. "Yes, yes, *Weapons Master*. What makes you think I would do anything for you?" she repeated.

"I don't expect you to do anything for me, Oyotsu. But I thought you would be happy to serve the empress." At that, Hanako stepped aside to reveal Mari.

"Your Majesty!" Oyotsu breathed in and stooped in a bow.

Mari's eyes widened. Hanako had said that rumors of a *yōkai* empress had spread, but as far as Hana Machi? Apparently so, judging by the look on Oyotsu's face. Hanako jabbed Mari with her elbow. "Act majestic," she whispered.

Mari stepped forward, hands outstretched. "Please."

Oyotsu grasped Mari's hands and stood at full height. Mari peered up at the striking woman. "It is an honor to have you at my doorstep," Oyotsu said. "Your likeness was explained to me, but they didn't do justice to your beauty."

Mari nearly winced at the platitude. *Thank you, but I fear your eyesight may need adjusting.* "And would it be an equal honor to host us for the night? I don't wish to put you out, but we are in need of shelter."

"Of course, of course!" Oyotsu opened the door wide, sweeping them inside. "Come in."

Jewel-toned pillows made of silk were laid out on the floor, alongside low tables displaying potted orchids. Incense burned along the walls, giving the room a hazy air. Curtained alcoves lurked in the corners.

Still covered in ash and blood, Mari felt dirty amid so much beauty and finery. Hanako made herself at home, falling onto one of the cushions. "I haven't felt silk on my skin in ages," she said, rubbing her smudged cheek against a peacock-blue pillow. Oyotsu clapped her hands, and the woman with whiskers on her chin appeared with tea and refreshments. A small fire burned, warming the space. Mari gazed into the flames.

"Forgive me, Your Majesty, but I don't have any rooms available

320

at this moment. My girls are occupying them with clients," Oyotsu said beside Mari.

Mari held her hands to the fire. "This is lovely. I don't wish you to go to any trouble on our account."

Oyotsu shifted. "Your Majesty —"

"Please, call me Mari."

"Mari," Oyotsu said. "I think you will find many who will go out of their way to assist you. You only need to ask."

Mari smiled, unsure how to respond.

Mari watched the woman's long neck as she retreated. She wished to call out to her. *Do not pin your hopes on me.*

It was the early hours of the morning, and Mari hadn't slept a wink. Ren had gone off to find some birds for breakfast. According to Hanako, *oni* didn't need much shuteye. Hanako snuggled in an alcove with the wispy curtain drawn.

Akira sat beside Mari. "You should try to get some sleep," he whispered. "We have a long journey ahead."

Mari's limbs were sluggish with fatigue, but her mind buzzed. "I don't think I could, even if I tried." Mari shivered, though a fire blazed in the nearby charcoal brazier. Akira draped a blanket over her shoulders. "I should have listened to you," she said, drawing the blanket in closer.

Akira kneaded his neck.

"Why are you not angry with me?" Mari asked.

Akira said nothing for a long time. "It seems as if you are angry enough at yourself. We are our own worst punishers." Light from the flames highlighted Akira's scars in orange and silver.

"You're right." Mari covered her face. "Everything went so . . . This is all my fault. I was wrong about Taro. All that love wasted . . ." She stopped with a sound of disgust.

"Don't say it. Don't ever say that. Love is never wasted," Akira said sharply.

"Even on a Cold Prince?" She kept her face buried so that Akira couldn't see it.

"Even on him." Akira leaned back, stretching his legs in front of him. He removed a throwing star from his belt and rolled it from finger to finger. "The night of your wedding celebration, I watched him, watching you. I observed a man whose love ran deep." Mari snorted. Akira's voice tightened. "It is not your fault. You saw the prince as you wished he could be. It's an admirable trait. You place faith in others."

Mari swallowed, unable to speak of it any longer. The wound Taro had cut was too fresh. She nodded to the gleaming star as Akira threaded it through his fingertips. "You didn't learn how to use those on our mountain."

Akira smiled like the edge of one of his stars, glinting and dangerous. "No. Hanako taught me."

"You've changed."

"So have you."

Mari smoothed her hands over her *hakama*. She'd had a bath and gotten new clothes. In a few days' time, she would be home, back in Tsuma. An isolated village untouched by time. "After we warn everyone, what will you do? Will you go on to the West Lands with Hanako?"

"I found a cause, and I'm willing to fight for it," Akira said.

"You'll join the *yōkai* Resistance?"

"It seems I already have." Then he added under his breath, "You're a part of it too, you know."

"And if I don't want to be?"

Akira shrugged, sliding his throwing star back into his belt. "You're a part of it — whether you want to be or not."

Mari brought her knees to her chest. The fire crackled and popped. Sparks flew from the grate. "I wish we could go back to how it was."

"But we can't. We've learned the truth about the world, and now we must speak it. Silence is the cousin of invisibility. I want to be seen. Don't you?"

Mari's chin jutted out, her old stubborn streak coming back. "I think I'll try to get some sleep now."

She curled on her side and brought the blanket to her chin. She knew what Akira was thinking — that his life could serve a greater good. She'd had the same musings once.

Another way.

Mari didn't have the heart to tell Akira that he longed for the impossible. She'd let him dream. For now.

CHAPTER 47

Mari

THE WALLS OF Hana Machi were thin lines behind them. Ahead ambled the dirt road leading up the Tsuko funo Mountains. They'd said goodbye to Oyotsu, and Hanako had told the brothel owner of the emperor's army. Hide. Be prepared to hide for a long time.

Akira leaned on a birch tree as he shifted the weight on his shoulders, a pack jammed with blankets and dried fruit, bare essentials for their journey. "We can travel the main road for a little while, but we should move into the forest by afternoon. We'll forge our own trail there."

"How many days will it take?" asked Hanako.

"Four if we stop to sleep every night. But we can make it in three if we hike part of the night." Mari looked into the rising sun. Wind rustled through the trees, beckoning her home.

"I've never needed much sleep," Hanako said.

Ren grunted in agreement.

Akira eyed Mari. She remained silent but lifted her chin, a subtle yes. The Son of Nightmares nodded. "Three days, then."

They started to climb.

Home.

The sky faded to a smoky sapphire. The smell of wood smoke permeated the air as the iron gates of Tsuma came into view. Mari let out a yell, dropped her pack, and ran. Hearing her, Animal Wives spilled from their homes. She ran past them, her legs carrying her through the village. A few feet from her door, she skidded to a halt.

Tears built in her eyes. *Home.* Most days, she'd dreaded setting foot into the cottage and seeing her mother. But at this moment, she couldn't think of a better sight to behold. She'd taken so many things for granted.

The door slid open, and her mother stepped out. "Mari?" Tami asked, hand to her chest. "Daughter?"

"Mama," Mari choked out.

They embraced, and in that moment, without a word spoken, all was forgiven.

The moment was short-lived. There was no time to waste.

"We need to talk." Mari gestured to the open door. "Inside."

Mari trailed her fingers along the walls of the *tatami* room. Her house. The village seemed so small now. From the corner, Tami watched Mari inquisitively.

Ren, Hanako, and Akira entered. Tami's nostrils flared at the guests but she didn't utter a word. With her three friends standing in solidarity behind her, Mari wove her tale. The sun set. A crackling fire was lit in the *irori*. Moths gathered, beating their powdered wings against the windows. Mari told her mother everything, how she'd conquered the Seasons and taken the life of a fellow *yōkai*. She even managed to keep her voice steady when she spoke of falling in love with Taro, and dreaming of *another way*.

Yuka brought refreshments, and other Animal Wives filtered in. Except for Hissa. Mari couldn't help but notice the absence of her friend. All eyes focused on Mari as she told of the army at their heels.

Noriko, an Animal Wife, leaned forward, the firelight on her cheeks. "And you say they are coming here?"

"I don't know for sure. But Taro will be searching for us. His only lead is my home. It is likely he will travel here, and soon. I've come to warn you. You must leave as soon as possible. I'm sorry."

A small cry broke from the back of the crowd. Yuka hushed and bounced Mayumi on her hip. "We cannot leave," Noriko said. A murmur of agreement ran through the group. Tsuma was sacred. The first Animal Wife had chosen this place. To leave it behind would be to abandon their history, a part of themselves.

Ren clicked, motioning at his collar.

Hanako nodded. "If you stay here, you'll be collared." Hanako fluttered a hand near her collar. "Fleeing is the only chance you'll have at freedom."

Noriko snorted. "And a life spent in hiding, is that freedom to you?"

"It is better than living in chains," said Hanako.

"I think they are equal," Noriko said.

Hanako did not argue.

326

Mari cleared her throat. "There is no choice. We have to leave."

Tami slowly shook her head, flames glinting in her dark eyes. "No."

Mari leaned in, her voice lowering to a whisper. "You can't possibly be thinking of staying. What about Mayumi?" The baby dozed in Yuka's arms now.

"Yuka and Mayumi can go. They should go. But the rest of us . . ." Tami looked at each Animal Wife. "We have the choice to stay and defend our home or slip away. My mother and my mother's mother are buried here. The first Animal Wife built her home here. The gingko tree that shelters us and gives us life is here — all on this mountain."

"I say it is better to live and fight another day," one Animal Wife called out. Some nodded. Others looked unsure.

Tami cleared her throat. "Each of you has the choice. Stay or flee. None will be judged for her decision." Her eyes landed on Mari, something unspoken in her gaze.

"And what will you do?" Mari asked her mother, though she knew the answer.

Tami smiled softly. "My life is here. To leave it would be my death. I will stay and defend my home."

Tears filled Mari's eyes. "Mama —"

"Hush, daughter; do not forget where you've come from, who you are. Do not forget who I am." With that, Tami's eyes melted to black, giving way to the beast inside. The Animal Wives answered the call of Tami's beast. Where Tami led, they would follow.

Hanako cleared her throat. "It doesn't matter. Whatever power we possess is negated by the priests. The moment they utter their curses, we will all lie down like clipped pieces of string."

"Not all of us." Akira spoke from the corner. He straightened, walking to the center of the room. "The curses don't affect me as much as most."

All eyes swiveled to Akira.

"What do you mean?" Noriko asked.

Akira's jaw clenched. "My mother is *yōkai*; my father is human. Just as I carry my mother's powers, I also carry my father's humanity. I can help defend against the priests."

"Why would you do that?" Yuka asked, her voice full of spite.

Akira shrugged. "I've chosen my side. It is with you, with all *yōkai*."

Ren clicked.

"The emperor is probably bringing a whole contingent of samurai and priests with him," Hanako translated. "How many do you have in this village? Forty or fifty? Our numbers are paltry compared to theirs."

Tami leaned forward, a dangerous curve to her smile like the glint of a knife. "Yes. But we are uncollared. With our beasts unleashed, we'll be able to conquer an entire army."

"And the priests?" Hanako asked.

Tami nodded toward Akira. "He can handle them."

Hanako snorted. "Maybe one or two, but not a dozen." She paused. "We need a plan, something other than brute force, especially if our goal is to push them back from the mountain."

How do you defeat an undefeatable army? An idea came to Mari with the ferocity of a spark. "We separate them," she said. All eyes turned to her. "The emperor pitted *yōkai* against one another, kept them separate. We shall employ his tactic. If we can get the priests sequestered from the samurai and vice versa, we have a chance at defeating them. Conquer the priests; conquer the army."

"We'll need weapons and explosive powder," Hanako said.

Someone cleared a dainty throat. Chika, a petite Animal Wife, held up her hand. "I have weapons and explosive powder." She blushed and giggled. "My fourth husband was the steel smith for his clan."

Hanako smiled, and it proved contagious. Soon the whole room was grinning. A plan was brewing.

Gravel crunched under Mari's feet as she approached her mother. Tami's eyes stayed fixed on the millions of stars twinkling in the sky. Mari had forgotten how brightly the night sky shone up on the mountain. In the city, smoke obscured everything. The moon was waning, just a sliver in the dark. A phantom. Ghost moon.

"Yuka is going to take Mayumi to the monastery and ask the monks for sanctuary," Mari said.

In the predawn hours, Tami had told each Animal Wife to fortify her home.

"That is good," her mother said.

"The only person I can't find is Hissa."

Tami blinked. "Hissa is gone. She left shortly after you. I tracked her as far as the river." Her mother's lips twitched. "I'm sorry."

Mari felt sick. *At least she won't have to fight to her death. At least she is somewhere safe. I hope.* She wished she still had Hissa's hair pick. It was all she'd had to remember her by. Mari swallowed, fighting off her sadness. She tried to focus on something other than the pain. "Everyone besides Yuka and Mayumi is staying," Mari said. "I am —"

Her mother cut her off with a sharp look. "You will fetch all of the copper coins, jewelry, and gold from under the floorboards, and you will run."

"What? No!"

Tami grasped Mari's shoulders. Her mother's eyes were wild. "You will obey me in this. It is my final wish."

Mari shrugged out of Tami's hold. "I will not." *Never let your fear decide your fate.* "I will stay and help." Mari's next words were biting. "What does it matter to you anyway?" How easy it was to return to old habits.

Tami's eyes blazed. "What does it matter to me? You are my daughter. My blood runs through your veins. I love you."

Mari bowed her head and sniffed. It wasn't the time for this conversation. An army marched toward them. But Mari couldn't help the words from spilling forth.

"When I was growing up, you were always so cold. So distant."

Tami pursed her lips. "I kept myself separate from you. I thought it was for the best."

"You never believed in me. You didn't think I would conquer the Seasons."

Tami's breath puffed out in foggy clouds. "No, the opposite. I believed in you too much. I knew you would triumph. I knew you would capture the heart of the prince. Since the day I first held you, I knew your life was bigger than Tsuma."

"You sent me away." *I almost died. I'll never be the same.*

"I set you free. You are the best thing I've ever done. And if I was cruel, it was only to prepare you for a world that is much crueler."

Mari's shoulders hunched. She knew it was true, had known since her mother's confession. But still, there was so much to forgive.

"You insist on staying?" Tami asked.

"Yes," Mari stated firmly. In her few precious moments alone, Mari had committed herself to living—or dying—by her friends' sides. What good would it do if she ran, and all she loved perished? She had to fight back.

Tami looked up. "It's going to be a beautiful day. Not a cloud in the sky."

Mari gripped her mother's hand.

Together, they watched the sun rise.

CHAPTER 48
Taro

THE IMPERIAL ARMY summited the mountain in the mid-morning light.

Taro led from atop a chestnut horse, its coat gleaming in the sun. He wore a cuirass, a vest made from plates of steel tied together with purple silk. His helmet was fashioned with antlers, twisting up to the sky, and a red metal mask. Satoshi flanked him on the left; his *shōgun* to the right. Both were clad in similar armor.

"The village — just five miles up the road!" a scout rasped, his horse galloping toward the group, then skidding to a stop. The scout dismounted the animal, slick with sweat, and bent over in front of Taro, trying to catch his breath.

"What else?" the *shōgun* asked.

"It seems they are expecting us. They have boarded up their homes." The scout straightened, still gasping for air.

"Have they fled?" Taro asked, lifting his mask.

"I couldn't tell, Your Majesty. I didn't want to get too close and spook them."

Taro grunted and let his mask fall in place.

"Your Majesty, we await your order," said the *shōgun*.

Taro's horse stamped a hoof, sensing his master's restlessness.

Taro felt the power behind him — five of his most favored *daimyō* leading five hundred samurai. A dozen priests. The trees filled with ninja. He'd brought an army fit to topple a mountain.

"We'll rest here today. We attack at sunset." The cloak of night was best for a hunt. "Make sure all know — the empress is to be taken alive."

"Your Majesty?" the *shōgun* challenged.

Taro gritted his teeth. "The empress is to be taken alive. All others are fair game."

Taro kept his eyes straight ahead. Somewhere just beyond the trees, Mari and her Animal Wives waited. Taro's heart sped up. By the next morning, it would be over. The mountain would fall. And Taro would dance on its ruins.

CHAPTER 49

Mari

DRIED LEAVES CRUNCHED under Akira's feet. At the noise, Mari stopped sharpening her new *naginata*, courtesy of Chika's weapon stash, and glanced up. She sat near the base of a flat rock, which rose from the ground like a pillar. Carved into the slate surface was the legend of the first Animal Wife. In front of her, a fire blazed. She'd built it earlier, adding red cliff daisies. Crimson smoke curled high into the sky. *I will return to the mountains. But if you should ever need me, find the red cliff daisy . . .* Hiro had said. Now Mari sought to collect on the debt he owed her. She prayed the *rōnin* would show, help her defeat an undefeatable army.

"I used to play hide-and-seek here." Mari sighed and let the *naginata* rest in her lap.

Akira wiped the dirt from his hands. He had spent the morning visiting his parents, urging them to run, then digging holes. An Animal Wife strolled by, her gaze lingering on him.

Mari's smile was melancholy. "None of the other children

would dare hide near the sacred shrine. And now it may be destroyed."

Akira circled the fire, then crouched, gripping Mari's knees. "You mustn't believe that. To believe something gives it weight and meaning. It taunts the gods and goddesses to turn it true."

"You are too optimistic."

He stared into her eyes. "I am not. I know lives will be lost. But we have a chance."

"And if we succeed, if we push back Taro's army? He will return with reinforcements. A fly may dodge a hand, but it is only a matter of time before the hand returns."

"We will make our stand, and if we succeed, we will go west and build an army equal to the emperor's." Akira put his hand on her shoulder. "And I think you should lead them." Akira paused, looking Mari in the eye. "You could have fled. Yet here you are."

Hanako and Ren appeared. They'd heard Akira's proposal. And they awaited Mari's answer. Could she do this? Join them — lead them?

She tightened her hand around her *naginata*. "I will fight, always, by your — *on* your — side." She felt Akira smile. She looked at him. At one point, she'd thought Taro completed her. Now she realized that he didn't. She was complete by herself.

Marriage and love, they aren't achievements. Mari stood ready to face Taro, ready to face a new life. The fireball of rebellion within her had broken free.

The whole village had gathered at Tami's house to eat. It was there they heard the first war drum, the hollow sound bouncing off the trees. The beat started out faint, a whisper on the wind, and grew louder as the minutes ticked on.

Mari's stomach dropped.

Tami stood, her hands trembling as she brushed them against her kimono. Even in the face of war, Mari's mother looked splendid in a silk gown.

Mari forced down the rest of her rice. Her fear gave way to scorn. How arrogant Taro was, announcing his arrival as if victory were a foregone conclusion. Blood heated in Mari's veins.

"The emperor comes," Tami stated.

"It's too soon," Hanako whispered. They weren't expecting him for another day. They needed that time to put the second part of their plan in place. Needed time for the *rōnin* to arrive.

Mayumi wailed in Yuka's arms as Tami ushered the mother and daughter out the door. "You must go now. Take her from here, and don't come back."

Mari followed, the rest of the Animal Wives spilling into the street behind her.

Yuka began to run, baby tucked in her arms. She leaped, tossing Mayumi in the air. The baby giggled, somersaulting through the sky. Yuka transformed into her beast. Just as Mayumi was about to hit the ground, Yuka grabbed her daughter up in her claws, then swept high into the air. She was already far away, her body just a silhouette, a gust of wings.

"That was amazing!" Hanako's voice pierced the silence. "Can you all do that?"

At once, the Animal Wives shed their human forms. To the

background of encroaching drums, they transformed into mighty beasts. Mari gazed at their twisting bodies, their cracking bones, their changing skin. Once again, she was on the outside looking in. After everything she had become, this was still something she couldn't be, not fully. But the stab she usually felt wasn't quite as sharp. She caught Akira's eye, and he smiled encouragingly. *I see you. I see all that you are. I see all that you are not. And it is enough. You are enough.*

The beast rolled under Mari's skin. *Accept me*, it seemed to whisper. *Accept me.* She closed her eyes. Her body hunched of its own volition. The ridges of her spine moved like a serpent under her skin. *No.* She didn't want this. Realization hit in a heady rush. It wasn't the beast that always rejected her. It was she who rejected the beast. *Because I never wanted to be an Animal Wife.* But now she realized, *It doesn't have to define me. It is a piece of who I am.*

Her back split open with a crack, and dark leathery wings sprouted and unfurled, black and pearlescent in the dusky sunset. Flesh turned itself inside out. Her arms elongated, and fingers tapered into thick black claws. Her nose and mouth fused into a beak. She blinked, and her eyes melted to black. Tough scales broke through her skin, and a winding tail snapped out from her spine. A mighty shriek burst from her beak. *I am Empress and Animal Wife and yōkai and whatever else I deem worthy and part of myself. I choose. No one else.* Mari looked again at the Animal Wives. Sisters. Mothers. Monsters. Beautiful beasts. Together, they shuffled their wings, ready to fly, ready to fight.

Shaking from their stupor, Ren, Hanako, and Akira took their places beside Mari. Hanako even risked running a hand over Mari's leathery wing. Fully transformed, Mari couldn't speak, but she could understand, and she could feel. *This is true freedom, to love oneself enough not to care what others think.*

"Is everything set?" Hanako asked Akira as she strapped a *katana* sword onto her back.

The Son of Nightmares nodded. Dozens of throwing stars lined his clothing, almost like armor. "I buried the pots along the road just as you asked. All Ren needs to do is light the thread and then . . ."

The drumroll drew closer. Mari's heart sped up.

"We all know what we are supposed to do?" asked Hanako. Nods passed around the group. The Animal Wives opened their beaks and shrieked, Mari along with them. "All right, then. All right, then. If we die tonight, we die together."

Mari beat her wings and lifted off the ground, leading the march to the gates. The Animal Wives flew just behind her, a dark, ominous cloud. They looked similar, but Mari knew her mother among them, felt her as a tree does its roots.

Ren ran ahead, a book of matches in one hand and a sickle and chain in the other. The first faint whiff of smoke reached Mari's nostrils. Her shoulders tightened, and her jaw set in determination. With her small size, she had learned that the element of surprise was essential. Taro had no idea what was in store for him.

CHAPTER 50

Taro

TARO HELD STRAIGHT in the saddle. Dirt kicked up around his horse's hooves. Shrieks, the sounds a cross between a horse, a bird, and a human cry, pierced the air. A murmur ran through the army, and they fought to steady their jittery horses.

The trees on either side of the road rustled as ninja jumped from branch to branch. One final stretch of incline, and the dirt road widened. Stones and boulders dotted the landscape. Wind whistled along the mountain slope. The air smelled of snow and ice, even though winter had long since passed. A gate came into view, its hinges squeaking in the wind. Taro spied rooftops but no lights. Had the village been abandoned?

"Something isn't right," Satoshi murmured. His half brother lacked the heart of a warrior. Priests relied too heavily on their curses. It was something the new emperor planned to rectify.

Taro scanned the area. Mounds rose up in the middle of the road as if a gopher had dug a very straight line. Taro's stomach clenched. He opened his mouth to order a retreat.

But it was too late.

Dirt and fire shot up, filling the air with smoke. One by one, tiny explosions erupted down the line.

The horses reared, spittle foaming at their mouths. The army split in half. Samurai on horseback fled in every direction. Priests retreated, deserting to the left. "Keep in formation!" Taro shouted into the chaos. But his cry was lost.

CHAPTER 51
Akira

AKIRA CHASED THE PRIESTS through the forest. He threw stars, the blades swiping through the jugulars of four priests. No care for their fallen comrades, the others ran on. Branches whipped at Akira's cheeks. He launched another star. Six priests down. *That's it, you cowards. Run right into my trap.*

Ahead, trees shook. Hanako and Ren dropped from the foliage, blocking the priests. The demon smiled, licked his fangs, and swung his sickle and chain.

The priests halted and began to chant. Instantly, the two *yōkai* crumbled. Animal Wives slid from the sky, the curses pulling them down. *Was Mari among them?* Fear took hold of Akira and nearly choked him.

The priests circled the Snow Girl and the demon. *Their defenses are down. Their backs are turned. This is it.*

Conquer the priests. Conquer the army. Now! Akira flung stars as quick and sure as lightning. Metal grazed the priests' necks, backs, stomachs. In minutes, they lay in a red heap. Gods and goddesses, their plan had worked. Far above the canopy, the Animal Wives shot back into the sky, shrieking in victory.

Ren assisted Hanako up.

"Everyone okay?" Akira asked.

"Check for pulses," Hanako told Ren and Akira. "I'll keep a lookout for samurai."

Akira toed the pile of priests and thrust their bodies over. He pressed his fingers to their necks, skin only slightly sizzling on contact with their tattooed skin. "They're all dead," he called out. He counted the bodies, noted the color of the robes — all gray. "One is missing. Satoshi, the High Priest. He's not here."

Hanako cursed savagely.

Akira's stomach churned. Smoke from the road explosions crept around their ankles. Night encroached. But no insects sang. The trees glowed, their souls trembling. He regarded Ren and Hanako. "Go help the others. I'll find him."

CHAPTER 52

Taro

MORE SHRIEKS, and this time they were closer. Taro resisted the urge to place his hands over his ears to blot out the noise. In the navy sky, black-beaked creatures swooped low. Ninja fired arrows through the trees. One of the creatures screeched as an arrow pierced its leathery wing, sending it spiraling to the ground.

As if connected, the creatures screamed in unison. They dove, swooping through the air, plucking ninja from the trees with their talons. They rose straight up until it seemed they were as high as the moon, then dropped the ninja to their deaths. Thick smoke covered the ground, obscuring the bodies.

"Your Majesty, we should retreat, regroup," the *shōgun* said. The whites of his horse's eyes glowed with terror.

"What would my father do?" Taro shouted over the din.

The *shōgun* hesitated.

"What would he do?" Taro insisted.

"He would stay and fight," the *shōgun* answered.

Black masses emerged through the smoke — the samurai returning. Taro urged his horse forward. A winged silhouette took shape in the fog. Then another without wings. The *oni*.

The demon drew back an arm, swinging a sickle and chain. The weapon left the *oni*'s hand. It whipped past Taro, through the *shōgun*'s neck plate, and into his throat. The *shōgun* gripped his neck and toppled from his horse.

The demon retrieved his weapon and retreated into the cover of smoke.

Taro slid from his horse. He was too visible above the smoke line. He drew his swords. "You hide like cowards!" he yelled, ripping off his helmet and mask. "Face me."

The winged figure moved in the hazy smoke. Taro froze, breath bated. His blood flowed heavy, as if weighted down by lead. The figure stepped forward, and, as it did, its body changed. Wings receded into its back; scales shimmered, then disappeared, replaced with skin; black fathomless eyes dissolved to brown flecked with amber. The demon handed her a *naginata*. Weapon in hand, she smiled. And he cursed the rush of blood that ran through him. The pleasure at seeing her. His wife. His empress. *Mari*.

CHAPTER 53

Mari

MARI UNSHEATHED HER *NAGINATA*. She was staring directly at Taro. The Cold Prince breathed deep, swords fisted in his hands. Samurai swarmed behind him, but Taro halted them with a single jerk of his head. Mari focused on him. Her stomach twisted in a vicious knot. *How did it come to this?*

Orange light flickered in Mari's peripheral vision. The ninja had set their arrows aflame. Mari heard a scream above her and knew another Animal Wife had perished. The beast tensed under her skin.

Taro must have noticed her flinch. "It doesn't have to be this way. Call off your rebellion. This battle can end without any more bloodshed."

Mari swirled her *naginata*. "You will leave this mountain and my village in peace?" she asked, brow arched.

Taro shook his head. "You know I can't do that. I ask for your surrender."

A terrible screech echoed through the mountain as another Animal Wife fell from the sky, this time on fire, a comet racing toward the earth. Gray smoke layered into black, bringing with it the scent of sulfur and burning trees. Around them, metal clashed against metal. Akira, Ren, and Hanako were fighting the army. Mari contemplated Taro's words. *No one else would have to die.*

Again, Taro sensed her hesitation. He took a cautious step toward Mari and let his swords drop. "You could come back to the Imperial Palace. Back to me."

Mari scrunched her eyes. She couldn't possibly have heard him correctly. *Back to me.* Be his empress again? She nearly laughed. She lowered her *naginata*. "What of my people? What about Akira?"

Taro's jaw twitched. "The Son of Nightmares killed my father. He must pay for his crime. Justice must be carried out."

"So stubborn in your certainty," Mari said through her teeth. Her hand clenched around the *naginata*. "And what of the *yōkai*? Would you remove the collars and reconstruct the empire so we are all truly treated as equals?"

Taro's swords scraped the ground. "I can't do that."

Mari blinked, and in that moment, she released any dream of a life with Taro. It flew away like a wild bird into the night. Perhaps it wouldn't matter, his half brother's betrayal. She couldn't trust him again. Not with so many lives at stake. Not with so much between them. "Then I cannot surrender," she whispered.

Taro grimaced.

Blood rushed through Mari's veins as she lifted the *naginata*. She crouched and swung out with the pole end, clipping Taro behind the knees. The move never let her down. Taro buckled, but, using his bent knees as a springboard, he somersaulted backwards into the air. He landed with an *oomph*, swords drawn. He rushed her.

They were back in the Spring Room, wielding their weapons against each other in an intricate dance. But this time no courtiers watched; no cherry blossoms lined the ring. This time there was the crackle of fire, the stench of burning bodies, the cry of falling Animal Wives. Violence. Destruction. *War.*

Mari blocked Taro's sword with the pole end of the *naginata*. She began to twist the weapon, but the movement was halted as a sudden pain radiated down her side. Taro's mouth fell open and he stumbled back, his short sword covered in blood. *Her blood.* Mari touched her side. A nasty gash ran the length of her torso. Not a killing wound, but enough to make her bend over and gasp. Cripple her.

Taro's swords clattered to the ground. "Mari?" He caught her by the arms, steadying her. Their eyes locked. For a moment, the melee muted. It felt as if everything were beginning and ending at the same time. His face spelled a lifetime of regret, of hurt, of sadness.

Blood coated Mari's fingers, and she grasped at Taro. Her ears began to ring. "Look what we've done to each other." *I could have loved you. I could have been your Empress of All Seasons. We could have found another way.*

A glint of metal flashed in Mari's vision. A throwing star sliced through the air. Mari cried out. With her last bit of strength, she pivoted her body in front of Taro, and the throwing star sliced across her belly. *A killing blow.* Mari crumpled in Taro's arms.

She grazed his stubbled cheek with her fingers. "Don't take me from here," she pleaded. *Don't take me from my home.* Taro's mouth quaked. "I didn't kill your father. The traitor is in your own house, in your own bloodline." She gasped. Her final words were spent warning Taro, trying to save the man she truly loved.

The whites of Taro's eyes turned red and watery. "Satoshi?"

Her eyes fluttered shut. She shuddered. An empress. Beloved by the Seasons. Chosen by gods and goddesses. Gone.

CHAPTER 54
Akira

A SOB LODGED in Akira's throat as he watched Mari fall. Tears marred his vision.

Heat blazed around Akira's ankles. The forest was burning. *Let it burn. Let me burn along with it.* He had killed his beloved. *No. No. No.* None of this could be real.

"Son of Nightmares!" the emperor boomed. Akira saw him through the trees. The emperor stood just above the smoke line, swords in hand. "Come and face me!" he screamed.

A shriek bent the air. Akira looked up. An Animal Wife circled above, swooped down, slashing at Taro's guard. Mari's mother. The other Animal Wives followed, swarming the samurai.

In the chaos, only Akira saw the knife fly through the air. He recognized the cut of the blade. It was the same knife Satoshi had used to kill Mari's servant. It sliced through Taro's armor and landed with a *thunk* in his chest. The prince staggered back. He dropped his swords, hands going to the hilt of the knife. Taro crumpled to his knees, inches from Mari's slain body. Blood seeped through his armor. The Animal Wives noticed the crippled prince and drew back, circling above.

They waited.

They watched.

The samurai dropped to their knees beside their fallen emperor. Ninja climbed down trees and alighted from the forest. They put their hands over their hearts. Taro's mouth opened and closed. He tried to speak, but no words formed. With the last of his strength, he crawled to Mari. Carefully, he pulled her into his arms. A boom of thunder rocked the mountain. Then he was gone.

Silence descended, eerie and heavy. The samurai and ninja had been trained to follow. What would they do without their leader?

Satoshi stumbled from the forest.

No. Akira reached for the star at his belt. *Empty.* He'd used the last one on the emperor — no — on Mari. Cruel fate.

A samurai stood. "The emperor is dead."

Sensing a new threat, the Animal Wives shrieked and dove toward Satoshi. A deep breath, and the priest began to chant. Burnt cinnamon suffused the air, turning to acrid smoke. The priest's words started low but grew in volume. The wind ruffled his robes as he reached to the sky. Akira felt the magic enter him, a burning tether that wrapped loosely around his soul. He could withstand it. The Animal Wives could not. Their bodies transformed in the air and dropped from the sky. It was a terrible sight. Samurai jumped back as Animal Wives landed, heaps of dust and broken bones. Preternaturally beautiful women littered the dirt road.

Between chants, Satoshi barked orders. He turned to a samurai

350

with a red tassel on his helmet. "Search the woods. Find all *yōkai* and collar them." The samurai hesitated. "Go!" Satoshi cried. "The emperor is dead. I am next in line. Heed me now, or turn against your empire."

Satoshi continued his incantations, sweating with the exertion. Mari lay near the priest's feet. Akira's eyes drew to her small, lifeless form. She looked so young, so vulnerable. So small in the fallen emperor's arms.

Samurai began to comb through the Animal Wives, collaring survivors. A group split off into the forest. Akira scurried up a cypress tree. He pressed his body against the trunk and watched over Mari through the branches. It was all he could do. Tears rushed down his face like hot waterfalls. It was the end for their people. And it was his fault. He'd killed his Animal Girl.

Suddenly, he remembered Hanako and Ren. They were still in the forest. *His friends.* He could do no more for Mari. Even now, a limping samurai was picking up her body. "Build a pyre, burn the bodies, and stay there until they turn to ash." Satoshi shuddered with rage.

Akira was jumping from tree to tree when he saw Hanako and Ren. They were alive but incapacitated, the priest's chants filtering on the wind.

Akira dropped from the trees. "We have to get you out of here," he said to them, although he wasn't sure they could hear him through their pain. "Samurai are razing the woods."

Hanako moaned. Ren shuddered.

"Mari?" Hanako groaned.

Akira shook his head, tears lighting his eyes. He couldn't bring himself to say it. *She's gone, and by my hand.* He crouched and helped Ren up. He looped an arm around the giant but couldn't stand with his weight. The demon slumped back to the ground. "I won't leave you behind." He tried again. No use. He sat next to the demon, panting and out of breath.

Hanako whimpered, and her lips parted. "H-h" was all she could get out.

"What is it?" Akira asked.

Hanako tried again. "H-hide."

"Hide?" Akira repeated. He jumped up.

Akira rolled Ren's body deep into the forest just as the first streaks of sunlight dawned. Then he carried Hanako. He laid the Snow Girl and the *oni* next to each other, covering them with branches and leaves. Then he climbed high in a tree just before the samurai arrived, trampling the forest.

The group fanned out, jabbing at the ground with their spears. Akira held his breath. *One. Two. Three. Four. Five . . .* Akira counted the seconds until the samurai left. He waited. Silent as the wind. He counted.

The sun rose and set. Flies buzzed and bit Akira's cheeks. The priest's chants finally halted. Below, the leaves rustled; Hanako and Ren woke from their pain-filled stupors, but they stayed put, sensing Akira's directive.

Wait. Wait. Wait.

Finally, the dawn came. A squirrel scampered in the branches overhead. Slowly, Akira climbed to the top of the tree. Smoke nearly covered the sun, but he could see that the army was still there, picking through the ruins of Tsuma. Everything was gone. *Mari's home. It was obliterated. A wasteland.*

All that was left of the village was smoke-charred ruins and a rusted iron gate. He scanned the road. Burnt bodies and tents. A handful of samurai had been left behind to raid the village. But there was no evidence of Satoshi, the new emperor. The trees nearest the road had darkened to crimson, transformed to *jubokko*, blood-vampire trees, common on the battlefield.

Akira felt something shift within him. Mari was dead, but her cause was not. Thousands of *yōkai* still wore collars. Akira would not rest until each one was destroyed. Every *yōkai* freed.

CHAPTER 55

Mari

DRIP. DRIP. DRIP.

Her nose twitched. The air was musty and dank. For one sweet second, she remained floating in the in-between. Then pain lanced her side and stomach, and she gasped. Her eyelids fluttered. Wooden walls. An oil lamp. The smell of rapeseed. She knew this room. The killing shed. The place where everything had started. And everything ended.

Drip. Drip. Drip.

"I think she's waking up." The voice was familiar.

"Give her some breathing room." Another voice, less friendly.

Memories gushed forth as a clock rewinding — the slice of the throwing star, a time of love and competition to the death, a journey along a dirt road, *rōnin . . . Masa. Hiro, red smoke.* She tried to shift, but her body wouldn't work from the neck down.

"Don't move." Masa wrung out a washcloth over a bowl. *Drip. Drip. Drip.* He swiped the cloth over her brow. The cold felt good against her throbbing head. "We weren't sure you were going to make it. Hiro noticed your fingers move." Masa smiled warmly.

"Hiro," she whispered.

The samurai moved into her line of sight. He frowned. Of course. "This shed was the only place I could think to hide you," he said.

Mari winced as pain shot up her side.

"I've stitched you up, and the bleeding has stopped. You've slept through the worst part. And I've ensured that there will be no fever," Hiro said, and held up a bowl with a thick paste that smelled of pine and cucumber.

"Night flower," she murmured.

"You'll heal, but you'll be changed," Hiro said.

Masa flexed his injured arm and winked. "Aches at the end of every day. What is broken can never fully be put back together." Masa paused. "We're sorry we didn't come earlier. We were halfway down the mountain when we saw the smoke. But better late than never."

Mari nodded, and tears leaked from her eyes. She had so many questions — about her friends, her sisters, her mother, Taro. Who had lived and who had died? But she didn't know if she was ready for the answers. If she didn't know who perished, they would stay alive in her mind a little longer.

"Thank you," she said, feeling the dark tide of sleep pull her under.

Hiro nodded. "I've honored my debt to you. A life for a life."

"A life for a life." Mari drifted off with a smile on her face.

She dreamed of wolves.

Her mother did love to hunt the canines. When Mari was young,

Tami took her hunting. It was the first time she'd seen her mother transform. Black scales against white snow. Her mother tracked a gray male to its den. There were no cubs. Just the male and its female, a smaller wolf with black triangle ears and paws. Tami had pinned the male and swiftly cut its throat so it wouldn't suffer. Then she shifted back to her human form, her skin absorbing the afternoon light. Together they carried the wolf back to Tsuma to share the meat with the clan.

That night, the female wolf came to the village. She'd tracked them all the way home. She clawed at porches and ripped plants from gardens.

Yuka killed the wolf.

Tami shook her head. "Such a shame. Some females don't know when to quit; they'll do anything for a male."

Mari had watched Yuka skin the wolf, a heavy feeling in her chest. Her eyes grew hot and gummy. She didn't think it was a shame. Mari thought sacrifice was the ultimate act of love.

The dream morphed into a black cave with echoing voices.

Men are conditioned to take. Women are conditioned to give. Her mother.

We're all monsters. No man, no human, will ever love us. That is the curse of the Animal Wife, never to be loved for who we truly are. Hissa.

I think we ought to be friends. I think it's the best idea I've ever had. Akira.

I believe in us, in what we can do together. Taro.

Mari woke with a gasp. "Are you in pain?" Masa hovered.

"My mother, my village, I need to see," she said. She fumbled with her covers, struggled to stand. But her body was too weak. She tried to call her beast forward, but it was injured too. It had fallen into a healing sleep.

"Easy, now," Masa crooned. "No need to tear your stitches. I'll take you." Masa tried to scoop her up but winced in pain. "My arm," he said, setting her back down. "I can barely lift a sword nowadays."

Mari squeezed her eyes shut. Helpless and alone. But then she felt herself being jostled. A gentle, strong arm hooked under her legs and around her shoulders. She opened her eyes and saw Hiro. Still sullen. Still frowning. *Hiro doesn't like anyone. He has two expressions: angry and less angry.* "Is this your angry or less angry face?" Mari grimaced as pain radiated up her side.

Hiro held her gaze. "You should not be going out. You need at least a month of bed rest."

Masa opened the door to the shed, and Mari squinted against the searing afternoon light. Fresh air stung her lungs.

"That way." Mari pointed to a path obscured by low-hanging branches. "It's a shortcut I used to take."

As they walked, Masa stayed in front, holding back branches, widening the path for Hiro and his precious cargo.

"I always wondered . . . Why did you do it?" Hiro asked.

"Why did I do what?" Mari bit out through the pain.

"In the shed."

Mari tried to look Hiro in the eye, but she couldn't move. "I am not beautiful. It was believed I would never be a true Animal Wife. My mother decided to train me for the competition. So I could at least become Empress, and an Animal Wife in my own way," Mari said. At the mention of her mother, she felt a sudden weakness.

Hiro grew silent, taciturn. The trees began to change, their trunks charred and black, their leaves gone. The scent of smoke clung to the air.

Mari thought of the battle, of Taro. There had always been inequalities in their relationship. Taro was human. Mari was *yōkai*. But more than that, it seemed Mari was always the one sacrificing. She'd faced death again and again. She had lost her ally, her friend Asami. All for Taro. And for *another way*. She'd been willing to change to fit in Taro's world with the hopes of transforming it. But now she realized she didn't need to change. The world did.

A muscle rippled in Hiro's jaw, and he spoke as if unable to keep his thoughts quiet. "They don't get to decide that," he said.

"What? Who?" Mari asked. They'd come to the end of the path. Tsuma's gate squeaked in the wind.

"The Animal Wives, anyone. *They* don't get to decide whether you're beautiful or not," Hiro said.

"Who does, then?" Mari asked.

Hiro looked down at Mari. "You, I suppose."

Mari had always known there was power in words. And Hiro's words struck her as revolutionary, even if she already had discovered their meaning for herself. *I am the only person who decides if I am beautiful or not, if I am worthy or unworthy.*

Masa stopped abruptly. So did Hiro. "Samurai," Masa whispered.

They peered through a thick row of branches. Tsuma was in ruins. The streets were scorched black, the cottages burnt skeletons, some still smoldering. Only the gate and the rock wall remained. Ashes fluttered on the wind. Figures unfurled from the steaming wreckage. Samurai in black lacquered armor were raiding the Animal Wives' stores.

Hiro stepped back, and a pinecone crunched under his heel. The sound echoed. The samurai paused and turned.

"Who goes there?" A samurai with a red tassel on his helmet moved forward.

Mari's whole body began to tremble. Hiro tightened his hold on her. He turned to run.

"Halt." Out of the corner of her eye, Mari saw the glint of a spear positioned at the back of Hiro's neck. More samurai broke through the trees. They were surrounded. *Had she lived only to die here, amid the ruins of her village?*

The samurai with the red tassel lowered his spear, then ripped the mask from his face. "Gods and goddesses, it's the empress!" he yelled.

The rest of the samurai removed their masks as well, eyes wide and unbelieving. "She lives," one said.

Mari held her breath. Masa's hands hovered over his swords. Mari counted more than twenty samurai. Her hands curled into fists, talons sprouting from her fingertips. The beast was injured, but it gave her what it could. They were outnumbered, and she was in no condition to fight. Weak or not, she'd try to claw her way out of this. She'd never give up.

Hiro adjusted his hold on her. "Do you think you can stand?" he murmured in her ear.

No. Even in the *rōnin*'s arms, her legs felt watery, useless. "If I cannot stand, I will fight lying down." This earned her a rare smile from the *rōnin*.

The samurai's expressions were as severe and forbidding as blocks of ice. They stepped closer. Hiro's grip on Mari tightened. In unison, the samurai placed their hands to their hearts and dropped to their knees, eyes shining with transparent emotion. "The emperor is dead," the leader spoke. At this, Mari's heart twisted in her chest. A choked sob escaped her as the memory came. The battlefield. Her bleeding out. Arms wrapping around her. Then a body going still. Had that been Taro? Had he, in the final moments of life, reached for her? Something in Mari constricted with certainty. *Yes.* Taro had chosen her in his last breath.

The lead samurai spoke again, voice echoing through the mountain. "The emperor is dead. Long live the empress." Keeping his kneeling position, the samurai looked up at Mari.

Mari bristled. Protests hovered on her tongue. *I am just a girl. I am not fit to rule. I am a pretender.* Just as quickly as the doubts came, she dismissed them. The corners of her lips curled up ever so slightly. "The empire is mine," she said, voice unwavering.

The lead samurai dipped his chin. "We await your command."

CHAPTER 56
Akira

THE FIRST TIME he saw her, he thought she was a ghost.

But ghosts didn't need *rōnin* to carry them about, didn't have samurai bowing to them. Ignoring Hanako and Ren's sounds of protest, Akira dropped from the trees, right into the center of the circle surrounding Mari. *She is alive.*

All at once the samurai stood, spears pointed at Akira's neck. The Son of Nightmares held up his hands.

"It's all right," Mari said, voice husky. Begrudgingly, the samurai laid down their arms. The *rōnin* adjusted Mari in his arms. The imperial samurai tensed, unsure of these samurai beholden to no master. "It's all right," she assured the samurai again. She patted the *rōnin's* shoulder. "He's just going to set me down so I might speak with my friend." With the utmost gentleness, Hiro placed Mari into a sitting position on a boulder thick with moss. The samurai took up different positions around her.

Akira flexed his hands at his sides. "This is my fault. You will never know how sorry I am."

Mari's eyes clouded with agony. "I think that you and I have apologized to each other enough for one lifetime. Besides, someone once told me, we are our own worst punishers."

"A thousand times over," said Akira.

"Then I won't add to your pain." Mari's eyes traveled past Akira, just beyond the trees, to Tsuma. "My mother?" Mari asked, her voice filled with tentative hope.

Akira shook his head.

"Yuka?" she asked.

Akira nodded. "She's alive." Mari's heart lifted, then dropped when Akira continued. "But she's been taken back to the palace. All the surviving Animal Wives have been captured."

The sun crawled against the sky. The two *rōnin*, along with the other samurai, stayed close to Mari. Akira wondered why the samurai stayed, what had incurred their loyalty, but his questions would have to wait. Tears snaked down Mari's cheeks as she thought of her people imprisoned in the Winter Room. "Hanako? Ren?" she asked on a final breath.

Akira managed a smile. Sticking two fingers in his mouth, he whistled. From a slope, the Snow Girl and the demon appeared.

"You're alive!" Hanako exclaimed, rushing forward.

The samurai tensed and moved to block the Snow Girl. But Mari had them stand down with a simple flick of her wrist.

Hanako halted in her tracks, but a winsome smile played on her lips. "Look, Ren," she said, taking a hold of the demon's hand.

Ren dipped into a low bow.

The sun had shifted, now merely an orange ghost on the horizon. Mari shivered and began to pale.

The brooding *rōnin* addressed the empress. "We should go. You need to rest."

Mari shook her head. "A little longer, please."

"We were going to the West Lands," Akira told her. "We were planning to leave tonight."

"Oh." Mari's brow dipped. "It seems I am still Empress." Wind ruffled her hair.

Hanako nodded. "Your place is in the Imperial City."

"There is much work to be done," Mari said.

Ren grunted.

Hanako interpreted for him. "Satoshi, the High Priest, has assumed the throne."

"He must be disposed of." *My people must be saved.* Mari's tone was regal, her command law.

"I imagine he'll be difficult about leaving," said Akira.

"Difficult but not impossible," Hanako said. "Especially if you have help," Hanako addressed Mari.

"Yes. I believe the samurai will follow me. But the priests . . ."

"Have either been killed or have fled. And if they return, they are no match against me," Akira interjected.

"I'd be even better equipped if I had a Weapons Master and an *oni* by my side."

Hanako smiled. She stroked Ren's shoulder. "I was born to fell an empire. Coups are a specialty of mine."

Mari breathed in. "It's settled, then. We will go east instead, to the Imperial City."

"We will reclaim your throne," Hanako declared.

"It won't be easy," Akira said, his soul lifting.

Mari shrugged. "We'll find a way."

THE LAST EMPRESS

FROM THE SKY, *Sugita watched the humans bow to a female yōkai in a forest near a burnt village. Anger darkened his face. This was not the will of the gods and goddesses. She did not bear the signature mark, the smudge between her brows. Yet the humans venerated her.*

"Ungrateful," Sugita cursed. He called for the lightning staircase, but it did not come. He cursed again and called for his sister Kita.

She approached him in the sky and gazed down on the bloodied battlefield. "What a shame," she said.

"Lend me your staircase, and I will smite them," Sugita demanded.

Kita clucked her tongue. "No, brother. I think you have done enough."

Their sisters Umiko and Aiko appeared.

"Help me destroy these mortals!" Sugita shouted.

"No, brother. We will govern from here," said Kita. At that, the three sisters seized control of the heavens and earth. But because the sisters knew what their brother never did—that true strength lies in compassion, they did not destroy him. Sugita was relegated to the skies.

While the female yōkai empress slept that night, Kita descended her staircase and touched the female's forehead. A smudge appeared. But then Kita thought better of it. She wiped the smudge away. "You do not need us. You will rule on your own."

The female yōkai, Mari, Empress of Honoku, marched to the Imperial City. In each town, each village she strode through, humans and yōkai alike joined her cause.

"Soon we will open our hands instead of clenching our fists," she promised. And her promise became the people's war cry. The banner they fought under.

When they arrived in the Imperial City, they stormed the palace and placed a metal collar upon Satoshi that would remain upon him all the days of his miserable, caged life. Besides the one he wore, metal collars were outlawed, melted in the streets while yōkai danced amid the flames.

There wasn't always harmony.

The female yōkai led the charge in two wars: the West Lands Uprising and the Gray Robe Rebellion. Stories for another time. Though she was regarded as mostly fair and just, there was rumored to be a dark side to the empress's rule. There was a man whom no one ever saw but all knew — the Son of Nightmares. An assassin. The bloody hand of the empress.

Still, her reign was known as the Golden Age. It was said the empress had loved her emperor so wildly, so deeply, that she never married again. Hearing this, the empress would smile knowingly and say, "We love our brothers. But not every happily-ever-after includes a man." And so it was.

An Empress for All Beings.

The Empress of All Seasons.

GLOSSARY

ashura — *yōkai*, demon with three faces, six arms, and three eyes

daimyō — a feudal lord, subordinate of the *shōgun*

dōshin — lesser samurai, performs job of prison guard or patrol officer

futakuchi-onna — *yōkai*, a two-mouthed woman

hakama — pleated trousers, worn over kimono

hari-onago — *yōkai*, Hook Girl

hashi — chopsticks

ibushi-ki — smoke pot

irori — a sunken hearth used for heating the home or cooking food

jorōgumo — *yōkai*, arachnid woman

juban — undergarment

jubokko — *yōkai*, blood-vampire tree

kamaitachi — *yōkai*, sickle weasel

kappa — *yōkai*, river child

katana — sword

kijimuna — redheaded, one-legged *yōkai* that dwells in Banyan trees

kimono — robe

kirin — *yōkai*, revered animal resembling a deer but with dragon scales

kiseru — long pipe

kodama — *yōkai*, tree spirit

komainu — lion dogs

kudzu — creeping vine where snakes hide

mon — emblem used to identify an individual or family

naginata — curved blade on a long shaft

namahage — *yōkai*, demon resembling *oni*

ninja — assassin

nunchaku — two sticks connected at one end by a short chain or rope

nure-onago — water girl

obi — sash

oni — the strongest *yōkai*

ono — axe

rōnin — masterless samurai

ryō — gold currency

sake — rice wine

samurai — warrior, usually serving under a *daimyō*

shachihoko — animal with the head of a tiger and body of a carp

shamisen — three-stringed instrument

shōgun — military dictator

shuriken — throwing stars

taiko — drum

tantō — small knife

tanuki — *yōkai*, raccoon-dog

tatami — straw mat

tekko-kagi — climbing spikes

tengu — *yōkai*, giant birdlike creature

uwagi — kimono-like jacket

waki-gamae — *naginata* position

wakizashi — small sword

washi paper — paper made from the bark of the gampi tree

yamabiko — *yōkai*, doglike in appearance with a voice that can
    mimic sounds, often thought responsible for echoes

yamawaro — *yōkai*, mountain child

yōkai — supernatural phenomena including monsters, spirits, and
    demons that range from malevolent to mischievous to harbin-
    gers of good fortune

yukata — a lightweight kimono

yuki-onna — *yōkai*, snow woman

ACKNOWLEDGMENTS

OVER THE YEARS I've written a lot of stuff. Each piece I remember differently, each challenged me in a new and exciting way and each has a very special place in my heart. I can honestly say this is the hardest I've ever worked on a manuscript, both in researching and forging an emotional connection. It hallmarks a rekindling of my cultural heritage.

My great grandparents emigrated from Japan. In another manuscript I wrote a character that is half-Japanese and half-white (like me). In it they say: "what a shame it is to have lost yourself before you're even born." In my life, I've often felt this way, disconnected from my Asian roots. So it is no coincidence that I created Akira, a character who struggles with his mixed-race identity, where he belongs and how the world perceives him. Much like Akira (and Mari) I never felt like "enough." This book was truly a labor of love. I owe so many people thanks.

All of my love to my family: Kiya, Mariko, Nathan, Liz, Dad and Mom. And Craig (husband), if I wrote all the ways I love you, we would need several more books. During the publishing of this novel, my life changed in a significant way. I welcomed my twin babies into the world, born prematurely at just thirty-one weeks. Before their birth, I spent a month hospitalized on bed rest. After, both babies were in the NICU for a month. The weeks in the hospital, the sleepless nights, the painful cesarean recovery — I'll never regret any of it. Yumi and Kenzo, you are my greatest blessings. I am so thankful to be your mother. May you never ignore your growing sense of disquiet. I'd also like to mention my fabulous mother-in-law, Elaine, who, along with my other family, sat with me for hours upon hours while I was hospitalized. You'll never know how grateful I was for all of your company. I hope this serves as my eternal thank-you.

I am deeply grateful to: all the staff at HMH Books for Young Readers who had a hand in publishing this book, especially Nicole Sclama, who worked tirelessly on this and who was incredibly supportive when my babies came unexpectedly early. Also thanks to Sarah Landis for seeing this puppy through to copy edits.

Very special thanks to Erin Harris for being a fabulous agent and career life coach. I appreciate you so much and hold you in the highest regard.

A team of experts helped fine-tune this novel. Thanks to Laura and Rebecca, my secret weapons. And to Jeremy and Misa, sensitivity readers.

Many books helped the world and characters of Honoku take shape: *Handbook of Japanese Mythology* by Michael Ashkenazi, *MFA*

Highlights Arts of Japan by Anne Nishimura Morse, Sarah E. Thompson, Joe Earle, and Rachel Saunders, *Japanese Art and Design* edited by Gregory Irvine, *The World of the Shining Prince: Court Life in Ancient Japan* by Ivan Morris, *The Book of Yōkai* by Michael Dylan Foster, and *Edo Culture: Daily Life and Diversions in Urban Japan, 1600–1868* by Nishiyama Matsunosuke.

And finally, thanks the YA community — the readers, bloggers, booksellers, book buyers, BookTubers, and writers.